Joel
Hope the readin'
is as much fun as
the writin'!

Ravin'

At The Moon

Steph Crane Halliwell
20 Dec 99

Ravin' At The Moon

A Novel

by Stephen Crane Kidwell

This is a work of fiction, the characters, their names, the events, are all products of the author's imagination, any resemblance to any person living or dead is purely coincidental

To my mom and dad
who told me for so many years
I could do anything I truly wanted . . .
I guess I finally believed them.

Prologue

THIS IS A STORY that explores some major changes that have taken place in our culture in the past couple of decades and, even though it's fiction, you may recognize someone you know or maybe even yourself in these pages. The years in question were pivotal for the masses in that customs and mores that had been taught for decades were not only in question but in a lot of cases changed out of hand. This proved to be extremely awkward for a lot of the people of those generations because they knew and liked the system as it stood and changing from long practiced ways proved to be almost intolerable to them. These changes in society and thought processes were echoed, or possibly brought on by, the music of the times.

Our story begins in the early Seventies . . . when the music died. The preceding two decades were rich, vibrant years during which the music of life was joyous and resonant, outrageous and inventive, intuitive and poetic . . . challenging conventions that had been handed down for centuries. The popular music of the Fifties and the incredible Sixties both mirrored and shaped the cultural changes of the time. It's possible that the music and the changes may even have created each other.

The music of government was one of deceit and treachery, beginning with the assassination of John F. Kennedy and continuing with the LBJ farce and that made-up war in the jungles of Southeast Asia. The music of society was a cacophony of wretched excess and conspicuous consumption. The music of business was underlined

1

by the booming bass of outlandish profits from an insatiable public appetite for the "good life." The music of women was a shrill anthem challenging a system that they had arbitrarily decided was insufferable . . . maybe because they had never learned it in the first place. The music of men was an etude of sorrow for what they intuitively knew was coming. Yet through it all, the music of celebration permeated even the darkest event or thought, a feeling of optimistic euphoria of things to come.

> . . . *Everything gon' be alright in the mornin', Da . . . Da . . . De . . . Da . . . Da . . . De . . . Da.,*
> *Boom, Boom!!!*

Marijuana came on as the substance of choice, along with some beer to mellow things out. The pill allowed everyone to join in a Dionysian celebration of life, albeit with the irony of excess. The questioning by the young people of the era continued and the answers, though better than "because I said so," were forever questionable. Eyes unopened for years began to blink and tear in the glare of new ideas. Ears mostly closed to new melodies began listening to the words as well as the instruments . . . the music of change was upon the populace.

Through it all drifted the pseudo-culture . . . those neither here nor there . . . the weekend freaks. During the work week they conformed to the "norm" or what they thought they had to be. On the weekends they became what they thought others (sometimes their own "other") wanted them to be . . . none of the honesty of the seekers. If they were east they went west, if they were west they went east. The hippest went back to middle America, the loons and non-thinkers to the coasts . . . or was it the opposite?? Anyway, the middle part became lighter while the coasts became darker . . . in spirit and thought and deed . . . the Oreo of the world.

Truth seekers, as they aged, began thinking about things that truth couldn't buy and about the elusiveness of what they sought. Some just gave in and went to work for, of all things, money. Others became weekend freaks. Some continued to seek truth in the substances at hand or the "new" substances that had cycled to the fore from the Twenties and Thirties (alot of those went the way of Janis Joplin, Jim Morrison, Jimi Hendrix, et al). A number of them decided to hide and watch, commenting only when prevailed upon.

Most of them, however, gave up the "wild" life for one more palatable to the established culture once the Sixties became the Seventies. Unfortunately, a whole bunch of them, in their confusion, made children and passed that confusion along to those Seventies babies. This caused absolute chaos in the Eighties . . . but that's another story.

Then came the pill, the greatest invention since the Salk vaccine, the savior of the modern world and something that would shake the very foundations of Twentieth Century existence. One of my best friends has a theory. He says that the pill was the downfall of the automobile industry as we know it. He holds that not only was the automobile the wheeled pheromone of the adolescent set but also served as transportation, playroom and, with any luck, bedroom. But with the advent of the pill, one no longer needed to own a big shiny vehicle to seduce women. One, in fact, no longer needed to seduce them at all. Probably what he was implying was that the pill was the beginning of the end of romance. Who needed to be wooed into something that was exciting and pleasurable if there were no consequences? By the way, when was the last time **you** went to a drive-in movie?

It is a commonly accepted fact that women invented romance, yet upon reflection, it is obvious that this is untrue. Men invented romance in order to ensure procreation and the continuity of the species . . . or was it really all just for the fun of it? Let's face it, most of the co-mingling gyrations that human beings go through are really the reward for enduring a very complex existence. What better way to vent frustration, relax, reward . . . than sexual pleasure. The only hang-up was that pre-pill sexual activity was only without penalty for the men. So it was men's lot to convince the women to go along for the ride, so to speak.

Simple, huh?? Not so! There was a time when food and shelter were payment in plenty for a man to "have his way," even though pregnancy was an inevitability. But somewhere along the line, some fool told the female how much man needed what she possessed and what power she truly wielded . . . and the competition began!

The fool in question obviously observed feline courtship and mating because that's about how the human ritual works. First, the males strut their stuff; then they fight among themselves; to the winner goes the spoils and finally, after he's used up all **his** energy,

3

she turns around and whips **his** ass. In modern times, this procedure is merely sedated and protracted. The spoils are just as fleeting but the ass-whippin' is much longer and more drawn out.

But back to the subject at hand. The advent of television didn't help things a bit. Television, which began taking the nation by storm in the Fifties, really got going in the Sixties. Evening programming gave way to afternoon and evening programming; which begat daily programming; which finally evolved into twenty-four hour programming. All of these time slots had to be filled and the TV moguls rapidly ran out of variations on news, sitcoms and variety shows.

Welcome the talk show and damn it too! It didn't — and doesn't — seem fair that, without qualifications of any kind, someone can become a talk show host and be allowed to stand up and espouse any view that they want in front of millions of inquisitive yet naive souls. It's probably why they put the freakin' things on so late at night . . . hopefully to limit their exposure.

So here we have these showbiz types busily analyzing life for the Average Joe and one of those poor misguided souls breaks down and cries on national TV . . . in front of millions of lonely people . . . lots of whom happened to be ladies. Now there are few things that a woman likes more than seeing a man cry. "It's healthy — you must release your emotions — it's natural" . . . . . . Daytime talk shows were born!!!

Ladies like to talk. They feel that this is the glue that bonds people together and it's true, because each of the sexes has a basic commonality. The problems begin when men and women talk to each other because both are afraid to admit that not only are they much different from each other but they really have very little in common . . . outside of the fact that each of them possesses half the pleasure mechanism.

In the late Seventies and early Eighties, women discovered (as men had much earlier) that with only half the procreative couplet you could still have fun — but it wasn't nearly the same. Men and women still needed each other.

The saga continued as communications increased and as is so often the case, the pendulum moved from extreme to extreme as it sought the middle. Women went from the relative security of a well-defined role in life that had existed since the beginning of time, to a search for the "real me." Men, reluctant to abandon a system so obviously right, resisted. Due to their innate persuasiveness (the same one that men invented romance over) women again prevailed and thus escalated the battle of the sexes.

Women failed to learn their new masculine role well. It just didn't fit them. They explained their ineptitudes at men's roles as "learning," men asked, "Why learn it at all?." The response was "You can learn my role as well!." Men said "I don't want to learn your role. Why don't we leave everything as it is?" The response was "You know why!" Echoing the same self-confidence bred into the species for milleniums, the men patted their mates reassuringly (and maybe wonderingly) and murmured "of course . . ."

Oh what a price future generations would pay for that "of course!" What travails, catharses, teeth gnashing and angst would plague the populace over this seemingly innocuous, though trite, acquiescence. For now, with that off-handed remark, man had indicated that he really understood what the opposite sex thought and desired. Yet, if the truth be known, three decades later as then, man really has no inkling of what goes on in a woman's mind.

Men believe that it is necessary to "look good" to attract women . . . but not at the cost of sacrificing masculinity. Looks are important to establish the pecking order. If you can't tote the gear, social conventions dictated, don't dress the part . . . . . . or I'll whip yo' ass!! In the Sixties, in deference to women's desires, men tried tie-dyed t-shirts, bell bottoms, scarves, earrings, etc., but it couldn't stop there. Women knew that the more **they** took off, the more attention they got. Unlike men, they could get as outrageous as they wanted with no one to whip **their** asses (as a matter of fact, usually the guy they were with would be the one to get **his** ass whipped). So they couldn't understand why their guys wouldn't go ahead and put on make-up and take off their shirts.

So, what was the answer to this dilemma? You guessed it, ladies got tattoos, shaved their heads and wore jeans with zippers in the front (penis envy?) And voila'!! Now, since women could dress like men, men could dress like women!!! "If you truly **love** me, you'll try to look nice for me" (read, "dress like I want you to"). Right?

Wrong! Love (which spelled backwards is evol) is an emotion that was invented and promulgated by women to insure their survival. From earliest history, men have provided women with sustenance and protection. Women have given men, in return, "love" (what better means of repayment than something as self-serving as

5

love?), while tossing monogamy into the bargain as fine print. This doesn't hold true for the rest of the animal kingdom, however.

In the animal kingdom males and females get together only during "mating season" (love/sex season??). Since this only happens at intervals, they don't always get together with the same mate. As a matter of fact, some studies indicate that, in a number of species, the female is impregnated by more than one male in the process. It's interesting to note that monogamy has never been proven in animals (even in wild geese and humans) and may be a part of this love thing.

Katherine Hepburn, a free and intellectual visionary, was quoted as saying that if men and women truly like each other perhaps they should move in next door and just visit now and then (amazingly acute insight . . . although somewhat animalistic). But for the mass of womankind, love, sex and monogamy have always been inseparable . . . a blessed trinity.

The children of the Sixties were known as the love generation not because they really loved everybody but because they made love a lot. Monogamy was not an issue. Of course this drastic shift in sexual mores was to cause major problems. One of the problems with making love a lot is that with the same person and no imagination, after a while it gets sort of routine.

You know, imagination is a wonderful thing. Someone, I think it was me, once described it as the ability to take the commonplace and make it something unique and exciting. This axiom must hold true in order for love to survive the test of time. For one thing, people change physically over time and, as with any species, the young are by far the most attractive, be they male or female. So, in order to prolong the attraction as aging takes its toll, a certain mindset must prevail. Not that you are with someone else (although in a lot of cases that may be the only thing that works) but rather that every day, instance, vignette is brand new and, therefore, interesting. Beings without imagination, and it is commonly believed that most animals fall into this category, must move from partner to partner in order to stay interested.

This, of course, doesn't do a whole lot for the classical definition of love. Like, on the other hand, is probably a better institution . . . a much less dangerous one for sure. Like is what the Sixties Flower Children preached and "unconditional like" might just be love. (If you meld love and like together you get live.) Love to the Sixties generation didn't have longevity attached to it and this violated one of the basic precepts upon which it was invented . . . a long-term commitment to survival. At some point in the Sixties a very dangerous and parochial rationalization was made, "if we like someone and subsequently make love (sex?)," it went, "and no commitment is required, then love **is** like and maybe commitment is not necessary after all."

That's fine when you are eighteen and great looking but it doesn't work so hot when you're going on forty and have two children . . . does it ladies?

It's kind of like the women's movement, whose response to the predicament of the going-on-forty divorced mothers with two kids and about a two-in-a-hundred chance of getting remarried was "We didn't know it would turn out this way. We didn't think it through. It doesn't make us a bad people. We had to find out who we **really are**, didn't we? We had to find ourselves!" Not a bunch of comfort considering that most marriages at that point were a fifteen year investment with a lifetime to go.

Like and love, of course, will always be a sticky wicket for men and women, kinda like politics. Politics is and will forever be a bar topic. I know, you've all been taught "don't argue religion or politics while you're drinking!." Well, that is an old wives' tale. In reality, the only time that any responsible person can speak on either subject is under the influence. The reason is really quite basic. Both institutions, by their very nature, are not only corrupt but also blatantly deceptive and disdainful of all mankind. However, the subject is politics here so let's get back to business.

Communications and technology accelerated at a dazzling pace in the seventh decade of the twentieth century. In large part because of this, people chose to question issues rather than blindly accept them. In earlier times, the "one bullet theory" in the Kennedy assassination would have been totally accepted by the masses. Likewise, the Kennedy boys' indiscretions with women other than their wives would have been quietly hushed-up and the whole family exonerated with an extravagant cash donation to a Catholic charity. That made-up war in Viet Nam would have been fought "to protect every man, woman, and child in this great nation of ours!!." Much to the politicians' chagrin, the children of the decade were not only encouraged to question that which smelled funny but also were bright enough to identify the outright bullshit that had been taught by the body politic since the turn of the century.

7

Now for an interesting dilemma. The generation in question knew instinctively that, even though it was the most easily rationalized way to live, living to the left of the party line was not working in most parts of the world. Liberalism (socialism?) is the banner of a group called the Democratic Party and the Democratic Party (which had run the United States of America for decades) was probably the cause of most of the problems facing them in the present and probably the future as well.

Most of these problems began with poor, addled Franklin Delano Roosevelt and his deranged accomplice, Eleanor. These two professed a penchant for social reform that would later prove more socialist than reformist. Not only was it their intention to better the world by taking from the rich and giving to the poor but in the process they felt it necessary for all of the people on the earth to be equal . . . not created equal, not given equal opportunity, but to literally be equal.

Unfortunately, reality dictates that no two people, cultures or races for that matter are equal nor will they ever be. All creatures are created differently, none are identical (which happens to be a synonym for equal) and all the attempts by these two self-styled visionaries and their antecedents to force equality on the masses have, predictably, failed miserably.

The results of this misguided sense of charity and goodwill toward others were, amongst other catastrophes; the Welfare System which would turn millions of Americans into slaves of their own greed and the Democratic Party; forced desegregation which would bring the level of education down for the majority . . . instead of bringing it up for the minorities; Foreign Aid which provided for those poor people in other lands who are starving and without shelter all the while ignoring those in our country who are in the same boat; Rule of the Minority, even though democracy is defined as the rule of the majority; and Tax and Spend Economics which stifles free trade and economic growth and also diametrically opposes one of the basic precepts that caused our forefathers to come to the new world in the first place.

It occurred to the thinking men and women of the Seventies that the above mentioned issues might well be disastrous if left unchecked but the economic boom of the era camouflaged the danger. Still, a number of the enlightened at the time acknowledged the fact that races and cultures, nations and states, even men and women were all very dissimilar in their likes, dislikes and reactions to stimuli. They also suspicioned that men and women might be at war with each other and somewhere in their deepest honesties suspected that this was an unnatural course of events. The saddest part of the whole affair was that a basic problem of the generation in question would not only escalate the hostilities but also make it almost impossible for them to rectify their differences.

Then came the event that would both stratify and, ironically, re-unite the people of this country and the world . . . the Viet Nam War. By gender, the response to it was quite diverse. The men, who had to fight the war here as well as in Asia, rebelled by protesting, burning their draft cards or going to Canada while the women got involved in politics and social reform. Since rebellion is a chancey business at best, like rolling the dice, and since it is always open season on them, there is no middle-of-the-road rebel. Rebels are heroes or goats, winners or losers, Democrats or Republicans, liberals or conservatives, Jews or Catholics (maybe even Methodists?!, Oh, noooo!) but all share a central problem: How to get their message across without losing their heads or hides.

Some chose to absquatulate (I love that word), some became conscientious objectors, some turned to drugs, some even stood up and challenged the system. In most cases, no matter what the answer was, the result was still the same . . . total disillusionment.

The AWOLs got dishonorable discharges (kind of fitting considering it was a dishonorable war) and subsequently were treated like martyrs by the women (lots of . . . um . . . **attention**, if you will). The conscientious objectors served their time at some veteran's facility and then went back to Fire Island or Key West or San Francisco. The runaways were granted amnesty by the same government that created the Selective Service System in the first place. The druggies have always been around and, as is their wont, used this latest affront to the collective intelligence as just another excuse for their addictions. The guys who risked their lives in Viet Nam, meanwhile, were mostly overlooked.

Oddly enough, the guys that challenged the system, the ones even higher on the women's lists than the guys with dishonorable discharges, those poor bastards had to change their identities and go underground to escape the slings and arrows of outrageous Hooverism. The irony is that, at the same time, their girlfriends were discreetly "lobbying" with the liberals or carrying banners by day and

9

partying all night long with some congressman about thirty years their senior.

The music of masculine politics during this period was the recognition of a moral wasteland in which small men became big men in the time honored, deceitful methods that their respective party had so carefully taught them . . . usually to the detriment of the masses. The music of women's politics was a blend of Sousa-type marches for questionable causes interspersed with whatever readily available romantic ballads there were that didn't include secular influence . . . and march they did!!

They marched for equality . . . now it's hard for me to understand why they wanted to step down from where they were to equality. It's pretty obvious that they had a pretty good handle on being more "equal" than men at the time. In the courts they were the weaker sex (read "more fairly treated"). In public they could speak their minds without fear of bodily harm, have "affairs" (rather than cheating) while everyone "understood," spout ridiculous views on topics that they weren't very well versed on and be listened to, and, finally, promote a movement whose inevitable conclusion would take them into a conflict with their natural partners which would threaten the very system that their forebears had worked so long and hard to perfect! In short, they could do anything they wanted to under the catch-all buzzword "liberation" and be applauded for it. Whew!! That's a lot to bite off in one little decade.

They marched also for a number of "rights" (as opposed to lefts). Animal rights is an interesting one. They marched for those poor dumb creatures who, since they couldn't think or speak, needed a "spokesperson"(???). They marched for gay rights for the she-men of the movement and for their he-girl friends . . . confidants, designers, and hair-stylists. They marched for abortion rights for all those freed from the moral and ethical restraints that our society has forever insisted upon. "What the hell," was their argument, "it was all his fault anyway, all any of them want to do is to get into our pants, right!!?!"

The right to be right, the right to be left, the right to change your mind, the right to be undecided, the right to be a woman, the right to be wrong . . . the right to be wrong??! Yeah, well if you can't justify it any other way, the way to do it is to "have the right"!!!

As most of you are probably aware, the end result of this "awakening" was total chaos. The moral fiber of a nation with no rules decayed rapidly. Free love brought about an erosion of the very romance that ladies were trying to re-invent, along with diseases that could maim and even kill. Drugs cycled out of the underground and back onto the streets where they could more easily debilitate the masses. The women's movement escalated the war between the sexes to new heights and the divorce rate soared right along with it. The number of lonesome divorcees at the singles bars accelerated at a rate that even the most seasoned traveling salesman could not in his wildest dreams comprehend. Singles clubs popped up everywhere. Places where single mothers and fathers approaching forty with children could share their problems with the group, then later go to a fern bar for a drink and maybe get lucky. The questioning of the system that began years before became the new cynicism of the coming decade. The music of the times began to have the same background beat which began to overpower the words more and more.

"Disco, disco man! . . . I wanna be a disco man!!"

Thus began the contrasting confusion of the Seventies . . . people were so intent on reinventing life that they forgot how to live. Ladies all of a sudden wanted to assume men's roles, convinced that it would enhance the quality of life. In response to this challenge of role identity, psychobabble blossomed as the intellectual music of the times. The resounding echoes of "I'm okay, you're okay — I need my space — you just can't seem to get in touch with your feelings" would color the period with splashes of unbelievable insanity.

No one took the time to verify who the new prophets were. Used car salesmen and other hucksters found new ways to live off the fat of the land. Who was Jack Rosenberg (est's Werner Erhard), anyway? And what were his credentials? The absurdity of the situation increased in direct proportion to its abnormalities and ambiguities. The more psychological pap the masses wanted . . . the more they got. Until finally, they were reduced to gelatinous globes of gibberish . . . anything goes if there are no rules.

Given the togetherness of the Sixties, how had all of this come apart so quickly? There may have been lots of questions and challenges in that decade but at least some meaningful conclusions were reached, some useful changes made. All things weren't done just for the doing . . . some had purpose. The privilege to be wrong was differentiated from the right to be wrong. Earning was still paramount to inheriting or, even worse, demanding. People were proud to be

11

what they were born and motivated to improve their lot in life. Stupid questions were treated as such or as obviously impaired views, not as profundities. Truth was sought after . . . not iced over with inane rationalizations. The deceptions and cover-ups that led to the searching Sixties became the banner of the Seventies . . . the music was fading fast.

Chapter One

JOSEPH VINCENT HEWS, a.k.a. Joey, was a Child of the Sixties, but the year was 1970 and today, Friday, August the thirteenth was his twenty seventh birthday. He rose as he customarily did, humming a melody, always a pre-disco tune and usually during his shower he'd begin to sing the words. He wasn't sure why these songs echoed through his head every morning and he really didn't care . . . after all, why should he?

Today's song was Van Morrison's "Brown-Eyed Girl," a tune that might have had something to do with his current live-in, tall brown-eyed Debra McPherson, senior drama major at SMU and madly in love with her Joey. He was going to graduate school and would get his MBA around Christmas. They were talking about the possibility of getting married (or maybe she was, while he listened), but a lot of things had been bothering him recently.

All his life he had been taught that first you get an education, then you go to work, get married and raise a family. He wasn't sure about all this go to work and get married stuff. Life up to now had been full of school, part-time work and partying. His love life had been hot and heavy, albeit varied, and his current girlfriend was great . . . but something was wrong with the whole scheme of things. There were a lot of things that just didn't add up when you really listened to people, especially women. Then again there were even more things that didn't add up when you listened to the preachers or all those college professors talk about life in their worlds.

Joey had been born and raised an optimist with a naturally cheerful disposition. Though not handsome in the pure sense of the word, he wasn't hard to look at and knew it. He was brighter than average and school had always been fun to him. Learning was not only enjoyable but also necessary. Reading a book a week and doing at least one crossword puzzle a day were mandatory and, even though he was intrinsically curious, he never questioned those Sixties tunes that played, over and over, in the auditorium of his head.

"You miiy, brown-eyed girl . . . . . ."

On this particular morning, it was off to Dallas for an interview with a nationally prominent consulting company. Graduation was coming on fast and it was time to look for work. Although he had never been in a hurry to get out into the real world, Hews was turning twenty seven this day and was under pressure from lots of folks (his included) to get on with it.

As he was standing under the shower head, rinsing off, he felt a cold breeze on his bare behind (a tush that he was quite proud of by the way) followed by the caressing touch of two warm hands. They traced the arcs of his buttocks and moved around front to encircle "Old Number Nine," who upon hearing his name called stood at attention straight. "Good morning" was fuzzily being murmured into his ear between little bites and kisses. So much for being on time for his interview. Oh well, every one you miss is one you're behind in the game of love and Debra was sooooo insistent!! Trotting to his car while she curled up for a little nap, he silently wondered what she had meant when she told him to hurry back so she could show him something.

The interview was in a typical North Dallas office tower. A mile high and modern with plenty of mirrored glass to reflect the shimmering Texas summer heat. The receptionist was East Texas wholesome and tried her best to put him at ease.

"Would you like some coffee, Mr. Hews?," She said in her best business school english.

"My name is Joey, my Dad is Mr. Hews and I'd like some Diet Pepsi if you have any. I've never been able to get used to coffee. First of all, it hurts your stomach, then it makes you have to go take a leak and it makes you hyper. Hell, I'm hyper enough as it is."

She looked at him as if he were from some other planet and went to fetch the drink. While she was gone, Joey took a quick walk

14

around the office. He figured if anyone asked, he'd tell them he was looking for the men's room.

The office was done in Neo-Jewish chic. Everything in bright colors with lots of gold and chrome around. The whole floor was split up into little cubicles with walls upholstered in rugs that didn't reach the ceiling. This caused everyone in the office to speak in muted tones so that no one could overhear anyone else's conversation. It occurred to Joey that all of the people in this office could be zombies, since nobody even looked up as he passed, much less asked him who he was.

By the time he got back up front, the cute little East Texan was back in the reception area with the door open peeking out . . . obviously looking for him. He smiled as he walked into the room.

"Bathroom," he smiled motioning over his shoulder with his thumb. "Too much Diet Pepsi this morning."

She gave him that same extra-terrestrial look as before and sat back down behind her desk. Glancing up every now and then to peek at him, she busied herself with little receptionist things like you see on television. Straightening things up on her desk, rolling a piece of paper into her typewriter, answering the phone which rang extremely infrequently; those types of things.

"Mr. Dingbat will see you now."

Mr. Dingbat?!!, he thought as he walked into the office that she pointed out to him. He could have sworn she had said that. Maybe it was just this whole bizarre scene or maybe he did drink too much Diet Pepsi this morning. At any rate, since he had already reconnoitered the area, he wasn't at all surprised by the guy's office or its decor. Ol' Dingbat was a typical striped tie, wing-tipped corporate stereotype who got right down to business.

"We at Doppler Brothers consider ourselves the very best in the consulting business and, from the looks of your resume, we think that you will fit right in, Hews! Of course, you'll have to cut your hair and take off those fruit boots, our clients expect us to look as if we're businessmen, not Hollywood actors."

Joey scanned the white shirt, conservative suit and haircut, wondering what mindless individual invented ties in the first place and figured that he must be the same yahoo that started wearing suits in the Texas summer heat. Actors, huh? Well, what kind of charade is this that you're putting on, moron?, he thought. "What's the job entail?"

15

"Basically, we take businesses that are sick and make them well," he smiled like a mortician who had just been contacted by a grieving but wealthy family. "Something you need to know, however, is that we are not very well liked by most employees since we usually must trim the work force in order to ensure profitability. For that reason, most of your work will be in towns other than Dallas . . . there will be a lot of traveling."

"So, what you're saying is that I'll be going into strange towns to fire a bunch of people that I don't know in order to save companies, right? Well, I have a question for you. What did you do before you came to work here?"

"I took an MBA from SMU, just like you're doing."

"No other work experience? Summer jobs?"

"Nope, worked part-time at a Chief Auto Parts store."

Holy moly! He thought, these guys want me to go out and give a bunch of people their walking papers and I don't even know who's good or bad, skilled or not. I haven't ever even had a real job. How the hell is he, or me for that matter, qualified to screw up some stranger's life like that? I think it's time to boogie.

On his way home, the first stop was the 7-Eleven for a six pack of cold beer. As he popped the top on the first one of the day, he reflected on what had transpired. His day really hadn't gone badly, he decided. A nice little bump-start in the shower to get the vital juices flowing and, even though the job wasn't right, the beer was cold. It was going to be a real nice sunset. Maybe a good night to go sit outside at the Quiet Man and have some knackwurst and sauerkraut, listen to some music, kibitz with some of the intellectual types. Probably best to work on the motorcycle if he was going dirt biking this week-end, though. Wonder what ol' Debra's got up her sleeve?

Well, she had a lot up her sleeve or actually on a piece of pretty high quality paper. What she had was the proof of a wedding invitation and both their names were on it.

"We've talked about it for the last two months and I'm ready, Joey."

She really looked **right** in the little mini dress with the late afternoon sunlight streaming through it (or did it have something to do with the six-pack?). Anyway, what the hell, he'd been with her a long time and she wasn't hard to get along with, why not?

Joey's eyes roamed up and down her marvelous body. Debra

16

was tall and willowy, with perky little breasts, dark eyes and the aristocratic, high-cheekboned face of a Neiman Marcus model, which she briefly had been.

"I'm ready too, darlin'," he said grinning, "but let me get a job first, okay? Hey, let's go ride with J. C. and them this weekend, huh?'

They had been riding motorcycles off-road together for several years now and everyone was pretty comfortable with each other's styles. Joey rode balls to the wall . . . to him the throttle had two positions, wide open and off. J. C., on the other hand used a little restraint. He liked to finish the ride in one piece. Might have had something to do with the screws the doctors put through his shin the last time he crashed and burned. Debra kept up pretty good and there were the usual motorcycle groupies who had all the latest equipment and looked great but were just there for the dreams.

Anyway, they rode hard all over the 5,000 acre ranch out west of Fort Worth that Saturday and in the rapidly falling dusk they built a bonfire and brought out the beer and weinies. Those clear summer nights around the fire were great for figuring out some of the solutions to the tough questions in life and Hews was full of them tonight. Not the solutions . . . the questions.

"Hey, J. C., talk to me about marriage."

J. C. and Joey were best of friends and Debra's sister was J. C.'s wife so they spent a lot of time together. J. C. grew up in North Dallas and made it to his Junior year in college before he knocked his ol' lady up. He graduated as quickly as possible and got a pretty good job but, along the way, he managed to sire two more babies and life got pretty complicated. Unfortunately, somewhere during this time his wife had started to take herself pretty seriously and that didn't help matters at all.

In the beginning, when they were just two young people who hadn't been careful enough, everything was fine. Then all of a sudden, they were the only ones in their group who couldn't go out on Wednesday night because they were saving money for the baby. Then he had to take a second job because she was tired all the time. Finally, they had to stop all sexual activity because it was getting close to time for the baby to be born. J. C. was only a year or so older than Joey but, in several respects, he had lived alot more.

J. C. took a long toke on some good old Mexican commercial grade pot and, after passing it to Joey, thought for a while before he answered.

"You know, I'm probably not the best person in the world to give you advice about that stuff. Most of the married things that have happened to me have just happened. Hell, it took me three kids in three years to figure out what was causing them. I couldn't tickle my old lady's ass without her blowing up like a toad, but I'll be happy to give you the benefit of my experience if you'll pass me that joint back."

With this, J. C. took another king-sized hit, popped open a cold beer and prepared to declaim. "Marriage is really a simple institution. Men don't have a whole lot of control over it. Women kind of make up their mind who they want and then they spend all their time plottin' to get 'im. If all else fails they still have an ace in the hole.

"Yeah?" said Joey. "What's that?"

"Well it's a physiological fact that, when your pecker gets real hard, a lot of the blood leaves your brain and you can't think too straight. They," he jerked his thumb over his shoulder at the women who were trying to throw J. C.'s squawling kids into a tent, "figured this out early in the evolution of mankind. They also figured out that if they kiss you just right or maybe even rub you a little, the result will be the same. So, if they want somethin', they just make you stupid and talk you out of it."

What J. C. hadn't told him was that the "pecker hard" thing was merely a method of response-reward training in which, when the penis no longer responds to the stimuli (as was rumored by the old farts at the VFW), there could be problems. With any luck, however, the patterns established through the years would continue after the demise of sexual urgency and the female could still control the situation. This method had been taught to the ladies, meticulously, generation after generation by their mommas and grandmommas before them. It was tried and proven over centuries of practice. Unfortunately, in their haste to change the order of things, the "new women" of the seventies literally screwed their way out of the situation.

Along with these new attitudes, several other factors conspired to cause seventies women to lose their edge in male-female relationships. As long as sex (love?) was a scarce commodity, it retained a bunch of its preciousness. After all, it isn't particulary hygienic, the parts in question aren't exactly pretty, the act itself rather fleeting considering all the posturing it takes to get down to it and the consequence of unplanned conception was always lurking in the back-

18

ground. Then along came some pretty effective birth control in pill form and, bang! (Or was it bang, bang?), sex was scarce no more! It was now a new "freedom" for women, no more could men hold it over their heads, now they could chose whether or not to enjoy.

Before the advent of the pill, women controlled most of the sexual activity in the world. They had to acquiesce before any how-you-call-it (that's cajun for poontang) took place. An amorous male had to use some form of coercion (romance, love, marriage, presents, money, etc) in order to score. But now there was a new "freedom" allowing anyone to go after it anytime, anywhere, with anyone that it occurred to anyone to go after it with.

The second thing that snuck up on them was the imbalance in the population. After a lot of men were killed in World Wars one and two, the Korean War, and that Democratic debacle in southeast Asia, women began to outnumber men. This put a strain on the whole value system that had been established over the centuries by clerics, educators and the legislature of the United States of America. The dilemma was, if society was going to honor a system that only allowed monogamy and there were more women than men, then a bunch of women were going to end up without love buddies. Since love-romance-marriage came about to insure survival of the "weaker sex," then, under this system, a lot of ladies damn-sure weren't going to survive.

Now some geek (someone should track he-she-it down and start systematically breaking off it's appendages until it disappears) stood up, pointed at the heavens above and, in a confident tone, hollered "men and women are equal!." Maybe it was trying to quote the Constitution of the United States and innocently omitted the "created" part of the quote. Whatever the case, the reality of the situation is that no two people are equal . . . all are different. Every single one of us is unique and any attempt by anyone to be equal to anyone else is not only futile but also an exercise in frustration. Apparently the geek stated its case with such conviction that a large percentage of its audience believed it.

Now modern science has proven that the masculine side of the human race is inherently the stronger but an independent poll conducted in watering holes across the nation has proven that the feminine side is instinctively meaner. This works well in the wild where she has to protect herself and her young but it's not so hot when she turns on another human being, especially her mate or her rival. In

19

the eighth decade of the twentieth century, mate and rival were, all too often, one and the same.

The final quirk that jumped up and bit them on their unsuspecting posteriors was that ladies began to get way too serious about themselves. Someone (probably a country and western singer) said that each of us is no more than a bug spot on the windshield of life and it seems that the women of the generation in question had forgotten that fact. Maybe they felt trapped because there weren't enough men to go around. Perhaps it was because they had gotten over their heads with the equality thing. Possibly, it was the realization that the sisterhood that they were in competition with were just as insecure about the situation as they were themselves. At any rate, they were definitely backed into a corner in their mind's eye and, as everyone knows, there is nothing more dangerous than a cornered animal, human or otherwise. So here we have a bunch of recently "freed," seriously angry, definitely cornered humans that outnumber their mate-rival-partners by about two to one on a given Friday night. Sounds like a conflagration looking for a place to conflagrate!

What could be done to avoid this head-on collision? Most commonly when it comes to humans the last solution tried in any situation is to look inwardly and alter the cause of the problem; to affix the blame on the causative factor, not the object of the consternation. So what can these vexed vixens do in the interim? Up jumps the dreaded "d" word; d-i-v-o-r-c-e!!

It really made sense when they reasoned it all out. If there was only one man for every two women and moral standards dictated monogamy, then each man would have to marry at least twice, thus the **necessity** of divorce. Since polygamy was illegal, divorce became accepted as a rational alternative and mate stealing began in earnest. The natural consequence was, once one mate was stolen, then the one who lost the mate was free to steal someone else's and, bingo, matrimonial musical chairs!

What everyone neglected to realize was that, no matter how you sliced it, there were still not enough men to go around and sooner or later, with or without children or marriage, lots of women would be alone. Sometimes it looks better to have half a loaf rather than none, but when it comes to marriage, none is probably the lesser of the two evils. The irony of the whole mess is that whether or not anybody had tried to change the situation, the result would have been the same.

This whole catharsis is a pretty complicated explanation of a simple observation of J. C.'s to his buddy Joey, and maybe it sounds sort of grim, but even though there was a pretty dark cloud over man-woman relationships in the Seventies, mankind intuitively knew that marriage was still the best way. It might also be the **right** way. So, after the words of wisdom from his ol' buddy and after giving the whole thing a good forty-five seconds of deep thought, Joey spoke clearly through the marijuana and beer induced fog, stating unequivocably . . .

"My friend, I believe I'm about to be your brother-in-law." J. C. wasn't really too surprised by this declaration since the memory of his own courtship was still fresh on his mind. As a matter of fact, he looked forward to having Joey to talk to as they strolled down the pathway of life, looking for those answers that no one has ever found. There is a certain security in numbers that seems rather appealing when you're navigating uncharted waters.

What Joey didn't know and J. C. couldn't bring himself to tell him was that recently he had begun giving all this he-ing and she-ing some pretty serious thought himself. Its not that his desire for his wife had begun to fade but here lately things had gotten pretty complicated. He wasn't sure that the complications wouldn't continue to worsen and become more severe as time went on. Certainly the cost was going to be high; physically, fiscally and emotionally and, for the life of him, he couldn't figure out how to tell his friend. Hell, it wasn't all that clear to him, given the fact that every time it all started to come together, every time a glimmer of the whole picture would announce itself in the back of his mind, every time his eyes would begin to glow with understanding, he'd get kissed or rubbed and after all that was over, it was time to take a nap anyway.

In the fall of 1970, Joey and Debra were married, not without some complications, however. Since neither one of them was a member of an organized religion, it wasn't easy to find a preacher too interested in performing the ceremony without some promise of future commitment. It seemed that modern churches, instead of being primarily committed to soul-saving these days, were quite interested in fiscal matters. Since they considered their services an investment, they were interested in future returns on the same.

This attitude coincided with all the "new" thinking not only in secular situations but in all facets of sociology. The questioning of the Sixties had wrought a Seventies monster whose mind-set was one of "try anything as long as it isn't status quo." In the past, as far as religion was concerned, this misconception had been controlled by that old Judeo-Christian standby: the guilt inducing, hellfire and brimstone Sunday Sermon. But some of the more well-heeled brethren were quick to learn that, with the advent of television, anyone with the wherewithal to buy some air time could reach a bunch of easily-leds and, with a minimum of persuasion, start some big-time money rolling in. As so often happens, they misconstrued this success in raising money with provenance of the theory that they espoused and, of course, the thing fed on itself until it got totally out of control.

Spiritual gurus began popping up with the same frequency as the psychobabblists and with approximately the same measure of accreditation. There was a time when churches were considered by the faithful to be the ultimate word next to that of God himself (herself, itself). Since that was the case, most men of the cloth exhibited a certain noble demeanor. This was reinforced by a strict code of ethics and behavior which was stringently enforced by their respective sects.

When radio was utilized as a method to reach out to more and more souls, these aspects of religion were still observed. However, with the advent of television an aura of showbiz pervaded the hallowed traditions that had been passed down for centuries. Instead of the Sunday Sermon, a sort of theological circus took to the air. If the "Ringling Brothers Religious Hour" promised a miracle, then "Barnum And Bailey For Christ" promised a miracle a day! Prayers were offered to everyone for everything as long as they pledged money. In times past, people had pledged faith and good works in exchange for favors from their Lord. Now they had to pay some guy to speak to the Lord for them and interpret their desires . . . a sort of spiritual agent, if you will. "Send $9.95 to me, get $100 worth of credit with him!" Well, pilgrims, how much of the Lord can you afford?

When the various secular conventions came to town, those arriving in private jets and the first class section of the airlines were no longer successful businesssmen come to buy their way into God's good graces. Those guys in silk suits, alligator shoes, Rolexes and $35 salon hair cuts were business men of sorts, but what were they doing with clerical collars around their necks? Worshipping the almighty dollar was taking on newer, broader dimensions! It fits that,

22

with the advent of the sterile Seventies, when the old values were being tossed aside for the "new morality," people should push their religion aside and just pay up for what they wanted.

Give money not presents for Christmas, "They know what they want, don't they? I don't!," "No sense in saying grace before meals, we don't eat together anymore, anyway." If you mess up and screw your neighbor's wife, buy another pew at the church. The only honest cleric of the period and perhaps to this day was the Reverend Ike. He was a black man who stood up and told his followers to give everything they owned to him; "You shouldn't need it anyway, seein' as how you was so religious!"

The ceremony finally had to be held in a Methodist church. It wasn't what the bride's mother wanted "Don't they have all of them candles and funny smellin' stuff and them pretty costumes on all those little boys in Catholic Churches?"

"Yes, Momma, but they also have lots of Mexicans!"

"Well, we don't want that then. What does Methodist mean anyway, I hadn't been to church in years. Your sister couldn't wait for a church weddin', besides, we couldn't hide her watermelon belly in a pretty gown."

"Mother!"

"Look, I'll just go get me a little drink and be right back."

Looking back on the whole thing many years later, that probably should have been Joey's first portent of things to come but, given the fact that he had already made up his mind, he just passed the old broad off as peculiar and went ahead on. He probably should have heeded that age-old adage "If you want to see what your wife will look like when she gets older, look at her mother."

This might have been the time to save the whole deal by exiting stage right, but just about that time, he got kissed or rubbed or something and then it was time to take a nap. When he woke up, she was gone and so were all the warning signs. If it hadn't been for the thoughtful look (read frown) on Debra's face, he wouldn't even have known the old crone was there, except maybe for that faint odor of ozone and cotton candy that would come back to haunt him again and again.

The next day, they booked a church for the first Friday that didn't disagree with the half-off plane tickets to Acapulco available on Braniff's "Summertime Savings Spree" and started with the real preparations. First on the agenda was a ring. Since Debra's Momma, although rolling in money, was by her own admission "tighter'n Dick's hat band," they went downtown to a discount diamond broker and then to a discount jeweler and, well, after a while Joey felt like they might just as well get married in a Walmart. When he mentioned this, however, he noticed that the temperature in the room went about twenty degrees cooler and, not wanting to get any further behind in the game of love, smiled sweetly and shut his mouth. Lesson Number One in the marriage manual now complete, he brashly moved on to Number Two.

Number Two was a lot harder to learn than Number One (if you have ever wondered where the word number came from here is your lesson; the word number literally defined is with less feeling or as in "If I don't get up and walk around a little bit, my ass is going to be number than a door knob"). Anyway, when they got to the catering part, Debra's Momma wanted to know why they needed food anyway.

"All's you need is plenty of booze and some "whore's dee ovaries" and ever'body'll have a good time!" Momma said as she petted her little toy poodle.

The tiny dog was groomed to a tee with little bows over each ear to match her trimmed and painted toe nails. The North Dallas "doggie salon" that Debra's Momma frequented had also shampooed and perfumed the little darling so that she emanated so much Chanel no. 5 that even Joey was getting turned on. All of this could not mask the fact that she was obviously in heat; the dog, that is.

"Momma, this is a wedding and our guests are not just here to get drunk! Motherrr, don't let that dog do that!"

Momma was letting the sex-starved little creature hump her leg. It was really a pretty crude thing to watch but the dog obviously was enjoying it.

"Ever'thang deserves to get a little now and then, sweetheart, and this little dog ain't never had none. So just you let her have her fun!"

Joey, by this time, was squirming in his chair and looking away. Debra's Daddy was doing the same but he had long ago lost the desire to stand up to Momma. How could this woman be doing this, Joey thought? I hope she doesn't bring her little toy poodle to the reception. Unconsciously, he started humming an old Frank Zappa number.

"Give me your dirty love, like your Momma makes her fuzzy poodle do."

24

'Ol Frank must have had the same kind of mother-in-law!!

"Honey, I'm paying for this and I say anybody not comin' to get drunk is a lyin' fool! Now, I'll just go and get me a little drank and we'll talk about it."

"Dammit, Momma, you think you know everything but this is my wedding and we are going to have a nice dinner and some champagne and go on our honeymoon!"

"Well, I'll tell you something, honey," her sweet Momma screamed back over her shoulder, "I'm paying for this shindig and I'm tellin' you what's gonna be served, where it's gonna be served, and who's servin' it! And it ain't gonna be in no damn Meskin' church, neither!"

At which point Momma went off in search of another drink and a match, since she hadn't had a cigarette in at least three minutes. Joey, not wanting Debra to feel too badly over her mother's foul mood, decided to jump into the fray.

"Relax now darling," he whispered, "the old bag will calm down in a few minutes and we'll work this all out."

At this point, Debra jumped straight in the air, grabbed him by the hair and started screaming. "Don't you ever call my Momma an old bag, you son of a bitch, she's paying for all of this! And dammit, we'll do it her way! You just take care of the things that you're responsible for and everything will be just fine!!"

With that, Debra ran after her Momma and slammed the door so hard that he could hear glass crashing in the kitchen. He started to get up to go after her, but all of a sudden some semblance of sanity struck him. Hey, fool, you didn't do anything wrong, they obviously are just nervous over getting everything right. It's probably a good time to run to the 7-Eleven for a cold six pack and give them time to settle down. Right?

Wrong! Although it had jumped up and hit Joey right between the eyes, Lesson Number Two ricocheted over his head with an almost audible whine. As he drove down the street he hummed a little more of Zappa's "Dirty Love."

By the time Joey got back to Debra's momma's house with his six pack, all the lights were out and Debra was sitting alone on the front porch, arms crossed tightly against her chest. He turned off the car and began walking up the sidewalk and all of a sudden she was on him like a cat.

25

"Don't you ever embarrass me like that again," she hissed, "you don't ever criticize my mother to me!"

"Hey, wait a minute, you were the one telling her how the cow ate the cabbage, all I did was agree with you!"

"Well," she sniffed, "I can tell my mother anything I want, any way I want to, but you just stay out of it!"

Now, what had happened here was that Joey had not only missed Lesson Number Two, he had also tried to apply the General Law of Womanhood and it had backfired on him. Lesson Number Two is; when a mother and her daughter are "discussing" a sensitive issue and you are tempted to speak up or are even **asked** to speak on the subject, immediately develope acute amnesia, choke on whatever it is that you are eating or drinking, or have an unexpected bowel attack and leave the room until the furor subsides. In no case offer an opinion of any type, or even an aside, for that matter.

The General Law, on the other hand, works in most cases but not in this instance. It states that when a female comes to a male with a problem, she is looking for sympathy . . . not a solution. This is one of the main reasons for the breakdown in man-woman relationships. The masculine response to any perplexity that arises, be it between man, woman or child, is to analyze the situation and find a way to correct it. This basic pragmatism which has served man so well in business, government, etc., through the years, just doesn't work when dealing with ladies under duress.

When she comes to her mate or boyfriend and says, "Oh damn! We've got to go to dinner with my mother and you know she's going to embarrass us and send her steak back at least twice!"

The first thing to come to mind with a man would be a solution.

"Well, let's go get Chinese. She doesn't know an eggroll from an asshole, anyway!" Wrong move.

The correct thing for him to do is to walk over to her with love in his eyes, hug her close and whisper, "I know honey, but when she does it, just look at me and smile and I'll handle it." Think about it.

Joey made two basic errors in a very short period of time. First, he got in the middle of a cat fight and, secondly, he applied the General Rule too late. He also got a couple of hints as to what was to come in the future, but as is the case with most of those in love (heat?), he missed them entirely.

Then again, the mysteries of life, although so obvious later on, are always hard to learn. The argument has historically been (from the feminine viewpoint) that these mysteries are the very foundation of the man-woman relationship and they are probably right because without mysteries to explain all the differences in their separate ways of thinking, they'd probably end up hating each other early on.

It seems amazing that in the seventies the Women's Movement decided to expose a number of these unknowns and, subsequently, set themselves back a few centuries. Maybe they thought that if men understood them better, they would treat them as they wanted to be treated all along. The problem with that train of thought is, in order for anyone to understand them, they would have to tell a whole hell of a lot more than they were willing or able to. As a result, men were more confused than ever and, since what used to work was no longer allowed, tried to swing from the hip. It's sad to report that very few of their attempts hit the mark, further exacerbating the problem.

The day that Joey and Debra were to get married dawned clear and bright. Joey got up early and took a shower humming a few bars of "Goin' To The Chapel." A few days before, Debra had moved in with her mother so that, as her mother put it, the marriage would be more "proper"(even though they had been living together for the last six months). Debra, on the other hand, thought that it would be a good idea for Joey to "miss" her a little before they tied the knot.

This brings up a point that we ought to examine here for a minute. There was a newspaper article the other day written by a guy named Jack Kammer in which he quotes a lady named Carol Cassell. It went something like this.

"Buried deep in the recesses of (women's) memories are years of messages telling us that sex is our most important asset if rationed, if kept out of reach."

Cassell in turn quotes Nancy Friday, author of that paean on womanliness "My Mother/Myself," "women have always derived power from witholding sex . . . . this power in women produces an enormous rage in men but since their need for us is equally powerful, they bury their anger."

This might just explain why, as men get older, their relationship with women changes. It also might explain why as they get older they tend to beat their wives more . . . you know, as the urge wans so the anger builds. At any rate, for some unknown reason, the women of the era seemed to be willing to give up this bit of control over men in favor of "free love." Or was it just that they had trouble with the new temptations afforded by the advent of the pill?

27

On the way to the church, Joey stopped to stock the car with cold beer for the trip to the airport after the wedding. When he got to the church the family hustled him into a little room so that he couldn't see the bride. What the hell, he'd see plenty of her later. The ceremony went off without a hitch with the exception of two notable events.

First, when the music started, Debra's Momma started crying. Not just crying but rather blubbering, snorting like an old sow rooting in the rutabagas. The crying, however, wasn't the issue to Joey. What really got him was that, as the noise escalated to an embarrassing 100 decibels or so and soiled hankies were flying everywhere, he kind of glanced around the church and all the ladies who weren't crying were smiling and exchanging knowing glances with each other. It occurred to him that the whole thing was an act. Momma was playing out her expected role to a tee and all her friends were acknowledging it as if it were serious and appropos. To Joey it was a bunch of nonsense; wasn't Debra's Momma just saying how happy she was for both of them? Women!! Yeah women, Joey. Maybe you ought to observe these incongruities and catalog them for future reference.

The second event of note came during the exchanging of the vows. When it was time for Joey to say his "I do," all of sudden all that came out of his throat was a croak like a frog out of water. Maybe this was a way of telling him something. Maybe by the very fact that he couldn't put into words what his mind was thinking, maybe what was happening here was extrasensory perception, maybe what was happening was an augury of future events, maybe it was just a sunspot. So what, a sunspot?

And so it began, this grand union. So had begun so many grand unions, all happiness and bliss; sunshine and blue skies; love and heat. Life stretched out before them like one clear, dry super speedway waiting for them to cruise down it wide open and hummin'.

"Get your motor runnin', go out on the highway, lookin'
for adventure, and whatever comes our way . . . ."

28

Chapter Two

ABOUT THREE MONTHS AFTER the wedding, Joey got his first job, working as an auto parts salesman. Debra's Momma was beside herself.

"What the hell did he go and get all that education for if he was gonna be a auto parts salesman? Sheeit! Your Uncle Melvin worked all his life in a NAPA store in Colorado City and he never could even afford a new car. He always bought our old used Cadillacs."

Momma failed to mention that her "old used Cadillacs" were second hand to begin with since she was too cheap to buy a new one. She had her husband buy them from his business partners after they got tired of them but she always made him get them from one of the partners who lived out of town. That way the people at the country club wouldn't recognize them as someone else's cars.

Joey himself wasn't too enthralled with being an auto parts salesman but he had been having a terrible time figuring out what to do with his life. The first few interviews had all been the same. Somewhere in each one, he started to smell a funny odor and he wasn't experienced enough to recognize it as fear. He'd smelled animal fear, the acrid spicy smell of blood, the sharp musty odor of snakes, the ozone that attacks women several times each month (now they called it PMS, but next week it would have a another name), but this one had a different bouquet. Kind of like mildew and athletic socks that have been used and then used again before they were washed. It was obnoxious but bearable and, as time went on, he would get to know it quite well.

It seems that in the business world, if an interviewee comes on as intelligent and strong, he is considered a threat by the interviewer. Young, strong, intelligent men tend to screw up the system by analyzing it and effecting change where necessary. Although change is a prerequisite to progress, it is almost always painful. In short, the old guys are afraid the young guys are going to come in and steal their jobs . . . which, of course, is a natural progression.

The end result was that he was getting very uneasy about going out in the business world at all. These people that were talking to him not only seemed unsure of themselves, but they also appeared to be somewhat ignorant of what their true function was in relation to their co-workers and their companies. Maybe the best bet, Joey thought, would be to take a teaching position. Certainly, most of the people who taught him were pretty unimaginative types who were really only a few pages ahead of the class in the textbook. He knew that, if nothing else, he was an interesting talker and should be popular with the students. Deep down inside, though, he knew that he should probably take a shot at making some large money.

The job itself had really come about kind of by accident. After his disillusionment with the big company interviews, one of the motorcycle groupies that he and J. C. had been riding with introduced him to his roommate who sold auto parts for a living. After looking the operation over, he decided to try it for a little while and off he went into the salesman's world.

It was quite a shock to his system. He knew something about cars and how they worked but he wasn't at all ready for the business world. Clinging to the high and mighty liberalism that he had cultivated in the classrooms and bars in his long educational career didn't help him at all in his new endeavor. It was hard to justify cutting his hair, much less putting on a suit and tie and some wingtips.

Nonetheless, the economic climate was right. Businesses of all types were flourishing, given the bank's new attitude since deregulation. The "oil bidness" was more lucrative then ever with prices heading toward $40 a barrel. Real estate was appreciating at an unheard of rate and everything looked rosy. So why not just jump out and go for it? People will always need cars to get around and they break down a lot in the Texas heat and it's not as risky as the "oil bidness," anyway, he reasoned.

The situation was further complicated by the owner of the little company that he went to work for. It wasn't obvious at the outset but the guy turned out to be of dubious gender. In the Eighties they would term this type of behavior "androgenous." In the Seventies, however, the guy was decidedly queer. Joey got his first inkling of this situation on their first sales trip.

In the car on their way to Houston (sales trips in those days were mostly by car), they got to talking about philosophies and that old nemesis, liberalism, jumped up again. Joey had been around a bunch of faggots in his life and his attitude was "live and let live" but he'd never been around a closet queen like this one before. He never once thought that the views he espoused on the way to Houston would come back to haunt him the way that they did.

Eight track tape players were the vogue in that time period and bootleg tapes were all over the place. Joey had bought a new Elton John tape, "Tumbleweed Connection," for the trip. You could buy them for $.99 at the 7-Eleven. He had always been a sucker for the written word and Bernie Taupin's lyrics were just about right for the state of mind that he was in. Unfortunately, the popular opinion being passed around in the music circles at the time was that Bernie and Elton were lovers as well as collaborators. Little did he know that this West Texas redneck that owned the company would misconstrue his musical preference for a sexual one.

By the time they got to Houston, it was late and the two six packs that they drank on the way down had made them a little drowsy. "Starvin' Marvin" checked them in at the hotel and, since he watched expenses closely, got them one room with two beds. Joey didn't think anything of it since it was all new to him, anyway. He did notice that ol' Marv liked to walk around without his clothes on a lot, but he also noticed that he spent an awful lot of the time looking at Joey in a strange manner and, as he smoked cigarette after cigarette, Joey noticed a definite effeminence in his motions with his hands which had exceptionally long nails. The good news was, after the long trip and the beer, they both fell into a deep sleep and the next morning went to work.

Their first stop was at Epstein Auto Supply and Joey was kind of nervous since he had never been on a sales call before. As they sat in the waiting room Marv said, "Just let me handle this, you need to see how it works."

Now, Joey had never tried to sell anything besides himself be-

31

fore but in the last week or so he had been schooled on several of the product lines that Marvin sold. He felt real comfortable with the ones that he was familiar with but what the hell did he know about automatic transmission parts, anyway? He was prepared to jump in if things went his way but he wouldn't be in a hurry to make a fool of himself.

Jacob Abraham Epstein had come up the hard way in the auto parts business. First of all, he was a Jew in a redneck's world. Cowboys don't have an innate hatred of the Jewish people like the Nazis do but they are quite wary of anyone who does not speak like them, cook like them and/or appears smarter than them. If you know anything about the Jewish religion, you probably are aware that they are real serious about "kosher." Kosher in the real sense of the word means clean and really that's the whole basis of their way of life. They like everything clean . . . everything. Cowboys aren't worried about how clean things are, they're more interested in whether the cows have water, how to stay cool in the summer, warm in the winter and how to make enough money to stay in the cowboy business.

So here they were sitting in front of Jake Epstein, one of the original guys in the business, and ol' Marvin was going to show Joey something. This wasn't some case study in some classroom, this was the real thing, the real job. And out comes Jake, all businessman bluster and Old Spice.

"So Marvin, what have you got to sell me today, . . . and who is this?"

"Well, this is Joey Hews and we're here to sell you everything that we have in the bag. We have radios, gaskets, . . ."

"Enough, enough already! Who is this young guy?"

"This is Joey Hews, he's young, he's smart . . . . . ."

"And he'll steal your business, Marvin," Jake said, "he's a lot stronger than you are and he'll do it."

"Now wait a minute Mr. Epstein, I have no intention . . ." Joey spluttered.

"Not now, but maybe later," Jake intoned, kinda like a lady who reads palms, "maybe after you figure this whole thing out. Maybe then you'll see what I mean . . . and when you see it, then you come call on me. But business, schmizzness. What are you selling me, Marvin?"

Well, it wasn't long until Joey came to call again and, when he did, he understood what Jake meant and Jake **did** listen. Their friendship was sealed and it continued for a long time. It wasn't until many years later that Joey realized how much that relationship meant to him. It's often the case that the least likely trees bear the most fruit. Jake didn't want to waste his time on any old salesman, but this young guy got his attention. He not only was enthusiastic, like Jake used to be, he was also intelligent, like Mac, and that was a plus.

"Mac" McDonald was an anachronism in the automotive business in the southwest. Not only was he probably the only Gentile that could put up with ol' Jake, but he also showed an innate propensity for business and an acute insight into people. His first impression of Joey was, he's all show and no go. This guy won't last fifteen minutes with Jake! And he was almost right, Joey almost didn't last fifteen minutes with the old man. But when the sales call was over and Jake had told him to come back someday, Mac knew that he would be alright.

Mac was an inherently gentle man, who wanted to only do right by anyone who was genuine. Maybe it was because of Jake, whom he called J. A., always beating him down. But that was the way that Jake had always been and would always be, and Jake had made a nice living for everyone that stayed around him. Anyhow, Mac's strong suit was perseverance and he might now get a chance to teach a little of that to Joey.

"Look, I'm going to tell you only once how to handle this situation," Mac said gently, "with J. A. there is no compromise as far as he is concerned. What you do is, you make him want whatever it is that you need to sell him and everything will be okay. And don't give him your best deal right away. If you give it to him up front, then you won't have anything to give him when he asks for more later on."

This sounded vaguely familiar to Joey, kind of like something that he should have remembered from some lost last night. Kind of like that rule you learned in fifth grade and forgot about all those years until suddenly it came back to you. The hard part to accept is that people really are all instinctively selfish; they have to be to survive. So why does anyone expect anything else? Why all of this soul-searching? Why all of this disappointment when people react exactly as everyone knew they would? Why this wishing that they weren't the way they were? You expect me to answer those questions? No friggin' way, Jack!

Joey took to the auto parts business like he was made for it or maybe he just took to the people. They sure didn't take to him too easily. He was sort of like Jake in some ways. He wasn't Jewish but he didn't hit it off with the rednecks right away. He had a feeling for business but no credentials. Rednecks didn't know credentials anyhow, all they knew was chicken fried steak and mashed potatoes; cold beer; dancin'; and gettin' a little booger now and then.

So out into the cold cruel world of business goes Joey the salesman. Probably the saving grace of it all, if now the cards were counted, was that Joey didn't know that he was about to enter the Great American Rut. He wasn't even aware that he was caught up in the system. It was just a way to make a living. It was only something that would be like a fleeting moment, something that maybe he would remember at some future date . . . but was he ever successful!

The money began to roll in and with the money came a house and nice cars and Debra's fickle Momma's respect. The easy way to get that respect, and interestingly enough the one that Debra chose, was to feather her nest with the type of house that Momma would "appreciate." Joey, in his ubiquitous desire to "take the smoothest path" and not ruffle any feathers, went along with Debra's choices on type of construction, interior appointments, etc. as long as he could choose where they lived. Naturally, he picked a pastoral setting as far away from Momma as they could live without Debra going absolutely bonkers on him.

This was how they ended up in a North Dallas type of home out in the middle of nowhere but close to a country club. Part of the trade off, of course, was that they had to have a barn and horses. The house did turn out quite nicely because the setting was beautiful up on top of the hill between Dallas and Fort Worth. They were close enough to one of those man-made lakes that are all over Texas to have a lake view and yet far enough away to avoid most of the trash that seems drawn to those types of recreational areas.

From the living area and from all the bedrooms there was a splendid view of trees and lake and barn and horses. As a matter of fact the house was absolutely rife with floor to ceiling windows . . . especially east-facing windows. Which, of course, for several nights in each month, if the sky was clear, were chock full of Ol' man moon . . .

All these things together helped make things bearable, but a dark image seemed to be lurking in Joey's subconscious, a gut-chilling foreboding that snuck up on him when he let his guard completely down. Like that moment just before you give yourself up to

34

sleep or the one just before you fully awaken. Like most people that have these extrasensory type perceptions, Joey was sure that everyone else had them just like him and for that reason never bothered to talk much about them to anyone else. Also, it seemed that everytime he did open up about them a little, people started finding a reason to leave or change the subject or something. This tended to bring on a slight tinge of paranoia to Joey's life but he discounted it as just a bit of temporary insecurity and, sure enough, most of the time it went away.

The more that he was around Starvin' Marvin, the worse the paranoia became. This guy was unreal. Joey, for the life of him, couldn't figure out how he had gotten into business, much less how he stayed in it. In the southwest men have an innate distaste for anyone who is less than macho, much less one who is gay. In the bigger metroplexes some of this was tolerated, but old Marv had been born and raised in a small West Texas town, a hotbed of conservatism, son of a used car salesman and his domineering schoolmarm wife.

He grew up straight, tall and handsome with a four pack a day cigarette habit that he acquired from his used-car salesman father. It wasn't until after college when homosexuality came out in the open and was almost socially acceptable that he discovered that, if you went both ways, you never went home alone.

He had moved from West Texas to "Big D" in the fall after his graduation from a small Junior college and he was completely in awe of the city. His first job was with a twice removed cousin who was in the auto parts business. After working in his store for about six months, a large manufacturer of mufflers offered him a job as a traveling salesman and he began to learn the salesman's nomadic lifestyle. After all those years being held captive in a small, dusty West Texas town where a newsworthy event was the passing through of an eighteen wheeler, the opportunity to travel in four very different states was a dream come true. It was during a sales trip to New Orleans that he learned how to "walk on the other side of the street."

New Orleans in the early Sixties was kind of a southern New York City. For that matter, if it weren't for the southern drawl, with your eyes closed it still could be mistaken for that city in the summertime. The accent is a combination of cajun French, Afro-American patois and redneck . . . heavy on the redneck. As a matter of fact, the locals say, the only thing that separates a coonass (cajun) from a

35

redneck is the Sabine River. At any rate, New Orleans was and is a haven for artists, writers and creative types of all sizes, shapes, and colors. As such in the Sixties, it was also a mecca for the stimuli that accompany most artistic communities.

Marvin was enthralled with the city from the very first time that he drove the twelve hours from Dallas to make business calls there. He loved the narrow crowded streets and the french architecture. He loved the little bistros and open air cafes that smelled of wine and cajun spices. He loved the people and their avant garde way of life. He also found out some things about himself that never would have occurred to him in Pampa, Texas.

His particular genesis began with a bisexual female artist in residence that he met in a place called La Boucherrie one cool fall evening. He had been drinking since early in the afternoon, celebrating the sale of a year's quota of mufflers to a large chain of installation centers that morning. She was sitting in a back booth and although not pretty in the true sense of the word, she was clean and attractive. As he came back from the restroom just a wee bit tipsy, he peeked over her shoulder at the drawing that she was creating and lo and behold it was a portrait of himself sitting at the bar. Stunned, he stood and stared for an eternity that lasted some thirty long seconds. When he could finally break away from the picture, he found he was looking directly into her black gypsy eyes.

"If you like it, why don't you join me?" she said solemnly.

"Only if I can buy you a drink and maybe talk you out of the picture."

"Buy me the drink and I'll think about it, cowboy," she said warming up just a wee bit.

Boy, stuff like this didn't happen very often in Dallas much less where he grew up. This might just be the right place for him to be. So, he collected his change from the bar and sat down across from his new friend who simultaneously ordered a double Cuervo Gold straight up with a lime back and began drawing him again. This time front on.

"You have great features," she said, "sorta like John Wayne, but more feminine."

Now being from West Texas where the men are men and the women like 'em that way, he was just a little put off by that remark but then again, as he thought back on it, he never had been much of one for manly endeavors growing up. When the other boys had been

36

riding horses or bulls or otherwise cowboying, he had preferred working at his Dad's used-car lot cleaning or selling cars. When basketball season rolled around and the coach wanted this tall lanky Texan to play, he had politely declined saying that his Dad needed his help at the car lot. This was mainly a product of his imagination since actually his Dad's was the only car lot in town and most of the locals would rather deal with him than with some city-slicker up in Amarillo. It also helped that the celebratory scotch that he had been drinking was starting to hook up and he was feeling a little magical at the moment. The idea that she thought him handsome and attractive was extremely seductive. Who gave a whit about the feminine part?

Not looking up from her work, she murmured, "You must be from Texas but where's your macho? Did you leave it in your other pants? Or could it be that I've finally found a sensitive cowboy?"

Her husky New Orleans accent and the magic of the afternoon made the suggestion of his sensitivity seem all that much more attractive and he found himself wanting to hear more. Hell, he was 600 miles from Dallas and more than that from his mother, he could damn sure be anything he wanted to be here in this wonderful town. At this stage of intoxication, combined with the ambience of the cafe and the funny fall New Orleans afternoon light, he began to have a delicious out-of-body experience. One where he was just an observer, watching a conversation between this semi-pretty, extremely talented artist and a John Wayne look-alike from Pampa, Texas. What a trip, he thought in his best North Dallas hip jargon.

"How many times are you going to draw me this afternoon?"

"As long as you'll sit and talk to me. It won't hurt if you'll buy me a drink now and then. Later on, maybe I'll take you to dinner and we'll go listen to a friend of mine make music."

Well, needless to say, Marvin had never seen such in his whole life. Here was an artist, a bona fide creative type person and she was coming on to him like a house afire. Sheeeit! This beat the dog out of sittin' in Daddy's Money on Greenville Avenue and looking for some SMU cheerleader type all coiffed and smelling of the latest musk from Neiman-Marcus' chic but cheap collection. He'd been through all that quite a few times and found it fun but severely lacking for some reason.

It seemed that after a Saturday night of sanitary almost sterile love-making and the obligatory Sunday brunch at some Greenville Avenue "in spot," he'd always end up with that same hollow feeling.

As if he hadn't really been there the night before, it had only been a dream and not a very vibrant dream at that.

After two more Cuervos and one more portrait, this time a silouhette against the last rays of the afternoon sun through the french doors of the cafe, she was ready to leave. Besides, although he was really enjoying all of this attention, Marv was chompin' at the bit to get on with whatever the evening was going to bring. He said he'd like to go to his hotel, freshen up and change out of his business clothes into something a little more casual. He was staying at the Downtowner Motor Inn right on Bourbon Street and it was only a short walk from the cafe. She said since it was close she'd just join him and off they went. He carried her artist's case and she held his arm as they ricochetted gently off each other on down the street.

When they got to his room, he went into the bathroom to shower. As he smiled at himself in the mirror he thought, I really **do** look like John Wayne! A quick shave, shower and out he popped to a sight that just about knocked him to his knees.

There she was propped up on pillows in bed, stark naked, with the TV tuned to an x-rated movie (you could get anything you wanted in New Orleans) with one hand twirling a taut brown nipple while the other idled around between her legs. On the ashtray next to her sat a still smoldering joint of some kind of exotic hemp.

She stopped stroking herself long enough to offer him a hit and smiling languorously up at him, murmured, "You took so long, I kinda got started without you. Want to join in?"

It only took a short while for him to "join in" and, much to his amazement and pleasure, they continued to "join in" for the better part of the evening. Dinner consisted of room service hamburgers, another x-rated movie to stir up the fire again, some strawberry shortcake which they ended up smearing all over each other before devouring it (and themselves) and, to top it all off, another cigar-sized joint. The grand finale was, while he was coming at her from behind while watching the TV over her shoulder, she reached back and insinuated his member into not its proper aperture.

Now this was something he had heard about and never in his life thought he would do . . . but, my god, did he ever like it! Ol' Marvin had finally found what he had been starvin' for all of this time. No more would he have that empty feeling afterward.

All of this took place on a Thursday afternoon and evening. On the following day, they went to breakfast and then over to her house so that she could freshen up. Afterwards they ambled around the French Quarter meeting her friends and talking. By mid-afternoon they were back in his room with the TV on and a fresh joint going and him trying out that new found pleasure again. Finally, after they had both exhausted their libidos, they slept until early evening. When he awakened she was already dressed and ready to go. Just to keep everything mellow they fired up one more little joint and burned it down before they walked out the door.

"Remember that friend of mine who makes music?" She smiled, "well, let's go see him."

They walked about two blocks down the street to another little open air bistro. Looking in, he could see a long-haired young guy on a stool who looked a lot like Cat Stevens and sounded even more like him. Upon recognizing her he broke into "Hard Headed Woman" which made her light up like a neon sign. Back to the Cuervo for her and the scotch for him. This was the way they whiled away the evening. Many drinks and many songs later they found themselves walking down the street all three arm in arm together.

"Let's all go up to your room, since it's so close," she laughed.

Boy, thought Marvin, I've read about this kind of stuff but I never thought I'd see the day when I'd be part of it. Golly bum! I ain't never had this much fun in my life! Well, he may have thought that, during the night before and the ensuing afternoon, he'd finally found what he had been missing but he was mistaken. For somewhere in the tangle of sweaty bodies in his room at the Downtowner, he ended up in that newly found place he liked so well . . . but it didn't belong to her, it belonged to the singer.

At this point ol' Marv decided on the spot (so to speak) that this was really what he had been missing all those years. Anyway, they spent the rest of the weekend engaged in drinking, smoking marijuana, eating and floundering around on and in each other until early Monday morning.

On his way out of town after kissing her (and the singer) good-bye, Marvin felt more content than he ever had before. He had finally found his true calling in life. Although still enjoying the company of women, he really preferred men.

It was several years later that he showed this side of his life to Joey. They had been working together for six or eight months when they happened to end up in New Orleans together and were staying at the same hotel where Marvin had found his true purpose several years previously. As fortune would have it, they had been working on a large account and just that very day had secured a substantial piece of business with them. Perhaps harkening back to that earlier time that meant so much to him, Marvin had suggested that they go down on Bourbon Street to celebrate. They ended up in the same little open air bistro where he and the artist had met the singer. There was another picker sitting on a stool singing folk music when they arrived.

"Well, partner, we gave 'em hell today didn't we?" old Marvin was flushed with the adrenalin rush that salesmen get when they make that big sale.

As fate would have it, the new business that they had written that day would end up being the springboard that put them into some pretty large money. Ironically enough, this event would also be the impetus that would cause Joey to eventually go into business on his own.

"What do you want to do tonight to celebrate, Joey?"

Joey, too, was riding the salesman's high and couldn't wait to call home and share his good fortune with Debra. "I think I'll run up and call Debra, change into some blue jeans, and then let's go to that little bar down at the Royal Sonesta for some crawdads and cold beer!"

With that they left the bar and headed for their hotel. As they got off the elevator, Marvin smiled, "I'll leave the door open, just come on in when you're ready to go."

After sharing the good news with Debra, Joey took a quick shower and changed into some blue jeans and cowboy boots. He had always been more comfortable in casual clothes and immediately felt more at ease than he had all day. Lately, he had had more and more trouble feeling comfortable around Marvin. It wasn't his speculation that Marvin was gay that bothered him but the little dark cloud seemed to be lurking in the background of his subconcious whenever he was around him these days. Deep down he knew, although he couldn't admit it to himself or anyone else, that sooner or later he and Marvin would probably go their separate ways. Right now, however, things looked pretty damn rosy.

As he walked down the hall toward Marvin's room, he hummed a little Crosby, Stills and Nash.

"Wooden ships on the water, very free . . . and easy."

Coming to Marvin's room he noticed that the door was open a

crack so he just pushed his way in. He could hear the sound of the shower behind the closed bathroom door and Marvin was nowhere to be found, so he pulled a beer out of the little pay-as-you-go refrigerator and turned on the television. In a few minutes Marvin came out wrapped in a towel and smiling like a Chesire cat.

"Get everything handled, Joey? Everybody okay at home?"

"Yeah, everything is just ducky. Let's load up and get some of that crawfish. I'm starvin'!"

He really wasn't all that hungry but he instantly remembered why he didn't like to be around Marvin in a hotel room. Ol' Marv was prancing around in the altogether as it seemed he did every chance he got when Joey was around. Joey fidgetted around with the channel selector and tried to concentrate on the television. Ironically enough, just at that moment the news broadcaster was doing a piece on the growing problem of gay-bashing in places like Houston and the Oak Lawn section of Dallas. About this time Marvin, still buck naked, struck a pose right in front of Joey between him and the television.

"How do you like the size of that equipment, partner?," he said, slurring his words just a touch.

Joey hadn't realized that Marvin was already a little tipsy but, what the hell, who cared? They had had a good day and everybody deserves to celebrate a little now and then.

"That's real nice Marvin. Now let's go get some of them crawfish and a cold beer."

He looked up and Marvin not only hadn't moved but he was looking Joey right in the eye with a look that Joey had never seen on a man before. At least not on a man looking into his eyes like that.

"Hey, Joey, you ever get it on with a man?" before Joey could reply he started talking a mile a minute. "Look, I'll do whatever you want me to do to you, or you can do anything you want to me, or I'll
. . . . . . "

By this time Joey had jumped up, spilling his beer all over the bed, and was backing rapidly toward the door with both hands stretched out in front of him. He'd been approached by queers before but never by anyone so frantic as Marvin was at that moment and it startled him. He stopped at the door and was amazed at how calm his voice sounded when he spoke to Marvin.

"Look, man, I really don't go for that kind of thing, so why don't you just get dressed and let's go. If you don't want to mess up our friendship, let's just forget this whole thing happened and go on."

"Aw, c'mon Joey, I was just like you and then one night right here in New Orleans . . . . . ."

"Goddammit, Marvin, I said cool it! Now, I'll be at the bar at the Royal Sonesta. You simmer down before you join me or don't join me at all."

"Whew," Joey thought as he hurried down the hall without looking back, "that was close. The sumbitch was nearly hysterical in there. He must have been drunker than I thought. Well, that should teach you something, moron, a faggot's got to be kind of screwed up to be that way in the first place, so it's probably best to avoid any situations where things like that can happen . . . especially with that loon."

In a short while Marvin showed up at the bar and acted as if nothing out of the ordinary had transpired. They had been there about a half hour when he started hitting on two middle-aged school teachers just in from Terre Haute who were at the bar obviously looking for some action. First thing you know he invited them over to the table for some of the crawdads and beer.

Joey tried to be polite but the one with the big nose kept looking at him like he was something good to eat and she hadn't eaten in days. Over and over he had to keep taking her hand out of his lap and putting it back in her own. Marvin in the meantime was helping his little schoolmarm unzip his fly under the table where nobody could see. I guess he's trying to show me that I must have been dreaming up there in his room, Joey thought, I think I'll just ease on out of here.

"Would you ladies excuse me a minute? I have to go to the bathroom."

Old big nose started to get up as if to follow him but Joey was past her in a flash. When she looked over at Marvin and her pal, big nose all of a sudden noticed what was going on between them and, as Joey made it safely out the door, she had already cozied up on the other side of Marvin and was directing **his** hand into **her** lap. That's perfect Joey thought, the sumbitch wants to jump my bones a half hour ago and now he's gonna take those two horny old uglies and do a menage a trois . . . figures. Wonder if I walked up and told them about that deal back at the hotel if they'd be so hot to go.

With this he slid back to the doorway and peeked in. There was Marvin looking right at him and right through him at the same time with a kind of half smile on his face while the one on his right worked feverishly under the table and the one on his left had a look very much like Marvin's on her face. They'll be just fine he thought, as he ambled on down the street to La Boucherrie for a nice relaxing beer before he went to bed. As he was sitting at the bar nursing his beer and musing on the events of the day, he noticed that the little bit of darkness had left his subconcious and he was at peace for the first time in a long while. Unfortunately, it wasn't long before it returned.

Chapter Three

IT WAS ONE OF those mornings several months later that the little dark cloud woke him with a start, shivering in apprehension. He had to get up early that day to catch a plane to an auto parts convention in Chicago and wasn't really looking forward to all of the boring sales meetings and the endless entertaining. In the beginning it had been a lot of fun; going to new cities, partying til late at night with customers and then stroking their egos all day long, but after a few years of this the routine was beginning to pale and Joey's sense of h umor began to wear a little thin. It also was beginning to go from fall to winter in Texas. That is a gray time of the year and with very little sun Joey had been getting a little depressed of late. With some snatches of "A Lighter Shade Of Pale" drifting in and out of his head, he stepped into a warm shower to try to break the mood. It didn't help much.

Debra came in as he was brushing his teeth. "Where are you off to this week?"

"Got to go to Chicago to the APAA show and I'm not really looking forward to it."

"Oh come on Joey, you love it and you know it. You like being on stage with all those people stroking your ego. Hell, you can't even take a dump without someone applauding at the end."

"Darlin', was it something I said or do you just want to give me another wonderful send-off as I go out to do battle with all those big shots?"

"You need to spend more time at home with me and not so much time in that damn business of yours. Last week it was Houston, the week before that San Antonio and now it's Chicago. Meanwhile, I get to stay home and clean toilets. It's just not fair."

"Isn't this a wonderful house we have?" Joey said gently. "And your new car and your horses and the tennis club and . . . . . ."

Debra came over and hugged him murmuring, "I just want things the way they were when we were in school. We never take the day off and just make love and hang around anymore. You work all week and then we go off and ride bikes all weekend and then back to work. Every vacation is with your business clients or my sister and all those screaming kids. We need new friends. I want you to take up tennis so that we can go to the club together."

This, of course, was the beginning of the "I need a change so you change" phase of the relationship. If it wasn't tennis it would have been western dancing or boating or gardening or something besides that which they were doing. This is one of the main differences between men and women, this looking for something new. The yen for something different is also the reason that women are such great consumers. They absolutely love change and the act of changing things, be they animate or inanimate. Lord Baltimore or Lord Chesterfield or someone said that men marry women hoping they won't change and women marry men hoping they will and, unfortunately, they are both sadly disappointed.

The good news is, that due to this quirk women are a great source of sales for all "new" or "improved" products. When men find something they like, they stick with it. Women on the other hand only live for something new. Maybe that's why men kept them under control for so many years. It might have been the only way to protect them from themselves. At any rate, marketing these days is merely a study of women's habits, for they are the great consumers. Between alimony and government subsidies, they also are the wealthiest segment of the market, but back to the emerging problem at hand.

Joey had been happy at work and play long enough. It was time to do something that Debra liked. Actually, she loved the camping and biking but they were not what Momma thought to be "class" avocations. Momma wanted her daughter to belong to a first class country club and drive a "big shiny car."

"That's why I married your Daddy, honey, because he had the biggest, shiniest car in town. You can learn to love any man, all they want to do is get in your pants anyway. What you got in the house to drink, baby? I think it's time for a little cocktail just to improve my appetite before lunch, dontcha know."

Momma, as usual, had had her "orange juice" (with just a tiny bit of vodka in it to cut the too-sweet taste of fresh oranges) this morning and was ready to move onto some scotch to get the awful taste of cigarettes out of her mouth. At one time she had been one of Dallas' leading real estate salespeople. When the boom was on everyone that could drive a Cadillac got into the business and, as property values inflated like a hot air balloon, the action was fast and furious. Momma missed the excitement of the real estate business and that's what she blamed the drinking on. She told everyone that she quit the business to spend more time with her family but, in reality, Daddy got tired of having to go and get her out of some building contractor's bed all the time. So he made her quit.

"Now, Daddy, I was just trying to get a listing on this beautiful new house he built and I got a little drunk. I was only sleeping it off before I drove home. Nothing happened. You trust me don't you, darlin'?"

Joey enjoyed going to tennis clubs almost as much as he enjoyed being on the receiving end of a fleet enema. He had never seen so many phonies in his life. They all ran around spanking themselves on their hips and giving themselves little pep talks as they missed this shot or that, all the time looking for that elusive top-spin backhand. But in the interests of domestic tranquility, he grudgingly agreed to start on Debra's new program the following weekend. He had good hand-eye coordination and the weekend biking was keeping him in great shape so he'd probably look good in those little outfits that they wore.

He came back from Chicago smelling of cigar smoke, stale beer and disillusionment. It seemed that when the automotive business had been smaller it had also been a whole lot simpler. Usually, the particular convention that he had just attended was a good place to see old friends from all over the United States and to write a lot of business with customers. This year, however, he had spent an inordinate amount of time defending his lines from rival companies as they tried to lure them away from him. Most of them were manufacturers that he had literally taken from no where to some major volume and, for that reason, they all stayed with him.

This type of crap was all new to him, however, and he did not

46

like the tone of the business. He usually thrived on competition but this stuff smelled of big company politics which, of course, was why he had avoided big business in the first place. Even with all the in-fighting, the convention had been exceptional for his business and it looked like he'd have another banner year. If he could only get rid of those little twinges of paranoia that kept creeping up on him when he wasn't looking.

In reality it was probably just the nature of the business that he was in. The auto parts business was finally becoming big enough to warrant the attention of all the shrewd business sharks that con-stantly cruised around in the ocean of commerce. As going home time neared he found himself actually looking forward to the tennis as a diversion from the dog-eat-dog world that he suddenly found himself a part of.

Ironically enough, when Joey and Debra walked into the tennis club that weekend, he was almost overwhelmed with those same feelings he had had at the auto parts convention. There was some-thing instinctively wrong with the people he met. They were nice enough looking but it was all so superficial. They huddled together in little groups and always quit talking if anyone came near. Suppos-edly they were there for the exercise but after an hour's play, the regulars all went to the bar where they smoked and drank for the rest of the afternoon.

Joey hooked up with a local insurance agent who played pretty well and was hip to all of the country club dirt. This was the stuff that *Cosmo* and *New Woman* were all about. It was hard to keep up with who was screwing who without a scorecard and it was obvious that several of the members were anxious for Joey and Debra to get into the loop.

Although he traveled a lot, Joey was pretty old-fashioned about extracurricular activities. He and Debra had promised each other that, if they really felt that it was necessary to mess around, they'd be honest enough to split the sheets first. The last thing they needed, as much as he was away from Debra, was to have to worry about one or the other cheating. Both of them, however, were very conscious of their looks and the shape they were in and some poor dissatisfied soul was always hitting on one or both of them. In the beginning they laughed off the whole business as a bunch of sorry old rich folks who were just bored . . . after awhile, though, Joey began to get a little tired of all the drunks pawing at him and Debra.

It was when they went to their first tennis "camp" that the real problems began. These camps were really just social events. They always took place at a beautiful but expensive resort and were a package deal. Ostensibly, club players went to them to improve the quality of play and the "camps" always featured a former touring pro. Someone recognizable to the public who was required to have a British accent, tennis being veddy veddy British, you know. But inevitably, the whole deal was to show off your new tennis togs, wristwatch and backhand.

Joey was more at home at a motocross or some other go-fast event. His idea of fun was a few beers around the pickup truck after an afternoon of racing. These tennis people liked to practice in the morning for an hour and a half, take two hours for lunch while they discussed every single stroke they had hit that morning, and play a couple of hours of tennis in the afternoon. Then it was off to the pool to have a few drinks and hit on each other's spouses til it was time for dinner. All this for three hundred dollars a day. Damn fine fun!

Joey gave it his best, both on the court and off. With no distractions, other than the usual country club clods, he actually had a pretty good time. It was springtime in the Texas hill country and the weather was beautiful; crisp, cool mornings and warm afternoons. He'd get up and run each morning, go hit some balls for an hour or two, then chase ol' Debra around the room for a little while after lunch. The evenings were filled with activities that he tried to avoid. Most nights they went into Austin for Mexican food and dancing. He had to be careful about that though because, even though he was a passable dancer, he really didn't like it all that much.

Women love dancing. A friend of mine's wife once said that, to women, dancing is a form of foreplay and she's probably right. Maybe that's why men get upset when their wives or girlfriends insist on dancing with strangers. That might have been Joey's first clue that something was amiss with him and Debra. It seemed that everytime they went out recently she would end up dancing with someone other than him, more likely than not lately . . . with total strangers.

They went to the Armadillo in Austin one night while they were at tennis camp. Willie Nelson was playing and this was before he became a big star so getting a good table was not a problem. There were two couples from the tennis camp along with Joey and Debra. One of the guys was obviously interested in Debra and was having a hard time hiding it. As the night progressed and he had had enough liquid courage, he finally stumbled over to ask her to dance. Joey saw what was coming so, just as the guy got to her, he grabbed her hand and walked her out onto the dance floor.

"Well, that was rude," she hissed in his ear.

"I really don't feel comfortable with you dancing with yahoos like that, darlin'. That sumbitch is drunk and on the make and that kind of stuff has trouble written all over it."

"Oh, come on! All he wants to do is dance. Don't you trust me?"

"Sure I trust you, darlin', but if he wants to dance let him dance with his own wife."

"Look, Joey, these people are just trying to be sociable and if he asks me to dance again, I will. I might even ask him to dance!"

"Debra, I'd really appreciate it if you wouldn't do that . . ."

Well, you guessed it. Debra went ahead and danced with the guy and he **was** drunk and after awhile he tried to sneak a little kiss. Joey pretended not to notice but when she kept on dancing with him he started to wonder a little. It looked like she was starting to enjoy this guy chasing her around. When he complained, she asked him why he didn't ask the guy's wife to dance. He told her he had no desire to dance with anyone but her and she said she was just having fun.

The evening ended with the drunk finally sneaking in a kiss and Debra getting mad and wanting Joey to beat the snot out of the guy. Well, if women admit that dancing is a form of foreplay, then why do they get mad when a guy wants a little kiss? Isn't that a part of foreplay too? And if they don't want to encourage that kind of stuff, why aren't they a little more particular about who they are foreplaying with? Needless to say, the ride home was quiet and extremely tense.

When they got back to the resort Debra wasn't in the mood to play one way or another and neither was Joey. Even though the deal hadn't come to blows it had really bothered him. He told himself that he could trust her but deep down in his subconscious that little bit of uneasiness started floating up toward the surface again.

"You know, honey, I'd really appreciate it if you wouldn't dance with strangers anymore. That thing back there at the Armadillo really upset me. I don't like the feelings it gave me, okay?"

"He was just drunk, that's all. Look, you don't own me. You can't tell me who I can or can't dance with. What's wrong with people dancing anyway?"

"What's wrong with people dancing is that when men and

women dance with each other they usually do it to get a little something started and that's why it often ends up like it did tonight. You've got to remember that a lot of times there are consequences when it comes to men and women getting together like that."

"Look, I like to dance and I like to be sociable and I'll do it when and where I damn well feel like it!" She screamed as she stomped out of the room slamming doors and drawers and anything else that it occurred to her to slam.

This kind of stuff had been coming up pretty regularly recently and Joey knew that it wasn't healthy. It had started with her insisting that he take her out on "dates" just like they used to before they were married. It seems that she was really interested in keeping the "romance" in their marriage.

There are several schools of thought on that subject. The traditionalists try to pretend that the initial heat of attraction doesn't decrease with time, it just gets misdirected. In actuality, the chemistry that brings people together in the beginning usually continues to be there but it changes with time and age. Its not as intense later on but it can still be satisfying.

When it comes to love, however, people, women especially, keep trying to recapture that first go-round. The one where your heart is pounding so hard that you can barely hear anything else and it's almost impossible to catch your breath. Where your mind is spinning deliriously and the tension in your pants is so delicious, you think that you are going to faint. Everything is sparky and sweet and when it's over the contentment makes you want to cry. It's a shame that with familiarity these feelings are never quite recapturable but isn't that true of all things? How come people accept it when it comes to sports or music or work, but not with love? If the body truly does change over time, then why do people expect the feelings to remain the same?

I was reading an article by a noted psychiatrist and marriage counselor and he says that after three months the heat will leave any marriage. He says that marriage is based more on acceptance than on lust, on like more than love. That when the passion isn't like it used to be, it isn't going to be like that again.

Now an awful lot of people have studied how to make love stay and no one has come up with an absolute answer to that question. But I do know one thing for sure and that is if you work your butt off trying to recapture any feeling that you once had long ago, odds are you will fail. Maybe it's better to just imagine those emotions because they were all spontaneous in the first place and trying to recreate them is futile. Besides, usually what is especially poignant to one person is not always as meaningful to the other, so the whole thing ends up wrong anyway.

The way to make love stay is really quite simple. All you need is imagination. Unfortunately that seemed to be in short supply in the seventies. The reason is that, due to all of the advances in technology in the preceding decades, most of the need for having imagination went away. Instead of being given a book to read, the seventies children had only to turn on the television to combat boredom. If it wasn't the tv, it was a video game or a computer or anything that didn't require a lot of thought. When the only toy that a kid had was something that he (she, it) made or inherited, imagination was necessary to turn it into something interesting.

It's the same with romance. After the initial heat is past, romance can become pretty routine. The sixties children, already jaded with sophisticated toys and surrealistic entertainment, didn't know how to respond to one-on-one situations. Not too many of them ever had the chance to stop and learn anything about relationships because, everytime they got bored, they'd have another diversion to move to. Their threshold of boredom thus lowered they were doomed to a life of change for change's sake. At this point it looked as if Debra, like so many other late-model ladies, was rapidly approaching her threshold of boredom.

Joey on the other hand was exercising his imagination to the hilt just trying to put up with Debra, her changing ideas and her screwed-up mother. Momma, these days, had taken to having long talks with her "baby." If only Joey could have been a fly on the wall during those conversations!

"Darlin', what's wrong with you, anyway? Joey out of town again?"

"Yes, Momma, and I don't know what I'm going to do. These days he hardly pays any attention to me."

"Well, it doesn't surprise me, honey, you bein' such a bitch and all. Why, you remind me of me . . . when I was a little younger that is."

And a little slimmer, Debra thought. Boy I hope that all the things that they say about daughters becoming like their mothers in their old age isn't true. Momma looks rode hard and put up wet!

"Momma, I'm starting to get tired of Joey always working all the time!"

"Darlin', he has to work all the time just to afford you, like your Daddy does with me. Now, if you're getting a little lonesome, go on out and get a little strange! Hell, there's lots of men would give their left nut to get into your britches!"

"Oh Momma, me and Joey made a deal that we wouldn't do that with anybody else . . . but there are a couple of guys at the tennis club that would like it. I just don't know!"

"Come on now, Debra! You seen how many times your Daddy has come back to me! The poor sons a' bitches are in **love**, honey. You can do anything that you want and they'll take you home and forgive you!"

It may sound cold, but Momma was right on two out of three counts. Joey was in love and her old man had taken her back over and over again, but that wouldn't necessarily hold true with Debra's mate.

Chapter Four

WHILE ALL OF THIS nonsense was going on between Debra and her mother, Joey was working harder than ever. It seemed that no matter how hard he worked or how much money he made, Debra could overspend him by about ten per cent. Since they had been married she had always handled the checkbook. She said he didn't know the value of a dollar. He just didn't want the hassle of an argument every time she wanted to spend some money.

This arrangement worked superbly while they were poor but all of a sudden when he started making some real money and she started bouncing checks, he got concerned. He had never been much for keeping up with the Jones'. It wasn't that he didn't like the finer things in life, it was just that all of the crap that really turned other people on wasn't very important to him. He had learned early on that the true beauty in life was in nature and there are a whole bunch of neat things out there for free . . . if you would only look for them, that is.

In Texas, that meant clear spring mornings and the soft, almost feminine sibilance of the Texas drawl, so out of place with the macho cowboy image that Texas men try to put on. One thing became readily apparent to Joey, the only real men in the Lone Star State were the cowboys. Even though all the city-folk made fun of them, those old rednecks were the only ones who had the guts to stand toe to toe with the local bad-asses . . . or any poor unsuspecting Yankee that happened along. It was neat to go down to the Longhorn Ballroom to watch some cowboy whup-up on a drunken loud-mouth and then walk off into the sunset, just like in the movies . . . and, oh, those sunsets.

Sometimes, after a long hot, hazy one hundred degree afternoon, the sunsets could bring water to his eyes. They looked like something out of a Georgia O'Keefe painting, all those pastel sun rays washed against the bold brushstrokes of gray clouds to the west . . . he never could figure out why he was the only one watching.

Anyway, the work continued at an ever increasing rate and even though the rewards were great, the income couldn't keep up with the outgo. One Sunday morning, about five years after they were married, Joey woke up after a particularly trying week and walked out to survey his domain. Jesus, it was amazing when you thought about it, from nothing to all of this. Twenty-five acres within shouting distance of both downtown Dallas and Fort Worth . . . horses, dogs, cars, a big house with a barn, and lots of open spaces . . . also lots of bills.

Each year he made more and more money, and each year he went further and further into debt. It was on this morning that he decided to take the checkbook away from Debra. He had a very understanding banker but he could see that even the most understanding fellow could at some point stop covering his account.

She walked out onto the veranda where Joey stood drinking a Diet Pepsi and was humming to himself.

"Somethin's happenin' here. What it is ain't exactly clear. There's a man with a gun over there, tellin' me, I got to beware . . . . . . think it's time we stop children what's that sound, everybody look what's goin' doowwn" . . .

"Isn't this wonderful," he said. "Just think a few years ago we didn't have anything. We weren't sure where our next nickel was coming from and now we have all of this. Who'd a' thought it!

"You know, Joey, all of my girlfriends are playing with a new tennis raquet that's a lot prettier than mine and we can get it wholesale from Dick's Discount."

"Yeah, well that's something we have to talk about. We have to start budgeting. I can't continue to cover all of these overdrafts at the bank and maintain a good credit rating. As a matter of fact, it's probably time for me to take over the check book."

54

"What do you mean, take over the checkbook? You don't know a thing about money. If it wasn't for me you'd spend us into the poor house!"

"Look, honey, we make more money than I ever expected to make in my lifetime, but we aren't getting ahead. I work harder and harder and we barely keep up. We have to slow down. I don't care about keeping up with anyone else, I just want to slow the pace down a little. Maybe we ought to go back to camping and motorcycles, god knows we had a lot more fun then!"

"You had a lot more fun then, not me! I've changed a whole bunch since those days and, besides, if we started riding motorcycles again and I got hurt, I wouldn't be able to play tennis. You've always told me, whenever I wanted money you'd just go out and make more. You said you were a money-makin' machine!"

He had said exactly that . . . but when he said it they didn't have diddly and he had just sold a bunch of water pumps to HiLo Auto Parts. This was five years later and he didn't feel nearly as invincible as he had then. It's real funny, he mused, how you go through all these glimpses of hindsight lucidity as you get older.

When he was younger, and that was only a few years ago, he literally exuded optimism. Everyday was a new opportunity, a new challenge, and one that he knew he was more than up to. This was in the beginning when it was all so easy he couldn't figure out why everyone wasn't doing it. Then, as time went on and that little bit of paranoia started to creep in, this selfsame optimism went to a cautious level of confidence. At which point Joey suffered a few of the downturns that are inevitable in life. Character builders, I think the guys on "Face The Nation" call them. They weren't really all that traumatic but they hurt none-the-less . . . most of them concerned business.

There is no higher high than making a big sale . . . but there also is no lower low than losing one that you have worked on real hard. On top of all that these types of defeats usually came in bunches for some reason (or maybe for no reason). After going through a particularly painful batch of defeats Joey slipped into a wee-bit of depression. Now, instead of looking in the mirror and admiring himself, he started noticing a line here and there, a bit of a sag in the chin, a little more forehead than he had yesterday, more face, and such a pretty face . . . or was it so pretty anymore?.

All of a sudden, instead of jumping confidently into the breach when a decision was called for, he not only paused but oftentimes would consult trusted friends for advice. This lack of spontaneity was not only a hindrance but also cause for consternation. He wasn't used to any kind of chink in his armor . . . nor were his friends.

It was probably during this time that he started paying more and more attention to those around him. It wasn't necessarily because of the changes in Debra (although that had occurred to him too), but things that had passed him by before stood out more glaringly obvious than ever before. Suddenly he started noticing that people might be laughing **at** him not **with** him. In the beginning he passed it off as his own insecurity but later on it became apparent that he might not be as well thought of as he would have liked.

When he didn't have anything and neither did any of his friends, there wasn't any reason for jealousy, but as time went on and success came so easily, a gap began to form between he and his buddies. He had been very generous with his friends from early-on. When he had money, everybody had money. As he became wealthier he started picking up more and more of the tabs for drinks and dinner that he and his buddies incurred. At the time, most of the guys that he hung around with were lagging pretty far behind him in the money department and, without his generosity, would not have been able to enjoy themselves nearly as often. This was especially true of Jimmy Jeff Stewart.

Jimmy Jeff was one of the first friends that Joey had made when he migrated from his East Coast upbringings to the plains of North Texas. His first stop after finding his new home had been a local bar for a few beers. Jimmy Jeff was putting himself through college playing guitar in a small-time band and they were playing that night. He played music about as half-assed as he did everything else and this would carry on throughout his life. Joey heckled him about his big nose and his lousy singing. Jimmy Jeff, in turn, gave him a ration of crap about his Yankee ways and they became fast friends.

Jimmy Jeff had always wanted to be in show business but since he really was as mediocre at singing as he was at making music, he never could make it . . . another Willie Nelson wannabe. He was a tall, soft looking, pear-shaped cowboy. You know, the kind you see on television doing all of those line dances where there are fifteen women and two or three men. The kind that wear designer jeans with Lucchese boots and a felt hat at the wrong time of the year.

Jimmy Jeff also didn't have either the great looks of a George Strait or the rugged good looks of Handsome Johnny Cash. He was a kind of a cross between Ernest Tubb and Alfred E. Newman.

Anyway, after graduating from college with a degree in art (the least demanding major he could find) he tried to back-door it into the entertainment world through advertising. His artistic talent proved as sporadic as his singing and picking. A little splash of melody here and there amidst great gobs of mediocrity. The money in the advertising business was about the same as that in show business, a whole lot for a few of those who were truly gifted and very, very little for all the rest. JJ fell right smack dab in the middle of the rest.

As long as Joey was starting up and didn't have a whole lot he and ol' JJ got on pretty well. They both married and did a lot of things together, but as Joey's career took-off and Jimmy Jeff's stagnated . . . Joey noticed that one of the one's laughing loudest at him was his old buddy.

Besides all of the money Joey had spent on JJ in bars and night-clubs he also had invested in the countless hare-brained easy money schemes that Jimmy Jeff forever dreamed up. It seemed that in Texas most men were preachers, welders, guitar pickers or promoters of some kind . . . in that order. Maybe what happened was that they progressed through all of the above and if they didn't make it in any of the first ones they just ended up as promoters. Joey, like most salesmen, was an easy mark for any other salesman . . . especially if that salesman were a friend. For that reason, he spent way too much on JJ's "big deals."

From the very beginning JJ had problems with his work but he had even more problems with women and, much to Debra's dismay, everytime he had problems of any kind he would come over to their house with a six-pack and sit in the kitchen all night pouring out his troubles to Joey and drinking up everything they had in the house. One of Joey and Debra's most frequent arguments was over this very subject.

It was shortly after the break-up of Jimmy Jeff's third marriage in six years and Joey had sat up with him until three A.M., listening to old music and his ol' buddy's tale of woe. It was as he was getting undressed in the closet, quietly so as not to awaken Debra, that she started in on him.

"I wish you'd pay half as much attention to me as you do to that ol' drunk!"

"What are you talking about? He's your friend, too. My god, the poor guy may be awful when it comes to women, but it's still a bad deal when any marriage comes apart. All I was doing was giving him a shoulder to cry on ... just like you'd do for one of your friends."

"Jeff's just an alcoholic who comes over here because he knows you'll buy the booze. I hope you don't end up like him, bouncing from job to job, marriage to marriage and not much good at either one of them."

"Come on, Debra, we've known this guy for ten years and we've had some good times together. He's just got it tough right now. He needs our help."

"He needs your help not mine. I've never really liked him anyway. Remember how he always used to embarrass me when we went camping and I'd out-ride him on the motorcycles? Remember how he ridiculed me when I beat him arm wrestling? What kind of friend do you call it when he makes fun of his best friend's wife?"

Joey started laughing remembering the outrageous way she had whipped him arm-wrestling. "Well, I guess it would be kind of hard on a guy to get beat by a woman in front of all of his friends," He laughed, "but see how pathetic he is. He can't really do anything worth a damn and here all his friends are making lots of money and doing lots of fun things while his life continues to slide down into the toilet. It's really pretty sad. I'm just trying to help an old friend a little."

"You want to help an old friend, come on over here and help me get to sleep. You look pretty nice standing there in your polka dot undies."

As always when a friend was in need, Joey rose to the occasion and Debra did, indeed, sleep well. Why was it then that Joey had such a hard time drifting off into the arms of Morpheus? Why did the little cloud keep trying to creep into his sub-conscious? Why did he feel so lonely and depressed when he started thinking about his old friends?

He lay there for about an hour musing on friends in the present and in the past, while Debra slept peacefully next to him. Every now and then she would make a little sound and move against him and the smell of her would waft out from under the covers. It occurred to him that this was probably the time when she **was** the wonderful woman he remembered when he was away on business, because for all her goodness (though somewhat limited by her selfishness in this department), she sure could be a bitch when she wanted to.

Then again, the older he got the more mysterious people became. As he lay there in the lonely darkness contemplating the changing life he was leading some snatches of "LaGrange" by ZZ Top rolled softly through his mind and gradually lulled him to sleep.

"Rumors spreadin 'round, that Texas town, bout the shack out by LaGrange . . . . you know what I'm talkin' about. Just lemme know if you wanna go, to that home out on the range . . . they got some nice girls, hah!"

Joey and Debra were quite different when it came to people. He had always been gregarious and outgoing while she had been shy and retiring. When he was in high school the other kids just naturally came by his house because they knew they would have fun there. She, on the other hand, could count her friends on one hand. His mom and dad were extremely supportive of all of his endeavors and treated his friends as part of the family. Her Daddy was out on an oil well most of the time while her Momma was constantly trying to seduce her teen-age boyfriends. Joey always believed he was good looking but, in reality, she was extremely so and he was, unbeknownst to himself, rather plain. Joey spent most of his time talking to people (he loved an audience) while Debra was self-conscious about her imagined gawkiness and could only come out of her shell after a few drinks.

Most people have a picture of themselves in their mind's-eye and usually this is the result of some event or situation that had a tremendous impact on their early lives. Whether that thing was real or imagined makes no difference because whatever it was that they saw was real to them, and it stuck in their minds. This is why folks who were once fat are always fat in their minds'-eye. Ugly ducklings may grow into graceful swans but they are still ugly ducklings to themselves.

This was the case with Debra. Besides having to struggle with an obviously deranged mother she also was burdened with a sister who, although just as neurotic as her Momma, was pretty as a picture from the day she was born. In high school her sister (two years her senior) was voted most beautiful, was the prom queen, was in the top third of her class . . . and was pregnant within a week of graduation.

Debra was gangly as a child, so near-sighted that she wore glasses from junior high school on and was in braces within two weeks of getting her glasses. Although she did well in school, she was only of average intelligence and when her periods began to come she developed a loss of concentration that would haunt her all of her life. In her mind she would always be a gawky, horsy looking, bespectacled, skinny girl with just the hint of a bad complexion.

For the first two years of high school, since she was taller than all but a handful of the boys, she was mostly overlooked on Friday and Saturday nights. At the school dances (she loved to dance) her height also was a disadvantage when it came to the slow numbers. Although she was really a pleasant person her braces and glasses put all but the geeks and nerds off, but in the summer before her junior year an amazing transformation took place. Off came her braces and glasses, in went contacts and, lo and behold, she developed real breasts. They weren't very large but they were shapely, had nice little nipples and . . . they were all hers!

Goodbye to the padded bras and swimming-suit falsies and all that embarrassment in physical education class. In addition her complexion, although always pretty clear, was now almost glowing without the hint of a zit! To top it all off, over the summer, her Momma had taken her to a make-up class at Neiman Marcus downtown and while there, a local fashion agent had noticed her and taken her under her wing. Immediately her height went from a liability to an asset. In a very short period of time she was doing catalog modelling and this eventually led to television. By the end of her junior year she was doing television commercials for local department stores. Needless to say, her junior year was the turning point from famine to feast in the boy department. Maybe if she had known the chaos that these changes would make in her life, she would have kept the braces and spectacles on.

Due to her relatively introverted personality she only had a few friends in her life outside family and family friends. But when this newly hatched swan hit W.T. White high school in the fall of 1965, she wasn't at all ready for the furor she caused. To all of the sexually precocious young men, most of whom had also blossomed that summer, she was, all of a sudden, extremely interesting. So much so that several of them even fought over the right to carry her books and take her home from school.

The girls on the other hand, most of whom were not close to her but at least had tolerated her in the past, now would not have anything to do with her. She noticed that, as she passed their little cliques, there was always the echo of serpentine sibilance and half-concealed bitchy laughter reverberating behind her in the hallways. From her viewpoint she was still the same tall, dowdy teenager that she had been at the end of her sophomore year, but to her classmates . . . Ooo-la la! She had come full circle from an awkward, homely, lonely sophomore to a tall, pretty, lonely junior. Meanwhile, her gorgeous, newly married, very pregnant sister began packing on the first of many, many pounds of "baby" fat.

With the first pregnancy, it was easy for Betty Jo, Debra's sister, to rationalize a few extra pounds, but after two more kids and three times as many pounds, the whole situation started to get out of hand. Debra's Momma, wouldn't you know it, was the instigator in the whole dilemma. Due to her overbearing nature (the same trait that made her so successful in the real estate market) Momma had to be in control all of the time and since J. C. and Betty Jo had gotten married and were on their own, she hadn't been able to exert her influence nearly enough to her liking. The only time she had any control at all was when the rapidly expanding family needed money and as time went on, those opportunities occurred less and less frequently. Then in the winter of 1971, bad fortune struck, J. C.'s father died. That is, it was bad fortune for J. C. and his family, not so for Momma.

J. C.'s daddy didn't have to die. He was actually quite healthy and not all that old. He just didn't trust doctors. In the winter of 1975 he got sick. It was during what they called in Texas a "blue norther." In the winter on the plains of North Texas it wasn't un-usual for the temperature to go up into the seventies or eighties if the wind would blow steadily from the south off the Mexican Desert for a few days in a row. Sometimes on these days you could look out the window to the north and all of the sudden the sky would begin to turn blue! Actually, the sky was blue-gray, but when you looked at it just right it was kinda' blue. Anyway, when a blue norther roared in during the months of January or February the temperature might vary 60 degrees in a single day. It was during one of these that J. C.'s daddy started feeling bad.

When his dad took sick 'ol J. C. was in Louisiana goose hunting with some business associates. When Betty Jo called to tell him that his dad had pneumonia and wasn't doing well, he reminded her that his daddy was only fifty-five years old, in good health and he also spoke about the wonders of modern medicine. Hell, nobody had died of pneumonia in years except for old people.

Well, up jumped the devil. Unbeknownst to J. C., his Daddy, upon taking sick with what he had diagnosed as the "croup," had gone to a pharmacist friend and asked him for some medication. The pharmacist, thinking that his daddy had gone to the doctor for the diagnosis and was just trying to save money on the prescription, loaded him up with some heavy duty antibiotics. As luck would have it, he really had influenza and the antibiotics, instead of curing him, merely made his body immune to their healing powers.

You guessed it, the influenza drove his resistance to an all time low and he developed pneumonia. When his temperature reached 104.6 and he was admitted to the hospital, the doctors unknowingly prescribed the same antibiotic the pharmacist had given him before and the infection wasn't even fazed by it. Shortly thereafter, in spite of all that modern medicine could do, he died.

The hardest part for J. C. was that, just before he left for the goose hunting trip, he had visited his dad who wasn't feeling too well at all and his father had told him he felt like he "could die." J. C. naturally took this as meaning that he felt real bad. Hell, it was the twentieth century and with all the advances in modern medicine, why should he stay home with a relative who had the "croup." Humming a little "Rockin' Pneumonia And Boogie-Woogie Flu" J. C. headed for the bayous to inflict war on the local goose population and any unsuspecting delta lady who happened along.

The second hardest part was that, when he received the call, he was in a coonass bar and the unsuspecting twenty-two-year-old cajun lady had appeared. Oh well, when things happen they happen for a reason right? Wrong, emphatically wrong!!

J. C. came home to a very confusing situation. To begin with he was loaded with guilt. Maybe if he hadn't been having such a good time in the bar with the Louisiana lady his daddy wouldn't have died. Maybe what went around truly did come around but how come it came around so quickly? Hell, he hadn't even gotten around to a dance much less a little kiss or a feel or some inny-outy. God wouldn't have struck his Daddy dead over a little conversation in a bar with a cute little dark-eyed cajun lady, would he? . . . Or would he?

He was met at the airport by his wet-eyed, extremely rotund wife who carried with her the awful news. Maybe it was the shock of the situation or the weeks' absence but he could have sworn that when he left he could still get his arms around her. As he followed her to the car he was sure that she was the same person that he had left so recently . . . but he couldn't believe that she (he?) had changed so much.

Maybe the most difficult part of the situation was that not only had J. C.'s dad's life insurance expired but also he was self employed and he had neglected to tell his son (or anyone else for that matter) that his business had been slowly going to pot. It seemed that ever since he had gotten involved with a local church he had put everything else on the back burner. Could it have been that he somehow knew what was to befall him in the near future? He hadn't been the best husband/father in this life. Maybe he was taking this opportunity to make amends for past sins, pave the road to heaven.

Anyway, his personal affairs were in a shambles and his dutiful son could see no other way but to quit his job and try to make something out of his deceased dad's equally dead business. This might have been the most inopportune time for these events to occur because J. C. knew very little about small business management. He knew that with the large oil company that employed him money was no object as long as the right people were convinced that what you were doing was the right thing. In recent months, J. C. had begun to become aware of what was what in his company. As a matter of fact he had just recently begun to really progress in the world of big business. The goose hunting trip had been his first real entree' into the political arena of corporate life and he fit in quite well.

Needless to say this little broken down business that he had inherited from papa would be quite a challenge for the boy. Not only was it strapped for cash but, due to Daddy's neglect, a number of large accounts had either been lost or were in the process of looking for new suppliers when he died. J. C.'s reaction to the problem at hand was to work night and day to try to save what couldn't be saved.

The irony in all of this is that what he had learned at the oil company would have served him quite well in that environment but wouldn't work worth a flip in the small business world. As a matter of fact he had been designated by his co-workers as an up and coming young man who was destined to do extremely well in the future.

He probably would have been able to take much better care of his mother and his family if he had continued there rather than try to save the family business. If only he had known. Combine all of this with the increasing pressures of his mother-in-law, his wife's personal problems and his new awareness of the world around him and it is easy to see major problems on the horizon. Unbeknownst to J. C., his old buddy Joey Hews was about to find out a little bit about life also.

Chapter Five

THE PART THAT JOEY was going to learn was a lot harder a lesson than J. C.'s. Well, actually it wasn't harder than J. C.'s, rather it was just **different** from J. C.'s. J. C. was only going to learn that things changed over time. Joey was going to learn that, a lot of the time, things change for the worse and that, in reality, Joey didn't have much control over it one way or the other. On top of that, there isn't much rhyme or reason to how things change. There doesn't appear to be a lot of selectivity in the process. Good doesn't automatically follow good. Bad things don't only happen to bad people. The whole program of change seems to be based on random selection rather than cause and effect. If that seems like a very cynical piont of view it really isn't. Well perhaps it is, but it might also be the most honest way to look at things.

At any rate what had happened to J. C. was what needs to happen to most of us every now and then. We all need some time away to look at things anew, to see our lives from another perspective or, then again, maybe some of us don't need that intrusion on our mind-made nirvanas at all.

What J. C. had come back to see was that his Daddy had died, his old lady had gotten fat, the responsibilities of children and family were a pain in the ass and all of the things that he had been taught were good, might not be so hot in the long run. This is probably the reason that a lot of people don't stray far from home. They really don't want the time to learn that what they have accepted as the way things should be, may not be the way things are at all. They know that if they come back to something that is obviously wrong they might have to make a very painful decision and this might be the nightmare that follows the sweet dream that they have been so carefully taught by mom and dad.

J. C.'s Daddy's funeral was the first one that Joey had ever attended and he wasn't sure what to expect. There were a lot of folks there that he had never seen before and they all looked so solemn. It occurred to him that, since the man was dead anyway, why should they all be so sad? Why shouldn't everyone be talking about how good a life he had had? Why were they all feeling so sorry for themselves, when in actuality it was him who had died? What a bunch of phony horseshit!

What they were really feeling was the fear that they might be the next one to go, that they might stand up for the final hymn and suddenly realize that it was their very own funeral dirge. These poor selfish bastards were actually so caught up in their own little paranoias that they couldn't feel anything for the unfortunate man that had just gone down. Joey, in an attempt to maintain the proper sad demeanor, tried not to think these inappropriate thoughts. He was sure that they could be read like little LED signs flashing across his forehead, that everyone in the room could see what he was thinking.

All of a sudden, it was as if a bolt of lightning had struck the chapel; with a flash, a little light bulb in his head went off. It wasn't an out of body experience, but it was the damnedest thing that Joey had ever seen. Everything went out of focus and then back into focus. All of the people in the church went from just being part of a crowd to assuming individual personalities. Joey could now see clearly, an aura (a halo of lifelight) around some of the people while a few of them looked gray and dead to his eyes. He wasn't sure whether it was all a dream or if what he was seeing was actually happening. How could he tell anyway?

He closed his eyes, shook his head and looked again and sure enough, there were the people with lifelights and there were the ones who were dead and didn't know it.

"Can you see it?" he leaned over and whispered to Debra.

"See what?" she whispered back, out of the side of her mouth.

"The aura that some of these folks have and the ones who don't. You can see it if you kind of look sideways at them. Kind of like at night. When you want to see something, you don't look right

66

at it, you kinda look above it or to one side or the other in order to see it."

"Dammit, Joey, I told you not to get loaded before we came to this thing. Why can't you be like everyone else?' This is a sad day. Why can't you pay your respects like the other normal people around you? Why do you think you are so special that you can see things that other people can't? Shit!"

"Look, Debra, number one, I'm not loaded and number two, this is the first funeral I've ever been to and number three, I can see some people who are alive and some people who are dead and just don't know it. Can't you see what I'm talking about?"

"You know, Joey, you are so full of shit, your eyes are brown!"

There had been a time in Joey and Debra's relationship when what he had just revealed to her would have been cause for consternation but nonetheless pretty profound stuff. Debra may not have accepted it as fact but she would have at least have regarded it as possibly neat if not something unique enough to merit further thought. The lesson here is that even though life has no basic form, to women, there is a cycle that all men go through .

It seems that, from a spousal perspective, men all go from dumb to semi-smart to smart to semi-smart to dumb and back again as time goes on. It's a shame that this is not only true from within but also from without. At this point in their relationship, in Debra's estimation, Joey was exceptionally dumb from without.

This might be an ideal time to examine this fundamental flaw in man-woman relationships. It has already been established that the male of the species is inherently the stronger. As such, usually in the beginning of a relationship, the man often confuses strength with intelligence. The female, during the initial glow (rhymes with halo), goes along with this scheme of things. As a matter of fact, she sort of convinces herself that he knows what he is talking about, even if he doesn't.

You can see it all of the time. In restaurants, bars, sporting events, movies . . . anywhere that men and women are together. Just listen up real close. Here will be some guy saying something absolutely absurd to some chick and she will look up at him with this far-away look in her eyes and nod as if he just told her the true meaning of life.

"You know, I read somewhere the other day that at M.I.T. they have taken rats and taught them to breathe highly oxygenated water.

I mean, they have been living in and breathing water for the past year!"

Not only does his girlfriend look up to him and almost swoon, but she tells him that he is probably the smartest sumbitch that ever walked the face of the earth. Now this is a very dangerous thing. Not only does she support his bullshit, but also there is a strong possibility that, if she continues, he might begin to believe it himself.

As a matter of fact this is all too often the case and the results are at the least traumatic and, more often than not, disastrous. After the initial glow of love (heat?) leaves the relationship, the same statement that earlier on had elicited such a positive response, now is cause for derision. The poor guy goes from being an absolute genius to the stupidest bastard who ever came out of Papolote (a small town in far south Texas known for it's snuff-dippin', red-necked, good 'ol boys). Instead of getting a reward for this unusually astute observation, he gets a behind the hand laugh, a roll your eyes to the heavens, a poorly concealed hmmph! Or an out and out sneer!

At his best friend's Dad's funeral, Joey had already passed semi-smart and was rapidly on his way to being a total dumb-ass in Debra's opinion. Couple this with the fact that she was on the brink of the early marriage doldrums and the results are almost predictable. Walk down to your local newstand and pick up the latest *Cosmopolitan* or *Ms.* and right next to the article on the search for that elusive orgasm that everyone talks about but no one ever seems to find, will be a big deal trying to justify why he got tired of her or she of him. The interesting part is that everyone including the protagonists can see the deal coming and no one has the gumption or energy to try to fix it . . . or maybe it's just lack of interest.

After the funeral was over they all went over to J. C.'s house to comfort the family. J. C. and Joey went out for some beer to kind of get away for a while.

As they drove down the street, Joey turned to his friend and said, "I don't know much about this funeral stuff, partner, but if there were anything I could do to bring him back I would. And if there is anything else that I can do to help you, you make sure and ask. Here maybe this'll take the edge off a little."

With that Joey produced a king sized joint of maui-wowee that he had smuggled back from his and Debra's last trip to Hawaii. (It's interesting to note that Texans can't say Hawaii. It usually comes out as "how-i-ya" with a long i. It's something like the Chinese with "r's" or the Negroes with "ask" and "question." There's probably a correlation there somewhere).

J. C. grunted in approval as he fired up the goody. "It won't bring him back, brother, but it sure eases the pain. Hell, to tell the truth, I didn't know him all that well anyway. We started drifting apart as soon as I was old enough to get around by myself. We just didn't think the same. I think he was closer to that church than to his own family. Sometimes I feel like I should have taken the time to find out what he was all about but everytime I tried to talk to him he'd try to preach back at me."

"I don't know about you but all that Jesus crap doesn't seem applicable to the life I know. I mean I believe that the ten command-ments and all that biblical stuff make for a nice story and a nice way to think about and live life, but it doesn't seem to relate to all the people I know or read about. What about you?"

The pot was having its desired effect on J. C. for now he could talk himself out of at least part of his grief. Joey too had spent many hours trying to make sense out of this life that we live and had come up against many of the same stumbling blocks that J. C. had. It seemed to him that people generally took one of two positions. They either explained everything unexplainable by attributing it to some "god" or spirit or something; or they just said they couldn't explain it.

Then, of course, you had the agnostics (wouldn't it be better to call them the apathetics?) who weren't going to take a stand either way. I wrote a poem once that suggested that agnosticism might be the best way to believe. It's interesting that the choice of words was "agnosticism might be." That's about as wishy-washy a bunch of claptrap as you can get.

Anyway, on to Joey, "You know we both came from the same generation and I probably traveled the same roads as you. We were brought up being taught that you have to believe in something. That there is some order to all this thing that we live. That if you live a good life and do good unto others, they will, in turn, do good unto you. But the very book that they cite as saying all these good things is so ambiguous and contradictory that they can use it to prove ev-erything and yet it proves nothing.

"Take the book of Job for instance. Here's this poor bastard that believes in and does everything he can according to his God's plan and all that happens is that he loses everything including his

69

health and his family. Now to me that is either an argument for how his God abuses his power and flat tortures the guy for fun or maybe it says that, basically, bad things happen and they aren't very selective about how or who they happen to. The more I live and learn the more I think that things just happen randomly. If you are fortunate enough to be dealt a good hand, then you are just fortunate and vice-versa. What goes around may or may not come around!"

J. C. came back, "Yeah, I know exactly what you mean. All of my Daddy's church friends were looking for this order in life so they could prove there is such a thing as perfection. Of course, they had to have perfection and order so that they could have this God that they needed. So which one came first? Most times, I think that God was invented by people, not that people were invented by God."

"One thing I know for sure is that, either way, people sure have messed up religion. I mean, look at my old man, here he gives up his business and his life for this thing he believes in and then he dies before he even has time to enjoy it. I hope heaven is what he thought it would be or that he even made it there at all."

"Well," Joey said hugging his old friend's neck, "as hard as he worked at it if it's there he's in it. Anyway, I guess we better get about living whatever this life is. Who knows, we might be next!"

For some reason, Joey's last observation seemed outrageously funny to both of them and they laughed until they cried. Maybe it was an hysterical reaction to the fear of death, or maybe it was just the pot. Whatever it was they both felt tremendously relieved by the time they got back to the house and, after a few beers, they let the old guy die.

Their obvious relief came much to the dismay of the rest of the family who, for some reason, wanted to hold onto their grief for a little while longer. Debra and her sister were especially pissed off by this seeming lack of respect for the dead on the part of their two husbands.

"What is wrong with you two?" Debra said as she cornered Joey in the hall by the bathroom, "don't you have any respect for the dead? Can't you feel bad like the rest of us for just one day?"

She probably shouldn't have used that particular choice of words even though it said exactly what she was thinking. It pointed up just how differently she and Joey thought about things. In his mind life was supposed to be an enjoyable adventure and grief and other bad feelings, although necessary in order to keep the good in perspective, should be dealt with and discarded as quickly as possible. Happiness and goodtimes, conversely, should be held onto firmly in order to fully appreciate them. Most of the events that he chose to remember brought a smile to his face even though some of them also brought a tear to his eye.

"As a matter of fact both J. C. and I have chosen to let the poor guy die and you might be happier if you did the same thing. It's not written anywhere that, since someone has passed on, everyone should ruin their lives because of it even for a day. I don't believe that that was the intention of his Daddy's or anybody else's God for that matter."

"Just what do you know about God, anyway, Joey?" Debra sneered back at him, "I've never seen you go to church. You don't pray before meals or anything. Life is not supposed to be all fun and good times. You work so hard at having fun you don't even know how to enjoy the bad times!"

That one really threw old Joey. How in the hell were you supposed to enjoy bad times?! Isn't that a contradiction in terms, an oxymoron, if you will? He had always suspected that some people might be goofy enough to think like that, but not Debra. Here he had spent the last five or so years trying to show her how it is possible to go through life with a smile on your face and, not only was she resisting it, she thought badly of him for trying to enjoy it all. Well, if that was what the Judeo-Christian ethic was all about, it was just one more reason for him to avoid it at all costs.

"The only thing I know about the God that all the church people talk about is that He (she, it) is to be feared and I can't live a life of fear. Fear is misery and there's already plenty of that around without mind-making some more."

At this point Debra gave him one of those looks that should be saved for someone who is trying to kill some small defensless animal, whirled around and stomped outside. She had taken up smoking again and was on her way outside to satisfy her craving.

This one mystified old Joey, too. Debra was intelligent enough to be able to read and comprehend and it had been finally proven, despite the tobacco lobby's billions, that smoking would definitely kill you and yet here she had started smoking again. Maybe it was her mother's influence because Momma was so addicted that she couldn't quit.

He was just as mystified by his friend Jimmy Jeff because he too chose to continue smoking even though he was smart enough to know better. Lately she and Jimmy Jeff would often smoke in front of him and scoff when he would make fun of them. This was brand new to him since, in the past, she was always belittling JJ and now she seemed to side with him against Joey. Also, he noticed that she wasn't so upset by Jimmy Jeff's visits these days. As a matter of fact, she seemed to look forward to them more and more. Strangely enough Jeff and she seemed to see eye to eye on more stuff than she and Joey did these days. It seems that 'ol Jimmy Jeff also had made some arbitrary decisions about things to believe in and they coincided pretty closely with Debra's.

Some of this came to the fore shortly after the incident at the funeral when Jimmy Jeff showed up one evening with a sack full of beer and a whole passel of troubles.

"Come on in JJ, what you got under your arm?"

"Brought some beer, figured you might be able to use one. Oh, hi Debra, how ya doin'?"

"About as good as I can considering I'm stuck with this jackass. You wouldn't believe what he and J. C. did after the funeral. They went out and got some beer and sat out back and actually enjoyed themselves while everybody else was in mourning. I can't understand how anyone could be so unfeeling!"

"Yeah," JJ agreed, "funerals are a time to pay your respects to the family of the deceased, not have a good time." He frowned at Joey.

"Now just wait a minute, if you think that you two are going to gang up on me you've got another think coming. Why am I all of a sudden such a bad guy. You're my wife and you're supposed to be my best friend. Why don't you both start acting like it?"

With that they looked uncomfortably at each other and quickly changed the subject to Jimmy Jeff's latest problem which was that he had lost his job again. After sympathizing with him for an hour or two and loaning him some money so he could make ends meet, Joey let him out the door about midnight.

When he went upstairs to bed, Debra was waiting up for him, "See, Joey, even Jimmy Jeff would have behaved differently at the funeral. Now can you admit that you were wrong?"

"You know, I'm kind of mystified by something Debra. All along you have been telling me how worthless Jimmy Jeff is. How he's nothing but a drunk and how he can't keep a job or a woman.

72

Now, all of a sudden, his opinion not only counts but it's more important than mine. What I want to know is, what brought about all of this change? He's just lost his job again, he's been divorced three times and he left here drunker'n Cooter Brown not twenty minutes ago. Doesn't look like he's changed much to me."

"Go ahead, make fun of your friend! Everybody is always wrong except you, you think you're so damned smart! Why don't you just own up to the fact that you're wrong and say you're sorry?"

"I'm wrong because I think differently than you and some poor misguided soul who have subjectively chosen to believe a certain way and I haven't? I'm wrong because you now have decided to side with someone who just a month ago was a dumbass drunk in your eyes? Listen to what you're saying. It doesn't make any sense!"

"Yeah, that's right! Go ahead and make fun of me just like you always do! You know you're not always right Mr. Smartass. And even if what I say is wrong, I have the right to be wrong!"

"You may have the right to be wrong but you also have the **responsibility** to recognize that you are wrong and do something about it. At some point, you have to own up to your mistakes. You can't just sluff them off by saying you have the right to be wrong. Do you also have the right to steal and lie and kill?"

"You son of a bitch!" And with that Debra turned her back to him and turned off the light.

It's amazing how big a king-size bed can seem when you're told good night in that manner. Joey knew that it wouldn't do any good to talk to her further this evening. These days when he wouldn't give in to her beliefs, no matter how far from reality they were, she took it as a sign that he thought she was ignorant or that he didn't love her. What happened to those times when he'd say something so simple and right, like tonight, and she would look at him as if he were a guru or something and give him a hug?

As you can probably see, all of this was going nowhere. Debra, like so many other lost souls, had made some arbitrary decisions about life, death and living that didn't necessarily have any basis in fact. Unfortunately when people do that, they close themselves off to life itself. Since they can't prove otherwise, why must they insist on an orderly much less perfect universe? Look around you, can you find anything that is truly perfect? Especially man made? It seemed to Joey that most of humanity's frustrations could be traced to the very fact that they were trying to explain an imperfect world in perfect terms.

Like mathematics, for instance. Given the fact that, in order for a bullet to hit anything, it must first go half the distance to that thing and then half the distance remaining ad infinitum, it can be mathematically proven that a bullet will never get to and therefore never hit its intended target. From personal experience everyone knows that is bullshit and yet people accept mathematics as being a "science." The difference was that Debra chose to accept all of this and Joey did not.

Joey went to sleep with an old Dave Mason song winging its way through his head. He wished that Debra were awake so that she could sing harmony with him.

"So just leave it alone, cause we don't see eye to eye . . . .there ain't no good guy, there ain't no bad guy, there's only you and me and we just disagree . . . ."

Chapter Six

WHILE JOEY AND DEBRA were having their problems a rift was also developing between him and his business partner. As time went on and Joey became more proficient at his craft, the gap between him and Marvin began to widen considerably. It was not necessarily that Joey was becoming more conservative (although, as a lot of people do as they grow older, he really was) but more that the people in his business were. Joey found himself spending more and more of his time insulating the most impressionable executives, be they customers or clients, from Marvin's increasingly bizarre actions.

Not only was he becoming more and more blatant as far as his homosexuality was concerned but he also was beginning to become noticably more paranoid about his age. With increasing frequency, Joey would pass Marvin's office and notice him sitting back in his chair, with cigarette smoke curling around his head like a halo (isn't that interesting) and looking intently into a little hand-held mirror that he kept in his desk drawer. As he peered deeply into the glass, he would slowly caress his face with his free hand and alternately smile and frown. If interrupted, he would look up and smile vaguely as if coming out of a coma or a deep sleep.

It was on one of those slow days in the middle of the summer that Joey finally had to confront him about their differences. Unfortunately, the day that he picked was one on which Marvin decided to bring his new boyfriend to the office to show off his operation. It was still hard for Joey to get used to the fact that ol' Marv treated these little sissy-boys just like a heterosexual male would treat the new girlfriend whom he wanted to impress.

As he entered Marvin's office, he walked through what seemed like a solid wall of English Leather before he noticed the boy-girl sitting on the sofa across from Marvin's desk. In the past, most of Marvin's lovers had been fragile little sissy boy types with big curvy behinds and just the hint of breast developement from all the hormones they had been taking.

This guy (gay?), on the other hand, must have gotten the hormone bottle mixed up with one loaded with steroids. He was all of six-feet four inches tall and at least two hundred forty pounds. He had a huge head of prematurely gray hair and a prominent lower jaw that was not only square but covered with a five o'clock shadow that made him look suspiciously like the Nicholson File man.

"Doesn't he have a marvelous smile?" Marvin gushed, with a dazzling display of pearly white teeth and limp-wristed gestures.

His new darlin' beamed back at Joey with a look kind of like a semi-tired, almost good-looking older lady at the only singles bar in a podunk town who has just attracted a guy about fifteen years her junior on a late Friday night. He was all silk shirt, too-tight pants and moussed hair and Joey could have sworn he was wearing make-up.

"Look Marvin, we have to talk but if you're busy we can do it some other time."

"Anything that you want to say, you can say in front of Patrick," he said, staring intently into his girly-man's eyes. "We have no secrets."

"Well, I don't feel comfortable talking business in front of people outside of the company." Joey said, "So, why don't we just wait until tomorrow."

"We'll talk right now or we won't talk at all!" Marvin spat out in catlike sibilance, "if you have something to say, say it now or go on and do whatever it is that you do."

It was obvious that Marvin was showing off for his friend at Joey's expense and today he just wasn't going to take it anymore.

"Ok, Marvin, here it is. Not only me but several of our manufacturer's are becoming concerned over your lack of attention to the business. They have expressed their displeasure with our agency and threatened to fire us if we don't straighten out our act. We need to start running this thing like a business not like a bunch of door to door encyclopedia peddlers. The market is growing and maturing.

76

We need to be more aggressive in merchandising and service, in order to maintain our core accounts."

Joey noticed that Marvin's face was pink bordering on red and that his hands were shaking as he attempted to light a cigarette that was already lit. He looked over at Joey with a squinty-eyed smile that wasn't totally caused by the smoke wafting up into his eyes and said mockingly, "Well, just what is it that you propose we do?"

"The first thing we need to do is hire more people. We need to cover the territory . . . . . . "

At this point, Marvin cut him off with a wave of his cigarette stained fingers, "Look, Joey, I gave you your start in this business and I've been in it a lot longer than you have. I've heard all of this poppycock about how we need to do this and do that before, and I'm here to tell you that you don't know what you're talking about. All of these manufacturers want us to overstaff in order to get more business but they're not willing to pay us for it. So just forget about it."

Well, it's now or never, Joey thought as he plowed on, "OK, that's fine but, in order for us to continue, it's going to be necessary for you to go back to work. I can't continue to carry this whole company by myself. I need some time off too!"

At this point Marvin puffed up like a foppish English lord and said, "I'll tell you what, if you want more time off, why don't you just take off, not just for tomorrow or this weekend but forever."

It was all that Joey could do to keep from jumping up and hitting Marvin but, after looking over and seeing the intensity in his huge boyfriend's stare, he immediately thought better of it. For the second time in his life he was amazed at how calm his voice sounded when he said, "I think we probably ought to continue this conversation at a later date. We're not going to get anywhere this afternoon."

"I meant what I said. If you don't like it, you can just leave!," Marvin shrilled in a decidely feminine falsetto, "We don't need you or your big ideas around here."

By this point he had his best "just you take that, you bully" look on his face, so Joey didn't press the point. He did take the time to clean out his desk on the way home, however.

That weekend, he went back to his office and copied everything pertinent in his files. He also took all of his personal effects and turned in an up-dated expense report. He wasn't real sure what he was going to do but, whatever it was, he knew he wasn't going to continue to do it with Marvin. It wasn't just the queers, it was more a basic difference in business philosophy.

Joey believed (idealistically) that if you were above-board in everything you did and if you worked harder than those around you, you must ultimately be the best at whatever you do. Probably if he had known how wrong he was he wouldn't have left at all. He would have just continued to take the money and sock it away for a rainy day.

The following Monday morning around seven-thirty Marvin called and asked what Joey had prepared for their regular Monday morning sales meeting. He responded that, since he was no longer employed he thought he'd just sleep in and then go hang out by the pool for a while. At this point Marvin got so incensed that he completely lost his temper. His voice went up about three octaves as he screamed into the phone. Joey had thought that he was hysterical that time in New Orleans, but now he yowled like a man possessed.

The last thing he heard as he hung up the phone was, "you bastard, you had your chance, you'll never get another dime out of me!"

Well, what did you expect, Joey thought, that the poor faggot would wish you good luck and settle up like a man? You didn't expect an emotional response from an acknowledged girly-man? Maybe Joey had expected an emotional response but certainly not one quite so violent. So now, what to do? Whatever comes next, Joey grinned to himself as he moseyed out toward the pool.

For about a week and a half Joey thought that he had died and gone to heaven. He'd get up in the morning and take a good run and then come home to chase Debra around a little. After a shower, they'd ride bikes or play tennis or go into Dallas just to look around. In the evening it was supper and television or more pool. Life hadn't been this grand in a long while.

By the end of the month, however, with no money coming in, Debra began to get a little anxious. "What are you going to do about a job, honey?" She asked one afternoon as they lay by the pool. "Aren't we getting a little low on money?"

"We'll be all right for a while yet. You know, I sure could get used to this way of life again. Why don't we go on out to Grand Prairie and ride bikes this afternoon? It's Wednesday and there probably won't be anyone else out there."

Joey was amazed by how easy it was to get back into the old ways, like back when they had nothing. Just get up in the morning and, if there were no phone calls, go on off and do whatever it was that melted their butter. He was also surprised at how Debra was taking all of this. Since he had been out of work, they were getting along just like old times. Lots of shared laughter, messin' around and seeing old friends . . . and all of this on a veritable shoestring budget.

These days they spent less in a week than they used to spend on a night out on the town . . . and had way more fun. Debra had quit counting how many beers he drank and instead drank right along with him. She also remembered how much fun it was to make love everyday, not only in the evening but in the morning too. His only concern was that she'd start to get worried about the money but, just like on this morning, he'd tell her not to worry and she'd drop the subject and go on and enjoy the day. It looked like he had passed dumbshit and was on his way back up the ladder toward smart . . . and all of this because he wasn't employed and they were "poor" again.

This idyllic lifestyle could have gone on forever if they had had enough money but, even before they ran out of that commodity, Joey started getting a little restless. He started missing the fast lane, making deals and riding that salesman's high. He also missed some of his friends in the business world. Then one day, about a month and a half after leaving Marvin, as he was trying to decide whether to go into town for a few drinks with his pals or just hang out at home, the phone rang. It was the vice-president of sales for one of Marvin's largest manufacturers.

"Hello, Joey?"

"Is that you, Ray?"

"Yeah, it's me and I've got to say I'm a little upset! What the hell is going on down there? I haven't heard from anybody in your agency for six weeks! We don't pay you guys all that money so that you can just sit on your collective asses and cash the checks. We expect some kind of communication . . ."

"Hey wait a minute! Slow down now Ray. I don't work there anymore, haven't in almost two months. By the way, it's a beautiful day here. How are things in Cleveland?"

He knew this would stop old Ray in his tracks because on the news this early September morning they had reported Cleveland's weather as cold with snow and freezing rain. At that moment, Joey was looking out the window at one of those bright Indian Summer days that usually precede Halloween in Texas. The temperature was in the low eighties and he was in his swimming trunks headed for the pool with the portable phone at his ear. Ray was the sales manager for one of the manufacturers' that Joey and Marvin had worked for and he and Joey had become good business friends over the past few years.

Ray chuckled as he looked out his window on the gloomy winter day outside. Then, as Joey's words soaked in, the smile turned into a frown.

"What do you mean you don't work there anymore? Nobody told me anything about all of this! What are you doing these days, anyway?"

"Right now I'm walking out to the pool to soak up some sun. I just got a new *Dirt Bike* magazine and I thought I'd catch up on some of the go-faster news for a while. It's a little early for a cold beer but I imagine that I'll get into a couple of those in a little while."

"C'mon, Joey, I'm serious. What are you doing or what are you going to do?"

"Honestly, Ray, I don't know. The conventions will be coming up in a month or so and I have been enjoying this rest so much, I thought I'd wait awhile to make a decision. As a matter of fact, I was going to check my financial situation this afternoon and go from there."

"Look, what's your schedule for this afternoon? Are you going to be at this number for a while?"

"Yeah, I'll hang around til you call back. What have you got on your mind?"

"Let me make a couple of phone calls and we'll talk some more. In the mean time, would you do me a favor and call Jake Epstein? He's got a problem with a stock adjustment and you get along with the old fart a lot better than anyone up here."

"It'll cost you a dinner and some cold beer next time you're in town but you know I'll do it. Same old deal? Two for one offsetting order and thirty, sixty, ninety on the terms?"

It felt good to get back into the swing of things after sitting idle for a couple of months, Joey mused, dialing Jake's number from memory. Business had always been fun for him. It seemed that he did the best with guys like Jake, who most of his competitors felt was a tough guy to deal with, so he was looking forward to his conversation with the old guy. I wonder what my buddy Ray has up his sleeve?, he thought. Well, I guess I'll find out soon enough.

That afternoon Ray called back and asked Joey if he wanted to start up his own company. Joey replied that, although he was flattered that Ray had asked, he would need more income than Ray's company could provide and Ray said he would call back the next day. Earlier in the afternoon, Joey had taken care of Ray's problem with Jake and Ray thanked him for it. Joey assured him it was a simple favor and said he would look forward to Ray's call the next day.

Later that evening, Joey and Debra went into town for dinner with Jimmy Jeff and his new sweetheart. This had gotten to be a regular occurrence in the past few years. JJ'd lose one and then somehow dredge up another one to listen to his bullshit for a while. Most of them were passable as far as looks were concerned but doubtful as far as taste went. It wasn't that Jimmy Jeff was a bad person but he was extremely self-centered and took himself awfully seriously considering his position in life.

When he came up with his new women, it was kind of customary to go down to a friendly place in Dallas that they all liked. Joey liked it because he knew he would have to pick up the tab and it was affordable. No sense investing a lot of money in one of Jimmy Jeff's chicks when you weren't sure of the longevity of the relationship.

Hebert's (pronounced A-bear's) was a bar and restaurant down in the Oak Lawn area that belonged to a friend of Joey's who used to be in the auto parts business. It had an old mosaic tile floor, tin ceiling and a long antique bar that had been imported from England. A fifty-pound bag of peanuts sat in one corner and they were free for the taking as long as you threw the hulls on the floor. You could find all types of people there depending on the night. They ranged from Harley riders to millionaires, bartenders to barflys and they all kind of fit in together. Rarely was there any trouble. Although limited, everything on the menu was good and the beer was cold. The place also boasted one of the best wine selections in all of Dallas, although no one ever knew why.

When they arrived at the bar Jimmy Jeff was already there, sitting by himself at a corner table that they liked a lot because it gave them an excellent vantage point from which to observe the continuous parade of people moving in and out of the place. This evening was a little slow, given it was the middle of the week, but you never knew what the night might bring.

"Don't tell me you already lost your new girl friend!" Joey laughed as he greeted his friend with a hug.

81

"That ain't my purse layin' there, pardner," he grinned as he sat back down.

"So what's new in the world of big-time advertising? Tell me you just landed a beer account so you can supply me with a case a day for the rest of my life!"

"Sheeit! We ain't doin' worth a flip down at the agency. Since the recession came on ain't nobody hittin' any big licks in the ad bidness."

Joey could tell from JJ's exaggerated Texas drawl that he must have found himself a cowgirl and, sure enough, out of the rest-room came this Dale Evans look alike complete with a Triple-X Beaver (hat that is), jeans fashionably frayed at the cuffs and a new pair of Lucchese roach killers (pointed toe cowboy boots so that you could get in the corners to stomp those poor little old la cucarachas). Her pants looked like they had been painted on and she two-stepped up to them to the beat of "I Didn't Know God Made Honky-Tonk Angels" blaring from the jukebox.

"Oh my God!," Debra muttered under her breath, "this oughta last about three minutes! Just look at that outfit!"

Joey glanced over at Debra in surprise because one whole side of her family were real-life ranchers and this new girl was dressed exactly like they would on a night out. He noticed that she had that slant-eyed Siamese cat look on her face that she usually reserved for good looking ladies that gave him the eye when they were out somewhere. Well, he thought, things have been going pretty smooth lately, maybe she needs to bitch me out a little just to keep things on an even keel.

"This is Billy Jean," Jimmy Jeff drawled as he kicked a chair out for her in good old John Wayne fashion, "like ya to meet my friends Joey and Debra."

"Please ta meetcha," she said around the wad of Spearmint she was chewing, "y'all from Dallas?"

She may have had the prettiest teeth that Joey had ever seen in his life. When it came to women, he was a teeth and fingernail aficionado. He had learned long ago that if a lady kept those two areas of her anatomy clean and neat, odds are the rest of her body would pass muster also. It was just habit that he still paid attention to detail since he hadn't been around anybody but Debra for the last six or eight years.

"Nice to meet you," Debra smiled icily, "yep, we're from Dallas, where are you from?"

"She lives in Fort Worth now but she's originally from Archer City, up near Wichita Falls." Jimmy Jeff answered for her, looking directly into Debra's eyes for a little longer than was comfortable for Joey. "She works for one of our clients and she says she's a passable barrel racer."

"Aw, JJ, ah'm not all that good but, if I win at the Cowtown Rodeo Friday night, I might could go on to the National Finals. Would ya'll like to come see me ride?"

She smiled all around the table and Joey found himself nodding yes. To his surprise, when he looked over at Debra, she was nodding yes too. They went on to have a pretty nice evening. Joey's buddy, the owner, came in and they got him to play country and western tapes on the sound system for the rest of the evening. And, even though it wasn't normally allowed, they and everyone else in the bar ended up western dancing wherever they could find room.

It started out when they played "Cotton-eyed Joe." Joey and Debra got up and started doing the old faithful dance and pretty soon they had the whole bar following them around in a conga line snaking between the tables. At this point Joey's buddy bought the whole place a round of tequila solos and it was off to the races. Everyone danced with everyone and, much to his surprise, Joey ended up with Billy Jean more often than not. She seemed to home in on him like a fly to honey and he truly enjoyed the attention.

On the way home Debra seemed a little bit quiet so he broke the silence. "Well, that was fun. It's good to see Jimmy Jeff is back in action. That little Billy Jean looks just right for him."

"Who are you trying to kid? She might be just right for you, hell, y'all danced damn near every dance! I thought you didn't like to dance."

"I don't all that much but the only time I danced with her was when she asked me to and that was only when you were dancing with someone else. Jimmy Jeff ain't got the rhythm God gave a preacher and I didn't want to just sit there like a bump on a log. You aren't jealous are you? Because if you are, I'm here to tell you that it would take someone a hell of a lot better than anyone JJ could dig up to tear me away from you, darlin'."

He looked over at her and maybe it was the light from the dashboard that made her look so funny. She had a look on her face that was more surprise than anger, more astonishment than jealousy, more puzzlement than hate. In all of his time of knowing her Joey couldn't remember anytime that he felt further from her than at that moment.

But then she shook her head a little, eyed him straight on and, with a look that could melt the coldest heart, said, "You truly love me, don't you Joey?"

"More than you'll ever know, darlin'" he said sincerely as he found her hand in the dark. She unbuckled her seat belt and moved over next to him so that she could rest her head on his shoulder and that's the way they drove home.

I may not have a job and who know's what tomorrow may bring but one thing is for sure, right now things ain't too bad, Joey thought as they cruised on into the Texas night with an old Tim Hardin song caroming gently off his somewhat bewildered psyche.

"If I listened long enough to you, I'd find a way to believe that its all true . . . knowin', that you lied, deep down while I cried . . . still I look to find a reason to believe."

Chapter Seven

THE NEXT DAY JOEY lay next to the pool trying to rest up from a long night of pretending he was eighteen again. God, it was great to be in heat (love?) like that, he thought. I haven't done any non-stop messing around in years. Debra was upstairs finally getting some sleep and he was sitting out in the sun with a yellow pad of paper prioritizing his life. When the phone rang he answered it so as not to awaken Debra and it was Ray again.

"Still out by the pool?," he asked, the jealousy in his voice so obvious that Joey couldn't bring himself to rub it in anymore.

"Naw, I'm sitting in my study trying to figure out what I'm going to do with the rest of my life (it was only a little white lie anyway, he **was** contemplating his fate at the moment). I don't want to whack my savings account too hard. You know, I haven't had a paycheck in a coupla months."

Joey was smiling to himself because, outside of the mortgage and the car payment, he'd hardly spent any money at all.

"I was serious the other day, Joey. We want you to go back to work for us. So I'll tell you what I did, I called some friends of mine in the business and I've got a couple more manufacturers for you to represent. Also, we'll advance you a few thousand dollars against the commissions that we're not going to pay Marvin, since he hasn't made a sales call in the last six months. It's not a lot but it will take you up until convention time and then we'll help you get some more manufacturers. You can have your own business. You don't need Marvin, anyway, you never did. What do you think?"

"First of all, I thank you and the other guys for thinking of me and for your help. Secondly, after you've gone to all of that trouble, I don't see any reason not to give it a try. Let me talk to Debra tonight and I'll call you in the morning. Okay?"

"I'll be waiting for your call, Joey. Let's go have some fun and sell something!"

All that Ray had known in his life had been selling. That is, if you got up every morning and went out and sold something, everything would be okay. If you didn't at least give it a try, then you weren't alive in his eyes. He especially liked Joey because in his mind Joey was the only guy who could work as hard as he could. Well, Joey thought, it will be good to get back into the swing of things. He was well-rested and eager to get on with it.

That afternoon, when he told Debra of his plans, she was a little apprehensive. She couldn't understand why he didn't take a job with an established company rather than start one of his own. He explained that all he was going to do was to give it a try for a few months and, if it didn't work out by convention time, he promised that he would get a "real job." At this point she agreed but noted ruefully that just bummin' around the last month or so had sure been fun. He couldn't tell if it was dread or anticipation glowing behind her sad-eyed smile.

The next morning he called Ray and told him that everything was go and that he was eager to begin. Ray outlined some projects for him to start on and also gave him the necessary information on the other product lines that he was to sell. With that, Joey began to write a business plan. Fortunately, he not only had learned the basics of the business from old Marv' but also a lot of the things that Marvin had done wrong. He knew that, if he applied himself and worked hard, he could probably bring the deal off and have his own company. That was not his intent in the beginning but that's the way it happened, or maybe that wasn't the way it was meant to happen, that was just the way it did.

The business plan was really quite simple. Since he didn't have a lot of money, he would be the only employee for a while and that would mean a lot of travel. So, if he loaded up the trunk of his car with samples, literature and files, he could take his portable "office" on tour. His routine was rudimentary, since he was centrally located in the territory, he set up four routes that looped through several major cities in each of the four states that he covered and each one ended up in Dallas. For four weeks straight he would leave early on Monday morning, make a loop and be home on Friday afternoon. The fifth week he would stay home, catching up on sleep, phone calls and paper work.

The next week he took off for the first tour. It really was good to get back in the saddle again and the reception he got from all of his old customers was especially rewarding. Most of them seemed to be genuinely happy to see him and showed it by ordering lots of merchandise. After a few months, however, the adrenalin high began to pale and things began to get rather tiring. The work was exciting but the driving was long and arduous and by the fifth week of each cycle he was more than ready for a few days at home.

By the time the conventions came around it was pretty obvious to him that the deal was going to work. He was doing a great job for all of his clients and, since most of the product lines used to be Marvin's, everything that he sold was familiar to him.

The first show he attended in his new role as "president" of his own sales company was in Chicago in mid-December. Since he was still on a pretty strict budget, one of his manufacturer's supplied him with a room and all of them made sure he didn't pick up any restaurant or bar tabs. Looking back on this period later in life, he would remember it fondly and maybe even yearn a little for those good old days.

When he reached Chicago he was greeted by an early artic cold front and a bunch of business friends wishing him good luck. He had been working extremely hard in the few short months that he had been in business, and had called on most of the major customers and a lot of the secondary ones in the territory. As a result not only did most of them remember him on sight but a large number of them also bought some of his products. This got his manufacturers extremely excited and, as they sang his praises to their friends at the show, he ended up landing some major new clients before he went home.

While all of this good stuff was going on, however, he noticed that some of his competitors were looking at him with a different light in their eyes. It seemed that when he first started with only a little business and two or three manufacturers, they wished him good luck and, in some cases, even offered him help. As soon as he began doing well, however, they began to get a little cold.

The guys that used to clap him on the back and buy him a drink at the social functions now nodded at him and kept to themselves. When one of them would come upon him talking to a customer they would try to hustle the guy away from Joey, more often than not in a rude or belittling way. Joey's response was to try to be nicer to them in hopes that his good manners would be repaid in kind, more of that "what goes around, comes around" bullshit. What he was about to find out was an important but discouraging lesson about men at work and human nature in general.

When people have plenty and life is easy, they actually live their lives like the Bible and all of those optimistic philosophical psychobabblist works want us to believe things should be . . . "Do unto others" ad nauseum. The pecking order is already set, everyone has his own little niche, and they can all be civil to each other. Just like in the animal kingdom.

When a pack of dogs has been together for a while there's no need for them to fight. They've already been through all of that and they know their place in the group. Introduce a new one, however, and, especially if he is young and aggressive, the fur is liable to fly. Interestingly enough an inordinate amount of the time the fighting is amongst dogs that have already fought in the past and sometimes this infighting is contagious.

This was what Joey was beginning to encounter in the business world, not only were the big dogs resisting his entering the group but they were beginning to fight among themselves. It was as if, since he was threatening them, they would see who was the toughest all over again. They fought for their superiority, they fought for supremacy, they fought for supercilliousness, they fought for stupidity. Yeah, they fought for stupidity, for plain old masculine asininity. You probably don't recognize asininity do you? That's not just a made up word, it's really one that just occurred to you.

Joey watched it all unfold with an amazed yet interested eye. It appeared that somehow he had started all of this but he couldn't see how. There seemed to be lots of business out there for everyone, if everyone were willing to work, that is. He certainly hadn't had any problems finding things to sell and people to sell them to. It was actually a lot of fun and he didn't mean anybody any harm. What those other guys were doing was wasting their time worrying about what he was doing rather than going out and working like he was. The reality was the harder he worked the luckier he got and the luckier he got the madder his competitors got, until finally a lot of them hated him or at least appeared to.

For the longest time he was astounded by the animosity that he had created by doing well. Certainly that was the antithesis of all that he had been taught as he grew up. His answer to all of this was to work harder and stay to himself. This of course only amplified the problem because, as he worked harder, he achieved more and, as he achieved more, the more he pissed people off. He was caught in a vicious and almost incapacitating circle because Joey needed other people to fuel his intense desire to please and the more that people put him down, the more isolated he became. The price of success was proving to be extremely dear and sometimes he felt like giving up. If it weren't for all the material obligations that he had accrued, he probably would have walked away from it right at that moment.

To add to all of this, Debra, alone once more for a few days at a time was beginning to get restless again. Later, in retrospect, he could clearly remember the look that she would get when it was time for him to pay an inordinate amount of attention to her. She would get a certain disdainful air about her that would disappear quickly anytime her eye would linger on another man, like it had with Jimmy Jeff at Hebert's. She also tended to become absent-minded and out of sorts more often. It didn't help that when Joey took his fifth week at home, he was literally worn-out and in need of peace and quiet while Debra, cooped up alone for the majority of the past four weeks, would be ready to hit the town and howl.

After one particularly trying road trip, Joey was lying out by the pool with his portable telephone and a cold beer, doing his expenses for the past month. This was something that every traveling salesman absolutely abhors. In order to feel better about it, he called it "creative writing" but everytime it came around he felt less and less creative. As a matter of fact, lately it had begun to really upset him. Maybe it was time to get out of the little office he had in the spare bedroom and open up a real one complete with secretary and staff to handle all of this business.

"Are you going to sit out there all day doing nothing or are you going to help me with this damn yard work?," Debra yelled from out front.

For some reason, she didn't or wouldn't understand that the demands of running a one-man show were pretty extreme and he couldn't just stop everything he was doing everytime it occurred to her to do something. It also bothered him, although he didn't realize it at the time, that when she did start this crap she sounded more and more like her mother.

When he was nudged into this impatient mood by Debra, or anyone else for that matter, strange thought sequences would come to him. They were strange alright but they also seemed to have some order to them. As if they came from an oracle hidden deep in the recesses of his mind. They also made a rather eerie sense of some of the mysterious ways that people live and act. For these reasons, he would sit and let them happen until they were finished. At times like these, he would go into a kind of trance which some people would think of as rude but everyone thought of as strange.

"Dammit, Joey, I can't take care of all of this heavy work by myself. This is your yard too! It needs to be taken care of today!"

"Just cool down a little Debra. We've got the rest of the week to mow the lawn and trim the hedge. Hell, we'll be the only people here until this weekend. There's no need to stop in the middle of what I'm doing to get it done. The yard ain't goin' anywhere!"

It had always mystified Joey why a woman's thought processes worked the way they did when it came to chores or other tasks. It seemed to him that there was little or no rhyme or reason to how they decided how to handle their work much less any kind of organization. Many were the times when he would come home off the road to find Debra running frantically around the house trying to straighten up all of the messes she had made as she tried to get all of the housework done on the day that he was to come home. Dirty dishes would be laying about, the stove door hanging open like it was sticking its tongue out at her, dirty laundry laying in insolent piles on the floor, the vacuum would be running and, usually, there were a couple of piles of weeds smiling wetly in the back yard. Debra would be on the phone and, holding her hand over the receiver, she would roll her eyes and whisper that she was on the phone for "the hundredth time today!."

He didn't have to hear all of the gory details to figure out what had happened. It probably went something like this. She had gotten up a little late because she had stayed up to watch Cher or some other important star on the Tonight Show. As she was getting some orange juice from the fridge, she noticed that it needed cleaning and so she removed the two bottom drawers and put them in the sink. About this time the phone rang and, as she was yakking with a

90

friend, she noticed the floor needed vacuuming and mopping. As she was vacuuming the kitchen, the phone rang again and as she was talking she saw the smoke curling out of the oven from the toast she had forgotten.

This, of course, caused her to observe that the oven needed cleaning. It took a little time to locate the oven cleaner and her rubber gloves and by the time she was half way through with that job the phone rang again. This time to get away from all of the mess so she could think, she took the portable phone and walked out into the backyard. As she talked, she began to pull a few weeds and, after hanging up, was soon weeding in earnest. A couple of hours later, the phone rang again. This time it was a friend asking for a recipe so that she could fix a nice meal for her husband who had been traveling all week. At this point she looked at her watch and, realizing it was almost five o'clock, began frantically trying to finish everything that she had started before Joey came home.

These homecomings were usually pretty strained affairs since, by the time he helped her get everything straightened out, she would be too tired or out of sorts to make dinner. Joey didn't particularly mind going out to eat even after four nights of eating out on the road. When they finally got around to it, however, neither of them would feel like getting dressed up for anything fancy, so they would just go to one of their usual hangouts. Now this didn't set too well with Debra because she didn't like "sharing" him with their friends and acquaintences the minute he got home. To avoid this he would usually give her the choice of where to go for dinner.

"Whew! I'm worn out. Where would you like to go for a little dinner and a cold beer, darlin'?"

"Oh, Joey, you've been eating out all week. You probably don't want to go out for dinner again."

"Hey, it's fine with me. You can't find decent Mexican food in Tulsa, anyway. Let's go get an enchilada and a margarita. You pick the place."

"I don't want to go to El Mercado again. We always run into all those boring business people there. Let's go to Esparza's in Grapevine."

On the way to the restaurant, Joey would sense a feeling of mounting tension build in Debra. So he often tried to lighten the mood by telling her of his work week and a few funny things that had happened to him. Unfortunately, this seemed to heighten the intensity of this evening.

"You always have so much fun out working while I have to stay home and work like the hired help cleaning toilets and mopping floors. Nothing interesting happens to me!"

"You know I'd love for you to travel with me, darlin', but everytime you do about halfway through the week you get bored with it all, remember? Tell you what, next week I need to go to San Antonio and then we can go on down to the Valley, call on some accounts and stay down on the beach in South Padre. Maybe go over into Mexico and just mess around a little bit."

"Only if we don't have to stay with that customer of yours with those two little pain in the ass kids! And I don't want to have dinner with that big fat guy and his wife. I've never met such boring people. All they can talk about is what they ate last week or what they want to go eat tonight."

"We've got to remember who pays the bills for us, darlin'. If it weren't for people like them, we wouldn't live nearly as well as we do," he said gently, "They like you a lot and it would really be kind of rude to be in town and not say hello."

"That's all you can think about, isn't it? Business, business, business! I think I'll scream if I hear anymore of your business bullshit!"

This particular type of conversation was almost a tradition with Debra when he would get home. He had noticed that it usually started about five weeks into his five week cycle. So, in order to try to make things better, he had begun to vary his schedule. Instead of travelling four weeks in a row, he'd go out two weeks, stay home a week and out two more; or out one week, home one week, out two weeks and back home; but no matter how he varied it, this same argument cropped up over and over again.

He couldn't figure out if Debra just plain detested the way he made his living or if she just disliked his business friends? Or did it have anything to do with any of that? Sometimes he thought that she just got bored easily but many years later, in retrospect, it became obvious that the real problem was that she lacked imagination.

Joey spent so much time trying to cure her "boredom" that he never took a few moments to find it's source. What appeared to be total revulsion for his business was just her inability to make each situation unique. She actually didn't want to enjoy what he had to do for a living much less tolerate it. Whenever he brought anything up about his work, she would automatically switch to a negative mind-set but, if he didn't talk to her about the subject, he wasn't "sharing" his life with her! Damned if you do and damned if you don't!

At any rate, he didn't know any other way to make the kind of living that they had gotten used to. Since he had started his own business and taken over the checkbook, they had actually begun saving a little money. He was working as hard as ever but now they were progressing toward the "good life." If only he could show her how to enjoy it. Of course, that was the little mind trick that so many of us play on ourselves. We don't want to change anybody, we just want to "show them how to enjoy life."

There are those folks who are meant to enjoy life and there are those who aren't and never the twain shall meet. Showing someone how to do something is exactly the same as trying to change them and that has repeatedly proven impossible. Ain't nobody gonna change nobody, no time . . . no how! But in our quest to make things better, to give the ultimate gift of happiness to spouses or friends (sometimes one and the same), we trick ourselves into believing that we aren't trying to alter anyone's behavior.

What a bunch of do-do! Of course we're trying to change them. We want them to be able to enjoy what we enjoy. We want them to smile when we smile, laugh when we laugh, cry when we cry . . . how self-centered can you get? Unbeknownst to Joey, he was about to find something out about being self-centered!

In conversation with Debra over dinner, she talked to him about her week. Most of the conversation concerned the tennis club and the problems of her girlfriends, many of whom were having trouble in their marriages. It seemed that the only way their husbands could afford all of the things that they wanted was to become workaholics and this put a strain on their lives because they were never home. The ladies, on the other hand, didn't want to give up their big cars, the tennis club and all of the trappings of wealth that they had "worked so hard" to attain. So most of them were at an impasse with their spouses. The unhappy consequence of this situation was that they started collectively looking for alternative solutions to their loneliness and a lot of those alternatives were not in any of their best interests.

The ladies consulted those bastions of feminine psychology, Dear Abby and *Cosmo*, and concluded that they needed counseling.

The counseling was usually quite expensive and this, of course, meant that the men would have to work harder than ever to be able to afford these new expenses. The counseling also took up a large part of the precious little time that the couple had together since they were either with the counselor in person or talking over what they had talked over in the counselor's office.

Later on, while the men worked, the ladies would gather after tennis or housework during the day and compare notes. Invariably, one or more of them would reveal that she was having an "affair" with anyone from the bagboy at the supermarket to the preacher and, sometimes, even to the counselor. At first, the ones who weren't messing around would be shocked but then as their curiosity became piqued they would think about the possibility of some of this kind of excitement in their very own lives.

Their rationalizations were endless and puerile.

"Oh, what the hell, he never pays any attention to me anymore, anyway! Patty has been doing it with her pool man for over a year and she says that it has made her sex life at home so much better!"

"Yeah, but remember that D & C that Shirley had to have after her dalliance with that young tennis pro?"

"You can't just start taking birth control pills after your husband's vasectomy!"

"I'll try it one time, I can always quit if I don't like it, no one will be the wiser!"

Ah . . . Ladies! Ladies! Ladies! That was the same thing you said about smoking and now look at you, sneaking cigarettes all day long and no way you'll ever quit. What about the ten pounds you were going to lose after you had each of your three children which now have turned into thirty? Think about all of those New Year's resolutions that lasted less than seventy-two hours or how nice you were going to be to your mother from now on, just yesterday. There is reason for discipline in life. The rules aren't there only for nuisance value. Crossing the line generally has a greater downside risk than any pleasure you can derive from it.

To add to the problem at hand, after shopping or over the phone at home, these ladies were constantly comparing notes with their friends. As they learned of all the adventures that their friends were experiencing outside of their marriages, their own uneasiness built. Until, finally, they found themselves fantasizing about the tennis pro or that old school chum that they almost went all the way with behind the high school gym that starry autumn night long ago. Now these liberated ladies must make a choice. Do I break the rules and try some of the forbidden fruit or continue in this miserable rut? Enter the self-help books!

Self-help books were obviously started by some "liberated" person who needed to rationalize his or her less than acceptable behavior to their critics. Most of these critics were theologians, peers, family or moralists of some type or another. The premise of these books is really quite simple. If everyone is doing it and you want to also, then there must be a way through someone else's logic that you can justify your actions to yourself and your family even though it is innately obvious that these actions are wrong.

Rationalizations are very dangerous things since they, like statistics, can be used to prove almost anything anyone wants. My favorite rationalization comes from a men's room wall and it goes something like this: God is love, love is blind, Ray Charles is blind, therefore, Ray Charles is God. Now if that makes any sense at all then I stand corrected on the whole "I'm ok, you're ok" thing.

Further on this self-help situation, the name is really a misnomer. Look at it this way, of all of the people that you know who subscribe to this type of hyperbole, which ones still subscribe to the same hyperbole three months or three years later? Aren't they usually by that time carrying a different banner, worshipping a different guru, psychobabbling in a different tongue? There are an awful lot of people out there who are willing to embrace anything that fits their particular modus operandi while not disturbing their lifestyle.

Let's face it, if you are going to do something that you are sure is wrong, you've got to have an explanation for your mother, friend, spouse, etc. that they will swallow. That takes care of the first episode because odds are, since they **are** your mother, friend, spouse, etc., they'll probably swallow any explanation that you have for your transgression . . . at least the first time. It follows,then, that if you are going to do whatever it is again, you will need a new explanation for everyone. Thus the need for all of the different self-help books. Shoot! If you only have one book to refer to, you only get one shot at all of the fun!

Well, what about the other side of the coin, the men? The men, as is their wont, went to the local bar and counseled with their friends. This wasn't always the best course of action because most of their buddies' were having the same kind of problems and things could get tense. Alcohol and anxiety have a way of turning into simple rage and this combination leads to some of the best bar fights that you have ever seen.

Another down side of this situation was that, with the advent of the pill in combination with the new "liberated" moral stance and the fact that women outnumbered men in most of the local bars . . . extracurricular entertainment was, all too often, readily at hand. The best case scenario was that the guy would get home a little late and a little drunk but purged of his angst and ire, convinced that he should straighten up and make a go of it "for his families' sake." The worst was that he wouldn't come home at all. As is usually the case with human behavior, most fell somewhere in between.

This is what happened with Joey and Debra. One night, when he came home a little tipsy and not quite purged of all of his bad feelings, she suggested that they go to a marriage counselor. Much to his surprise she already had one selected. As a matter of fact, she had been seeing this "therapist" for several weeks without Joey knowing about it.

The counselor came highly recommended by a girlfriend of Debra's who had recently gotten divorced and the counselor was a divorcee' herself, although not so recently. Her credentials were impeccable. She had undergraduate degrees in sociology and psychology and, in addition, an elementary school teaching certificate. She also had a thriving practice in a chic north Dallas high rise and an hourly rate of $120.

"You've been going to a shrink? Why didn't you tell me? I had no idea that you were having problems, darlin!"

Now, this wasn't entirely true. Joey knew that most of Debra's friends were having marital difficulty and he really had no reason to believe that she wouldn't identify with them. His mistake was in thinking that she and their marriage were strong enough to not be influenced by her semi-flaky, going-on-forty friends. It's another interesting part of human nature, that other people's troubles can become so important to some people that they actually become their own troubles. Even though, up until that time, they hadn't really had any troubles! It's almost as if trouble is infectious. He could almost hear the conversation now.

"How's it going, Ralph?"

"Not so hot, I think I'm coming down with divorce."

"That's a shame, everybody in our neighborhood's had it. Why, I just got over it myself!"

At any rate, Debra thought it would be a good idea if Joey went to see this lady and then the two of them could go together. As luck would have it, Joey had taken some courses in psychology in graduate school and had learned that most of the married couples that go to counseling end up getting divorced themselves. Needless to say, this new turn of events had him quite unsettled.

"As a matter of fact, I have been upset with you and our relationship for some time now," Debra said, not looking at him. "All you do anymore is work, work, work. We never have any time alone."

"Look, darlin', I realize that some of your friends are having a tough go of it with each other but that's no reason to make their troubles ours. All of this work, work, work is beginning to pay off and real soon I'll be hiring some salesmen to take the pressure off me. Things will ease up and we can go back like it was last year when I didn't have a job, remember?"

With this he put his arms around her but she spun out of them and walked over to the window, arms crossed over her chest. Again, without looking at him she said, "You keep saying all that stuff but you know you're never going to slow down. You love all of that traveling around being a bigshot with your American Express card and your phony-baloney salesman shit! I need a life too!"

"Look at all of the wonderful things we have, darlin'," he countered in that condescending tone that adults reserve for small children. "This beautiful house, your horses, the tennis club, a husband that loves you and doesn't screw around. Why, I bet an awful lot of your friends would love to trade places with you. You know if you try hard enough, you can find something wrong with anything . . . nothing is perfect. What's most important is to recognize the relative worth of the whole picture, not the little imperfections in this part or that."

"Don't try to con me with all of that rational bullshit," at this point she was getting a little testy, "everybody knows that you went to graduate school. It's not as simple as all of that. I'm not happy with the way our life is going. We need to change some things!"

"Look, we're in the top one per cent in the nation in income and net worth. We take at least two vacations each year that cost more than most people make on an annual basis. When I'm not at work we play bridge, tennis, ride bikes, do everything together.

Everyone comments on what a wonderful couple we are and how we are so obviously in love. What is it that we need to change?" Joey knew he was getting in too deep but, as usual, he didn't know how to get out gracefully.

"I don't care about all of that. I want to go out on dates and get some romance back in my life. All of my girlfriends have the same problems. You men think that everything bad can be solved with a good screw!"

"Aw come on, Debra, I told you about letting someone else's problems become your own. You know better than to let those things get to you. Besides, a little poontang sounds like one hell of a starting place . . . if not a solution!"

Sound familiar? We all know these kind of arguments and we all know that they never go anywhere. It's not because anyone is right or wrong for there isn't any right or wrong in these man-woman things. Men and women just think differently.

Women depend on "feelings" to carry them through life. Whether the "feelings" have any basis in reality makes no difference. Men, on the other hand, due to their innate pragmatism, need explanations based on fact. They are uncomfortable with arguments based on the way someone feels. It's important for them to have proof in order to resolve an argument.

Maybe the answer to all this is in a theory that was making the rounds recently. It holds that underwear is the cause of all arguments between men and women and it seems like a reasonable premise. It states that disagreements don't happen when both parties have their underwear off. Just on that note, can you remember the last argument that you had with the opposite sex with your underwear off? As a matter of fact, the next time you smell the ozone in the air or get that look that you know so well, run up and pull your mate's underpants down and see if that helps. If it does give me a call. If doesn't, don't call me, I have troubles of my own.

But let's get back to Joey and Debra and the "I'm not happy so we need to change" or the "things are going too good, let's change something" syndrome. This phenomenom has been observed by millions of people but it only begins to count when you get a little older.

Probably the reason is that as the initial heat (love?) begins to fade there is time to consider other aspects of a relationship besides when the next romantic interlude will occur. It's really a shame that this happens with such boring predictability but what's really amazing is that more people don't warn each other about it so that future generations can somehow avoid it.

For the life of me I can't remember anyone sitting me down and saying, "Now, listen up here, pilgrim. There's going to come a time when this sweet wonderful young thing that you're about to hook up with is going to come up to you and say some things that are going to sound totally out of character to you. At this point you must find a way to change the subject to something that she will enjoy. That way you will help her take her mind off herself for awhile and maybe even make her feel a little bad about these unfounded 'feelings' that are causing her to act so weird."

The way some of my Jewish friends handle it is, they go out and buy their mate something way too extravagant for their standard of living. They know that her conscience will bother her (especially if he paid retail) in a few days and she will return it. But by that time she will have forgotten whatever it was that set her off in the first place. I don't personally recommend this to just anyone. You could go to debtor's prison if you are with the wrong person.

Joey's major problem in this arena was that he had not only never been through anything like this but also had never had anyone preview this type of behavior for him. It wasn't in any of the case studies that he'd read in college; no mention of these ambiguities in Psychology 101. His Mom and Dad certainly had not made him aware that this type of thing would come up after a few years. So, like the bulk of the male population at that time, he was mostly on his own. It was at this point that he should have remembered the General Law of Womanhood. Remember? "When women confront men with a problem, they are looking for sympathy . . . not a solution."

How simple it all would have been if he had just walked over and given her a hug and told her he loved her. But just at that moment the phone rang and it was one of Debra's friends who was going through a divorce after getting caught in flagrante delicto with a local used car salesman. Debra asked if they could take her to dinner and Joey was so relieved to get out of their impasse that he agreed.

As they were showering up for dinner, Joey almost successfully invoked the General Law but, unfortunately, as he hugged Debra and told her he loved her, "OLD NUMBER NINE" betrayed him and she went off in a snit again. One of the things to remember about the General Law is that it's real dangerous to try to use it with no clothes on because natural biological urges at that time are inappropriate in a woman's mind.

"Damn you Joey! You come on so sweet and then all you want is a piece of ass! I almost thought for a minute that you really did love me! What a piece of junk you men are!"

With that she fled the bathroom taking only time enough to slam everything within reach that was slammable. It's amazing how many things women can find to slam when the occasion calls for it. Joey thought that he had seen them all but when she slammed down her make-up sponge and it made a loud splat! . . . even he was impressed. He smiled down at his still erect member and shook his head. He wondered how many of her girlfriends would be happy to have a man who still was so in love (heat?) with them. He knew the one they were going to meet for dinner would probably love it. Oh, well!

They met Mary Ann at one of those chic north Dallas wine bars where everyone looks like a picture out of *Vogue* magazine. All of the diners wore the latest in fashion and couture and the hairstyles bordered on the ridiculous. They had to turn up the music in places like this because everyone is so busy trying to see who is there that they don't have time to talk to each other. Besides, who wants to talk to someone who doesn't have anything to say anyway?

Joey wasn't very comfortable in these types of surroundings even without the added pressure of a recently divorced, extremely pretty, very wealthy, obviously horny woman sitting across from him. The lady was dressed to kill and, even though she was ostensibly with friends, could hardly keep her eyes off Joey as she recited her tale of woe. Debra, sensing the attraction that her friend had for Joey, got that cat-eyed look that she reserved for anyone who showed interest in him.

Oh, great, he thought, first we have these problems at home and now after she has about two more Harvey Wallbangers I'm going to have to dodge another barrage of bullets. It's just not my day! With these thoughts in mind, he got up, excused himself and headed to the bathroom.

On the way to the back of the restaurant, he was stopped by one of Debra's tennis buddies. He kind of recognized her face but had never seen her in anything but tennis clothes. Besides, when he had passed her at the tennis club, they had only been nodding acquaintenances.

"Hi, Joey," she said as she grabbed his arm and pulled him close, "you here by yourself?"

He couldn't even remember her name but she looked at him like a starving Ethiopian who had just found a still-warm smoker loaded with prime rib and potatoes.

Trying to be courteous, he replied, "No, Debra's up there with Mary Ann and we are going to have dinner. By the way where's . . .?" He couldn't remember her husband's name.

"You better look out for old Mary Ann over there. She just got unhitched and she's liable to tackle you and jump all over your bones. Speakin' of that, me and Ken split up about a month ago and you don't look so bad to me either, honey!"

She was laughing as she said it but at the same time looking him directly in the eyes with the same look he had hoped to see on Debra's face when they were in the shower earlier that evening. Boy, he thought, I don't know if I can stand it if things get any hotter.

About this time he felt a hand pulling him backward away from the bar and as he looked around there was Debra. The cat-eyed look had gone from smoldering indifference to flashing Siamese. Oh man!, he thought, here I am trying to get away from one scorned lady who needs another scalp for her totem pole only to have another one grab me and in the middle of it all, my pissed-off old lady walks in. Dammit to hell!

"Hi, honey. I see you've found Barbara. Whatcha' all talkin' about?"

"Barbara was just tellin' me that she and Ken are going to part ways but, actually darlin', I really need to take a leak so I'll just leave ya'll to get caught up. Hope everything works out okay, Barbara."

With that he tried to saunter casually to the bathroom but he could feel Debra's eyes boring holes in his back all the way. Well, hell, he thought, just a little while ago she was telling me what an inconsiderate piece of junk I was and now she's mad because I was talking to one of her friends.

Wrong, Joey, you were talking to one of her **divorced** friends. One of her **recently** divorced friends and she had not **recently** approved the conversation. So no matter how innocuous it may have seemed to you, you, at this point, were consorting with the enemy. There was one thought that kind of flitted through Joey's mind that later on scared him to death and that was: if she wasn't all that happy with him and someone else wanted him, why was she so pissed off?

As he walked back from the men's room, he noticed that Debra was back at the table with Mary Ann while several of Debra's friends from the club were huddled around Barbara. It was obvious that, if they weren't all talking about him, they sure were waiting for him to come out of the restroom for some reason. He hadn't run a gauntlet like this since high school football. Well, what the hell, he thought, in for a dime, in for a dollar!

"What happened, Barbara, did the tennis club burn down? Or is this ladies night out? I haven't seen this many good-looking women in one place since my senior prom!"

Joey smiled at all of them but didn't let his glance linger on any one of them, knowing that Debra and Mary Ann were taking it all in.

"Well, whatever happens, Joey," Barbara smiled like a cat with a little mouse between it's paws, "you probably best not be hanging around us, at least not when Debra's around. She seemed to be a might pissed off about us talkin' a minute ago. After all, you're married and we ain't!"

With that, they all broke out in nervous laughter glancing sideways at Debra and Mary Ann at the same time. Joey quickly gave them all another smile and strutted on over to his own table. Well, he thought, for better or for worse those bitches still think I'm attractive. I hope the dinner goes a little smoother than the hors de'oeurves did!

As fate would have it and much to his chagrin, that was not to be the case. By the time he got back to the table, Debra and Mary Ann were deeply involved in a conversation in which they were not only discussing Barbara in terms that would make his dear mother blush, but they also were including him in the diatribe from time to time.

"Now hang on a minute girls," he said trying to be casual, "if you're gonna pick on me at least let me sit down and defend myself!"

"Yeah, sure Joey, why don't you just go on over there and hit on my newly divorced friends! Sometimes you are such a fool!"

"Whoa! Wait a minute, Debra, your girlfriends pulled me in there to talk to me, I was only being polite! Look, if I were going to mess around with them, I would at least have the common courtesy to do it when you weren't around. Anyway, I've never particularly liked any of your friends from the tennis club . . . present company excluded, of course." He said, turning his best little-boy smile on Mary Ann.

Mary Ann, of course, picked right up on the action. After all, this might have been one of her best friends but all's fair in love and war. Especially in love, and right now, as far as Mary Ann was concerned, love was a pretty scarce commodity. So she responded as only a recently scorned woman would.

"Calm down a bit there Debra! You ain't got nothin' to fear from Joey, although I would kinda look out for Barbara. She hasn't had a lot of love for you since you whupped her butt in that singles tournament last year. I would say, though, if you're bored with him, and all those things you told me about him are true, he might suit me juust right!"

With this she turned one of the sweetest, nastiest smiles that Joey had ever seen right square on one of Debra's bitchiest faces. At this point, Joey damn near threw his arms up over his face to try to protect himself from the onslaught he knew was forthcoming. Much to his surprise, it never came. With an unbelievable amount of self-control, one which he had not seen demonstrated recently, Debra somehow managed to keep from cold cockin' both of them and to their amazement managed a smile. It wasn't a pleasant smile and her lip did quiver a bit but it was a smile nonetheless.

After that, the rest of the evening went rather smoothly. But through it all the tension remained, since Debra was busy defending her turf. Joey couldn't turn around without noticing one of the tennis bitches giving him an openly inviting look. Jesus, he thought, if a fellow were looking to commit adultery, this would be one hell of a place to start!

When they had said their goodbyes and walked out in the parking lot, Debra grabbed him as he was opening her door. Fearing the worst, he kind of flinched but, instead of taking a swing at him, she laid a good old-fashioned french kiss right smack on his lips. Along with it she executed one of the finest bump and grinds he had felt in a long time. It seemed like an eternity before they broke apart, breathless, looked at each other like two starving animals and went right back after it again.

"Take me home right now, Joey!" She gasped as they broke apart again. "Take me home!"

Joey threw her in the car and ran around to his side which she already had open for him. As they turned out of the parking lot she already had her pants down and was fumbling with his belt. Needless to say they only got to the first semi-secluded parking spot they could find before they jumped all over each other. Later on, driving home with her head on his shoulder Joey thought, maybe all of those games at the bar were worth it!

When they got home from the restaurant, they couldn't get enough of each other. It was as if they weren't going to see each other ever again. They were half-naked when they got out of the car and totally naked by the time they got to the living room. So they made love (sex?) on the couch. After a short nap, they went to bed and as they crawled under the covers she smiled at him and off they went again. Finally, totally exhausted by the tension of the evening and all of the sex (love?), they fell into a deep sleep hugging one another for dear life. Joey fell asleep grinning with happiness but if he could have guessed what was to come, he probably wouldn't have been so happy.

Chapter Eight

JOEY WOKE UP EARLY, as confused as he was refreshed. Damn, he thought, in the shower earlier in the evening he had been wrong to get aroused, but the rest of the evening and into the wee hours it was okay. For the first part of the evening she acted like she was trying to get rid of him and then, when someone else looked like they wanted him, she held onto him for all she was worth. Boy, this is going to make great fun for that friggin' counselor.

He was softly singing some of the words of "Just Stopped In To See What Condition My Condition Was In" by Kenny Rogers and the First Edition when he said to himself, Oh yeah! The counselor! Up until then, he had completely forgotten about the counselor. He was getting a wee bit leery about going back to see her but after the first visit with him and Debra together, she had suggested that for the next few visits Joey should come alone. He wasn't a believer in counseling in the first place and saw the whole thing as a nuisance. He also saw a light in the counselor's eye that made him uneasy.

That afternoon he finished his paperwork and got in the car for the ride to the counselor's office. On the way he almost stopped for a six pack thinking what a bunch of crap all of this was. Maybe what I ought to do is go sit out behind J. C.'s shop til it gets dark, play a little hooky. A six pack and a sunset is probably better therapy than what I'm gonna pay this chick $120 an hour for. That was probably the truest thought that had passed through his mind in recent months.

When he got to her office it was around five-thirty and he knew that Debra, who was playing tennis, wanted him to meet her about seven-thirty for dinner at the club. As he entered Phyllis Bowen's office, he noticed that the receptionist had already gone home and the lights were off. The door to the "doctor's" office was open.

"Phyllis," he called, "you in there?"

"Come on in Joey," she called back, "I'll be right with you."

He walked into the dimly lit office with the view of downtown Dallas out the large picture window and was surprised at how pretty that view was. In his preceding visit the drapes had been pulled together. She had her back to him and was talking on the phone in a soft monotone. He sat down and took in the scenery, not paying any attention to her or her conversation.

When she finished, she spun her chair around and hung up the phone, one of those late model deals that looked like something out of Star Trek. He noticed that she had it hooked up to a recorder and wondered if she also recorded their meetings. She straightened up her desk, took out a pastel legal pad complete with a matching pen and smiled at him.

"Well, how are we doing today, Joey?," she asked, not in doctor fashion at all.

"Just fine, Phyllis, and you?"

"Couldn't be better. By the way, wasn't that you and Debra I saw necking out in the parking lot of The Rose last night?"

"Yeah, we kind of got carried away. Didn't know the whole world was watching and I guess we just didn't care. I think she was a little upset by some of her friends in the restaurant. You know a lot of them are either having trouble or getting divorced and they were kind of letting me know about it. I try not to get involved in those situations too much."

"Why is that Joey? Are you afraid of them or yourself?"

Oh, oh!, he thought, this thing is getting out of hand already! You've got to remember that you're talking to a shrink! These people will climb on anything you say and make a big deal out of it. He looked out the window again as he composed his thoughts. "I don't think I'm afraid of either one but it has been my experience that when someone is having trouble at home they might say or do things that they wouldn't normally. As a friend of mine once said, the only way that most people know to get out of a bad relationship is to start another one."

106

That wasn't too smart, Joey, he mused watching her eyes light up, she'll have a field day with that. It sounded like something right out of *Red Book* or *Self*. From the look on her face this was going to be an interesting conversation.

"That's an interesting point. I notice that you have a Masters Degree in marketing. You didn't happen to take some psychology courses along the way, did you?"

"As a matter of fact, my undergraduate degree was in behavioral science which as you know is really just psychology applied to business situations. I find people fascinating in or out of business."

He was looking right into her eyes when he said this and was surprised at what he saw. She wasn't looking at him like a professional at all or maybe like a professional, but not a professional **doctor**. There seemed to be more than a passing interest in her look but then she was supposed to be interested wasn't she? Joey noticed that she really wasn't all that bad looking if she would scrape off some of that makeup and let her hair down.

"You know, with all of the education that you have, you might be better qualified for my job than I am myself. Why do you think that you and Debra are having problems?"

"Hell, I don't know. I wasn't even aware that we were having any problems at all until right after you found out. We don't get along perfectly all the time but we've always been able to work things out. I just figured that since most of her friends were having problems, she decided she'd have some too. Isn't it fashionable these days, what with all the divorces and all this liberation crap, for people to go to therapy or counseling or something?"

"Yes, I get alot of that these days," she laughed gently, "and I hope that's the case with you two. I'm a little concerned about Debra, however, she seems to be a strong person but she has such a difficult family."

"If you're talking about her mother, that has been a concern of mine also. Her mother is about as screwed up a person as I have ever seen. If it's wrong she has done it and she seems to delight in everyone else's failings also. I don't consider her too hot a role model for her children or anyone else's for that matter. She sure makes life miserable for Debra and her sister. I guess it must be tough loving someone and not being able to stand them."

"Wait a minute Joey, you've got to remember that, after all, this is her mother we're talking about and she will defend her to the death. That's just the way women are. And sometimes the defense can destroy a man-woman relationship because she has to choose between her mother and the man she loves. Unfortunately, Debra appears to be the type who will choose her mother the majority of the time."

Joey felt as if someone had just thrown a bucket of ice water over his heart because he had already sensed what the counselor was putting into words. When he and Debra had first started going out together she had accepted everything he said or thought as being the ultimate answer on most subjects. Lately, however, she was leaning more and more toward her mother's opinions. Maybe that was the reason for this counselor. Maybe she figured she needed an impartial observer to intercede and clear up some of the questions that had been perplexing her so.

"I'm afraid, Joey, that, from my conversations with her, an awful lot of the endurance of your relationship will depend on your patience and understanding. Not only of Debra but also her family because she has made it pretty plain that you can't have one without the other. Now, I know that that is contrary to the way that lifetime priorities should be set but, unfortunately, that is the way she has set hers. I'll be damned if I can explain to you why she feels that way. I wouldn't have a bit of trouble in making you number one in my life!"

Now Joey was having a hard time even looking at her because all of a sudden he noticed that they were all alone in her semi-darkened office and there was some kind of soft jazz playing in the background. He quickly looked around the office and saw the big paisley couch and the bar with what looked like a bucket of ice with the neck of a bottle sticking out of it. He looked back over the desk at her and she smiled that smile again. Unconsciously, he smiled back and was kind of relieved at the feeling it gave him (or maybe it was the lack of feeling that was reassuring).

"Why don't we get a little more comfortable?," She gestured toward the couch, "Maybe have a little wine. There's no need for us not to be friends. I only have a few more things I want to discuss with you and then I'm going to call it a day. Do you like Piesporter?"

As she poured the wine she continued, "As I was saying, Joey, your patience and understanding are either going to make or break your marriage. It's not that there are any major problems right now but the warning signs are all there.

"You've probably noticed that she sides with others more than you lately. That's quite common, by the way, especially as marriages begin to age and some of the initial mystery begins to pale. Also, she's under a lot of pressure in the upscale society that you have thrust her into. There is a lot of peer pressure in the north Dallas crowd that you two have chosen to run in. She is beginning to feel that you might be getting a little tired of her and may just be looking around a little bit yourself."

Joey sipped his wine, settled back into the chair and let out a long slow sigh. So this is the way this kind of stuff starts, he thought. Well, Debra picked this lady and I paid for it so I think I'll just ride this old horse till she falls and see what happens next. So he loosened his tie, sat back and let fly.

"You know it has always been taught to me that marriage, or any relationship for that matter, is a two-way street. That the duration of the situation is determined by the whole, not by any one facet. So why is it that, all of a sudden, it is totally up to me how this thing comes out? How is it that we need an ultimatum all of sudden? I know that we have had some lingering arguments that seem to crop up from time to time without resolution but I haven't considered any of them insurmountable. Do you know something that I don't?"

"I know that Debra is unhappy with her life and in reality she has no reason to be. I also know that you are a very attractive, wealthy, intelligent individual who is very appealing to her recently unhappily divorced friends. And to top all of this off, her mother, who is extremely unhappy with her life also, has been bad-mouthing you because you won't give in to her egocentricities. I think that Debra is feeling pressure from all sides including you and, at some point, if it doesn't ease up, she will look somewhere else for relief."

"Hold on now, Joey" he was sitting straight up in his seat on the couch, and Phyllis was motioning with her hand for him to sit back, "this doesn't mean she is contemplating anything rash, she is just uptight. Maybe you two need a little time apart."

The last sounded even less convincing in person than it does in print. What kind of lame rationalization is this?, Joey thought. Either she loves me or she doesn't. I'm not going to settle for any of this late-model psychology. I don't need any "time apart" (read affair) and neither does Debra. It was at this point that a picture of JJ and Debra flashed in the back of his head and right behind it a picture of she and Peter dancing together that night in Austin. Involuntarily he shook his shoulders as if coming out of a bad dream.

"I guess I need to explain something to you, Phyllis. I may

seem to be something that I definitely am not. To begin with, Debra and her Momma chose our north Dallas lifestyle, not me. That's why we live out in the country. I'm really a very simple person. I like Texas sunsets and cold beer and the least complicated life that I can get away with and still live well. I don't screw around and I could not accept it if Debra did. I'm just not interested in all of that extracurricular activity. I have watched an awful lot of people go through that thought and life process and all of them, without exception, have failed miserably. As a matter of fact, as a "professional" counselor, I'm surprised that you would even suggest such a thing!"

"You know, Joey," she intoned in her best professional manner, "this is the seventies and society has come a long way in the last few years. What was unacceptable just a few years ago is quite the contrary now. We have progressed to a point where suppression of any kind is being looked at very closely. Women are much more liberated these days. We can speak as we please and live as we please, not bound by man's outdated dogma."

As she was saying all of these appalling things she kept sliding closer and closer to Joey until he could smell her perfume and see the glow in her eyes which were riveted to his. If I didn't know better I'd think that she was taking a shot at me, he mused. Now wouldn't that be the cat's ass! Here I am paying this woman $120 an hour to take care of my problems and she wants me to take care of **hers.** Well, let's just see how serious she is!

"You mean to tell me that you women really believe all of that drivel in all those magazines and self-help books? I thought it was just a bunch of movie-star crap and you all just used it for entertainment, like the soap operas."

"We women are as serious as death when it comes to love, Joey. Love is one of the most important things in life to us and, when we think that we are being shortchanged in that department, we can do some very drastic things. The one thing that men can't seem to get through their thick little heads is that with women there are no rules. The game is constantly changing and we will stop at almost nothing when it comes to getting what we want."

Whoa! Joey thought, this sumbitch is stronger'n dirt! She may be that serious about love (heat) but she ain't gonna find any of it with me. The way things are heating (loving?) up, I better back off before this deal gets out of hand.

"Damn!," He said, looking at his watch, "I'm supposed to meet

Debra at seven-thirty for dinner and it's almost seven now. Boy, the time just flew by. Well, thanks a lot for the wine and the conversation. When do we meet again?"

He was standing by now and fumbling for his car keys while she smiled crookedly up at him.

"How about Monday, same time." She stated rather than asked, the whole time leering mockingly at him.

Ah, this is the challenge phase! Next it'll be, "what are you some kind of queer or something? I'm a woman, Joey, with a woman's wants and needs!" He could picture the whole thing now. Well, if she was that lonely, why couldn't she keep her old man around? Why did she need to hit on married men whose wives were baring their souls to her?

"Okay, I'll see you then. You just want to bill me or do you need a check?"

"Just come by on Monday at five-thirty, Joey, and plan on staying a little longer," she sighed resignedly, as if some boring or unpleasant reality had just dawned on her, "We can probably wrap this thing up with one good session."

As he drove back to the club he didn't know whether he should be flattered or disgusted. It was obvious from the way that she had come on to him that this wasn't the first time for her. Besides, he wasn't that attracted to her anyway. He had been approached by women before in his marriage and, to his credit, always resisted. Maybe I'll just tell Debra that I don't think I'm getting anything out of this deal and stop going. He knew, though, that she would probably insist on him seeing it through and he would probably go back on Monday. Perhaps, he should bring old J. C. along as a witness.

When he got to the club, he found Debra's car and parked close by. As he walked by the indoor courts he saw her playing under the lights with a guy who looked vaguely familiar. To his consternation, it was the same guy who had hit on her that time in Austin when she had wanted Joey to whip the guy's ass for trying to steal a kiss. I wonder what that's all about? he marveled as he walked upstairs to the bar for a beer.

Debra came up a few minutes later, kinda out of breath and, when she saw Joey, looked apprehensively back over her shoulder but no one was back there. Flushing slightly, she gave him a big smile and a kiss.

"That was quite a workout!," She giggled. "Peter is warming me up for the club singles championships. We played three hard sets this evening. What's that you're drinking, a cold beer? That sounds wonderful to me! Would you get me one?"

As Joey walked over to get her a beer he noticed Mary Ann and several of the ladies from the restaurant the other evening sitting together at a table. They waved casually and said hi but he noticed that they all were watching him intently as he went back to sit with Debra. She was nervously smoking a cigarette as he approached.

"I don't see how you can do that after a good workout. If I tried to smoke after running, I'd probably fall over dead!"

He was trying to be funny and serious at the same time but Debra was having none of it.

"Look, Joey, I don't make fun of your beer drinking and you don't make fun of my smoking." She snapped. "I'm a big girl. I know what's good for me and what isn't. I've had a wonderful evening so far. Let's not spoil it, okay?"

He noticed that while she was talking to him her eyes were darting all around the room and he turned to look around as well. There was her tennis partner, Peter, sitting with her friends and talking animatedly. From time to time he and the girls would all break out in almost hysterical laughter like a flock of startled geese. Joey looked from them back to Debra and didn't like what he saw. This whole scene along with what had just transpired in the counselor's office was making him pretty uncomfortable. From the look on Debra's face she wasn't too comfortable either.

"Say, why don't we split and go somewhere else for dinner? I've been here all afternoon. Maybe you could follow me and we can stop somewhere on the way home."

With that they gathered up all of her paraphenalia and walked out waving goodbye to all of her "friends" along the way. These processions are getting more and more uncomfortable, Joey thought. I must really be getting paranoid. It's as if we are always the center of attention. I can't get any good vibrations from any of them. I should have gone ahead and beat the dog out of Peter that time back in Austin. That last thought took him by surprise and he wondered about it all the way home.

The next Monday was extremely busy as most Mondays are and he almost forgot about his appointment with Phyllis the psychologist. Instead of getting there on time, he was about a half hour late.

As he pulled into the parking lot, he wasn't surprised to see her car still there.

"Sorry I'm late," he said as he let himself into the office.

She was already over on the couch with a glass of wine in her hand. He noticed that she had also poured one for him and it was on the coffee table in front of her. Wine had never been a favorite of his but, in all honesty, he didn't like the unspoken romantic connotation that went along with it.

"It was Monday all day today! I thought the phone would never stop ringing. You wouldn't happen to have a cold beer, would you? I'm nursing a terrible dry!"

"No problem, Joey, look in the little refrigerator behind the bar. I think you'll find what you want back there. I've had one of those Mondays, too. I got here at seven thirty this morning and I didn't even have time for lunch — had to eat on the run."

Even though it was the end of a long work day, she looked as if she had just stepped out of a relaxing bath. Not one hair was out of place and her makeup looked recently applied. On top of all that, she smelled good enough to eat. Enough of that kind of thinking, Joey, he mused, you've got all the problems you need as it is. He popped open a beer and took a seat across from her on one of the bar stools.

"Have you thought about the things we talked about last week, Joey? You know about Debra's priorities and what your role probably will have to be in the future?"

"As a matter of fact, I haven't given it a dime's worth of consideration. It seems like these days I don't have the time that I used to to delve into those things. I just kind of take everything one day at a time."

"Maybe it's time for us to have one last session together, all three of us. When we do I'd like you to exercise as much patience as you can muster. I'm afraid that the things I'm going to have to say to Debra aren't going to be much to her liking."

"Then why say them at all? Maybe I am not reading all of this bullshit correctly but off hand I would say that Debra chose you thinking that you would say what she wanted you to say. If you don't, do you honestly think that it will serve any useful purpose?"

Phyllis smiled knowingly and shook her head gently to and fro. "For someone who comes on like he doesn't know anything about women, you know one hell of a lot! That's exactly why she chose me. She thought that, since she couldn't change you into what she

113

and her mother wanted, maybe I could help, me being a woman and all. You have most of the qualities that women look for in a man. You are decent looking, faithful, a good provider and well thought of in business and the community. The problem is you are not controllable."

Son of a bitch, Joey said to himself, this can either do a lot of good or a lot of harm! Either way it sure has backfired on poor Debra. If she believes what this woman is going to tell her, she's got to choose between her Momma and me. If she doesn't, she'll think that the counselor and I are in cahoots and have ganged up on her. The problem is that, whichever way it falls, I lose. In the meantime, look at this picture!!

Phyllis, who obviously had had more than one glass of wine, was standing by the bar and tuning the stereo with one hand while she tried to unbutton her blouse with the other. As she turned around to face him she pulled her blouse open to reveal two plump though somewhat sagging breasts . . . and that's the way he left her. The one thing that would stick in his mind as he re-lived this scene over and over in the ensuing months was the joyless but acquiescent look on her suddenly tired face. It only took him a few minutes to exit the whole sad scene. Dammit, he hollered at himself, what do I do now?!!

This particular dilemma was solved for him later that evening when he confronted Debra with the results of his meeting with Phyllis. When he got home, Debra was sitting in the kitchen talking on the phone with one of her friends. He kissed her lightly on the cheek and went to the refrigerator for a cold beer. He smiled as he waited for her to get off the phone but she seemed a bit uncomfortable with him there so he walked upstairs to change clothes. About the time he had changed and taken a leak she walked into the bathroom where he was buttoning his old denim shirt.

"How'd your day go?" She asked.

"Fast and furious," he chuckled, "typical Monday. By the way, I guess I had my last solo meeting with the counselor today. She says we need to have one last meeting with her together in the next few days. I guess she's found out all she needs to know about both of us."

"Well, I hope you understand how I feel now that you've talked to an impartial third party. I brought it up over and over again but you were too busy with that business of yours to pay any attention to me. It seemed no matter how hard I tried to tell you, you just wouldn't listen."

She was looking at him so aloofly confident that he couldn't help but burst her balloon.

"On the contrary, she said that resolving our problems would depend mostly on how patient I could be with you. She also said that you probably wouldn't like what she has to say to you when we meet together."

"Well, since it's obvious that you two got along so well together, maybe we don't even need to waste the money going to see her again. She'll probably just try to tell me that I'm wrong, anyway, and I know I'm right. She doesn't live with you all of the time like I do. You probably charmed her right out of her pants with all of your psychological bullshit!"

Boy, if she only knew how true that almost was! Maybe I should have taken the old girl up on it, he thought, since it looks like I'm going to be accused of it anyway!

"Let me tell you something, Debra, in this case I agree with you. I really didn't find her all that competent and I'm not sure that she has any answers that would help us anyway. We have to work this thing out ourselves. Besides, we didn't have to try too hard to get along in the beginning of our relationship, no reason why we can't do it again. I'll tell you what, I'm willing to wipe out all the bad stuff and start out fresh if you are."

With a tear in her eye, she nodded in agreement and he took her in his arms. As he hugged her he looked over her shoulder into the bathroom mirror and found her staring right back into his eyes. With this they both broke into fractious laughter and hugged each other for real.

"Anyone for tennis?" He mumbled, as he carried her into the bedroom, thinking all the way that he had dodged the bullet again.

Chapter Nine

FOR THE NEXT FEW weeks things couldn't have been better for Joey and Debra. They got along just like old times and nothing seemed to get in the way of their fun with each other. It helped that it was the middle of November and the holidays were coming. This always signaled a slow down in Joey's business and he used the resultant free time just goofing off and shopping with Debra. Life was good again and, in an attempt to keep it that way, Joey took one night out in the middle of every week to give them each a breather. Most of the time he and J. C. would just go out and shoot some pool or drink beer and talk while Debra would play tennis with her friends or visit with her Momma.

It was on one of those nights out and Joey and J. C. were at their favorite local bar. After shooting a couple of games of pool and drinking a few beers, they sat down at the corner of the bar to talk. Actually J. C. sat but Joey liked to stand when they talked.

"Well, J. C. tell me how it's going. You gonna make it through the first of the year or what?"

J. C.'s business had not been going so hot and the recovery he had hoped for didn't seem to be on the horizon. Betty Jo had gotten a job and that helped . . . but she had also packed on so many pounds that she was fat as a town dog and that didn't help at all. These nights out with Joey and the few weekends that they spent camping and biking were just about the only entertainment they could afford in recent months. Joey knew it was wearing thin on his buddy and he

116

wished that there was something he could do about it, but he knew there wasn't. Everybody's gotta either get it together by himself or not.

"To tell the truth, I'm just makin' it day to day. Nobody's called any notes or anything yet but there ain't much business out there and I got a bunch more competition these days. The customer base isn't growing and they keep us biddin' against each other so that none of us make any money. The next few months will either make me or break me. In the mean time, why don't we have another beer?"

"What would you do if you had to give up the business? Have you given any thought to anything else?"

"I guess I'd have to go back to work for one of the oil companies. I really don't have any experience in anything else. Hope some of my old friends in the business have done well. Maybe they can help me out. Guess I ought to give a couple of them a call over the holidays."

"Yeah, at least Christmas gives you an excuse to contact them. If I were you, I'd do that toot suite. It's amazing how quickly people forget you when you're gone. Holy guacamole! Look at this little race horse comin' in the door. Here hold my wallet and checkbook! No matter what happens, don't let me have 'em back till she leaves!"

Joey pushed his wallet and money clip at J. C. who put both hands over his eyes pretending not to watch her entrance through his open fingers. Both of them were laughing their fool heads off as in the door marched a little darlin' about twenty years old who was just as cute as a button and dressed like a street walker. She obviously knew that all eyes were riveted on her as she walked right up to J. C. and Joey like she had known them for years.

"Somebody gonna buy me a drink or what?" She said, giving both of them a dazzling smile.

Joey was the first to regain his composure, "Sure thing darlin', what are you gonna have? How about a nice Double Cuervo Gold con limon y sal so's you can catch up with us? " He winked at J. C., as he waved the bartender over.

"That sounds great to me. How about some nachos to go along with it? I haven't eaten all day. My name's Taffy, what's yours?"

"I'm Joey and this is J. C." He said nodding at his old friend. "Come in here often?"

"Only with J. C." she smiled as she watched Joey execute a classic double take and gape incredulously at his buddy all the while shaking his head in disbelief. J. C. turned a deep shade of red and

117

ducked his head, grinning like a George Burns look-alike. Joey couldn't keep from looking one to the other with his lower jaw hanging down around his belt buckle as they hugged and laughed at him. Well, doesn't this just take the cake, Joey thought, ol' J. C. got him some poontang on the side. Coulda' fooled me! he thought and, as he usually did in nervous moments, he excused himself and went to the bathroom.

When he came back out, J. C. and Taffy were still grinning at each other as they crammed nachos into each other's mouths. Joey shook his head again, not believing what he saw. This little sucker coulda' stepped right out of the pages of *Penthouse*, he mused with just one little pang of jealousy which he quickly shook off. Well, my ol' buddy deserves a little treat what with all the things he's been through lately.

His happiness quickly turned to apprehension as pictures of Betty Jo and J. C.'s kids passed through his mind. I hope he keeps his wits about him, I've never known a hard dick to have a conscience! That'd be all that we'd need. Here it is Christmas coming on, he's goin' broke, his ol' lady's gettin' fatter by the minute and he's havin' a ball with some twenty-year-old darlin'. I haven't seen him this happy in five years he thought as he smiled at both of them. As if on cue Taffy excused herself and went to the ladies room so that Joey and J. C. could talk.

"Ok so you've been holding out on me! What's the deal?"

"Actually I met her right here when you were in Chicago a few months ago. I came in for a few beers after work and here she was. Just lives around the corner. I was a little late getting home that night or should I say that morning. You didn't hear about that?"

"Naw, things weren't so hot between Debra and me then so I guess she never said anything to me about it. You aren't planning on doing anything rash are you?"

J. C. stared off into the distance with a far away look in his eye that was really all the answer that Joey needed. It's just a matter of time, he thought, if it isn't this one it will be another. Dammit, why can't Betty Jo get her act in order? But way down deep in his heart he knew that it was way too late for that. How many people have you known who let themselves go to pot that ever recovered enough to keep it together?

"Let me tell you, buddy," J. C. said sincerely, "it gets harder and harder to go home all of the time. I don't think Betty Jo is ever going to get her act together. It's not the weight you know, she's just turned into a complete slob. Since she took that job, which we can't do without by the way, she has completely forgotten how to cook or clean the house. That's why we haven't been able to go camping on the weekends anymore. If I didn't get her and the kids together on Saturday and line out the housework, I'd be afraid to look under the beds or go out in the garage. The cockroaches would probably carry me off."

With this last he tried to laugh but it didn't come out too well — more like a frog strangling or a cough or something. Joey could tell it hurt him a lot but he could also see that he was getting close to making a major decision. From a selfish standpoint this new turn of events pissed Joey off royally. Here he was back on the right track with Debra and now J. C. and Betty Jo were about to have problems which he knew would soon turn into his own. Dammit! There just isn't any winning in this game, is there? He had to admit, though, watching J. C.'s little love bunny bouncing up to the bar from the bathroom, all smilin' and sweet smellin', if she made **him** an offer it would be hard to refuse.

It had been a long time since the thought of someone else had even crossed his mind but this one sure piqued his curiosity. Probably, it was because he knew that it could be done but, at any rate, he could feel a tingle start way down low that he usually reserved for Debra. Why would you **even** get that kind of notion, he thought, you don't need any more problems than you are already going to have.

They stayed at the bar another couple of hours laughing and doing a little street theater for J. C.'s darlin' until about ten o'clock when Joey decided that he had had all of this good time he could stand and got up to say goodbye. He was a little startled when the chickie got up too and gave him a hug that would easily polish a rodeo cowboy's favorite belt buckle . . . a little startled and a whole lot impressed (with himself that is).

It is a proven fact that any and all attention that men get from women is because of their own irresistable charm (in their own minds, anyway) and Joey was no exception. J. C., knowing his buddy only too well, was smiling like the fox that just left the chicken coop. So Joey hugged him too and exited stage right, chuckling and swaggering on down the line like a cross between John Wayne and James Brown.

J. C. caught his sleeve as he was about to open the door and said with a wink, his little darlin' grinnin' over his shoulder, "If anybody asks, we stayed till about midnite, ok?"

"Midnite or one o'clock," he winked back as he jumped into his car and drove off into the night with ol' J. C. waving and smiling in the rearview mirror all the way down the block.

It started Joey thinking about times in the past when he had found some new bar poon' and was taking her home for the first time. As he drove on into the night with the cool night breeze blowing in through the window, he found himself singing an old Chicago number.

"I'm so happy, that you love me, life is lovely, when you're near me, cry sweet tears of joy, make me smiiiiile, yeah!"

But when he turned down the final road home and approached his driveway, it brought everything back into perspective. He wouldn't ever know that feeling again. A mixture of happiness and melancholy swept over him like a wave and was gone as quickly as it came. By the time the car was parked and he was turning the key in the lock, things seemed relatively back to normal and he went upstairs looking forward to crawling into bed with his Debra.

It wasn't many days later that the expected problems between J. C. and Betty Jo started rearing their nasty old heads. Debra was still Betty Jo's main confidante even though they didn't see each other nearly as often since Betty Jo started working again. So Joey wasn't surprised when Debra mentioned that there might be trouble in her sister's camp. He was dumbfounded, though, when she started giving him the specifics one night when they were out having a beer together.

"Looks like we're going to have a nice Christmas," Joey beamed, "just got the news today that we are going to get that new account on ignition parts. Should be worth an extra hundred grand next year that I hadn't counted on. Looks like this may mean the big time for us."

"Well, it doesn't look so hot for my sister's family," Debra frowned.

"What's the matter, his business take another turn for the worse?"

"Yeah, that's not doing so well either but there are worse problems. I can't believe it! My sister is having an affair with a guy in her

120

office and the things she is telling me! For all I know, she may be having affairs with several men. She is giving me all of the gory details and it sounds like something out of a porno movie. She has done some things that I would never dream of her doing or even thinking of doing for that matter. I mean, she does it in the morning with J. C. and that afternoon she's doing it with the other guy!"

With that, Joey damn near swallowed his whole beer, glass and all. It was all he could do to keep from spewing the thing all over the table. Who in the world would think that anybody could be attracted to ol' Betty Jo. She had an attractive face and all but, man!, she had packed on a bunch of pounds and . . . well, I'll be damned! This sure ain't the way I thought it would be! I wonder what the hell I should do now?

"Now wait a minute! Is this guy married?"

"Of course he is and I don't think she's thinking of leaving J. C. for him but there is that chance. The thing that mystifies me is . . . who would be attracted to her like she is now?" She said echoing his thoughts of the moment before. "And the way she talks about it! It's like talking to a sailor on leave!"

"I don't know what to say," Joey mumbled and he didn't. He had a pretty good handle on how he was going to react to the news about J. C.'s infidelities but this one had caught him completly off his guard. As he started to regain his composure he managed to ask, "What started this whole conversation between y'all?"

"We were kind of talking the year over, it being close to New Year's and all, when all of a sudden she said she had something to tell me that I had to keep secret. I thought maybe she was going to tell me that she had spent too much on the kids for Christmas or something but she said she just couldn't get into the Christmas spirit. Now I can see why! This has been going on for sometime and she's having trouble looking J. C. in the face. She wanted to know if I thought she should tell him or not."

"What did you tell her?" Joey wanted to know.

"I told her that I have known several women at the club who had had affairs and that usually they passed and maybe she ought to wait awhile," she said carefully," especially if she wasn't planning on taking up with this guy or anything. After all, an overweight woman going on forty with three kids is not a real hot prospect for remarriage. Besides, it's probably just a phase she's going through. She can't be too happy with herself or have much self-esteem the way she's let herself go. I thought maybe she was just experimenting to see if she could still attract a man but I think she's really enjoying it and, like I said, this may only be the tip of the iceberg."

"What makes you keep saying that?" He said, expecting her to bring up the deal with J. C. "What else is there?"

"It's just the way she talks. It's like maybe she has more to tell me. I don't know. It's just a hunch I have. Also, when I talked to her on the phone this morning at work, someone came in and kissed her and the guy she told me about wasn't even in town at the time!"

"Well, kiss my como se llama!" With this he started laughing in amazement at her obese sibling's carryings on. Debra, just as put off as he was by this surprising turn of events, joined in and soon they were laughing uncontrollably like two kids sharing their first joint.

When the laughter finally subsided and both of them were wiping tears from their eyes, Joey was back in the same fix again. What in the world do you say about something like this? You can't condone it but it is so surrealistic that it's hard to get upset about. Especially with someone as pitiful as Betty Jo was at the time. This was probably the most fun she had had since before her marriage. On the other hand, knowing what he did about J. C. and his girlfriend, it was even harder to get mad at her. Damn, Sam! This thing is getting more and more screwed up the farther we get into it. I've got to be careful, he thought, not to spill the beans **on** either of them, **to** either of them.

Later on, when Joey had the time to reflect on this turn of events with no one else around, it became obvious to him that this was just round one of the battles to come. Sooner or later one of them was going to slip and spill the beans to either J. C., Betty Jo or both of them. At that time this whole thing would start all over for Joey and Debra. Eventually, of course, they would probably have to take sides. Emotional situations such as this demanded that each side try to justify why they stepped over the line. It is unusual for both sides to fess up to their misdeeds and this usually fractionalizes their immediate families.

The sad part is that, unless someone were living with them as everything came down, how the hell were they going to know what truly went on anyway? Why not just say I'm sorry for both of you, I hope you can work it out? With this in the back of his mind it wasn't much of a surprise to Joey a few weeks later when they were over at Debra's sister's for a casual dinner, that J. C. brought up the subject again.

They were standing out behind the garage barbequing some chicken and drinking beer. Joey hadn't told his buddy anything Debra had told him and holding it all in was about to kill him. It wasn't that he was taking sides, it was just the tension from trying not to let anything slip that was eating him up. Most of the time Joey would have to start up the conversations between him and J. C. but this time he just kind of bit his lip and, sure enough, J. C. started right in.

"Looks like I'm going to have to give up the business and go out and find a real job. We can't continue to get by on what Betty Jo makes, what with all the kids in school and, besides, I need to get out of town a little bit. I feel the need to mosey around a little without having to worry about someone running into me from behind every-time I stop to look at something. You know what I mean, Joey?"

"Yeah, I've always held that a little time away from home now and then makes everybody appreciate each other a little more. That's why, when I'm home a lot, I make sure I have something to do by myself every week. When I have to travel that kind of takes care of itself. Maybe you ought to find a sales job of some kind."

"That's exactly what I thought too and I think I found it today. I won't have to travel a whole long way away from home like you do but I ought to be able to get in a few good road trips every month or so. Of course, I'll probably also have to entertain customers once a week or so."

With this he smiled and gave Joey a wink bordering on a leer that could not be mistaken. Joey smiled and winked back, quickly looking over his shoulder to make sure that they weren't being over-heard. It looked like the chicken had a few more minutes to burn and the beer was holding out pretty good, so he plunged ahead.

"You still doin' that deal that I saw you at the bar with a few weeks ago or did all of that cool down?"

"Sheeit! It's stronger than ever brother! You know how those young girls are. It takes an older guy to teach them a few things and pretty soon, they just can't get enough. I stay home these days just to get a little rest. By the way, you haven't heard anything have you? Anybody getting suspicious?"

He couldn't bring himself to tell his friend that his ol' lady was so busy takin' care of her own deal (deals?) that she didn't have time to worry about his. It's hard to look over someone else's shoulder when you're always looking back over your own. Oh, well what's good for the goose . . . .

"No, if she knows anything, she hasn't said anything to my old lady. At least Debra hasn't said anything to me. I don't know if she would even if they had talked. You know how those women are, kinda like us." He grinned back at J. C. who was busy burning the chicken.

"Let me tell you, pardner, you ought to try a little strange now and then. It makes you a much better husband. Everybody needs a little guilt so that he can put up with his ol' lady's bullshit. Some guys do it by gambling or spending money on guns or cars or somethin, but I think strange is a better deal . . . and there's lots out there. You been over on Greenville Avenue lately? You can't beat 'em off with a stick! Well, looks like this chicken's done so we better get on inside. Let me know if you hear anything that I need to know, will ya?"

"Yeah, you just be careful," Joey said with worry smeared all over his face because he knew that no matter how things worked out it was going to be tough on his pal.

The rest of the evening went relatively smoothly with no hint from J. C. or Betty Jo that anything was amiss. On his way out the door Joey marvelled at how relaxed they both were with each other while he was a nervous wreck. Their sneaking around was taking more of a toll on him than it was on either of them! What a way to live, he thought as he and Debra rode silently home.

The next evening Joey had a business meeting and dinner so Debra went over to her Momma's to visit. This time she was startled to discover that Betty Jo had also been confiding in Momma. Momma, of course, couldn't be happier that she was being included in the loop. As usual, she was enjoying her daughter's unhappiness and the possibility that she could meddle in Betty Jo and J. C.'s affairs. Debra, on the other hand, was afraid that her Momma would spill the beans to J. C. in order to try to mess up his life.

"Well, it looks like Betty Jo has some problems, darlin'" she smiled slyly at Debra as they sat down to talk. "Who would have thought that your big fat sister could still attract a man? Why, she must weigh two hundred pounds these days. Have you seen her with her clothes off lately? She was in the bath tub the other day when I went over to help her clean house and she looked like a beached whale."

"Now Momma you know how hard it is to lose weight after you have a baby. Besides, she mainly eats because she's nervous and right now is a pretty nervous time for her."

"Let me tell you something, Debra, she better be careful 'cause,

124

if she loses J. C., she's gonna have a hard time finding someone else. That guy she's screwin' ain't gonna stick around if she gets free. He's only doin' her because it's convenient. It's not like it's love or somethin'."

"You're probably right and that's why we've got to make sure that J. C. doesn't find out. We were over there just last night, though, and they get along like nothing is the matter at all. I'd be nervous as a whore in church if I had something like that going on but it doesn't seem to bother her at all. Did she tell you all the gory details?"

"Yes and for the life of me I can't picture any of that goin' on. You'd think a man could do better'n to crawl in the rack with her. Where'd she learn all of that stuff she does anyway? She been goin' to the skin flicks or somethin'? I know I sure never taught her any of those things."

"In my day we just did old standard masculine superior with lots of kissin' on the mouth. Now that she's brought it up, though, I might like to try some of those things. You know, like when the man kisses the woman down between her legs. Daddy don't go for any of that shit, him bein' from West Texas and all. Joey ever do any of that kind of thing to you?"

"This is Debra you're talkin' to not Betty Jo and I don't feel comfortable talkin' like this to you. You know that! And I don't like talkin' about her doin' it either. It kind of turns me off. Well, let's hope she gets through it with no one the wiser."

"Like I told you before darlin', there ain't nothin' wrong with gettin' a little strange now and then. It keeps your vital juices flowin'. One a these days you'll remember what I've said and get a little yourself."

With that they got on to more important subjects like what kind of "new" car Momma was going to get and when she and Daddy were going to Palm Springs.

A few nights later, Betty Jo called Debra and wanted her to come over. These days that was one of the things that Debra least liked. It wasn't just the tension from the secrets that she had recently been told, but more the ugliness of it all. If this was the stuff that was supposed to turn her on, it was missing the mark by a mile. As a matter of fact, everytime they talked about her goings-on, it turned Debra off so much that Joey was the one that paid for it. Recently, he had even suggested that she only go visit her sister when he was out of town. He figured it'd work better than a chastity belt.

125

As had been the case recently, Betty Jo was full of surprises but most of them had to do with her tawdry sex life. When Debra walked in she was on the way to the bathroom and, as she passed her in the hall, she handed her a book to look over. It was a late model sexual self-help manual that was literally a guide to female masturbation. Up till now Debra didn't think that she needed anything of this type but her natural curiousity overcame her so she opened it up and started to read. The next time she looked up, Betty Jo was sitting across from her with two glasses of wine already poured and smiling like the cat that ate the canary.

"Thought you might like to see some of the reading I have been doing lately. Interesting, isn't it?"

"Have you tried any of this stuff? I mean, I have always thought that my sex life was doing pretty good but after reading this I might be missing something. You don't have a vibrator and all of those icky toys, do you?"

"Nope. You don't need all of those things. All you need is to rub yourself the right way and it all works out. You know most men don't understand that they aren't built to satisfy a woman. They only have the equipment to satisfy themselves. They think that all of our pleasure is in direct relation to the size of their parts."

"Can I borrow this book? I'd like to take it home and read it. Now, don't be looking at me that way," she giggled nervously, "I just want to read it! I'm not much into sex without men."

Well, Debra **did** take the book home and, at the time, she wasn't much into sex without Joey. But one night when he had been gone for several days and she had had some wine after tennis, she tried a little self stimulation and it worked. Oh, how it worked! I wonder if this really does make you blind? She thought as she gave it just one more whirl (or should we say twirl?) before she fell asleep. That night she slept so soundly and was so refreshed when she woke up, that from then on when she was a little tense at bedtime and Joey was out of town, she would employ her newfound release. It was only a matter of time before she brought the subject up to Joey.

She figured the best way to do it was to show him the book. It was a little dog-eared and she kept forgetting to return it to her sister but she promised herself she would buy her a new one the next time she saw it at the mall. She chose one night when he had had an especially hard day at the office and said that all he wanted to do was curl up in bed with a good book and get a refreshing night's sleep.

126

Before he could get started with the latest *Dirt Bike* magazine, she shoved it under his nose.

"What's this?," he said, just a little shortly.

Usually when she gave him somehing to read it had to do with organic gardening or how to build a fence or something and tonight he wasn't interested in that kind of crap. But when he read the title, he looked sharply over at Debra.

"This looks like something your sister would read." He said seriously.

"That's exactly what I thought when she gave it to me," Debra replied. "But I went ahead and read it anyway. Go on and read a little of it before you just put it down. Then let's talk about it for a minute."

"Look, Debra, you know how I feel about this kind of trash! Your sister may need all the help she can get as far as sex is concerned but we surely don't need any . . . do we?"

The last went from a strong statement of fact to a semi-weak question as Joey thought about what he was looking at and what he was saying. With only the slightest glance over at Debra, he commenced reading in earnest. After a few minutes, he looked up.

"Okay, what is it you're trying to tell me? That all of this time you've been missing something? That your sister has shown you that something is lacking between you and me? Damn, Debra, things have been going so good and . . . . . . !!!"

She cut him off with a gentle smile and a wave of her hand.

"Stop it, Joey! Stop it! You know I love to make love with you and it has always been good for me. I wouldn't fake that but I have just found how to make things a little bit better. I wanted you to see it so that maybe we could try a few little things."

And try a few little things they did. Much to Joey's surprise, it only made things better for his sex life and seemed to be even better than that for Debra. It was like she had suddenly found a new toy that she had been looking for most of her adult life. All of a sudden they were back on two-a-days again everytime he was home. With this kind of encouragement, of course, Joey seemed to find more and more reasons to travel less and less.

It was after one of the marathon love-making sessions that they seemed to be having lately and they were both lying back enjoying that after-pleasure contentment. Debra got up on one elbow and smiled one of those oldtime smiles at Joey.

127

"Boy, it's a good thing that I didn't find out about all of this stuff in high school. I'd have been knocked up quicker'n Betty Jo!"

Needless to say, that statement didn't give Joey a whole lot of comfort. If it would have put her out of control then, what would keep her under control now? In this permissive new society, with everybody "doing their own thing," he might have to stay a little closer to home. Let's hope she learned all of this new stuff in that book and not from one of those jerks at that damn tennis club, or worse yet with his old buddy, Jimmy Jeff Stewart!

Knowing it wasn't healthy, he immediately dismissed that thought from his mind. He knew that if he didn't know about it, it didn't happen and besides he couldn't do anything about it anyway. It was drawing close to Christmas and everything was going so good, he thought, why spoil it with crap like that?

That brought up an interesting thought to Joey and he contemplated it as he lay back relaxing a little bit at a time. Life is really like a dream, he mused, the most meaningful things happen so quickly and are usually interspersed with so many inanities that a lot of the time we miss out on the good parts. Also, it seems that, as it is with dreams, a bunch of the time people imagine the worst things that can happen to them just when everything is going well. I wonder if it's only me or does this occur to everybody? Things really are going good with us, maybe I'm just reading J. C.'s troubles into my life. There's probably no reason to get worried about Debra. With that, he dismissed all of these thoughts and drifted off into a dreamless sleep . . . not without that little dark cloud slipping into his subconscious, however.

Chapter Ten

CHRISTMAS IS A VERY traumatic time of the year for most people, but especially for women. I overheard a conversation in which a guy was complaining that Christmas is supposed to be a joyous time of the year and yet for his wife it is always a time of great distress. Rather than celebration, the mood is one of apprehension and tension. A time when a civil answer seems to be a herculean effort and any form of hanky-panky is totally out of the question.

The reason for this is quite simple. As with Debra and Betty Jo, the end of the year is a time for evaluation for most people, especially the female of the species. It's a time to look back on what has happened versus what was expected during the previous year. As is the case with most of us, they have been taught to set goals a little higher than what they know they can attain. So naturally whatever it was that they were supposed to achieve was miserably missed. This unrealism can only cause problems because how can you be happy if you worked all year toward a goal and didn't make it? And how can you ever make it if you continually set it too high?

Debra frowned as she stirred her keoki coffee with one of those little swizzle sticks with reindeer on them that they are always putting out around Christmas time. She was sitting in TGI Fridays on Greenville Avenue waiting for her sister to join her for dinner and she was thinking how stupid it was to take her overweight sibling out for more to eat. They had been doing this every year for so long that it was more tradition than anything else, but it still didn't make any sense.

She also wasn't looking forward to their traditional "Christmas Talk" which was sad enough without being colored by all of the new developements in her sister's "love-life." It was sad because Betty Jo would be depressed since she hadn't lost any of the weight that she had been trying for the last ten years to lose. And because even though both of them had tried as hard as they could, they still couldn't put up with their mother's eccentricities. They knew that they were supposed to love her but they couldn't accept the fact that they could love her and never actually like her at all.

Probably the hardest part of anyone's coming of age is sometime after their teenage years when they have to decide whether or not they like the ones they love. Not only do people have a hard time making this determination with their families but it also parellels their married lives. Like and love just don't necessarily go hand in hand. As a matter of fact, the two might well be mutually exclusive. Like is easy when everything is new and hot but as a relationship cools down (and they always do) a lot of the time what used to be cute becomes stupid; what used to be unique is assinine; what used to be funny is now intolerable. Maybe imagination should also encompass the ability to remember things in a softer, less critical light. It would probably help make love stay . . . but back to Debra and Betty Jo and the girls' Christmas get together.

Betty Jo came blowing into TGI Fridays like Dick Butkus breaking into the backfield in the Super Bowl, her Estee' Lauder having a tough time masking the odor that the overweight have after a hard day at the office. As usual she was about forty-five minutes late and she apologized profusely as she sat down, red-faced, and gave a big sigh.

"I'm sorry, I know it pisses you off when I'm late but it pisses me off too. This is the worst time of the year for me. What with my job and getting all the shopping done for J. C. and the kids as well as the rest of the family, there just isn't enough time in the day. Besides, I can't get into the Christmas spirit this year with all the you-know-what going on and all."

"Slow down Betty Jo, this is supposed to be fun. We have all evening to just relax and enjoy each other's company. Order a drink, kick off your shoes and take a few deep breaths, then we'll talk."

Debra looked around the restaurant and was happy to see several of the young guys trying to make eye contact with her. At this time of year she tended to get a little insecure as the realization hit her that she was about to get another year older. Just this evening as she was putting on her make-up she noticed several new wrinkles around her eyes and she had to try on three different outfits before she found one that fit the way it should.

She couldn't believe she was already in her thirties and still didn't have any children but with all the trouble she saw her friends having with their kids she just couldn't make up her mind to do it. Joey's business had stabilized as had their relationship and she knew that whatever she wanted he'd go along with but that was such a big step and so much responsibility for such a long time!

"So how are J. C. and the kids? Have you gotten all of your Christmas shopping done yet?"

"I thought you said that I should relax and then all you want to talk about is my family. You know it's amazing, you think all your life about getting married and having a family and then, after you've got it, you spend the rest of your life trying to get away from it. Take my word for it, don't ever have kids. There is no more thankless job than being a parent. No matter what you do when you have as many kids as I do, someone is always upset, and if it isn't them it's your husband who's pissed off."

With that she rolled her eyes and tried to laugh but all she did was spill her drink down her front. This caused her eyes to well up with tears and suddenly Debra could see that she was on the brink of crying. Debra helped her pat dry the areas of her front that she couldn't reach and tried to comfort her with a little humor.

"Look, I'm not gonna buy you anymore drinks if you're just going to pour them on your tits. They're supposed to go in your mouth!"

Her attempt at laughter although sincere came out sincerely shaky and Betty Jo wasn't helping things with the look on her face.

"It's a wonder that I can even hold a drink as nervous as I have been lately! The tension of this holiday is just killing me! I think the kids caught me talking to you-know-who on the phone the other day and I don't know whether to make up a story about it or just let it drop. Everytime Junior looks at me, I could swear he knows everything that is going on, and I know that I look guilty as hell. What would you do?"

Debra knew that they would probably have to talk about this

subject before the evening was out but she hadn't planned on getting into it this early. Then again maybe if they jumped right into it they could get it over with that much quicker.

"I know exactly what I would do if I were you, just like I told you before. I'd quit seeing the guy immediately and never do it again. So far you have been lucky because no one is the wiser but if you do it long enough someone is bound to catch on. No matter how you slice it, you have done about as good as you ever will in your life in the family department with J. C. and the kids, and there isn't much of a market out there for overweight ladies going on forty with three kids looking for romance."

"It's not as easy as that," Betty Jo frowned morosely, like a giraffe trying to eat a peanut butter sandwich, "you see there's more than one."

"Dammit to Hell, Betty Jo, have you gone crazy? Are you into some kind of menage a trois or something? What do you mean there's more than one?"

"I don't mean at the same time, it's nothing like that really. I just have more than one boyfriend. When you were in high school you had lots of boyfriends and so did I."

"But we weren't married and we damn sure weren't going to bed with them!"

She knew that the former was true but from the look on Betty Jo's face she could tell that the latter wasn't necessarily so. Well, what do you say now smartass? Your sister has turned out to be the town punch and she doesn't want to stop and you're sitting here and you ain't so pure either, are you? Just what were you doing with old Peter when Joey was out of town, huh? And what kind of hanky panky are you and Jimmy Jeff up to anyway? And who are you gonna blame it on this time? Lord knows, you can't blame it on yourself! Ah well, just save it up and blame it on **him** the next time he gets drunk and snores!

Oh my! Things used to be so easy and now they're getting so confused, aren't they? Why is it always that way? Yesterday everybody had everything so together, so cut and dried, so simple. But today everything is different, everything is disconnected, everything is so . . . well, it's just so . . . well, dammit, I can't help it if he is so self-confident, no, if he is so sure of himself . . . no, if he is such a know-it-all . . . no, if he is so . . . . . . RIGHT! Damn you anyhow, Joey!

It's a hard deal, isn't it, Debra? You love him and you can't stand him. He's brilliant but he's so stupid. He doesn't mess around but all of your girlfriends want him to. He won't respond to your moods the way he's supposed to. Why can't he see that he really isn't all that smart? As a matter fact, he's really no smarter than you are. That's it! You're just as smart as he is! And he's stupid! He loves you, but how can he?

You know, when you think about it, the real problem is your sister. She's the one who's all fouled up. Look at her! She's fat, she's married with three kids, she's got her mother's personality, and she's doing all of the things that you are trying to believe you wouldn't do . . . things that you couldn't do. But why are you thinking about those things, then? Why does your mind play these tricks on you? Why do you think you want these things when you really don't? Or do you?

"Debra, Debra are you listening to me?" Betty Jo was almost shouting in order to get her sister's attention. "What's wrong? Maybe we should forget this whole thing and just go on home."

"I'm sorry, I'm all right. I just kind of drifted off there for a moment. You understand, don't you?"

Betty Jo nodded yes and the amazing thing was that she did understand, as only a sister or another woman could. She understood that now that modern women had finally gotten all of the freedoms that they had demanded, they'd have to figure out what to do with them. Things weren't so simple anymore. There had been a time when every action had elicited a very well-defined response. A reaction that was not only easily anticipated but also quite welcome when it came. Now choice had reared it's ugly head and with it came responsibility and selfishness.

"I've been doing that a lot recently but at least I have a reason to," Betty Jo was smiling now, wickedly.

Well, maybe not wickedly but definitely leeringly. As if gloating over the fact that she, the fat one, could have more intrigue in her life than her sibling, the skinny one.

"I was thinking just this evening on the way over that the end of the year is right around the corner and what a year it's been. If you would have asked me what was going to happen in the future last year, I sure wouldn't have answered the way I would have to now.

"Last year I promised myself that I would lose weight, quit smoking and become a better housekeeper. This year I don't think it's possible for me to even consider New Year's resolutions with all the shit I have going on!"

133

"Speaking of New Year's," Debra chimed in, welcoming the change of subject, "do you guys still want to have that party that you invited us to last month? You know we have a few others to go to but we'd love to end up at yours."

This wasn't really a lie, just a wee bit of truth stretching. Going to her sister's party late on New Year's Eve seemed something akin to walking up close to an accident to see the blood and gore. For some reason, there was a little black cloud hanging over that thought.

"Oh, yes! We're still going to have the party but it won't be a real big one, just family and close friends. You know, I've been thinking about what you said and you're right. I really do have to get out of these things that I've gotten myself into. And I'm going to do it soon. As a matter of fact, I'm going to get everything straightened out before the party. You just watch me!," She said as she ordered another drink and lit a cigarette, a look of triumph on her face.

Oh my God! Debra thought, another impossible New Year's resolution! And such a deep sadness washed over her that it was all that she could do to keep the tears from rolling down **her** cheeks. What ever happened to the time when everything was fresh and new? When nothing was as soiled and dirty as her sister was now. When something so futile as her sister's resolve still had in it a ray of hope. How was Debra supposed to live her own life when she had such a tough one to live with her family? Well, by god, her sister had come to the right place for support when she came to Debra. She'd help her through the rough times to come and back to the good life that she deserved!

Careful now Debra! In order to help someone else, you've first got to have your own act in order. If you don't, there's not enough time to live both of your lives and make anything out of either one of them, both will undoubtedly suffer. But these thoughts were the farthest things from Debra's mind as she responded to the pitiful soul sitting across from her. For this year, as with every year in the past (although she had forgotten that part), she felt closer to her sister and her family than ever before and she was going to do her damnedest to right all of the wrongs that she had ever inflicted on any of them or that they had inflicted upon themselves.

Now we've come to the reason that a lot of people have such a hard time with Christmas. Not only is it a time to review the past year and discover that no matter how good we feel about ourselves,

134

we've missed our goals by a mile but also it's a time to set new, equally unreachable ones.

As is the case with most people, Betty Jo and Debra both had forgotten that the feelings they were now having were quite similar to the ones from every other year that they could remember. And that their response and resolve were also as heartfelt and strong as they were in the past. That the futility of what they were feeling was the same for them as it was for all mankind at this time of year as they search for the perfection that doesn't exist for anyone. That they would probably make these impossible demands on themselves again was a certainty . . . as was the probability that they would be in this same situation next year and in the years to come. The fleeting peace of mind derived from this trite exercise might be worth the effort for a few days though. At least through the holidays, after that, who cares?

Debra and Betty Jo continued on with their new resolve and went ahead to plan their Christmases and Betty Jo's party. After that they talked about their individual resolutions and they promised each other, tearfully, that they would help one another achieve their goals. And, as happened every year, this lip-service to their fallibilities gave them each the comfort that they needed to face the holidays with confidence, knowing that next year would be the one in which they would finally get everything on track the way they had always hoped it would be. With that they paid the bill, hugged each other and went home to their respective spouses, full of renewed faith in themselves and all of humankind.

Christmas dawned as it most often did in Dallas, bright and windy, chilly but not cold, with that obtuse glare that the sun has when it's winter in southern climes. As a matter of fact the brightness makes some people teary-eyed and sleepy, tending to drift off in thought so that everyone thinks they are really inattentive and not in the spirit of the day. Joey had an especially hard time with Christmas in the south.

To him Christmas was cold and frosty if not snowy, with that special smell of wood smoke and winter. When you walked into a house the soft warmth and the kitchen smells almost made your eyes wet and the feeling could penetrate even the iciest of hearts. But in all of his Christmases in the south, he just couldn't seem to recapture those holiday essentials and this Christmas with all of the family goings on was certainly no exception.

Their families, like so many others around the world, liked to follow a specific routine which called for the holidays to be held every other year in the respective spouses' families' homes. This year it was Debra's turn and the festivities began with the Christmas dinner which was usually at Debra's parents' house . . . a very tense situation to say the least. Tense because Momma had a very tough time with the end of the year, too. She not only had a bad time thinking about what had transpired the year before but also because she was about to get another year older.

If she thought about the year in review at all (which Joey seriously doubted), it would be impossible for her to be honest about it without falling into a deep depression. This of course would be deepened by her out-of-control drinking. What usually happened, however, was that she would turn into a sickeningly sweet, extremely dramatic, darling of a mother, grandmom, mother-in-law. The only area in which she would be herself was with Daddy and as a result he would take a remorseless emotional beating throughout the period. This probably explained why he usually would not appear until dinnertime on Christmas Eve and have to go immediately back to work at 4:00 P.M. on Christmas day. There were even years when he wouldn't be able to be at home at all . . . never, however, when Joey was in attendance.

They were greeted at the door by Debra's Daddy who was still in the coveralls that he had worn that day out on the oil well. His warm handshake for Joey was equalled by his awkward hug for his daughter. He always had trouble showing feelings for his children . . . maybe he should have had sons so he could just punch them on the shoulder or something. With that Daddy blustered off to the bathroom to shower and clean up as Joey and Debra went out to the kitchen to see if they could help Momma.

Momma, as was her style on holidays and special occasions, was hiding out in the kitchen camouflaging her drink behind the flour canister (which by the way had never held anything more important than the quart bottle of scotch that Daddy didn't know about) and cooking up traditional meals for all of those assembled. Joey could tell immediately (and predictably) that she was loaded to the gills by the phony wall-eyed grin that she had for them as they walked smiling through the doorway.

"Anything we can do to help, Mother?" Debra asked with that

136

tremulous quaver that she reserved for people who could, but might not, hurt her. "Do you need Joey to do anything?"

Joey knew that with any luck she might have something for him to do outside or maybe need something from the store so that he could take a ride. As if she knew it was Christmas, she asked him to go to the store for some beer. Damn, he thought, what did I do to deserve this? Maybe Santa Claus really does exist! To add to his delight, as he was walking outside, in walked J. C. and the two of them decided to take the ride together. As they walked out into the cool Dallas Christmas afternoon grinning and clapping each other on the back, neither one could think of anything less than happiness and good cheer.

This little excursion was relatively uneventful with the exception of the fact that the cute little girl behind the counter at the 7-Eleven obviously would have liked to go along for the ride and J. C. thought that might be a good idea. This led to a discussion of J. C.'s home situation which really wasn't too comfortable for Joey. It all started when Joey gave the girl a hundred dollar bill in payment for the two cases of beer that he bought. She immediately made a cute comment and the games began.

"Oh my, do you boys always run around in such good company? I've always admired Benjamin Franklin! It might take a few minutes to get you change from this safe so why don't y'all make yourselves at home?"

"Don't mind if we do, honey," Joey shot back, "but you'll have to hurry. Me and J. C. are nursin' a terrible dry."

They all chuckled a little as the clerk counted out the change. J. C., however, had that look on his face that he usually reserved for Taffy or some other unattached young thing.

As they walked out of the store he said, "Damned if there ain't a whole lot of poontang out on the loose these days. If we didn't have to go back for dinner, I'll bet we could have a hell of a time with that little sumbitch."

"Maybe you but not me," Joey said, semi-seriously, "I've got all I can handle just keeping up with my ol' lady."

"Well I sure as shit don't," J. C. replied. "Getting it on with my ol' lady kind of reminds me of bein' out at the farm. As a matter of fact, I'm thinkin' seriously of just disappearin' for awhile . . . if not forever. Don't be amazed if one of these days you look up and I'm AWOL."

"What the hell you talkin' about J. C.? You ain't goin' nowhere, at least not without me!"

"You might be surprised, and it might be in the very near future," J. C. smiled smugly (it's a lot easier to smile smugly than to say, "smiled smugly"). "I've been giving it a lot of thought lately."

"Oh, c'mon, J. C., it's just that time of year. Don't take yourself so seriously. Hell, you've got a wife and a shitpot load of kids. I think we probably need to get out and go bike riding just the two of us."

Joey kind of looked sideways at his buddy, not liking the tone of his voice.

"Hey, don't worry about it, brother. Right now we've got two semi-goofy women and one definitely goofy momma-in-law to put up with. After that it's New Year's eve and then we're home free," he said, opening a couple of beers.

Handing Joey the first one, he smiled, "Merry Christmas, my friend."

Joey smiled back as he tilted his cold beer and responded in kind, "Merry Christmas, J. C., and may all your Christmases be bright!"

With that, off they went . . . riders of the new frontier, soldiers of misfortune both, frick and frack the stepbrothers, the one and onlies . . . yeah that's what they thought. At that point in history they were the only ones. The only ones that counted that is . . . the chosen pair, Cain and Abel, Oral and Jerry, you know the ones. J. C. and Joey, attitudes adjusted, were on their way back to the wake that their wives called Christmas. Pity that they couldn't come back in a more somber (maybe it's sedate) mood. So that they wouldn't be so out of synch with the rest of the party.

By the time that they returned, Momma was well on her way through the quart of young scotch she hid in the flour canister and Daddy was just getting out of the shower. The daughters of the evolution were orbiting around their Momma as if in some kind of slow motion slap-stick dance routine, carefully catching everything that Momma was in danger of dropping or spilling. But she held up well, not dropping anything or getting real goofy. She didn't eat, however, complaining that making all of the food had taken her appetite away, when in reality she just didn't want to spoil her empty-stomach, holiday scotch buzz.

All in all things went pretty well, all the gifts got opened and were oohed and aahed over just like in the movies. About three-thirty everyone started looking at their watches anticipating Daddy's leaving at four o'clock to go back to work on the well and Momma going to take a nap being "totally exhausted" by the festivities of the day. The sisters hugged goodbye and that was that. Joey sighed with relief as they got to the car without one major Momma altercation.

When they got home Debra surprised him with a little holiday love play and then drifted off to sleep. As he lay there in the afterglow reflecting on the day, he was overcome with a feeling of uneasiness . . . almost dread. It seemed ironic that a festive period was always so tense and unpleasant. There just wasn't any feeling of family togetherness with Debra's bunch. They all tried so hard just to be civil with each other and had to be so careful to avoid a scene with their "beloved" Momma . . . maybe the let down was just a family hangover. He looked over at Debra peacefully asleep beside him and tried to assimilate some of the serenity that she exuded. Unable to do so, he got quietly out of bed and, opening a cold beer, went out into the December dusk to see if the pale winter sunset might help heal his troubled soul.

Chapter Eleven

A WEEK LATER AND it was time for New Year's. New Year's was not just a traumatic time for Debra and Betty Jo, it also affected Joey. He never could get into the celebratory spirit. It seemed silly to him to get all dressed up just to go out and watch a bunch of non-drinkers get drunk. Invariably, the ones who lived the cleanest lives would get extremely inebriated and do things entirely out of character for them. Then, until the next New Year's party, they would use their besotted behavior as an excuse to explain why they didn't drink. Someone described New Year's Eve as a drinker's amateur night but to Joey it looked like something out of a high school horror story.

This particular eve was no exception. First they went to Debra's Momma's so that all of the relatives and friends could see that Joey and Debra were doing well. It was early when they got there and Joey could already see that few if any of those assembled would make it to midnight. Momma was three sheets to the wind already and Daddy was right behind her hoping that maybe before she passed out he might get lucky. One old coot actually was dancing around with a lampshade on his head just like in the Sunday comics. The good news was that they didn't have to stay long since they had several more parties to go to. The bad part was that the next party they had to go to was at the tennis club and Joey didn't relish that one at all.

When they got to the club, the format was explained to them. Since they all loved tennis so, the party would revolve around a round robin mixed doubles tournament. Each match would be only one set so that each couple could get to play every other couple in a short period of time. This way they could get out of their dress-up clothes into tennis clothes, get all sweaty as they tried to mix tennis with alcohol and, finally, get back into their dress-up clothes to go on to the next party. Joey and Debra did surprisingly well, considering the boozing and confusion, and ended up winning the damn thing. There were some occurences of note, however.

Most of the recently divorced tennis ladies were there with their new paramours . . . if they had one to show off, that is. But the ones who were in the divorce process for the most part were alone and in a hurry to get out of there since they didn't have a partner of the opposite sex and had to couple up in order to play. So, to soothe their obvious discomfort at being "fifth wheels," they got to drinking stuff like tequila soloes and/or assorted other lethal concoctions. Several of them got real happy, several real sad but without exception they all got hornier than a four peckered billy goat.

A couple of them homed in on Joey right off. Mary Ann was the first one to pat him on the ass as they changed sides during their match and, after that, couldn't seem to walk past him without rubbing him somewhere. Soon he noticed that not one of the single ones had managed to pass him by without some kind of gesture to let him know that they were not only approachable but available. In the beginning it was a source of great pleasure as it boosted his ego by leaps and bounds but as Debra became more and more aware of what was going on things began to deteriorate rapidly. It got to the point at which Joey, in order to avoid getting fondled between matches, would grab a beer and sneak off into the men's locker room for a few minutes rest. This ploy was shattered toward the end of the evening when Mary Ann, by this time completely and uncontrollably drunk, followed him into the locker room and tried to pull him into one of the stalls in the men's room.

"Look Mary Ann," he giggled, trying to be casual, "this is really not the time or place for this. If anyone came in right now there'd be hell to pay. Why don't you save this for some nice young dancing boy from one of those clubs on lower Greenville Avenue. I'm sure you could show each other a thing or two."

"C'mon, Joey," she breathed harshly in his ear, "you know I've always wanted you. Let's start the New Year off right. Nobody's gonna know any different. The way I feel now it'll only take a coupla minutes anyway. Here!"

141

With that she turned around drunkenly and started to take off her clothes which gave Joey the opportunity he needed to escape. Wouldn't you know it, as he pushed his way out the locker room door, who was coming in but that idiot from Austin, Peter. As he brushed on by him, Joey couldn't resist one jab at the unctuous little schmuck.

"Better hurry in there, Peter, I'll bet even **you** can get lucky tonight!"

As a matter of fact, by the time Peter got in the door ol' Mary Ann, who was so drunk and in heat that she could hardly control herself, much less see, grabbed him thinking that it must be Joey who had reconsidered and was coming back to finish what she had started. By the time she recognized Peter, they were already past the point of no return and neither one saw the need to stop. Au contraire, the sounds of their frantic coupling could be heard by more than a few of the assembled masses as both of them forfeited their final match. One of the older guys, hearing all the commotion, walked in on them writhing on the floor and after watching for a few minutes returned to tell his wife who told her friend, etc. Soon everyone, including Peter's date knew what was going on. Much to Joey's surprise, Debra seemed more upset than Peter's companion about the episode.

"C'mon Joey let's get out of here. These women are all acting like a bunch of bitches in heat. I've had enough!"

Fortunately for Joey and rightfully so, Peter was going to take the heat for what almost spoiled his whole evening. In their haste to get out of there, they just grabbed their clothes and bolted, neither one wanting to be involved in the festivities any further but for very different reasons. Joey, of course, was just happy to get away without Debra observing his part of the scene in the locker room. Debra, on the other hand, was afraid to trust herself not to climb all over Peter for flaunting his singleness in front of her. Although she had no real claim on him, she knew that he was very interested in her and was probably trying to make her jealous by messing around with Mary Ann. She also knew that he had succeeded . . . and, much to Joey's good fortune, was prepared to punish him for it.

When they got to the car they decided to change right there in the parking lot before going to Betty Jo's. Looking over Joey's shoulder as he untied her shoes, Debra saw Peter come out of the club, obviously looking for her. Quickly, she pulled Joey to his feet and started kissing him passionately on the lips and neck while she massaged his awakening manhood. Pushing him backwards into the car, she started pulling off his pants as he did the same for her, and, hiking up her skirt, climbed up on him like a monkey up a palm tree. She lifted up her blouse and pulled it down over Joey's head burying his face between her breasts so that he couldn't see her smile as she watched Peter, face beet red and mouth set in a tight white line, turn on his heel and stalk angrily back into the club. That ought to show the son of a bitch, she thought, as the ecstasy of the moment started to catch up with her and carry her away.

"Happy New Year," Joey murmured dreamily into her ear as they started to come out of the afterglow," do we get to do this at all of the parties? If so, I'll have to pace myself."

Debra smiled that cute little sideways smile that women do so well and said, "Maybe, if you play your cards right, I'll meet you around midnite in the back bathroom at Betty Jo's. Just like old times!"

With that they hurriedly dressed and tried to freshen up as best they could on their way to Betty Jo's. It had gotten so late that they decided to pass on a couple of other parties that they were supposed to attend. Joey stopped and bought some cold beer while Debra put on one of their favorite cassettes and so they drove into the night, sippin', grinnin' and singing their hearts out to the music.

When they got to Betty Jo's, Joey drove around back and parked behind the garage. As they listened to the end of one of their favorite songs, Joey pulled Debra to him and began to kiss her a lot like she had done to him in the parking lot. Before she could even think about it, she looked back over her shoulder to see who was watching them and the resulting guilt she felt when no one was there quickly put a damper on her passion.

"Not now, Joey, I said around midnite in the back bathroom," she smiled weakly. "Let's go inside and liven up the party!"

With that she grabbed the cassette from the radio, jumped out of the car and, before he could even open his door, disappeared into the night. Joey sat back for a minute reflecting on the situation. Why is it that everytime you think you have it all figured out, when you finally see the whole picture, someone (in this case someone decidedly female) jumps up and throws you a curve. Well, maybe not a curve, maybe more like a screwball.

What the hell was this all about anyway? Smooth one moment

143

and then rough the next, almost as if there were an undercurrent of change going on. Something that no one had explained to old Joey. Could it be that he was missing something so important that nobody was letting him in on it? Perhaps it was just his imagination, this probably wasn't anything to be concerned about. It was just women . . . or perhaps the **difference** between men and women.

So he got up and followed Debra (or at least the path through the dark that she had made) into the house. What he came into was more of a wake than a party. The people were all sitting down, which was usually the sign of a dull situation. J. C. was in the garage just kind of moping around, like something major was on his mind. Betty Jo was mixing and mingling with the bored looking guests, trying to get some kind of celebration started. When J. C. heard that Joey had arrived, he came out of the garage with a cold beer and a smile.

"Glad you could make it buddy! Here, have a drink! Happy New Year!"

His smile and gesture were genuine but the rest of his attempt at good cheer fell flat on it's face. Obviously there was something troubling him and from the frown/smile that he was wearing it was something that probably merited a "garage talk."

"Thanks pardner and happy New Year to you, too! Whatcha got goin' on in the garage?"

He smiled at J. C., all the time herding him back into the garage. He hoped that the relief on J. C.'s face wasn't as obvious to everyone else as it was to him. All of a sudden he looked like someone who had just been told that a long lost girlfriend had surfaced with an unbelievable inheritance and his high school photo in her pocket.

"As a matter of fact, I don't have a damn thing going on out here but at least it's quiet and peaceful next to the bikes. Remember when we used to camp out every New Year's? How we would all save our Christmas trees and carry them out to the campground on the top of our vans then pile them all up and make a bonfire and bring out the beer? That must have been a hell of a sight! That caravan of cars and motorcycle trailers headed west with Christmas trees on top of all of them, man! Those were the good old days!"

His smile was so sad that Joey had to look away. "Yeah, that beats the daylights out of going to a bunch of tired-ass parties and watching all these unhappy people pretending that they're having a good time. Next year, if I can talk my old lady into it, I'm going up to the Red River just like those good old days."

Joey must have forgotten that he had said the exact same thing last year and the year before. Each fall when he brought it up to Debra, she vetoed it out of pocket. Said she was afraid that she'd get hurt biking and that she didn't like camping anymore.

"I'll tell you what, old buddy, why don't we just load 'em up right now and head that way? We could get up there around midnight, start a nice fire, have a couple beers and sleep till the sun comes up. Then ride our asses off all day long and do it again tomorrow night."

J. C. clapped Joey on the back as they both chuckled ruefully at the thought of the good times they had had and probably wouldn't have again.

When they walked back inside, everybody was gathered in the living room trying to play charades. Joey rolled his eyes at J. C. as they watched one of the amateur drinkers try to act out the Joe Buck strut from "Midnight Cowboy" while maintaining some semblance of equilibrium. Twice he fell over the coffee table and twice Joey helped him back up. Finally he just went over and sat in the corner with a dazed look on his face while his wife glared at him from across the room. What fun, Joey thought as he headed for the kitchen for something to eat and a beer. J. C. followed him in and stood looking out the window for a few minutes.

Finally, taking a deep breath, he turned and said. "I know we can't go right now but how about we load 'em up in the morning and go ride, just me and you, nobody else?"

"That's fine by me, Debra probably won't want to go anyway. I don't need to sit around tomorrow watching football and eating. I'll go talk to her about it right now."

With that he walked back into the living room in search of Debra. He found her in the dining room, talking earnestly to her sister. When they saw Joey coming, they both looked as if they had just been caught talking in study hall.

"You girls talking about me behind my back again," he smiled at Debra, "or can you share the dirt with your old pal Joey?"

"It was just a bunch of girl talk. You wouldn't be interested in it, I'm afraid. Have you tried this dip, it's great with a tortilla chip."

"Hey, Debra, me and J. C. were talking about loading up the bikes in the morning and going riding. We don't have any other plans, do we?"

"Oh, great!" Betty Jo blurted out as she hurried out of the room.

145

Joey turned back to Debra and said, "What was that all about?"

"Forget it Joey, you wouldn't understand. She's just a little uptight about the party and the time of year. Besides, why didn't you invite us? Are women just a pain in the ass? We used to be good enough to go riding with y'all all the time . . . why not now?"

"Hey, wait a minute! We've been asking ya'll for the last three years to go camping for New Year's just like old times and everytime ya'll have pooh-poohed the idea. So J. C. and I figured that you wouldn't want to go this year either. This party jazz is for the birds just like it's been every year and I can guarantee that I won't be doing this again! If you want to go, we'd love to have you. Now, I'm just speaking for me but you know J. C., he'll be happy if everybody comes along."

"That's just not good enough, Joey, Betty Jo is feeling real left out right now, what with ya'll just hanging out in the garage and all. Why don't you guys want to join in the charades and stuff. That used to be a lot of fun. You were always the life of the party. What's the matter, Joey? Gettin' a little old and conservative?"

She tried to make it sound cute but the sparkle in her eyes didn't come off as teasing or flirtatious, more like taunting or mockery . . . and it was making Joey increasingly nervous.

"Look, Debra, I don't know what's going on here but if the truth be known, if anybody should be feeling left out it should be J. C. and with the way you're acting maybe I should be too. I don't know what the hell is going on between you and Betty Jo but don't try to pull me into it. Why don't we just go on home and get some rest so that we can go up to the river and have a good time tomorrow instead of spending the day stuffing ourselves with party leftovers and watching a bunch of football games on television?"

"We can't leave now, the party's still got to last until the ball falls. Besides, we leave now and this thing is really going to turn into a drag. C'mon, I'll get you a beer and you start livening this thing up. Make Betty Jo and J. C. laugh a little. Do a real good job and I'll meet you out back at midnight like I promised!"

Again she tried to be cute and give him that little sideways look that she did so well and again it just didn't quite come off. Joey, by now as nervous as a long tail polecat in a room full of revolving doors, headed for the kitchen to get his own beer. Dammit! he thought, I better go out there and liven things up a little just to get these crazed ladies off my ass!

146

By the time he got to the refrigerator, J. C. had caught up with him and from the look on his face, he, too, could feel the heat. Joey opened the door to the fridge and both he and J. C. grabbed a couple of beers. As if they had rehearsed it, they opened their beers in unison and handed the open one to each other. Again, like mirrored images they both tilted up their beer, chugged the whole thing down, threw the cans in the waste basket and grinned like possums in the moonlight.

"Now, that's more like it," J. C. grunted as he opened his other beer and belched loudly, "now, let's go on out there and face the music. I can make it a couple more hours, can't you buddy?"

Joey opened his beer, chugged it down, pulled two more from the cooler and smiled at his old friend. "We either liven this shitaree up or we'll turn this deal into a Phillips 66 station. If we got to stay up we may as well have a little fun. Grab that bottle of tequila and let's go in there and dick with the non-drinkers a little. New Year's is always a time for either laughin' or cryin' anyway."

With that they both took a deep breath, puffed out their chests, put on their best life-of-the-party smiles and headed back out to amateur night. As the chug-a-lugs hooked up, Joey fell into a number of his old street theater routines with all the fuzzy puppy stories and ethnic jokes. He was loose enough to pick on everyone there at least once and the ones that laughed were rewarded with a pull off the bottle of Cuervo Gold he was carrying around like the first prize trophy at a beauty pageant. Soon the amateurs that weren't sick were acting out all those fantasies that they would regret for the rest of the year and the resulting din was approaching 100db as midnight neared.

When the clock struck twelve Joey, Debra, J. C. and Betty Jo all put their arms around each other and yowled a real loose version of Auld Lang Syne which everyone joined in with at one time or another. As Joey and Debra snuck off for their back bathroom rendezvous, Joey noticed, over his shoulder, that J. C. and Betty Jo, backs to each other, were headed to opposites ends of the house.

Even though it was fun, their back bathroom love-making lacked the intensity that both of them had imagined there would be and left them feeling a little bit awkward and empty. Before they went back to the party, Joey tried to interject a little bit of tender smooching but Debra was having none of it.

"Let's get back, Joey, everyone will be wondering where we've been."

"The hell with 'em," Joey murmured in his best Robert Redford imitation complete with the crooked sexy smile.

But Debra pushed right past him and, leaving the door wide open, hurried on down the hall. Joey, in turn, finished putting his clothes back on and, giving himself the luxury of one rueful look in the mirror, walked on back to the party shaking his head in disbelief. Damn! he thought, do you ever get to know anything about life and women or is everything always brand new? How the hell are you ever supposed to anticipate anything, when there are no constants? Going through life is like going through a shit storm, he mused, sometimes you can dance between the drops and never get any on you and sometimes you can't avoid the downpour no matter what you do.

When they got back to the party most of the ambulatory guests were helping the incapacitated ones into the back seats of their cars so that they would soil only the floormats with whatever was left inside them. Joey made sure that the ones that got behind the wheel weren't totally befuddled and at least knew their way home before he would let them leave.

With all the guests gone, Joey, Debra, J. C. and Betty Jo went back inside, gave the house a quick clean up and had a New Year's drink . . . just the four of them. As they drank, they reminisced about years gone by in a sad sort of way and promised themselves that next year they'd try camping again just like old times. From upstairs the kids, obviously still awake, gave a resounding cheer. Joey and Debra smiled at each other but J. C. and Betty Jo just looked thoughtful.

As they hustled down the sidewalk to the car, Joey turned and hollered back at J. C., "Give me a call when you wake up and we'll see about that bike riding. Maybe we'll all go!"

J. C. nodded and waved absently as he quietly closed the door. Even though it was a typical mild Texas New Year's night Joey shivered as he unlocked the car. Ain't life grand!, he thought as he pointed the car home.

They got in bed about 3:00 A.M. and when the telephone rang Joey could swear that he had only been to sleep for an hour or so. As it turned out that was exactly what had happened. The clock by the phone gleamed 4:45 in its big red letters as Debra answered it. Joey rolled over and tried to go back to sleep but the sudden change in tone in Debra's voice made his eyes bounce wide open. It sounded like she was talking to her sister and it didn't sound good.

148

"What's going on?" Joey said, but Debra put her finger to her mouth and shook her head as she gathered the phone up and went into the bathroom. Oh, brother, he thought, this obviously is man-woman trouble. I wonder who got caught with whom? It wasn't too long before he got the whole gory story.

It seems that after everyone was gone and Betty Jo and J. C. had gone to bed, she had made some references to "your annual New Year's poontang" and something had snapped inside J. C. Not only was he not in the mood for his "New Year's poontang" but he was in the mood to pack his bags and get out of her life. This, of course, had upset Betty Jo greatly since she had just made her mind up to straighten out her extracurricular situations and here he was leaving her. Their talk didn't last long enough for her to even state her case, however, because as everybody else was cleaning the house after the party ol' J. C. had been cleaning out his closet. According to her the whole scene lasted about five minutes and he kissed her goodby just like he did every morning when he left for work. He did say that he'd call her in a day or so when he got everything sorted out and gave her some money to handle the bills.

"Well, what do you think?," Joey said, as Debra finished her recap of the early morning events. They were lying in bed, she with a Pepsi and he with a beer (what the hell, they'd been partying just an hour earlier).

"I don't know what to think," she sighed, "where do you think he could have gone? Wait a minute, he doesn't have a girl friend does he?"

With this she turned on the light and looked him straight in the eye with that "you better tell me the truth" look with which only she and Joey's mother could intimidate him. For just a fleeting instant Joey toyed with the idea of trying to fabricate a story and then thought better of it.

"Hell, I don't know! I saw him at the bar one night with some cute young darlin' but I left before he did and I don't know if he went home with her or not."

He had started out real good but his finish was kind of weak and it was hard for him to meet Debra's eyes. This is not real good for the home team, he thought, but if I try to make something up it's gonna sound phony. So he continued on hoping to stumble on the right explanation or some way out of the trap.

"Now that you mention it though, I wouldn't be at all surprised if he had something going on. I've just done my best to avoid the subject since you told me about Betty Jo. I'll probably be able to tell you in a day or two though, because I'm sure he'll call me one way or the other. We were supposed to go riding today, remember?"

Now what he was saying was the truth, it just wasn't all of the truth. Here it was early early in the morning after about eighteen beers, there was a major trauma in the family, he still had about a half a package on and he was supposed to think clearly. It occurred to him that he might be back in the shit storm again and he definitely wasn't dodging the drops too well.

Debra considered what he said and, although she suspected that he might just be concealing a few little facts, was really too tired to tear into his butt this early in the morning. She desperately wanted to know, however, what her sister's chances were for getting back with J. C. because she knew in her heart that if she lost him, ol' Betty Jo was going to be **her** albatross for a long time to come.

"Look, darlin', let's just go on to sleep and we'll talk about it in the morning. There's nothing we can do about it tonight, anyway."

With that he rolled over and pretended to fall into a deep sleep, happy to have skirted the issue for now. It was a while, though, before he really got to sleep and when he did he didn't rest very well at all.

Betty Jo, meanwhile, wasn't doing so hot herself. As a matter of fact she was rolled up in a blanket on her empty bed staring out at the drab gray dawn coming in her bedroom window. Things sure had worked out differently than she had expected in the last few hours and they weren't to her liking at all. She couldn't remember the last time that she had felt this alone and the gray morning twilight wasn't helping matters at all. She rolled over to look at something different and noticed that the wall looked like someone had thrown a bowling ball at it. The wallboard was dented in and the plaster was cracked and littered the rug. As she turned over on her back to try to get some sleep, the light sneaking in through the cracked door set off little rainbows in her tear filled eyes. She quickly wiped them away as her eldest son stuck his head in the door.

"Where's Dad," he whispered, "aren't we going up to the river today?"

"I don't know, honey. Maybe he went to the store or something." With this, great big old crocodile tears began running down her cheeks and she had to turn away as she said, "We had a little argument, Junior, and Daddy left for a while. I'm sure he'll call in a little bit and tell us what we're going to do."

Actually, she was way off the mark on this issue as he wasn't going to call for awhile. This, of course, was hard on Betty Jo but it was also extremely hard on the kids. They all tried to pretend that he was gone on business but it didn't help much.

J. C. called Joey on New Year's day about four o'clock in the afternoon, obviously drunk and having a hard time concealing his feelings. As they talked he kept swinging from one mood to the next but all of them were fairly upbeat. He said that he had been thinking about leaving for a long time and figured that he may as well start the New Year out right.

"But what about the kids, J. C.? How are you going to support your family and yourself? Two people can live more cheaply than two separate families, you know. Why don't you just go on back home and tough it out for a while? Hell, you've put up with it for a long time now, why is it so intolerable all of a sudden?"

"You won't understand it, Joey, until you're going through it yourself and I hope you never have to. This ain't exactly the easiest thing I've ever done in my life. But I've thought about it and thought about it and I can't see any other way out. Sure, I probably could have toughed it out but I want more than that out of life. I want to look forward to going home instead of dreading it. I want to be proud of my old lady instead of trying to pretend I'm with somebody else. I want to be responsible for only my screw-ups not somebody else's. I want to be free!"

"That's all well and good, ol' buddy, but we all feel that way from time to time. The unfortunate part is that what you're describing doesn't have anything to do with marriage and a family and if you'll look around real close you'll see that you have already committed yourself to both of those institutions. Now, I don't claim to be a marriage counsellor or anything but it seems to me that two fairly rational adults with children ought to be able to work out their differences at least long enough to allow them to finish raising their kids together. You know how hard it is for kids who don't have full-time parents."

There was a long pause on the line and Joey knew that he had struck a chord. Even though this was the era of the "me generation," J. C. had enough common sense to know that his buddy was right. The signs of the breakup of the traditional family unit were every-

151

where in their seventies society. Crime was up, drugs were openly available to school kids and the divorce rate was approaching fifty per cent.

"You're probably right, Joey, people should be able to work things out." At this point, Joey began to smile over the phone thinking that his buddy was seeing the light. That wasn't to be, however, as J. C. continued on, "but I'll tell you what, I think it will be easier on the kids being with their mother without me than being with me and their mother the way I am now. They've got to be feeling the tension between us all of the time and I know that can't be good. I'm going to have to try it my way for a while and just see how things come out. I know I can't continue the way things are now."

Damn! Joey thought, so near yet so far. He could tell from the resignation in his friend's voice that he had given himself up to the seventies selfishness. The sense of blind responsibility that had been the hallmark of the previous generations just didn't apply anymore. The rules had been hashed over so often by so many different "experts" that now there didn't appear to be any rules at all. Confused by all the "free thinking" (read laziness) of this new decade, more and more people were using the same flawed rationalizations that J. C. and Betty Jo were using to justify shirking the responsibilities of family and society in order to go off and "find themselves." Unfortunately, in the process of finding themselves, most of them lost a great deal of the quality in their lives.

Joey was extremely upset for his friend and his family because he had seen more and more people in recent years go through this kind of schism and he couldn't think of many that had come through it for the better. As a matter of fact, at this particular moment, he couldn't think of anyone who had come up with anything positive out of a situation like this and he tried to tell this to his friend.

"J. C., both of us have seen this kind of thing happen more and more frequently recently and I bet you can't point out one instance in which anything positive has come out of it. Both sides always end up unhappy and, in the process, the ones taking most of the beating always seem to be the kids. I know it sounds like I'm preaching and, yeah you're right, I don't have kids but dammit from where I sit you're headed down a deadend street!"

For the life of him Joey couldn't figure out why he was arguing so strongly for his buddy to go back home. Looking candidly at J. C.'s life Joey knew that he too would be tempted to leave especially if J. C. knew what Joey knew about Betty Jo and her sordid sex life. But J. C. had his sordid side too, Joey thought, damn, here we go again! Deep down inside Joey knew it was all wrong but how come there wasn't just one person to blame it on.

In the past there had always been one person to point at when it came to man-woman problems. Now you had to point at both of them and getting one person to compromise was hard enough, how in the hell were you going to get two of them to give in long enough for anything meaningful to come of it? The thoughts were coming so hard at Joey right now that he was beginning to get a headache and couldn't really think straight enough to continue.

"Look, J. C., why don't we get together in a couple of days and talk about this some more. Maybe together we can get all of this sorted out. By the way, you want me to say anything to Betty Jo? I think she and the kids are on their way over here right now."

"Yeah, I need a little help there old buddy. Try to calm her down as much as you can but don't give her the impression that I'll be back home any time soon. The kids are going to be real upset too. I guess what I'm trying to say is unless something real radical happens, I'm gone for good. There just ain't no turnin' back. I don't know for sure where all of this is goin' but I do know one thing. Where ever its goin', I'm goin' along for the ride!"

Yeah right, Joey thought, you're goin' along for the joyride and I'm going to be stuck with your irresponsibilities. He knew intrinsically that whatever Debra's sister's problems were, they were soon going to be his also and this afternoon was just going to be the start. Here he thought that he had found a way out of the typical New Year's day college football and leftovers rut to go motorcycle riding and instead he was going to get his first dose of the nineteen-seventies home-therapy blues! Ain't that a hell of a note!

"I'll do the best I can, I promise. Well, I see them coming up the drive now so I guess we better hang up. How can I get a hold of you? Or do you just want to call me in the morning?"

"That's probably the best thing, me calling you. That way you don't have to do any more lying than necessary. Speaking of which there probably isn't any need to be talking about Taffy right now. By the way, I'm not staying with her if that's what you're thinking although I will be over there from time to time. She really isn't the reason that I'm leaving. OK, so she's part of the reason, but that's all. Anyway, I'll call you tomorrow, okay?"

"Yeah, that's fine. Oh, and J. C. . . . everything's gonna be alright my friend. You know that anything you need, you can count on me, okay?"

In reality, Betty Jo wasn't going to be over for awhile but Joey was now so confused that to continue the conversation would have been useless. From the way that J. C. was rambling toward the end of their little talk, he obviously was having the same problem. As Joey sat there musin' over the confusion, in walked Debra who had been discreetly listening in to their conversation on the other phone.

"Well, that didn't sound too encouraging for Betty Jo, did it Joey? And, by the way, who is this Taffy?"

Oh no, Joey thought, now the cat's out of the bag. Why didn't I think that she'd be listening in on the other phone? Dammit!

"That's the one I told you I saw him at the bar with but he said that wasn't the reason that he left and I believe him (in his mind, he wiped the sweat off of his brow). It looks like neither one of them can keep their pants on away from home. By the way, since you took it upon yourself to listen in, you're sworn to secrecy on this deal too. You can't be running back to Betty Jo and telling her anything that J. C. tells me, especially not now. If you do he'll stop talking to me and we can't have that (this time, in his mind, he gave himself a little pat on the back for quick thinking)."

Debra thought long and hard about J. C. not talking to Joey and knew that what he had said was right. She couldn't disrupt the communication process no matter how much she wanted to tell her sister. Maybe she could just tell her selected parts of what was going on. No, because then some of it was bound to get back to Joey or J. C. and that would tear it right there.

"I'm certainly not going to run to her right now with any more bad news than she's already had. But what are we going to do to help her? She's got enough problems without J. C. leaving. What are we going to do? What are we going to say? What's she going to do?"

Those are all excellent questions, Joey thought and even though he had the answers, he knew Debra didn't want to hear them. So instead of answering them, he invoked the General Law of Womanhood.

"I love you darlin'" he said as he hugged her and closed his eyes in silent acquiescence.

Chapter Twelve

BETTY JO SHOWED UP about ten minutes later and it was obvious that she had had a tough night. She was dressed in an old soiled warm-up that hadn't seen the washer in a while and she wasn't wearing any make up. No one wanted to comment on her appearance in this situation but she looked kind of like an aging Western European milkmaid at Saturday morning milking after an extremely demanding Friday night. From the look on her face, she was in a mood to be the pamperee a little bit and she didn't really give a damn who would be the pamperer. Whatever, Joey thought, the way she looks this sumbitch is going to have a hard time finding anyone to even think about giving her any attention much less show it.

Debra jumped up and embraced her sister with that tender aloofness that only sisters have for each other and motioned for Joey to take the kids and get them settled. Getting them settled involved taking them into his pool room (the only room in the house that he had declared off-limits to anyone under twenty-one or anyone, for that matter, that he didn't feel could be trusted with his prized possessions) offering each one a soft drink and, god forbid, joining them in a game of eight ball. He thought it was the least he could do for his best friend in absentia, J. C.

"Uncle Joey, where did my Daddy go? Y'all promised last night that we could go riding up at the river and we've been looking forward to it all day. Why won't he come home? Mom's been in her room all day and won't talk to us. What are we gonna do?"

As Junior was asking these questions and looking Uncle Joey straight in the eye with that lost puppy look, his siblings were wreaking havoc on the pool table and anything else that they could get their hands on. Dammit, Joey thought, how the hell am I supposed to answer these questions while those little bastards are tearing up the pool table?

"Junior look, I'm not going to pull any punches. You're gonna have to grow up kinda fast and neither you nor I have any control over it. Your Mom and Dad are having a hard time seeing eye to eye these days and I'm sure you know about that, don't you?"

Junior looked quickly over at the other kids and, seeing that they were not paying any attention to the conversation, lowered his head and whispered, "I've heard them arguing over little things for a while and Mom's been acting real strange. Sometimes she gets phone calls and goes into the bedroom and closes the door. And then again, sometimes Dad comes home real late at night and they argue. Why do they do that?"

"Hell, I don't know. For some reason, it seems that after a while people just can't seem to get along together anymore. The only thing I can tell you is that you just gotta love 'em both and hope that everything works out okay. Look, no matter what happens, you know how to get a hold of me and I'll always help you all I can, okay?"

That particular ending was so weak that he couldn't meet Junior's eyes anymore, especially since they were now brimming with tears. He had to quickly avert his gaze to keep from joining the little guy in big old sobs.

Man, oh, man!, he thought, I hope old J. C. is enjoying his freedom because this whole deal has sure put me in a trap. Looks like I got a family to raise no matter what I do and I'm willing to bet that I'm gonna be missing out on at least as much poontang as he's gonna get in the near future. This is just not the way it's supposed to be. I didn't have kids so that I wouldn't have to raise them and yet I can't just leave the poor little buggers out in the cold.

By this time Junior was hugging his uncle Joey for dear life and sobbing wetly into the front of his shirt. Joey, as only a father figure could, was suddenly sobbing right along with him much to the consternation of the younger kids who were staring in shiny-eyed amazement. Of course, it didn't take long for them to join right in and soon Debra and Betty Jo were standing in the doorway wondering what the hell was going on.

156

Joey, looking up briefly, was surprised . . . almost shocked by the looks on the two sisters faces. Both were dry-eyed and looked kind of put out by all the ruckus in the poolroom. Both were also looking at Joey like he was something that not only looked bad but also smelled that way. He, in the meantime, was trying his damndest to calm the children but to no avail.

Betty Jo came over and yanked them away from him like an irate mother saving her youngsters from a child molester. Joey looked over at Debra for support but she was glaring steadily at him with a look that could kill. Joey threw his hands in the air with one of those, "hell, I don't know what's going on" looks and tried to smile but he accidently knocked a picture of Momma to the floor and it broke into about a million pieces.

"You were supposed to play with the kids not upset them! What in the world is wrong with you, anyway? Don't these kids have enough problems without you upsetting them further? Dammit, Joey, all you think about is yourself!"

Debra's tone and the awful scowl on her face immediately set the kids off again and this time it was impossible to get all three to stop crying. Everytime one would stop, one of the other ones would start right up again and off they would go. Joey in the mean time was experiencing chapter four in the "Manual Of Other People's, Especially Your Wife's Immediate Family's, Marital Problems."

Finally, in order to settle himself down a little, Joey stood up and started shooting pool. This got everyone's attention. The younger children were immediately distracted by the action and Junior was looking for anything other than his mother's attention at the moment. Debra and Betty Jo were annoyed by the apparent callousness that would allow him to shoot pool in the face of such a major crisis but at the same time fascinated by his prowess.

All in all, it proved to be the right thing to do. Joey was lucky enough to make some pretty tricky shots and, as he noticed that he was onstage, spiced things up with some lively poolhall patter. Soon everyone was having a pretty good time.

Debra and Betty Jo went out to the kitchen and got everybody a drink. Wine for themselves, soft drinks for the kids and even a cold beer for Joey. Joey started a mini-round-robin tournament going with everyone involved and, with the tension lifted from the evening, kind of began enjoying the festivities himself. It got so good that after a couple of hours Betty Jo loaded up her brood and

157

went home stating optimistically and slightly drunkenly that "everything would be all right in the morning." Debra and Joey, of course, agreed and gave everyone a kiss and a positive hug to send them off, all the while looking doubtfully at each other.

"Well," Debra said, getting Joey another beer from the fridge, "what do you really think about the whole situation?"

The beer was a signal for Joey to sit down at the kitchen table and talk for a while. He did so with some reluctance because, even though he had extricated himself from the earlier problems, oftentimes these late evening kitchen table talks had proven to be disastrous for him. It all harkened back to that age old male-female problem, the differentiation between facts and feelings.

It's probably time to talk about this subject for a moment because this might possibly be one of the answers to the war between the sexes. To women, feelings (hunches) are the most important things in life. They consider them more important than reality. As a matter of fact, to them, they are reality. It's interesting to note that people are considered sane when they can differentiate between feelings and reality and that, when they can no longer tell the difference between the two, they are determined to be insane.

To men, on the other hand, the most important things in life are facts. Men have a hard time basing their lives on anything other than fact, and, consequently, are constantly searching for truths to live by. This of course makes communication between the sexes kind of interesting for how can people communicate when the rules are different for each of them?

Although he had never thought through this disparity between feelings and reality Joey knew intrinsically that communication between he and Debra was a pretty touchy issue. So when it was time for them to have these little talks, he always tried to lay down some ground rules in order to avoid conflict. This, naturally, was the wrong thing to do because instead of avoiding conflict it seemed to lay the ground work for it.

Debra always wanted to know why it was that they had to have ground rules before they could have a discussion about anything of any relevance. Weren't they both **adults**? As a matter of fact, weren't they both **intelligent** adults? Now really, weren't they both **rational** intelligent adults? And being rational, intelligent adults couldn't they simply have a casual conversation about these things without having to establish some kind of cockamamie protocol? Suuuure!

"I mean, really now, Joey, why can't we just talk a minute about some family problems without having to observe all of these rules. This isn't a board meeting, you know, this is just you and me talking about my sister and her stupid freaking husband who obviously is going through some kind of mid-life crisis and has found some young bimbo who is about fifteen years younger and fifty pounds lighter than she who he is shacked up with and doesn't know if he is going to come back home and own up to his responsibilities or not! It's not like a meeting with the lawyers over a will or anything!"

At this moment the only thing as blue as her face was the language she was using. It was interesting to Joey that her corollary was that of a lawyer and a legal document because he could see that, if this discussion were not properly handled, it could end up with exactly that kind of scenario for him. As was usually the case in tense moments, he tried to lighten up the conversation with a little humor and, as usually happened when he tried that particular method at times like this, it fell flat on its nose.

"Shoot, Debra, he probably just decided to go bowling with the boys, got drunk as a skunk and couldn't drive home. I'll betcha' he's sitting at the house waiting for them to get home as we speak!"

The weakness of his humor was only accentuated by the frailty of his smile. Things were going down hill at a rate approaching the speed of light and from the look on Debra's face, it was obvious that she wasn't in a light-hearted mood. This was one of those times that he wished he could be the fly on the wall that everyone always talked about. Instead, he felt like the pile of manure that the fly would prefer sitting on to the wall.

"Goddammit, Joey, we need to talk about this, so quit trying to clown around and let's get serious! Don't you realize that this whole thing has gotten pretty strong? Don't you see that J. C., damn him, has finally gotten sick of my fat, lazy sister? If we don't do something about this he isn't going to come home and we're going to have to baby-sit her, her kids and my Mother for the rest of our lives! Doesn't that mean anything to you?"

For just an instant, Joey thought seriously about telling her exactly what that meant to him and then he thought better of it. There is a time for truth and there is a time for reality. This, obviously, was a time for neither of the above. This was a time for being creative in thought, word and deed. This was a time to dazzle her with rhetoric; to do a dance so distracting in its beauty and complexity that she would forget about the problem at hand in her overwhelming awe of him. This was the time to confuse her totally so that she would get the migraine headache that could be his only saving grace. Either that or he could quickly run out and buy her something that he couldn't afford . . . or shoot her. It only took him a moment to consider all of these options and, inhaling deeply, he plunged ahead on.

"You're right darlin'. I guess we need to concoct a plan of action before this thing gets too much more out of hand. Let's look at the facts now. He has left home but he hasn't talked to her or anyone else but me about what his intentions are. He may stay away for a week or a month or he may come home tomorrow with his hat in his hand. I know that he will be talking to me soon, hopefully tomorrow. Probably what I need to do is to go meet him and try to get some idea of his plans. Then we'll figure out what to do from there."

Debra took all of this in but Joey could see that she was still disturbed about something. She had that look on her face that generally preceded something bad for him. It was sort of like that look your mother used to get just before she asked you where that *Penthouse* magazine she found under your bed came from; or the look your Dad would get after taking a phone call from your girlfriend's father. Joey decided that he better get to dancin' before she said what was on her mind.

"But you know there is one constant danger here and that is that we let this thing insinuate itself into our relationship. We've got to remember that the problems they are having are theirs not ours or they could easily become ours. I know it's going to be hard to be impartial but we've got to try. We have to be the most important thing to each other, darlin'. "

With this he grabbed Debra by the shoulders and gave her a long tender kiss. Unfortunately, he moved a little as he began enjoying it and she didn't interpret his movement correctly. Or maybe she did interpret it correctly but wasn't interested at the moment. Anyhow, when he felt her tense up against him, he quickly disengaged himself before old number nine betrayed him again and walked over to the window to regain his composure.

This was just the beginning of what would prove to be a very long winter for Joey. The breakup of any family is a hard thing for everyone involved, especially if you happen to be on the periphery of the problem. It seems that being a principal in the action is easier because at least you know what's going on from moment to moment. When you're on the outside but still intimately involved, you get all of the necessary information long after you need it. This is great when it comes to hindsight. Which is probably why it seems that your friends always have such good advice after the fact. They get to pass judgment after everything has occurred and we all know how much easier it is to assess a problem after all the facts are in.

So there sat Joey trying to keep everything together for two very opposite reasons. On the one hand he was motivated by his love for J. C., his friend, and the knowledge of what havoc a marital break up would wreak on all involved. On the other hand, he felt terrible for Betty Jo because her life would probably take a turn for the worse if J. C. didn't come back. On the third hand (??), and most importantly, he felt desperately sorry for himself because the worst their lives could turn wouldn't hold a candle to the grief he knew he would endure over the deal.

Fortunately his selfishness was overridden by his concern for J. C.'s kids because he hadn't seen many kids that turned out well in single parent families. He was a strong believer in the family unit. He knew that children need both parents for a number of reasons, the most important of which was balance.

It seemed to Joey that all of life involved balance. Aristotle called it moderation. The Christians call it temperance but they narrow it down so much that it really isn't livable. He'd found this out a lot lately. The more you narrow your viewpoint down the harder it is to live under whatever it is that you are considering.

Temperance is defined as moderation, restraint or abstinence in that order according to the American Heritage Dictionary. Now most people have been taught that when you look up a word the first definition is the most acceptable and the second less acceptable, etcetera. Well, the Christians (and most other religious groups for that matter, let's not just pick on them) all seem to agree on one thing and that is that temperance refers to the last definition, abstinence . . . and that is the most extreme definition of the word. Well, I'm no expert on religion but one of the few quotable quotes that I will take credit for is "extremism in any form is a question not an answer." Unfortunately, most of the organized religions lean toward some extreme or the other, like with the word temperance. If there is confusion as to the meaning, why not take the first definition (moderation) or the middle definition (restraint) rather than the last (abstinence)?

161

Poor old Joey's dilemma was that he was trying his damnedest to maintain balance in his life while everybody around him was going to one extreme or the other. He knew inherently that this whole fiasco was going to jump up and eventually cause him a lot of grief, even though he hadn't done anything to deserve it, but at the moment he chose to dwell on the problem at hand not what was waiting for him down the road. With that in mind, he suggested that he and Debra sleep on it and maybe tomorrow things would take a turn for the better. After all, there wasn't anything they could do about anything anyway until they talked to J. C., was there?

Joey awoke the next morning feeling strangely refreshed, considering the tension of the last few days. After his morning run and shower he headed to the office and sure enough J. C. had called. He didn't leave a number but he did promise to meet Joey for a beer at their favorite mid-week hangout. The rest of the day was a blur of Monday-morning-after-a-holiday problems and when he finally looked up it was cocktail time. He called Debra, told her where he would be, that he might be late, for her not to meet him and fled the office.

As he walked through the door of the bar, he patted himself on the back for telling Debra to stay home because there sat J. C. with his little slut puppy on his arm and a smile as big as Texas on his whore dog face. He looked so happy that Joey couldn't help but smile as he hugged his friend.

"Hate to see that your personal problems are tearing you up so bad, pardner, here let me buy you a beer to ease the pain!" He smiled as he waved to the bartender.

He was amazed to see that J. C. just kept right on smiling the whole time as he looked Joey straight in the eye.

"You're right old buddy, times are tough, but when the times get tough the tough get goin . . . and I'm a goin'!!"

With that he toasted Joey with his beer, gave his little darlin' a hug and sauntered smugly off to the men's room.

Joey turned to Taffy, looked her right in the eye and said "Well, what are y'all gonna do now, honey?"

She smiled sweetly back at him, took a sip of tequila from the shot glass in front of her and replied demurely, "Whatever comes next."

By this time the bartender was there with the beers and, after that got straightened away, J. C. came back so their conversation ended just about as it had begun. Joey didn't know whether or not he should initiate anything personal with the little darlin' around so they just engaged in jokes and small talk until it was time for her to go to the bathroom. Strangely enough, when she got up to go Joey realized that he was actually enjoying talking with her. Maybe it was more that he was dreading talking to J. C. about his dilemma . . . but after she got up he kinda wished she hadn't gone.

Looking down into his beer glass, he kind of let the side of his mouth fall open a little bit and the words tumbled out onto the bar in a crescendoed pile, "You got any plans yet, pardner? Anything you want to tell me? Or is it just too early to talk about anything serious? Stop me if I'm walkin' where I shouldn't and be assured anything you tell me goes no further than this table!"

Even though it rained out in a jumble of consonants and vowels, J. C. was able to reassemble the letters in his mind and turn them into thought forms that he could assimilate. In other words, he could see that his buddy was extremely nervous about the situation and probably under great pressure from his wife and sister-in-law and that he needed J. C. to give him a little something to take home to them.

"Well, I don't have a whole lot to report, really. I can tell you for sure that I won't be going back home as a married man and that I miss my kids. I can tell you also that I will be calling them and Betty Jo tomorrow but I don't want you to tell them that. And I can also say that the day after tomorrow, I'm going to the lawyer's to file for a divorce. Oh, one other thing, I might need to borrow some money for a little while just to tide me over until this thing is done. Think you can help me out?"

"Sure I can help," Joey said as he let out a long sigh of relief, "I'm just happy that you have a plan. I mean, I'm sorry that you have decided that you and Betty Jo need to split but I know that you have given it a lot of thought and . . . . . ."

At this point, Joey looked up at J. C. who was grinning like a Cheshire cat and kind of let his speech trail off. His face turned red as he realized that what he was saying didn't really need to be said at all. That J. C. was dead set on what he was going to do and that he didn't need Joey to tell him that it was okay or even to pass judgment on it for that matter. As a matter of fact, he looked so comfortable with his situation that Joey quit worrying and actually relaxed enough to start enjoying himself.

"Are you done now Joey or do we have to go through all that 'you have responsibilities' bullshit again." J. C. laughed. "Believe me, I have thought this thing through over and over and I know that I have made the right decision. Look, it's going to be a little tough on everyone, me included, but I think everything will work out for the best."

"It seems to me that marriage was invented when people only lived to be thirty-five or forty years of age. That way people got married when they were eighteen and stayed married for life. I have noticed, though, that in a lot of cultures they had more than one wife. Now in my case, I think that I have put my lifetime in and I'm ready to move on. I haven't felt this good about anything in a long time!"

I can tell that you are happy about being free again, Joey thought to himself. Who wouldn't be in your situation? Here you got married before you even got out of school, had three kids before you figured out how to make them stop coming and had to struggle to help your family get squared away. Hell, that doesn't leave much time for living! But what about your kids and Betty Jo? What about me? I know it's selfish but I'm the one who's gonna have to pay for your freakin' party, damn it!

Just as quickly as he started, Joey stopped feeling sorry for himself in the glow of his buddy's newfound happiness. Watching his cute little bimbo prance back from the ladies room all full of herself and J. C... and watching J. C.'s eyes light up like they used to a long time ago but hadn't in the recent past, Joey couldn't help but think that things were pretty right with J. C.'s world. He smiled as big as he could but suddenly got in a hurry to leave. The barroom was beginning to feel awfully cramped and stuffy. He stood up so abruptly that he almost knocked everyone's drinks over.

"Is there anything you want me to tell anybody?" He asked, "I need to get my ass home. I've got a meeting early in the morning in Houston and I haven't even packed yet."

"Yeah, tell Debra that I'm fine and that I'll call Betty Jo and the kids tomorrow night at home. And, Joey, I'm sorry if this thing has upset your life but I've got to go through with it. Maybe someday you'll understand."

"Hey look buddy, everything is cool with me. The only thing that is bothering me is jealousy. Deep down we all want to be free."

With that and a wave, Joey turned on his heel and almost

164

sprinted for the door. He hadn't felt this claustrophobic since the time the elevator got stuck in Chicago and it took the janitor fifteen minutes to get it fixed. By the time he got to the car he was sweating as if he had just finished his early morning run and he noticed that he was breathing through his mouth. What the hell is going on here? He thought. Why is my body responding to my mind like this? This whole shitaree isn't my problem, anyway. Dammit!

When he got home Debra was waiting for him at the kitchen table with a cold beer ready. Again he fought the claustrophobia back. The last thing he wanted at this moment was to have to report every last little detail of the evening to Debra and then have to re-hash it about three times so that she wouldn't run to the phone and upset Betty Jo. He thought seriously about what to say to her for a minute and suddenly realized something kind of weird. He could distinctly remember driving home but, at the same time, he realized that his mind had gone blank for the entire ride. It was the first time he could remember that he had not had a single thought for a long period of time. If he had he would have rehearsed what he was going to tell Debra so that everything would come out right. As it was, it looked like he was going to have to do this thing a capella and that was not a comforting thought.

Debra gave him a big hug and the cold beer and led him to the table. He noticed that she was dressed in one of his old tee shirts with not another stich on underneath which absolutely drove him wild but he knew that that was just a promise to encourage him to tell her everything that had happened at the bar. Grabbing the cold beer and taking a long pull on it, he prepared himself for the worst.

"You were there for a long time, Joey. What did J. C. say? Is he going to come home? I thought you'd never get here!"

She was so excited by the situation that she didn't ask anything about Taffy, thank goodness, because if she did he would try to avoid the issue and, if she pressed him on it, he would have to tell her the truth.

"Well, I've got good news and bad news." Joey sighed. "The good news is that he is in good spirits and he has a plan. The bad news is that it doesn't include Betty Jo. I'm afraid they are going to be separated for sure and, unless something drastic happens, they're going to get a divorce."

With this part of the conversation taken care of, he took another long pull on his beer and, noticing it was gone, got up and walked to the refrigerator for a fresh one.

"Want anything while I'm up darlin'?" He said over his shoulder, afraid to look her in the eyes.

He knew that what he had just said was a nightmare come true but he thought that it was probably best to get the worst part over with as quickly as possible. This wasn't one of the best ways that he could have handled the situation in Debra's mind. Of course, if the truth be known, there probably wouldn't have been any good way to handle it. One way or the other he was going to have to hear about how stupid her sister was and how macho J. C. was and what an idiot he was for good measure. There just wasn't any way around it.

When he turned back around she was girding for action. Instead of remaining in her seat she was standing with her back to him looking out the window at the black winter night with both arms stretched out in front of her, hands resting on the window sill. Since she hadn't answered him, he had gotten her a beer also, just in case it might help soften the situation.

When he asked her if she wanted the beer, he could see every muscle in her back from her butt to the nape of her neck tense up as if she were a body builder showing off for the judges. Fearing an explosion of some magnitude, he took the seat farthest from her, sat back and took a long slow drink of beer.

She spun around like Lauren Bacall in some old Bogart film and proceeded to vent her frustration on him. "Goddam him anyway, the son of a bitch! He hasn't been worth a shit as a provider or as a husband since the day they were married! All he was good at was making her pregnant and when the babies came he wasn't any help at all!

"And Betty Jo, damn her ass! We all told her that if she kept letting herself go, he wouldn't stick around. And sure enough after every baby she gains another ten pounds and then she is so upset by the weight gain and the fact that she doesn't turn him on anymore that she goes and gains another forty pounds."

"Oh! And you! I'll bet you didn't help the situation did you? You can't stand any of my stupid family, can you? You're probably enjoying this whole thing, aren't you?"

"Now, wait just a minute, Debra, this thing isn't my fault at all. I had nothing to do with it . . . then or now. And I'll be damned if I'll take the blame for it!"

He looked down and he was white-knuckling the table in front of him and he noticed that he was out of breath. At which point, he started making a conscious effort to control himself. At least long enough to try and calm her down. Which, from the set of her mouth and the way she was glaring at him, was not going to be a piece of cake.

"Look," he said as calmly as he could, "I thought we weren't going to allow your sister's or anyone else's problems become ours. I've done my best to try to get J. C. back home but I'm telling you he's made up his mind and he isn't going to turn back now. I haven't seen him this happy since I've known him. It's as if someone has lifted the weight of the world off his back!"

The minute the words left his mouth, before he even looked at her expression, he knew he had made a major faux pas. Not only had he spoken truth, which was neither called for nor wanted by Debra, but he had also neglected to respond as another woman would. Naturally, this would have been an especially hard thing for him to do since he wasn't a woman but, to Debra at this moment, that had nothing to do with anything. When he finally did look up, she was wearing a sneer that would have done Elvis Presley proud in Blue Hawaii or maybe Elizabeth Taylor in Virginia Wolf. In any case, he knew that this conversation wasn't going to be any short term thing. Not if he wanted to remain in the status quo that is.

All of a sudden one of those errant thoughts that you always fear will announce itself at about one hundred decibels or flash across your forehead like a neon sign no matter how hard you try to suppress it crossed his mind. Maybe, just maybe, it wouldn't be so bad to be in J. C.'s shoes right now. He was sure that J. C. wasn't listening to an irrational diatribe from some stressed-out woman right now. Or at least if he was, he could just stand up and walk out on her, not bound by any considerations other than whether or not he chose to listen to it. Odds are no matter what he was listening to it wouldn't preclude him from getting a little poontang before the night was out, anyway.

"Well, I'll tell you what Mr. Bigshot. Whether you like it or not it is going to **become** our problem. As a matter of fact, it already **is** our problem. Who do you think is going to have to listen to all of Betty Jo's troubles from now on? Hell, she can't take care of herself much less the children."

"You know my mother is just going to gloat over this whole thing. I can hear her now . . . 'Betty Jo I told you from the start he

167

was no good. Why didn't you just have an abortion like I told you to. I would have paid for it and then you wouldn't have to go through all of this garbage. You just wouldn't listen to your mother would you?' . . . and then she'll start in on me, I know she will!"

Well if you know she is going to give you a bad time, why don't you tell her to mind her own damn business or just avoid her, Joey thought, for once knowing better than to voice his opinion. You better start covering your own ass, though, buddy, because if you don't she sure as hell is going to try to make you just as miserable as she is. Since he didn't know quite where to go from here, Joey intuitively invoked the General Law Of Womanhood.

"Hey, look Debra," he said soothingly, "we both know this is going to be a tough row to hoe but we can come through it together. The first thing we need to do is get ready for when he calls her and the second is to prepare her and your momma for when he files for divorce. If we work together on this, we can probably keep everybody calmed down enough to get through the damn thing. Here, drink this beer and relax a minute. Let me put a little music on, we'll work this deal out somehow."

He said this last with a smile and a confidence that he didn't feel in the least but he thought it came off fairly well. At least Debra sat down, shut up and drank her beer. He put on some old Crosby, Stills and Nash that they used to listen to around the camp fire up on the river and pulled two more beers out of the fridge. Maybe I can get her a little bit drunk and take her mind off of all of this stuff, he thought as he sat down next to her and gave her the beer. To his surprise she not only took it but gave him a dazzling smile.

"You're right you know," she grinned tilting back the beer, "we've all known this would happen sooner or later the way things were going. I guess we need to just make the best of what ever comes along. And this time I'm not going to let my mother get to her or to me," she said with firm resolve, "I'm going to call Betty Jo in the morning and tell her to take a sick day. Then she and I are going to clean her house and get her on a diet and exercise program. Maybe I'll treat her to a haircut and a facial. She'll enjoy that won't she?"

"I think that is the best idea you've come up with all evening. The best thing to do is to attack this thing on the most positive note that you can. We can lick this thing if we try hard enough. All it will take is some time and attention, speaking of which, it's getting late

168

now so why don't we give each other a little time and attention before things get too hectic."

With this final thought he put down his beer, hauled her to her
feet, kissed her in his best Clark Gable fashion and waltzed her off
to the bedroom. Surprise again, she went off meekly and almost sub-
serviently and made love to him as tender as a lamb before she went
quickly to sleep. As he lay there staring at the darkened ceiling, he
didn't know whether to smile or to frown.

Chapter Thirteen

THE NEXT MORNING DEBRA woke up to find Joey already gone and a note on the kitchen table saying that he had an early meeting in Houston but that he loved her and he knew she was doing the right thing. She immediately called Betty Jo and caught her just as she was going to take a shower and get off to work.

"Betty Jo, why don't you take a sick day and let's get your house cleaned up, literally and figuratively. You haven't been taking any time for yourself in the last year and it wouldn't hurt to disappear for a day, what do you say?"

She tried to sound as enthusiastic as possible but wasn't sure if she was coming off that way or not.

"What happened, Debra? Did you talk to J. C.? Is it bad news? Come on, let me have it. I'm a big girl. He's not coming back is he?" She whispered into the phone, "I know he isn't and I'm not sure I want him to, anyway. Neither one of us needs to keep living the lie we've been living for the last two years. Yeah, I'll take the day off and we can do those things. I guess it's high time I got my house in order."

She said this last with such resignation that it took all of Debra's strength and resolve to stay upbeat. But she knew she had to or the whole situation would go to hell. At least Betty Jo was honest enough to admit what was really happening. It was almost as if she had been listening in on Debra and Joey's conversation of last night. Debra decided to let everything lay where it was, told Betty Jo she'd be there in forty-five minutes and hung up. She wasn't sure what she was going to say to her sister but she figured she'd just play it by ear and hope everything worked out all right.

By the time she got over to her sister's house, Debra was humming a happy tune. The thought of all the good she was going to do for her sister was taking her to a higher high than she had been on in weeks. The sun was shining and the birds were singing and everything was going to be all right! When she pulled up in Betty Jo's driveway, however, she had a slight sinking spell. The front yard hadn't been worked on recently and the paint on the windows and trim was faded and peeling. The garage door was gaping crookedly open where someone had broken it and the windows beamed the sunshine back into her eyes in oily, rainbow colors. Although she had tried to tidy herself up, Betty Jo looked as careworn as her house when she opened the door.

"Looks like we've got some work to do, doesn't it sister? Where do you want to start?" she said looking around at the filth and disarray with obvious distaste.

Debra tried not to look too dismayed as she maneuvered her way through the clutter to the kitchen. "Tell you what, Betty Jo, I've always worked my way through the house from the kitchen out. Why don't we try that to start?"

With this, she opened the cabinet under the sink only to jump back with a shriek as a cockroach as big as a horny toad charged her as though it was going to knock her over. As Debra stomped the sucker flat, she hollered over her shoulder "and call the pest control people while you're at it. That damn cockroach almost ran me over on his way out!" Gritting her teeth in disgust she scooped the carcass up with a paper towel and deposited it in the first of many garbage bags that they would use that day.

Both of them were taken by surprise when they heard the knock on the front door. Debra because she realized that she had been yelling at the top of her lungs and Betty Jo because the house was in such sad shape. But neither one of them was prepared for what they saw when they opened the door. For there stood Momma replete with do-rag, bucket, mop and broom obviously ready to jump right in and give them a hand. This was all the more remarkable since Momma hadn't cleaned her own house for the last decade or so (ever since Daddy had struck it big in the oil bidness).

As a matter of fact, Momma had astonished them all by keeping

171

the same maid for as long as they could remember even though she treated her like a second-class citizen. First, she wouldn't allow her to park her car in front of the house, rather she had to hide it in the back alley. Second, she wouldn't feed her lunch, instead she made **her** cook for Momma and bring her own food from home. And finally, when the holidays rolled around, not only did Momma give her a tip that would have seemed paltry to the lawn boy but also she would insist that she put on a rented maid's outfit (black dress, white apron, white cap and white shoes) and serve at their Christmas party.

"Well, what have we got here?" Momma laughed her big old whiskey laugh, "you girls got somethin' planned for the day? Did your ol' Momma figure y'all out or what?"

By now they were all laughing so hard they were almost crying, hugging and patting each other . . . and then they **were** crying, in happiness that is, hugging each other and then pushing each other away to look at one another and then crying and hugging again. Men have always had a hard time with this particular feminine behavioral trait. Why do women cry when they are happy? Why don't they laugh or chuckle or grin or smile? It seems that the only time they do those things is when they are with men. Is their true happiness really sadness? Is that why they have such a bad time on holidays or any other time that is supposed to be merry? But then you would think that the opposite would also be true, that at sad times like funerals and things, women would laugh. Well, that doesn't seem to work out either. They do tend to giggle when they lie, however.

Ironically enough, the fact that men don't understand these anomalies is just as hard to fathom for women as their behavior is to men. Women believe that men can't understand feminine behavior because they are "insensitive" and "not in touch with their feelings." That the woman's obviously converse behavior is normal and that, even though masculine behavior at these times makes more sense, men should "understand" why the feminine gender chooses to act so peculiarly. How are men supposed to innately comprehend these ambiguities? And why can't women explain to men why they respond so disappropriately to certain stimuli? And if they can't, in fact, explain these things, why are they so critical of men for not responding "correctly" when they act that way? Of course, if these questions could be answered, there really wouldn't be any reason for this book, would there?

When this emotive trio finally finished with their semi-hysterical release (maybe **that's** the reason they cry when they're happy, laughter just isn't enough release for their emotions), they all had to sit down for a moment and have a cup of coffee to talk it over. As they tenderly rehashed every little detail of the previous few minutes, they struck up that bond that is so rare in mother-daughter relationships. One that, if it could only be recalled on demand, would probably herald the end of all physical and mental strife in the world. One that would probably prove to be the reemergence of family unity and sisterly love. One that could allow Betty Jo and Debra to finally get along with their eccentric ol' Momma. Even though this would prove, as always, impossible, they all enjoyed it for a few poignant moments, anyway.

Momma was the first to come out of the euphoria of the moment and look around the kitchen. What she saw was actually a little bit worse than what she had imagined it would be on the drive over. The place was truly in a shambles and time was a wastin'. As was her wont, Momma felt it necessary to take charge and, in the spirit of the moment, Debra and Betty Jo were willing to become her two little helpmates just as in some imagined yesterday.

"Okay girls," Momma intoned in her best schoolmarm english, "let's get down to business. Betty Jo, you go call Truly Nolen and tell them to get over here and spray tomorrow after we finish cleaning up this pig sty. Debra, let's you and me get to emptying out all of these cabinets and washing everything in them. Oh, and Betty Jo when you get off the phone, strip all of the beds and start a load of wash. We'll have this place squeaky clean in no time!"

With her speech completed, Momma fell immediately into the physical therapy that all three of them needed at the time. Sometimes it is best to let the hands take over to heal what the mind can't seem to . . . and heal it did. Not only did the house get a cleansing that it so obviously needed but also their souls seemed to get washed out in the process. By the time the kids got home from school, they were greeted by a house that was in order for the first time in a long time and a family that seemed to have recaptured its meaning also. Oh what a joy it was to see everything so together and in place.

It only seemed proper to Momma, after what was to her a tremendous expenditure of time and selflessness, that they have a little meeting with the children to lay out the ground rules for their "new" family. The evening before, in preparation for her mission of mercy, she had taken the time to bake some Toll House cookies. Laying these and some soft drinks out as bait to attract the kids to the kitchen table, she prepared to tell them how things were going to be "from now on." The only problem with the whole scenario was that Momma's new deal and her daughter's new deal were not one and the same.

"Come give your grandma a hug, Junior," she said, kind of like a gypsy trying to lure in a tourist, "Look at these cookies that I baked for you."

Now, Junior had fallen for this ploy before and the result had always been some kind of trap, so he was a little wary at the onset. He approached the table cautiously like a dog approaching a tidbit offered by a complete stranger, sidling up to the table just out of arm's reach. Of course, when he got the first home-made cookie into his mouth, just like the dog with the first little hand fed morsel, he was hooked and grandmom had him. This little act was repeated by his two brothers and a quorum was rapidly reached.

As soon as she had the children assembled, Momma called for the rest of her brood. They, too, had seen this particular scene played out before and were as reticent as their offspring to approach the sacrificial altar. But, chocolate chips being the Trojan Horse that they are, soon all of them were gathered around the conference table, chattering happily around mouthfuls of squishy dough and bits of chocolate. Momma, observing smugly that she had outwitted all of them again, began immediately to declaim. "We have all had a beeootiful day here, children and children," nodding alternately at her brood and her after-brood, "and we have done a wonderful job of getting this house in order. Now it's time to get ourselves in order, too."

With this her voice went up about ten octaves and her face began to color as she sat up much straighter in her chair. She had only had three or four drinks this afternoon but as the day grew darker so had the drinks and the last one was a Jim Dandy. Those folks who grade their drinks by color would have called this last little number a deep mahogany. As a matter of fact, with each sip that she took, her face became alternately more flushed and more resolved. Everyone in the room, instinctively recognizing what was to come, shrank downward and backward in apprehension.

"From now on we are going to have a little bit 'a responsibility and order in this house. Everyone is going to have a job to do and, by God, they're going to do it! Now your mother, who has obviously

174

lost her husband, your father," she said this with such vengeance that no one in the room knew who she was more pissed off at. Betty Jo or J. C., "is now goin' to be the provider around here. As such, she is gonna' have to get her fat ass to work ever' mornin' and bring home the bacon. Now I've made up a list of chores for you kids to do to keep this place lookin' just as good as it does now and I'm sure I speak for her when I say if ya'll don't do 'em, there'll be hell to pay!"

While the kids took this onslaught as all kids do when they are being lectured, with that laconic, bored-interested look, their mother and her sister got increasingly agitated. The snide little remark about losing her husband hurt ol' Betty Jo pretty bad since she wasn't as used to her Momma's sharp tongue now as she was when she was growing up and exposed to it more often. But when Momma started in on her kids, like she used to do to the girls in those good old days, it was all she could do to hold herself back. Unfortunately, they were just coming off one of those once in a million good experiences with Momma and she didn't want to ruin it with a scene. Also, she knew that without her Momma and Daddy's financial help in the very near future, things were probably going to get very uncomfortable. So she decided for the time being to keep her mouth shut.

By now, Momma had launched into her lecture about how tough she had it when she was a girl and how lucky kids were these days. You couldn't prove it by the looks on the faces of the kids she was addressing, however. Junior was staring out the window obviously wondering how much longer he would have to put up with his grandmom's drunken rambling. The two younger boys, becoming more bored by the minute, went into a pinch, push and shove match which threatened to escalate into a fist fight any minute. Betty Jo, recognizing all these signs as the beginning of the end of their little soiree, leapt into the breach.

"Momma, I'm sure you've made your point to the boys and I'm sure that they will behave themselves and help out in the future. This whole thing hasn't been easy on any of us, so maybe we should talk about some of the good things that can come of all this. Like the facts that we have a nice house to live in and food to eat and, most importantly, each other to love."

Betty Jo was smiling that crippled-lip smile that says "I was hoping you'd understand and cool it but I know you won't" while Debra was rolling her eyes and warily watching her mother for the signs of the inevitable inebriated eruption she knew was in the making.

Momma's eyes, already red and watery from the effects of her deep mahoghany drink, began to narrow and bug out alternately as she prepared for the climactic ending to her drunken diatribe. Although both Betty Jo and Debra knew what was coming they hadn't a clue as to how to circumvent it nor had they ever been able to stop one of her "hissy fits" in all the years that they had known Momma. The thought did cross Betty Jo's mind, however, that almost every pleasant occasion that she had enjoyed with her mother had ended this very way.

"Well, I'll tell you something, honey. Things ain't gonna be so Goddam rosy around here in a month or two. You can't eat love, you know! It costs a lot of money to live these days and you don't make enough to keep a family of field mice alive much less three growing boys and a mother that eats enough for two people. So don't be so damn smug about everything!"

By this time Momma's face had become a florid purple with every vein from her hairline down to her heaving bosom threatening to explode in a venomous reaction to her thoughts and words. The boys, each startled out of their individual diversions by the heat of the onslaught, were now paying strict attention to Grandma's every word. Debra and Betty Jo were looking at each other with the same "help me, please" look on their dispirited faces and, at the same time, searching for a safe exit way or word. They both knew that they had to end this scene but they also knew that whoever stood up and did what had to be done would pay for it in spades at some point in the future. Debra, always the stronger of the two and the one with the least to lose in this particular squabble, finally took the plunge.

"That's enough Momma, dammit! Here we've had this incredible day together and you have to end it like this! Why can't we all just give each other a hug and call it a day. I'm sure that Betty Jo and the kids will work out a schedule to make sure everything is taken care of and it'll all work out okay."

Much to the relief of Betty Jo and the children, this was just the distraction that they needed to make their escape. While Momma homed in on Debra like a crazed bull heading for the toreador, Betty Jo exited stage left shooing her brood before her. Debra in the meantime, began to execute the first of several diversions that she had mastered over time in the hope that one of them would at least slow Momma down enough for her to make her own getaway.

Holding her hands up before her and giggling nervously, she

began. "Just calm down now, mother. Isn't it about time for Daddy to come home? I thought he was due in from the well today. Since it has gotten so late and I'm sure you're as tired as we are, why don't we all meet at El Fenix for some Mexican food. We can go in there dressed just like we are and all get home and to bed early."

This gave Momma pause and for a moment, as her alcohol and nicotine addled mind mulled over her daughter's words, she was overcome with a brief flash of lucidity. Her mood rapidly shifted from almost uncontrollable rage at her fat, helpless daughter and the situation that she knew would end in misery for her, to one of benevolent empathy for the plight of all divorced women who suddenly become single heads of multiple child families. The melancholy that overcame her at this revelation brought a flood of tears to her already bloodshot eyes and, for an instant, she looked so sad and vulnerable that Debra jumped up and ran around the table to her. At this point, Momma lost track of where they were in the disagreement and, thinking it was over, gave in to the hugging and "I love you's" that were supposed to follow such events in her judgment.

Momma was not unlike a lot of women in the way they interact with their daughters and there is a very plausible explanation for this phenomenon. By their very nature, the female of the species is in direct competition with all other females from the time that she becomes aware that there is an opposite sex. In nature, from the time of puberty, all females are vieing for the available and, more importantly, desirable males who in most species are in short supply. This includes her own family and/or offspring and explains why, as with Momma, a lot of women routinely flirt with and try to attract their very own daughter's boyfriends; why, when it comes to matters of dress, they are so harshly critical of others of their gender including relatives; why, when it comes to morals, they can't find anyone who lives the way they believe they live their own lives; and it ultimately answers the question of why women feel more secure with men friends than with women friends.

At any rate, as Momma and Debra were engaged in the ritualistic making up that follows these types of altercations, in walked Betty Jo who immediately sized up the situation and with an audible sigh of relief joined right in. Amongst more tears, hugging and murmured "I love yous," the battle drew to a close. Momma by this time was so worn out from a full day of housework, alcohol and profound feelings that she begged off dinner, stating that she needed to go home and rest. Neither Debra nor Betty Jo put up much of an argument fearing further sentient confrontations over the currently unsettled condition of Betty Jo's life. They helped mother out the door with all of her utensils intact. (Momma was very protective of her things. As a matter of fact the less valuable the thing the more she seemed concerned over it). As they waved her a good-bye from the front porch, they turned and gave each other one of those "saved-by-the-bell" grins.

With Momma out of the way, the girls scrounged up enough food for the boys' dinner and went into the living room for a glass of wine and a little conversation. After they had each settled in and started on their second glass, they reviewed the days' events. As they compared notes, the one thing they could both agree on was, no matter how good things seemed with Momma, given enough time they would go to hell in a handbasket. It appeared that every time things got going real good, Momma seemed compelled to disrupt them. She just couldn't tolerate anyone else's happiness without trying to inflict some pain on them. Both girls wondered why things had to be that way.

"Let me tell you something that you need to know, Betty Jo," Debra said, getting down to business, "we like to think that Momma means well and as far as anyone else is concerned that's the way it is but, in reality, Momma is just plain mean. Look at what she has done to Daddy, look at what she has done to us and I'll tell you what, there's no tellin' what she'll do in the future. Her whole miserable life revolves around her own selfish desires and if anyone or anything gets in the way she'll stomp on them just like I did that cockroach in the kitchen today.

"Now, she's gonna get real interested in your life as long as there's no man to get in her way and you're gonna have to put up with it for a while. At least until you can get your feet back on the ground. Because if you don't, she ain't gonna help you at all and from where I sit, you're gonna need all the help you can get."

"Aren't you being a little hard on Momma, Debra? After all, she's always been there everytime we've needed her . . . although I will admit that her help has never come without its price." This last with a rueful smile that reminded Debra of a circus clown.

"Yeah, and that price is usually just a little bit more than anyone can afford," Debra laughed sardonically, "just like today. I don't know about you but I thought that scenario with the kids was just a little much. It's like I said, she made everybody feel good with her help and her cookies and then she had to make everybody feel bad with her drunken diatribe. I hope we inherited more of Daddy than we did of her."

Debra was still smiling but, with that last comment, the smile was more of a grimace of pain than a sign of pleasure. All that aside, however, she really wasn't prepared for her sister's next comments.

"Oh, come on, she really isn't all that different from everyone else's mother. You two are just so alike that you always clash. I don't know who is the more hard headed, you or Momma. I mean, either one of you gets an idea in her head and you can't beat it out of there with a stick. And the way you treat your men . . . I'm amazed Daddy and Joey take all of your bullshit when you two get stupid."

"Whoa, now, Betty Jo, both Momma and I still **have** husbands, we haven't run ours off yet! Maybe you should have learned a little from the way we handle things."

"That's a pretty cruel thing to say, Debra. After all, you have always been the one in the spotlight, doin' those commercials and all. I've been stuck here with three kids and a hyperactive thyroid that makes me fat and miserable. Now just because my marriage is falling apart is no reason to rub salt in the wound."

"I'm not rubbing salt in the wound, but you've got to face some facts in your life. The main reason J. C. left is because you've become so lackadaisical in your life. You're fat because you eat too much, just like your house is dirty because you don't clean it enough. You can't just blame your misfortunes on everybody and everything else. You have to do something about them. You need to get your act straightened out or you're gonna end up a whole hell of a lot lonelier than you are now!"

While Debra was caught up in her oration, Betty Jo couldn't help but think how much she resembled Momma. Maybe just a tad less raunchy, Betty Jo thought, but for someone who doesn't want to end up like Momma, she sure is on the way. Reflecting back just an instant, several vignettes from former times flashed through her mind. In them, Momma would be off on one of her tirades and suddenly Debra's face would take the place of hers. Instead of feeling dread at these thoughts, Betty Jo felt pleasure or vindication, almost elation at the similarities between the two. These good feelings were rapidly replaced by guilt, however, and now Betty Jo had to look away, as from a misjudged child or a lie that was too hard to face straight on.

179

"I may end up lonelier but I sure won't end up meaner. Look, why don't we talk about something else. We obviously don't agree on Momma or her ways. Besides, I'm tired of fighting. It seems like that's all I have done since I don't know when. I thought when the holidays were over everything would be all right and look at the mess I'm in. I don't care about what caused all this shit, I just want a way out of it."

"We just got you started on that part. Look how nice and clean everything is and didn't we have a fantastic day? Well, for the most part, anyway. If I were you I'd try to get in touch with J. C. and see what his plans are. If he doesn't have anything good to say, probably the best thing for you to do is go out and find a lawyer and get started on whatever it is you have to do to get this thing over with. Maybe Joey can get him to come see you."

"Oh, he'll be back all right. He left most of his clothes and all of his personal stuff here. But I know in my bones that our marriage is over and I'm not sure what to do about it. I could be real bitchy about his little girl friend but I haven't exactly been a saint the past few years myself. I wish we could just erase all of that and start over again. It sure wasn't worth the cheap thrills that I got out of it. Take it from me, most things that look real good on the outside, aren't."

Between the wine and the toll taken by the emotional roller coaster that she had been on for what seemed like most of her life, Betty Jo was on a steep downhill slide and Debra wasn't helping much. It was a good thing that she didn't have a mirror to look into at the moment because the image that would reflect back at her wouldn't help the situation either. What she would see was a once pretty but now obviously care-worn thirty something and obese mother of three boys who was not ready for the single parent experience. Her tired eyes had black bags under them from sleepless worrying and her hands were red and peeling from the nervous tension that seemed to always be with her. Her brow was wrinkled and her mouth twisted in a permanent frown that couldn't be erased even with an attempted smile.

Looking up, she gave Debra a half-hearted smile/frown and said, "Not a pretty sight is it? Well, whatever it looks like from the outside isn't half as bad as what it looks like from the inside. But you don't want to hear all of these bad things, do you? You've got a wonderful husband who obviously loves you or he wouldn't put up with your selfish ways, no kids to take up all of your time with their

180

petty inconveniences, and enough money so that you don't have to worry about every dime you spend. Count your blessings, sister, because if you're not careful, you could be in the same fix I'm in!"

In a pig's eye, Debra thought defiantly, there's no way that I could end up like you are now. First, I wouldn't ever let myself go like you have. Second, I'm not going to have any children. And, third, if there's going to be any divorce in my life, I'm going to be the one in control of the situation. It's just like Momma says, you keep them in love with you and they'll do anything you want them to. You just let yourself go so bad that J. C. found someone shinier than you are, that's all.

"I know it's tough, Betty Jo, but everything will get better. You'll see. Why don't we get together after work tomorrow and start in on an exercise program. We'll begin walking a few miles and work up to jogging. Maybe we can get the kids involved too. It'll help take their minds off the goings-on around here. The best defense against this kind of stuff is to get busy."

So began a new era in Betty Jo's life. Every afternoon she and Debra would get together and, if the weather was good, take long walks and talk their heads off. When they couldn't do that they'd go over to Debra's club and, while the kids played tennis or swam in the pool, they'd work out on the Nautilus machines. The exercise was good for their bodies (especially Betty Jo's) and even better for their spirits. Betty Jo, while certainly a long way from svelte, was becoming at least passable and, as she lost part of the weight she had acquired, was not too bad to look at at all. Much to her delight, she even occasionally attracted the attention of some of the dirty old men at the club.

Debra, in the meantime, while helping her sister through her tough times was creating some for herself. As she paid more and more attention to Betty Jo, she paid less and less to Joey. He took the opportunity to really apply himself to his work and the monetary rewards got better and better. He did notice, however, that the travelling was getting pretty old and that he began to miss Debra and their time off together.

Chapter Fourteen

IT WAS ONE WEDNESDAY morning in the late fall when Joey woke up in a hotel room in Houston and it took him what seemed like forever to determine where he was that he knew he needed a break from the action. As soon as he ascertained his location (about sixty seconds, although it felt like an eternity), he got on the phone, canceled all of his appointments for the rest of the week and after packing his bag and calling his office, he got in his car and headed home.

By the time he turned into the driveway it was late afternoon on an overcast day in Dallas. The drive through the newly leafless trees was as gray and dreary as the sky and the house was dark and somehow foreboding instead of friendly and warm. There were no lights on at all and, when he entered the house and called Debra's name to no answer, he was disappointed that she wasn't home.

Joey picked up the phone and called the tennis club but no one had seen her that day. So he dialed Betty Jo's house but after the phone rang ten times, he decided that they must be together somewhere. Finally he called J. C. to see how he was doing.

"J. C., it's Joey, how ya doin' pardner?"

"What do you say, you old rattlesnake? Where the hell are you?"

"I'm at home. I woke up this morning in Houston, couldn't remember where I was and decided that I needed the rest of the week off. Exercising my authority as an up and coming business executive, I just canceled everything and boogied on home. I can't seem to find Debra anywhere, so I thought I'd call you and see if I can buy you some dinner or at least a couple of beers."

"That sounds like a winner to me pardner. I'm takin' a night off from all the young starlets tonight. Why don't we meet at The Rose in about a half hour?"

With that Joey wrote out a quick note to Debra, threw his suitcase in the closet and headed for town. He was looking forward to getting caught up with his old friend since the only side of the continuing saga of J. C. and Betty Jo that he was getting these days was coming from Betty Jo through Debra. He'd been out of town so much recently that he'd lost touch with most of the happenings on the home front. This thought triggered a small alarm in the back of his brain and he vowed to spend more time at home and less time working in the future.

As he walked into the bar, he found himself smiling in the anticipation of a few beers with good ol' J. C. Waving vaguely at a couple of people who looked obscurely familiar, he gave J. C. a big hug.

"Damn, it's been a coon's age since I've seen you, J. C., you look great! Have you lost some weight or what?"

J. C. did, in fact, look better than he had in years. He had lost about twenty pounds and changed his hairstyle to something a little more fashionable. He had never been much of a clothes horse but someone was sure dressing him a lot better these days. Not only was he color coordinated but also his new duds fit him so as to accentuate his recent weight loss. He looked tanned and fit and, when Joey glanced at both of them together in the bar mirror, he was disappointed to see that he himself looked pale and puffy, almost frumpy in his wrinkled business suit.

This triggered the second alarm of the evening and he promised himself that not only would he begin sticking around town more often but also watch what he was eating and begin working out the first thing in the morning. In the meantime, he decided not to look in the mirror again that evening.

"Well, tell me all about it J. C., how goes the war?"

J. C. smiled a wry smile and shook his head, "I thought you'd never ask, my friend. You want the real story or would you settle for some salesman's bullshit?"

Not missing a beat nor waiting for Joey's answer, he continued on, "It started out a little tough and I think it's going to get tougher," he said. "Not with Betty Jo, I think she's resigned to her fate and she says she likes being single. The tough part is the kids. A couple of months ago when I first split, her Momma and Debra went over to the house and helped her get everything cleaned up and in order. She had the best of intentions as far as keeping it that way was concerned but she hasn't changed much and the place is going down-hill fast. She says she can't handle the kids, that they won't help her and do what they're told. I may have to move back home and take them and the house over or it may all go back the way it was."

"By the way, she's out looking for an apartment tonight but I don't know if Debra's with her or not even though they're thicker than thieves these days. The last I heard from Debra she was dead set against Betty Jo movin' out but I don't think that's gonna' make any difference. They've been reading a bunch of that self-help non-sense here recently and all they talk about is "codependence" this and "me" that and "self-esteem" this to the point that she really doesn't have much room for anybody else in her life, much less three growing boys. What the hell is it with late model women, anyway? What happened to the mothering instinct? I think she's actually looking forward to leaving and living without the kids."

This was just the first of many incredulous conversations that J. C. and Joey would have in the near future on this very subject. As developements continued to unfold, both of them would be incessantly astounded by the change in thought processes that had taken place in the women in their lives. Both of these men had been raised by relatively conservative mothers who had happily accepted their roles in life. None of the self-serving, real-estate selling, man-hating propaganda that Debra and Betty Jo had grown up with.

They were satisfied that they had been put on earth to get married, have children and build a fortress of warmth, love and security for their families. If it had been necessary for them to go to work to help provide for their brood, they would not have hesitated for a moment. But, for the most part, they adhered to the beliefs taught to them by their mothers before them. It seemed reasonable to them that what had worked for their mothers should be good enough for their own lives and those of their daughters-in-law. Although they were open to contemporary ideas and new ways of living, they were reluctant to blindly embrace the radical thinking of these "new women."

They were especially wary of the concepts that these seventies ladies espoused because there seemed no definitive direction or cohesion to them at all. The overwhelming presumption on which all of these new ideas appeared to be based was one of extraordinary selfishness which of course left no room for the family unit that they believed in so completely. The same family unit, by the way, that had preserved and protected the human race for as long as anyone could remember.

Although steeped in the pragmatism that exemplified the masculine of the species, Joey and J. C. believed what their mothers had taught them over the years. They were not at all hesitant to take a shot at something novel or unique but they would at least think it all the way through to its conclusion before jumping in with both feet. Most of the new ideas that they had seen had also had some new consequences attached to them and, as they continued to mature, they found out that it was much more comfortable to learn from someone else's mistakes than from firsthand experience. They didn't believe in change for change's sake and were startled by this untried direction that their wives and their wives' friends seemed to be taking.

"Maybe it's just a ploy to get you back in the house. It could be she thinks that once you get back home you may realize how much you missed her and the boys and that you won't want to leave. Maybe this is a last ditch try to save her marriage, old buddy. By the way, think there's any chance of that?"

"That's the strangest part. I thought exactly the same thing in the beginning but I can tell you from talking to her that she hasn't got the slightest inclination in that direction. And I can also tell you that, from talking to the kids, they don't give a damn if she leaves or not. They think that she's a fat slob who only cares about herself. You know how selfish kids are and she is so busy finding the "real me" that she hardly gives them the time of day. This whole thing is working out kind of back-asswards. I thought I'd be the one living in some little apartment with her getting everything and now she wants me to have it all."

While J. C. was filling him in on all of the latest poop, Joey was carefully observing every facial expression and move that J. C. made in order to try to assess how he was really taking all of this stuff. Much to his surprise, he had never seen J. C. so calm and positive in the many years that he had known him. Instead of acting like this was going to cramp his style now that he was a single man, J. C.

looked as if he were anxious to get back home and raise his family. This could be the best thing that ever happened, Joey thought, maybe with J. C. back rearing his own brood it will take him off the hook. The more J. C. talked the happier Joey got and J. C.'s spirits seemed to soar right along with his.

"To tell you the truth, I've been feeling real guilty about leaving the kids like I did. You know, Betty Jo's a good old girl and all that stuff but she can't take care of herself much less a family. She isn't making enough money to keep her in junk food and she's so heavy that she's tired all the time. She and Debra started working out a couple of months ago but that didn't last long and now she's gotten into this new woman thing . . . to tell you the truth, I probably got out just in time. I think she's thought herself into a corner and there ain't no savin' her now. If she's trying to prove something it sure isn't to me. It's got to be for someone else."

In the end this would prove to be most prophetic comment of the J. C. saga . . . it was true that Betty Jo was trying to prove something to someone other than him. She was trying to prove something to all of those mysterious spirits that had been haunting her all of her life. Her "mother" for instance, not the one who had just visited her recently but the one that she dreamed about, the one who was only there in her mind; and the "father" that was really at home and not out on the well; and the "boyfriend" whose breath always smelled like spearmint gum and who never pointed out how fat she was and was always happy to see her even when it was her period; and the beautiful "children" she had always wanted who loved her so dearly and loved her only for what she was, not for what they wanted her to be. Yeah, she was trying to prove it for something or someone else but by the time that she had all of this proved, who the hell was going to know it anyway?

It sure wasn't going to be Momma. She wouldn't know love if it smacked her in the face . . . much less any other feeling, for that matter. She was so consumed by her own selfishness that she would never have time for anyone or anything else. And now J. C. was gone and no matter what she did she couldn't hurt him. He'd already seen the other side and was no longer under her spell.

Maybe she could prove it for Daddy, maybe he would finally show her that he loved her. She could almost smell his aftershave as she thought about him giving her the hug that she had never gotten. He was so close that one Christmas . . . but then Momma had come in all drunk and . . . and there were those children. J. C. suddenly realized that he had been lost for awhile and that he was actually in a bar with his old buddy, Joey. "Sorry, I went away there for awhile, pardner. I was just thinking about Betty Jo and it sure was sad. That might have been the first time that I really could empathize with her in a long time. You know, it's a shame that she couldn't have been here to share it with me," J. C. said with an ironic, lopsided grin.

To Joey, who was sitting across from J. C. wondering what was going on in his head for what seemed like forever, this last remark seemed awfully cold and callous. As a matter of fact, he looked across at his friend and wondered where it had come from. He knew that the way that he heard the thought couldn't have been the way it was meant. After all, J. C. was a much more tolerant man than Joey had ever thought about being and there was no way that he would have been that cruel to Betty Jo. So Joey knitted his brow in puzzlement and looked hard at his pal.

"If you really feel that way, why don't you call her and tell her? She would probably love to hear that you were thinking of her and that you understand how she feels."

"She doesn't want to hear what I was thinking, Joey. I'm telling you she's hung up on this "me" thing and that wasn't the part that I was empathizing with. I was feeling all of those experiences that she missed while she was growing up. The ones that resulted in the way she is thinking now. I'd be willing to bet you that she has been so disappointed in the fact that life isn't like the picture in her mind from what she's been taught and read that she's become cynical about the whole system."

"When you stop and think about it, men stop believing in fairy tales at some point in their lives while women keep right on with the facade forever. It's as if they don't want to see the real world at all. Women are afraid that if they lose this aspect of their thinking, they will lose their femininity."

"Have you ever read any of those women's publications? You know how they sort of look at the world through a gauze filter so that all of the rough edges are smoothed over and things have a kind of ethereal look and feel? How husbands come home and spend long hours talking to them about their new hairstyle, gardening and so and so's wife that they absolutely despise? And understand it all?! Reality is a tough old booger bear and, when all of the facade is stripped away, it can be extremely traumatic for women."

187

"That's about where I think Betty Jo is at the current time. The trouble is, when you are traumatized like that its not the time for rational thought or decision making and she's making some pretty profound decisions right now."

"Hey, J. C.," Joey blurted out as the third alarm of the evening rang shrilly in his subconscious, "you don't think that Debra is falling for any of this psychobabble do you? That would be all I'd need right now is for my ol' lady to get caught up in that crap, too."

"All I can tell you, old buddy, is that they are closer than they have ever been as long as I've known them. That doesn't mean that Debra is as irrational as Betty Jo but they have been spending a lot of time together and you know how people get when they're upset. The one that's the listener a lot of the time gets caught up in the one that's distraught's feelings and substitutes them for her own."

"Oh man, don't even start thinking like that! We don't need **two** divorces in this family. I hope I don't have to go through a bunch of those inane rationalizations this evening when I get home. I'm really not up for all of that tonight."

Neither one of them wanted to continue with this uncomfortable conversation at the time so they went on to other things. J. C. brought Joey up to date on his love life and Joey brought J. C. up to date on all of the latest jokes he had heard on the road. Finally, after they had had a few more beers and a whole bunch of laughs (some of them nervous, some phoney and some genuine), they decided to forego dinner since Joey was tired and needed some rest. Actually, he was anxious to see if Debra was really into all of this Betty Jo stuff and how it would affect his life.

They got up from the bar around ten o'clock and hugged each other goodby with that shake-your-hand-and-clap-you-on-the-back routine that men do (the psychobabblists call it male bonding or some designation of that ilk) and walked out the door laughing at each other and the turns their lives were taking. Joey left J. C. at his car and, after reiterating that everything was going to be all right (both of them with more hope than confidence), kept walking down the sidewalk of the little bar and restaurant strip center toward his car. As he passed another one of his favorite haunts to his surprise he came upon Debra's car parked out front. After circling it once to make sure it was hers, he went inside to see if he could find her.

He was a little bit put off to discover her sitting in one of the

188

back booths enrapt in conversation with none other than his old buddy, Jimmy Jeff Stewart. There were a couple of half-empty wine glasses and some pretzels in between them but they were both leaning forward almost nose to nose in conversation so intense that they never saw Joey coming.

"Well, what a pleasant surprise," Joey grinned as he slid into the booth next to Debra, "I've been lookin' all over for you darlin'." How you doin' Jimmy Jeff? It's been awhile since I've seen you!"

His smile was not returned by either one of them but, for some reason he couldn't nail down at the moment, it didn't surprise him. Instead, they not only looked stunned at his appearance but also not real happy with the fact that he had broken in on their conversation. As a matter of fact, they both seemed to be having a bit of a problem composing themselves and Jimmy Jeff was fumbling with something under the table.

"What in the world are you doing here, Joey?" Debra giggled nervously, as alarm number four went off in Joey's head. "We . . . I didn't expect you back until Friday."

"Surprise, surprise y'all. I woke up this morning in Houston and decided that I have been working way too much and not spending enough time with the people that I love so I just up and came home. I tried to find you but no one knew where you were so I met J. C. for a couple of beers at The Rose and was on my way home when I saw your car out front. Whatcha got under the table there, JJ?"

"Aw, it's just an ol' book I been readin'. One of them self-help things that are goin' around these days. It ain't much."

"Well let me see it a minute. I didn't realize you were into that kind of bullshit. I always thought you were a little bit more savvy than to rely on crap like that. Let's see what the latest new ideas in human relationships are."

"Like I said Joey, it ain't much. I don't think you'd even be interested in it. Hey, look! It's almost ten-thirty and I got to be at work at seven in the mornin'. One of those early mornin' staff meetin's don'tcha know. I better get my fat ass on home. See ya'll later. Give me a call Joey and we'll go have a beer or somethin'."

With that and a wave, Jimmy Jeff gathered up his books and was out the door in a flash. Joey looked around at Debra who was very carefully studying the table and decided he'd better get up and order a beer. As he stood at the bar waiting for his drink, he noticed Debra heading for the restrooms.

189

"You want another drink, darlin'?" he called into the mirror at her image in front of him.

"Yeah, I'll take another glass of wine," she replied not looking at him. She seemed kind of preoccupied with getting to the ladies room. Almost as if she was headed to shelter in a storm or away from Momma when she was on a tear.

Joey carried their drinks to the booth and sat down to reflect on the rather startling events that had just taken place. He had not expected her to be with JJ and, even though he expected them to be surprised, he hadn't counted on the reaction he had gotten. Both of them seemed genuinely upset by his arrival. Almost as if he had interrupted something that he was not supposed to be in on. Stop thinking that way now Joey, he thought, don't make something out of nothing. But the same fourth alarm buzzed in his mind again as he pictured Debra giggling nervously when he sat down. She always giggled when she told a lie.

When Debra approached the table from the bathroom she was an entirely different person from the one who had left him just a few minutes ago. She gave him a dazzling smile when he looked up at her and, as Joey stood up to let her in the booth, she gave him a welcome home kiss that made him nearly forget all about the preceding developments. What the hell, he thought, if I had been sitting here talking to one of her friends, her walking in would have set me back a little too. But then again I probably wouldn't have been sitting in here at ten o'clock at night with one of her friends while she was out of town, would I?

Joey knew that this kind of thinking was harmful but he was feeling pretty uncomfortable about the whole thing and he couldn't seem to shake the disagreeable feelings he was having. So he hugged her again and told her he loved her. She reciprocated in kind and gave him another one of those hungry-horny kisses that made him want to carry her out of the bar to the car.

"Well, what did ol' JJ have to say? Lost his job again or just his girlfriend . . . or both?"

His attempt at an amused grin didn't entirely fail but it was pretty obvious that he was very uneasy at the time. Good friend, husband, provider, loverboy Joey needed some stroking! Debra smiled and wiggled a little closer as she caressed his leg under the table. She got close enough so that he couldn't really focus too well on her face and the rubbing and the sweet smell of her was taking his mind off his deleterious condition. Unfortunately, Debra giggled anxiously again as she began telling him of her evening.

"To tell the truth," she tittered uneasily, "I was on my way home from shopping when JJ honked at me and waved me over into the parking lot. We talked for a few minutes, mainly about you, and he said he was coming in here for a drink and why didn't I join him. I knew you wouldn't mind so I parked my car and trotted on inside. We started talking about this and that and the next thing I knew in you came.

"He's really gotten into self-evaluation and improving himself and he got out those books to show me what he had found out about himself. It was really interesting. JJ is not nearly the person that I thought he was. He's really much more complex than I would have believed. And, yes, he's without a girlfriend now and says that he's going to change jobs again. But let's talk about you. Why did you come home early?"

Joey wasn't at all satisfied with her answer but he wasn't sure that he wanted to pursue it either. Knowing how shallow and self serving Jimmy Jeff was there was no telling what he had on his mind or what he said to Debra for that matter. Add these facts to his disconcerting conversation with J. C. about Betty Jo and Debra and Joey could smell major problems in the wind. It was probably good fortune or maybe the combination of beer, rubbing, loneliness and libido, that caused his mind to drift down below his belt but in time it would only prove to postpone his undoing. Putting aside the decision as to whether or not to pursue the JJ discussion, he took the easy way out.

"It's just like I told you, I woke up this morning in a strange bed in a strange bedroom and it just didn't set well with me. I have been getting increasingly tired of travelling and being away from you and our home. I miss you more and more these days and I'd really like to cut down on my out of town time. I'm going to start looking for somebody to help me out and maybe even sell the business to first thing tomorrow morning."

Debra brightened even more as she heard these words of vulnerability. This was what all of the psychological drivel that she and Betty Jo had recently embraced was all about. If Joey would only show that he was in the least bit emotionally crippled, things would work out all right. The whole premise of the seventies psycho-culture was built on human frailty and the blending of male-female emotional reactions. Unisex, androgyny, and homosexuality, though abhorred by theologians, society and the common man for eons, could now come out of the closet and be accepted as the neo-feminists tried to make men and women one and the same.

The first to embrace this new way of thinking were the "artistic left." Those folks on either coast who were truly confused as to their sexuality. As *Cosmo* and *People,* those bastions of latter day truth-seekers, began to pick up on these misconceptions, the general populace followed right along. Soon the talk shows were rife with outrageously coiffed and bedecked dandies who espoused maniac-ially skewed observations on any and every subject imaginable. The immediate impact wasn't felt in all arenas of society because most of the talk shows of the period came on long after the most impres-sionable members of our culture were fast asleep. As time went on and the word spread, however, soon all facets of civilization were tinged with this obviously contaminated thinking.

Upon reflection, and in the light of 20/20 hindsight, it really was necessary to foster and nurture these ludicrous irrationalities since they were the fodder that fueled the psychiatric machine that was making so much money for the media. Really now, how could all of the sensationalist publications, those dirt bags written off long ago by all but the most deficient in judgment and good sense, exist and even flourish without this new proclivity to believe the most implausible suppositions. This kind of outrageous thought process was expected from those particular periodicals but all of a sudden the whole world was being bombarded by this insanity in all milieus.

Weakness was now strength as the men in the fern bars soon found out. For if men showed that they were "human" (read prone to feminine feelings and weaknesses), they immediately were branded by the new women as sensitive and therefore desirable. It is interesting to note that the qualities that have always been desirable in the masculine segment of the population, the ones that ensured survival and the proliferation of the species, were now set aside in the quest for a new way of life.

It seems rather presumptuous in retrospect to think that years of human development could be so radically redefined by such a dis-tinctly impaired minority. To take the stand that the opposite of what had been proven over time to be the correct order for society and without any rational substantiation other than "it doesn't have to be that way" could only create havoc in the world. And Joey, in his physically and emotionally weakened state, was falling right into the trap.

"That's exactly what Jimmy Jeff and I were talking about all evening, Joey. When you give yourself up to the pursuit of the almighty dollar you also give up your humanity. There are more important things in life than cars and trucks and planes and big boy's toys. When you can't remember the last time you noticed the trees blooming in spring because you were always thirty thousand feet above them in an airplane going to some business meeting, you lose a very vital part of life. Sometimes it's better not to have so many material things but have a better quality of life."

Dammit, Joey thought, that son of a bitch Jimmy Jeff is trying to justify his inability to make a living or keep a relationship alive with a women by belittling my success in business. Isn't that always the way, he mused, you give someone all that you can afford to try to help them enjoy their dismal lives and the next thing you know they want everything that you have. Well he'll damnsure have a tough time taking my stuff away from me. I've worked too long and too hard for all these material things that he professes are unnecessary. Besides, isn't it natural for us to always try to improve the quality of life? Isn't that what the human spirit is all about? Isn't that what drives the human race?

"Well, where would you like to start, darlin'? I could just quit my job and take a position as a day laborer. Get up every morning, punch in at seven-thirty, punch out at five and come home to a cozy little apartment. Of course, we'd have to give up the tennis club and our house and the horses and these nice cars and take up something more cerebral like watching television or reading *National Enquirer.* We'd have a lot of time to think about spring and summer and fall and winter since we wouldn't have any money to go anywhere or do anything."

"Look, Debra, I'll admit that I've been overdoing the work thing here in the last few months but you know part of the reason is that you have been so busy with your sister and the rest of your family. I figured you needed to spend time with them in order to help them and yourself. At the same time, some tremendous opportunities in my business presented themselves and I decided, not really consciously, it just kinda happened, to take advantage of them."

"The good news is that things have worked out well and we have a lot to look forward to even if you and Jimmy Jeff don't think that material things are important. I'll tell you what, he may think that there is beauty in poverty but I'm not going to try it on his advice. At the rate he's going, all we're going to have to do to experience deprivation is to watch him anyway. If he blows one more job in this town, he'll learn all of that insanity that he's preaching firsthand."

"So you think that you can really find self-fulfillment in all of these material things that we are accumulating? You don't think that the quality of life is better when you have less distractions? When things aren't so complicated and fast paced? You don't think we were really better off when we had less?," Debra was really intense at this point.

"Let me put it this way, darlin', your sister is about to uncomplicate her life. Do you think that she is going to find happiness in her new world? For that matter, do you think anything is going to be that different, except for the fact that she is going to be awfully lonely and awfully poor. I'll tell you something, and you can quote me on this, she is just about to see what misery is all about. Maybe we need to get her and Jimmy Jeff together. In a year or two they will probably tell us something a whole hell of a lot different than what they're preaching today!"

With this last parting shot, Joey got up and went to the bathroom. When he came back out, he was surprised to see the booth empty. He looked outside and saw Debra walking toward her car. Thinking that she was getting something that she had forgotten, he sat down and ordered them each a drink. When he looked up again it was to see her tail lights winking at him as she drove away. Well ain't that a bitch, he thought as he finished his beer, laid some money on the table and walked out. What the hell is going on here?? On the way home, all alone and wondering why Debra was acting so strangely while knowing innately what the general trend was going to be when he went through the door, Joey pondered why he was going through all of this again. It seemed that everytime things were going the way that all the books on men and women talked about, something like this would come up and nothing that he had read was relevant. Reason was blown out the window and insanity prevailed. The good news was, after all the fighting was over the sex was usually pretty damn hot. The bad news was, it was always after the fighting and less and less worth it as time went on.

Cruising slowly up the driveway trying to resist the impulse to turn around and leave just as he had left Houston that morning, Joey

194

steeled himself for the trials ahead. Imagine his astonishment when he pulled into the garage and Debra's car was not there. Thinking that she might have had trouble along the way, he immediately turned around and retraced his route. Then to be sure he hadn't missed her, he drove back a different way and when he still didn't find her he retraced it again. Finally, about an hour later he gave up and pulled into the garage only to find her car there.

Oh man, he thought looking at his watch, now she'll think I stayed out just to piss her off. He walked in the door to total silence and only the light over the kitchen stove to welcome him. Finding no one at home downstairs, he carefully ascended the steps, not knowing what to expect. He rounded the corner into his bedroom taking each tenative step more carefully as he went and there was Debra, all propped up in bed with her night light on, smilin' like a 'possum in the moonlight.

"Where've you been, Joey? I thought you'd never get home!"

The malevolence in her eye was so strong that he had to look down and walk away. He found refuge in the closet as he took his time disrobing. Damn, he thought, what in the world is going on here. I've seen her mad before but this time the distaste in her eye is more than I can stand. I'm glad she doesn't have a gun.

All of a sudden he realized how seriously he was taking himself and almost laughing out loud he peeked around the corner of the closet to see if the coast was clear . . . and there was Debra peering around the corner right back at him not a foot from his face stifling her hysteria with her hand.

"Had you goin' for a while there, didn't I?" She giggled, "you didn't know whether to shit or get off the pot, did you? Come on let's go to bed."

Joey was so relieved and, at the same time, addled that he forgot everything that he had thought about on the way home. As he crawled between the covers she immediately began hugging, rubbing and kissing him and, naturally, when all of that was over it was time for a nap anyway, wasn't it? Strange how this all works out, he thought as he drifted off into a deep sleep.

What had happened to Joey wasn't all that strange or far-fetched. It is just hard for men to comprehend the cerebral mechanizations of women. Or maybe it isn't so hard to comprehend it, it's just hard to fathom them. Or maybe it's really "e," none of the above. That's a nice cop-out isn't it, none of the above? Well, why wasn't it any of the above? Why didn't any of this bullshit have anything to do with any of the bullshit that came before? Why was all of this so confusing? But then again, why was all of this happening?

Looks like it's back to the "mysteries" of womanhood. Those unexplainable idiosyncrasies that differentiate between the sexes. The secondary reasons that men and women are attracted to each other. For without the mystery the lure of one for the other would probably be vastly diminished. In the seventies the changing attitudes of modern women coupled with the increase in and the refinement of communications was auspiciously bringing an end to the majority of these enigmas.

Chapter Fifteen

JOEY AWOKE REFRESHED BUT still ill at ease. In an attempt to shake off his funky mood, he jumped into a cold shower. As he danced around under the icy darts raining out of the shower head, a Fleetwood Mac song began playing in his mind. All of a sudden he stopped dancing and humming as he realized that the music hadn't played in his head for a long, long time. When he took a few moments to deliberate on this revelation, he noted that life used to be a lot better when each day started with a song weaving its way into his subconscious. He had felt for some time that something had been lacking in his lifestyle but, up until now, he hadn't quite been able to put his finger on it.

So now you come back, he mused, I wish I knew how to turn you back on just in case you go away again. Shaking his head in puzzlement and relief he smiled inwardly at himself and went back to suds and song. After a few more minutes of the chilling blast, Joey jumped out of the shower, towelled himself briskly and started to sing out loud.

"Well, I been 'fraid of changin', cause I've built my life around you . . . but time makes you bolder and people get older . . . an' I'm gettin' older too . . . So if you see my reflection in the snow covered hills . . . . will the landlslide bring you down??

Even though he felt much better, the ominous tone of the

words of the song started him thinking about the events of the night before. It galled him that all of the wonderful things that had happened in bed last night didn't begin to make up for the unanswered questions that had plagued him on that weird ride home. It made him very uncomfortable to think about getting back into that conversation with Debra again. He thought about J. C. telling him several times in the past "As you get older you'll learn, with women, if you don't want to know the answer, don't ask the question! There are some things it's just best not to know." Maybe this is one of those times, he reflected as he went into the closet to dress.

By the time he got downstairs, Debra had gotten up and gone out to tend the livestock, so he got in his car and drove down to the barn to say goodbye. As he drove up to the door and had to holler to get her attention, he wondered if she would have missed his goodbye or if it was only a nuisance to her. One of those "honey do's" that are necessary when you are married to someone, like taking out the trash and Valentine's Day . . . when she came out of the barn the look on her face made it obvious that he didn't want to ask the question and, after a perfunctory goodbye, he drove on to work, singing "Landslide" in earnest.

Having left Houston so abruptly, there were a lot of explanations necessary to start off the day and he wasn't at all in the mood to make them. In order to seduce himself into getting it done, he decided that the sooner he made his excuses, the sooner he could leave. Hell, it was already Thursday. Maybe he oughta take the rest of the week off.

Buoyed up by that thought, he put his head down and with a deep breath dialed the first number. The next thing he knew it was two o'clock and he was finished. Telling his secretary that he was off to an appointment, he almost sprinted to the door to avoid any further conversation and/or telephone calls. By the time he made it to the car his smile had changed to a frown but that soon faded as the music started in his head again. He drove to his old favorite midweek hangout, ordered a beer and made a bee line for the phone. It took all of about thirty seconds to talk J. C. into playing hooky along with him.

"Boy, you just don't give a damn anymore, do you pardner? You up and bag out on all of your appointments, come home early and then take the day off. It's a good thing you're friendly with the boss or you'd be in a world of shit!" J. C. smiled with relish as he ordered a beer, pulled his tie loose and unbuttoned his collar.

198

"Ah," he sighed, easing back in his chair. "What prompted this moment of lucidity in your otherwise workaholic life?"

"Funny you should ask that, J. C., actually I'm gettin' kinda' bummed out about all of this Jimmy Jeff, Debra, Betty Jo and self-help senselessness. I fended off most of that stuff when it went through the country club last year but now it looks like she's really become serious over some of this confabulation (another really wonderful word). She's lookin' at me real funny these days and I want to trust her but I'm not sure I can. What do you know about her and JJ? Have they been spending a lot of time together recently or do you know?"

"Hey, look old buddy, it's pretty obvious from my track record that I don't know much about this man-woman stuff but I will tell you one thing, if you look hard enough for something bad you'll find it. I didn't even look for it and it came around and found me. Now don't you go out and foul up what you two have got going with each other. Of all the people I know, you guys have the best chance of making it of any man and woman that I have ever seen so don't go messing it up by doing something stupid."

"Hell, JJ is just a poor misguided drunk who doesn't have much to look forward to. Most of the women that he attracts leave him after they see through his bullshit which usually lasts about three dates. Anybody with any brains at all wouldn't give him the time of day. C'mon, pardner, Debra at least has enough common sense to see through that phony act of his, doesn't she? "

"I wish I felt as confident as you do about her, old buddy. I'm telling you something weird is going on here." At this point the intensity in Joey's eyes and voice made J. C. sit up and take notice. "I mean, I'm no expert on the female sex, no man is, but I will tell you that there is trouble in my camp. I haven't seen anything like this in all of the time that she and I have been together. She looks at me differently, acts curiously and tricks me everytime that I let my guard down. Maybe it's just the fact that I have been away from home a lot recently and the paranoia is catching up with me but I could swear to you that something bad is going on in my home. You know me, I'm not much for emotional foolishness but it's bothering me none the less. What do you think?"

"I think it's what you just said it was, a bunch of emotional foolishness. You don't have anything to worry about, especially from anyone that I know. Remember all of that conversation that we had about how when one woman is having trouble it tends to infect all of her friends and they all have trouble? It sounds like you may have some of the very same problems that you are worried about her having. Why do you want to create problems? Don't you think that they'll find you quick enough anyway? Just because I have chosen to get my marriage over with is no reason for you to do the same. Hey! I'm starting to sound a lot like **you**, aren't I?"

With this J. C. broke out into a nervous laugh which caused Joey to join right in. Although his wasn't nearly as genuine as J. C.'s because he still had that bad feeling in the pit of his stomach. You know, that dread that you feel when you don't know why you feel it. The cold ball of quease that rolls around right under your heart just when you've forgotten about the bills that were due a week ago or the problem with your boss or employees. The little worry wart that turns your bowels into water if you let it take you over. Most of the time he could turn it on or off at will. Sometimes he'd turn it on just to teach himself a little humility when he was getting too full of himself. But this was the first time that he could remember when he couldn't quite make it go away and laughter wasn't helping a bit.

Fighting back the hysteria that was trying to sweep him away, he got up and headed for the security of the men's room, that porcelain port of safety during times of emotional storms or embarrassment. He had been hiding out in the bathroom during periods like this as long as he could remember. The cold tile floors and mirrored walls somehow comforted him as they reminded him with their images and echoes that he was still alive. Standing in front of the urinal in that familiar hand-on-hip pose that men know so well, the anxiety that he had been feeling seemed to drain out of him as he relieved his bladder and ceremoniously flushed his troubles right on down the drain. On his way out of the john, he waved at the clown that grinned back at him from the mirror. Boy, I'm glad that's over he thought as he went back to his beer and his buddy.

"If you don't mind, I'll tell you something else that's bothering me, my friend," Joey said as he sat back down, "and you tell me what you think again? Ok?"

J. C. smiled wryly as he thought about what was to come. Even though it probably wasn't anything but imagination, his friend **was** worried and listening to his tale of woe wasn't much of a price to pay for all of the things that Joey had done for him. He could almost anticipate the story as he reflected on the events in his own life in the recent past. Thinking smugly that at least he didn't have to put up with any of that married crap anymore, he let out an audible sigh.

"C'mon, old buddy, lay it on me!"

"Okay, remember last night when you went home. Well, I was walking down the sidewalk to my car when I saw Debra's car parked in front of The Pub. So I went inside to say hi and who is she sitting with but ol' JJ and believe me the two of them are right up in each other's faces talkin' about somethin' that looked to be mighty heavy duty. They didn't even see me until I said hello and when I did they both looked like they'd been caught with their hands in the cookie jar."

"I sat down next to Debra so she couldn't leave and caught ol' JJ tryin' to hide this book under the table. He told me it was one of those self-help things but he wouldn't let me see it and, even though he knew I was going to buy him a drink, he got out of there as fast as he could. I don't know, the whole thing threw me off."

"Anyway, when he left, I got up to order a drink and, as soon as I moved out of the way, Debra scooted into the bathroom. Now I didn't know what to think! When she came out, she started huggin' up on me and changin' the subject so that I never got a chance to ask her what was going on when I came in. Then I kind of took a little jab at all of this bullshit that JJ is apparently feeding her and went to the bathroom myself."

"Imagine my surprise when I came back and saw her walking out toward her car! Well, you know me, I figgered she forgot something and ordered us another drink. The next thing I know, she's driving out of the parking lot!"

By this time J. C. was leaning forward in his seat as he began getting into the story. The smile that he started out with had cycled from smug, to fixed, to crooked . . . to gone, as he started to see the pattern developing. A feeling of *deja vu* overpowered him as he struggled to keep a calm, almost disinterested look on his face. Joey continued.

"So I paid the tab and headed on home. Well, when I got there she wasn't home yet. Thinking that she'd had car trouble or needed gas or something, I retraced the route we usually take but I still didn't see her car. So I tried a different way and then back home again. By now it was after midnite and this time her car was in the garage. As I went upstairs, I started thinking, oh shit! she'll think I stayed out late just to piss her off and sure enough when I walk into the bedroom . . . Well, if looks could kill, I wouldn't be sittin' here tellin' you this story. Anyhow, I split to the closet to dump my clothes and when I peeked around the corner there she was laughing at me, like she'd been joking all along or something!"

"Don't tell me, Joey," J. C. grinned wryly, "then she jumps your bones and off you go to sleep, feeling like you just dodged another bullet. Sounds to me like she just outsmarted you, buddy. You know, there probably isn't anything to all of this stuff, but if I've said it once I've said it a thousand times. If you don't want to hear the answer . . . Don't ask the question!"

This last they finished in unison and it made them both laugh but again Joey's was forced and unfulfilling, kinda like last night's sexual encounter. Only last night, Debra was Joey and Joey was J. C., or vice versa . . . or something.

"At any rate," J. C. rambled on, this time not so sincerely, "I wouldn't worry about it too much. There's no telling what is going through her mind what with me and Betty Jo's deal and all. I'm really sorry that my situation is causing you so many problems but it's too late now, man! The good news is, it'll all be over pretty soon and everything should go back to normal . . . whatever that is." This last trailed off lamely into the beer and popcorn that J. C. was cramming his mouth full of as he talked.

Joey could see that things weren't going to progress too much from here so he changed the subject to work and J. C.'s girlfriends and such. He tried to get into the conversation and forget his own troubles but he found himself looking at his watch so much that he finally gave up and, picking up the tab, called it a day.

"Well, I better get on home," Joey said looking up from his watch. "You know how it is with us old married farts. If I don't get home soon my old lady will be bitchin' for the rest of the week. Anything goin' on this weekend with you?"

"Yeah, I got a sales meeting up at Lake Murray this weekend and I'm gonna sneak Taffy into my room. That way when it gets real boring, I'll just tell everybody I got the green apple two-step and take a little break. It'll beat the hell out of spending the weekend with a bunch of hairy-legged old salesmen whose only entertainment is drinking free beer and lying about how much they can sell! Hey, look, everything will probably be all right in the mornin' anyway. She probably is just tired of you bein' gone so much. Why don't you stay home a little more for awhile? That ought to straighten everything out. I'll talk to you when I get back on Sunday . . . maybe stop by for a beer on the way home, okay?"

"Yeah, come on by. I don't think we've got anything planned. We'll probably just be hangin' out."

They got up and gave each other a hug and headed for the door. As he walked to his car, Joey was relieved to see that it was still light outside. He didn't think that a ride home in the dark would suit his mood too well. Turning the radio up as loud as he could stand it, he headed on home hoping that maybe the noise would make him stop thinking about all of this stuff. Maybe if he didn't bring it up again, it would all just go away. Suuure, Joey!

When he pulled up in the drive, he was dismayed . . . no, kind of pissed off, to see Jimmy Jeff's beat up pickup truck parked in front of the house. He considered this while putting his car in the garage and tried to lift his spirits by thinking that maybe ol' Jeff was just the diversion he needed to lighten the tone of all of the extraneous rhetoric that seemed to be enveloping him these days.

He walked inside determined to be upbeat and nonchalant and it almost worked. Until he saw Debra and Jimmy Jeff sitting at the kitchen table talking in earnest and this time ol' JJ didn't even bother to cover up the book that was laying on the table between them.

"Hey, what's goin' on y'all? How you doin', JJ? Anyone for a cold beer?"

"Bring us both one, Joey, "Debra replied, "all of this talk is makin' me real dry and I know Jimmy Jeff won't turn one down! But neither one of us is going to get anything to drink till I get a kiss! C'mere, you sweet thing!"

This gesture would have been just right if it wasn't for the fact that the whole time she was talking to him, she was looking sideways at JJ. Who, in turn, could take about a half a second of her eyes before staring fixedly out the window. Pausing for just a beat too long as she continued to try to get Jimmy Jeff's attention, Debra recovered quickly and beamed up at Joey like he was a piece of candy or somethin'. Not wanting to take a chance on another scene and still buoyed up by the toll that the moment was taking on poor old JJ, Joey bent over and gave her a good one, right on the lips.

"My, my, Joey but you sure haven't forgotten how to kiss. Run over and get us a beer quick, honey, now I'm hot **and** dry!"

With this she started giggling and JJ got up uncomfortably and walked to the refrigerator. "I'll get the beer while y'all get all your foolin' around over with. Sheeit, remember y'all are performin' in front of a man that's been starved for any kind of female companionship for the best part of a month! Hold it down, now, will y'all?"

Jimmy Jeff was trying to be funny but his eyes weren't laughing as he turned around from the refrigerator. Debra, on the other hand, was giggling as if she were the Queen of The May. Joey joined right in with the laughter if only because it was making JJ so uncomfortable. As he opened his beer, he wondered why he had put up with the sumbitch all of these years! The goddam leech only came over to drink his beer or mooch something else, anyway.

Just before he got carried away with the feelings in the room, he thought to himself, whoa, Joey, this isn't going to do you any good. No matter what is going on here, you've got to keep your cool!! Walking quickly to the table he picked up the book before Jimmy Jeff could get back from the refrigerator, opened it to the overleaf and found an inscription to Debra from JJ.

Debra,
> How long does it take you to look at a horseshoe?
>> Jimmy Jeff

The inscription was obviously in reference to an old joke that Jimmy Jeff liked to tell about how fast a cowboy threw down a horseshoe that had burned the grunt out of his fingers, once he discovered that it had just come out of the blacksmith's white hot forge. Turning back the cover to look at the title, Joey discovered that the book was, in fact, one of those self-help pieces of garbage that he had seen reviewed in the *Dallas Morning News* recently. It seems it had to do with people who were trapped in a marriage that they really didn't want to be in but didn't know how to get out of. At the end of the book was a list of scenarios that purported to make the task a lot easier.

"Jimmy Jeff!" He declared, "how thoughtful of you to give this book to Debra! Now, do y'all want to tell me just what the hell is going on here or do I need to come over and talk to you up close and personal?"

"Hey, look, Joey," Jimmy Jeff stammered, backing toward the door, "me and Debra were just talking the other night . . . To tell the truth, she brought it up . . . anyway . . . "

"Now, just you wait a minute, you yellow bastard! I didn't

bring anything up!" Debra was beside herself, screaming like a woman possessed, "You're the one that started talking about how Joey was gone all of the time and didn't I get lonely and how all Joey could think about was the almighty dollar, remember? Don't you go blaming all of that bullshit on me!!"

Jimmy Jeff was now backing hell-bent-for-leather for the door with Debra in hot pursuit screaming at the top of her lungs.

"Come back here and own up to what you've been telling me, you asshole! Tell Joey what you were saying as he drove up! God-damn you Jeff, if you really believe all of that shit, come back here! Be a man for once in your life! "

By this time, Jimmy Jeff had made it through the door, jumped into his battered old pick-up that seemed to start of its own accord and was backing out of the drive spinning gravel as he went. Debra, in the meantime, stopped her screaming, started sobbing in great huge shudders and, spinning around quickly, grabbed Joey and hugged him tightly, keeping him from getting outside.

"Oh, Joey, stay with me! Stay with me please! I'm sorry, so sorry! I can't believe I was listening to all of his bullshit but he sounded so sincere, so lost, like a little boy . . . but nothing happened, I swear it! Oh, I can't believe he can be so two-faced. Can you ever forgive me for being such a fool?"

By now the whole thing was playing like a second-rate soap opera and Joey wasn't having a whole lot of it. It seemed to him that somewhere in some lost nightmare, he had already played out this scene. Not only was the dialogue phony but her blockade of JJ's escape almost seemed staged to him. Dammit, he thought, I knew the bastard was up to something but I didn't think he had the audacity to try anything like that in my own backyard with me around. Now I've got to go find that son of a bitch and beat the livin' shit out of him!

The rage in Joey had him so pumped up that he was shaking like a leaf but suddenly a particle of rationality insinuated its way into his subconscious. Wait a minute, now, old buddy, it takes two to tango, you know. Maybe you better ask some questions and listen up real close to your old lady before you go out and make a fool of yourself. Jimmy Jeff isn't going anywhere in a hurry. Besides, you know where to find him. Let's just take a minute to think this whole thing over!

But as you have probably figured, he never got the chance to think too much about anything for Debra immediately broke into "the great diversion" again. The one that has made midgets out of martyrs and suckers out of supermen. The one that made Adam eat the apple and almost made old Jimmy Jeff eat crow. The one that caused all those guys to kiss Medusa and was about to eat Joey's lunch. That immorality that was so blatant and yet so covert, so obvious and yet so hidden, so anticipated and yet so unexpected.

It was a little later, after the nap that always follows this particular farce, that Joey started to think about what was happening to him. About all of the signs that he had been ignoring for whatever reason. About all of the illusions that he had been creating for himself in order to ignore the obvious. With this last thought he startled himself completely out of a deep sleep. Instantly awake and alert, he found himself sitting bolt upright in bed, sweating profusely and wanting, although not wanting, Debra to be right there with him. Fortunately and unfortunately, the bed was empty next to him . . . she was nowhere to be found.

And now Joey was in a more difficult situation than he had ever encountered. For here he was a stranger in his own house. Afraid to get up and go look for his wife, friend, lover . . . afraid that she would be his ex all of the above. Afraid that what he had witnessed this very evening was not just a bad dream but something that he would have to re-live in the morning or the next day.

Throwing caution to the wind, he rolled out of bed and headed for the bathroom, hoping that the door would be closed and locked. This, of course, was to no avail and the very room that had given him so much comfort in the past was now cold and barren. Its porcelain majesty no longer beckoning but now rather foreboding as if waiting to swallow him up in gelid indifference. Well, piss on you he thought, grunting savagely at the demons in the bowl in front of him. Take that you bastards, he farted at those sneaking coyly up behind him . . . and still no relief.

Creeping quietly down the stairs, he was relieved to see a light on in the kitchen and there was Debra, sitting at the kitchen table in one of his old sweatsuits totally immersed in that damn book that Jimmy Jeff had left for her. The thought raced through his mind that he might have been the world's biggest fool for not throwing the friggin' thing away when he had it in his hands earlier in the evening. Glancing quickly at the clock, he saw that it was almost three-thirty in the morning (well past both their bed times).

"What are you doing, darlin'?" he whispered softly.

Unfortunately (or maybe fortunately) she was so absorbed in

whatever it was that she was reading that he startled her. Whooping loudly in surprise, she threw the book straight in the air and he caught it reflexively just like in the movies. Without wasting a moment or an effort, he spun around and kicked the garbage compactor open. Continuing with his piroutte, he hooked the terrible tome into the compactor's gaping maw with a move that would have made Kareem Abdul Jabbar (nee Lew Alcindor) jealous. Jumping straight into the air and giving forth a scream that would have done Bruce Lee proud, he executed a side kick at the door and, simultaneously, hit the mash button.

Spinnin', grinnin' and spreadin' his arms wide, he genuflected deeply and exclaimed, "I think you've had enough of that bullshit, darlin' and I know I have. So, why don't we just go on up to bed and forget all about this evening?"

Poor old Joey, unbeknownst to his frazzled psyche, had stumbled upon a feminine hallowed ground, an area of inviolate sanctity impententrable by mortal man. A ladies arena of stale phrases, trite cliches and witless witticisms that belong only to those who really want to believe in them. So, out damn spot (or really out damn Joey) and take your macho bullshit with you! Can't you see that you have just denigrated one of the last bastions of femininity? The self-help publication that helps no one? The answer that only causes questions? The "for my eyes only" that's only for your eyes? What hast thou wrought? The look on Debra's face could curl linoleum.

"Dammit, Joey, I wasn't finished with that book," she spat the words out angrily with a look like someone who had just knocked back a shot glass full of vinegar," and I'm going to finish it, too! It might not hurt for you to do the same thing!"

Joey knew instinctively that he was caught in another one of those now or never situations that had been popping up with regularity of late. He wasn't sure how he kept getting into them but once he was there he didn't know how to get out of them, so, giving himself an instant to marshal his thoughts, he dove in with all of his might. Thinking fleetingly that the best defense might be a strong offense, he pulled himself up to his full five-feet-eleven and proclaimed boldly in his best announcer's voice,

"We might as well talk this over, Debra, because it's obvious that you are not aware of what JJ is trying to do to you and to us. I've already read the reviews on that platudinous piece of psychobabble (his p's were working well for so early in the morning) and the unanimous verdict is that, not only is it poorly written by a writer of dubious credibility, but it also lacks any basis in fact. Apparently the asshole who wrote it suffered through a particularly bitter divorce and used the book to vent his hatred toward women in general and matrimony in particular. Sound familiar? Sound like our old buddy, Jimmy Jeff? C'mon, Debra, wake up! Don't let the dumb shit talk you into something that you'll regret for the rest of your life!"

"He isn't talking me into anything! And just because some people don't like what's in that book doesn't mean that it isn't worth reading. I think that you have to read everything in order to know anything! I mean, why don't you read it first before you condemn it?"

"Look, darlin', the damn thing starts out like all of that psychological crap with a premise that doesn't agree with anything rational that has been said or written in the last few decades. Then it attempts to prove this guy's personal hatreds with a bunch of gibberish that makes absolutely no sense. He's trying to be abstract enough to peak the curiousity of some poor souls who are stuck in bad relationships while not saying anything of any worth to anybody. The sum total of the message is that, if you have a problem with someone who you started out loving, the best way to solve that problem is to leave and try it again somewhere else. That's a pretty shallow way to look at things, isn't it?"

Joey continued, hoping against hope that at least part of what he was saying was getting through to Debra's mind which at the time was closed tighter than the doors of a whore's heart.

"Of course, that fits right into old JJ's modus operandi. Hasn't it ever occurred to you that the reason that he goes through jobs and relationships like a dose of salts through a widow woman is that he hasn't got the courage or the intelligence to recognize his own shortcomings and do something about them? Can't you see that for some reason he'll probably never be able to explain he's decided that he wants something that is totally verboten to any man of any gumption?"

"Real men have a code that all of them that are worth a shit have observed throughout time. You absolutely do not, under any circumstances, come between a man and his wife while they are trying to work their relationship out. Not only is it considered in bad taste but also the depths of cowardice to try to entice a married woman who is confused about her situation into another relationship. The response in most Latin countries is to snuff the offender immediately. In most other places, a duel or some other challenge of honor is called for but no where is this type of behavior tolerated by any man with any balls at all."

Instead of listening closely and seriously to what Joey was saying, Debra had a cocky sneer on her face that, had it been on a man's face, Joey probably would have knocked it off with a right-left combination to the head. For an instant, the heat of the moment almost caused him to do it, anyway, but using just about all of the restraint he had left in his tired body, he checked himself at the last moment and instead walked to the refrigerator for a drink.

Debra took this opportunity to make her side of the argument. Unfortunately, it seemed that she and Joey weren't arguing about the same thing because she lunged ahead as if she hadn't heard anything that he had said previously.

"The book says that men and women don't necessarily have to remain with the same person forever. As a matter of fact, it might not even be natural for them to do that. Actually, people that stay together for a long time are freaks of nature. After a while people are bound to get interested in other people. It's natural to want to be with someone else from time to time. There's nothing wrong with it! All the guy does is give you some ways to make things easier on each other!"

"What in the hell are you talking about? Don't you realize that what you are saying makes absolutely no sense at all? You know that JJ is not a good source of information dealing with any major life decisions. Hell, he can't even run his **own** life worth a shit much less tell you how to run **yours**! And then he brings you some kind of claptrap from some kook with absolutely no credentials other than he just got shit on by some middle-age-crazy woman and you suck it up like a sponge, the whole time ignoring anything that I say that makes any sense. You can't be happy if you give up moral discipline in order to salve your selfishness! Don't you see that?"

"I'll tell you what I see! I see that our relationship is getting more and more stale as time goes on. I want to get some excitment back into my life. I want to go out on dates and go dancing and out to eat with some new, interesting people. I'm tired of business, business, business. I'm tired of boring business conversations and even more boring business people . . ." she said this with such phony sincerity that she had to look away as her words caught up to her.

209

"Well, how do you propose that we maintain our standard of living, then?" Joey jumped into the breach. "You think that houses like this and lifestyles like ours grow on trees? You think that I like working my ass off while you're out riding horses or playing tennis or shopping . . . or plotting behind my back with a complete nothing like Jimmy Jeff Stewart? You haven't listened to a thing I've said, have you? You know something Debra, sometimes, talking to you . . . I may as well be ravin' at the moon!"

"I should have known that you wouldn't take the time to see my side of the situation." Debra jumped back into the fray. "You think that, just because I'm playing tennis or riding horses or shopping, I'm having a great old time, don't you? Why don't you take the time to see what I really need? How can you think that just because you provide all these wonderful things, that I'm gonna be happy? Why don't you ask me what I really want?"

After a long pause and a deep sigh, Joey asked that most questionable of questions, "Okay, Debra, maybe you're right. What is it that you really want?"

So now Joey had fallen into that peculiar masculine trap that all men encounter from time to time. When men listen to women complain about their ways for an extended period of time, they tend to become apathetic and attempt to examine the problem from the woman's perspective. This usually leads to some hasty soul searching that raises doubt that, even though they have thought their side through and it makes more sense than the "feelings" upon which the feminine stand is based, there is a possibility that they could be wrong. This male fallibility is not only confusing but, if men come around to the feminine way of thinking, it almost inevitably causes women to lose respect for the men. Instead of solving the problems, whatever they are, the poor bastards now become wimps!

Debra, geared up for a long impassioned argument over what she instinctively knew was a bunch of selfish doubletalk on her part, was taken aback by Joey's sudden change of course. What **was** it that she really wanted, anyway? Did she want a divorce? Did she really want to start dating other men? Did she want Joey to leave? Did she want him to stay? What did she want?

Giving him a look that could only be the product of some internal blackout, she said in her best Joyce Brothers demeanor, "I don't know what I want, Joey, can't you see that? And I don't know if you could give it to me, even if I *did* know what it was!"

210

If you think that Joey was totally mystified by this outburst you are absolutely right! Not only did the words not make any sense but the more he thought about them the more confused he became. Do women just say whatever it is that's on the tip of their tongues, he thought, do they ever think about the consequences of what they are saying? She did ask me to ask her what she wanted didn't she? Why did I assume from that remark that she knew what she wanted? Is she crazy or is she trying to drive me crazy? By this time, Joey's head was spinning so badly that he couldn't concentrate much less make any sense of what he was hearing.

"Look, darlin', I'm really tired now and I can't seem to think too straight. Why don't we just go to bed and we'll talk about this tomorrow?"

Sensing her advantage, Debra took one last shot at making her point . . . whatever it was. "Just because I don't know what I want doesn't mean that it shouldn't be important to you! And it doesn't make me just another stupid woman, either!"

Whew! Joey thought, this thing is going downhill fast. I wonder if I'm hearing her correctly because, if I am, she is definitely a few sandwiches short of a picnic. Joey walked over to the window to try to get away from her antithetical diatribe . . . and that was when he noticed the moon. The orb itself was so huge that it almost filled the east facing picture window that he looked out every morning to watch the sun rise. But it was the color of it that really set him back. It was sort of an icy blue gray that misted over into itself . . . and underneath the colorization was the hint of a face with an expression that seemed to keep changing from a smile to a sneer to a frown.

Damn! Even the man in the moon is getting into the act. Joey looked down to see every hair on his arms standing on end. A chill ran up his spine that was so vivid in sensation he was sure that Debra could feel it as well. After it passed a tremendous weariness came over him and he knew he had to go to bed.

"Are you listening to me, Joey? I'll bet you haven't heard a word that I've said, have you?"

"I have but for some reason I can't seem to concentrate too well right now. I'm so tired I can hardly stand up anymore. Let's just go to bed, Debra. This can wait til tomorrow."

Not waiting for her response, he walked out of the room and up to bed. Within thirty seconds of crawling into bed he fell soundly into a deep dreamless sleep. If Debra came to bed after him, he never knew it.

He awoke in a while and she wasn't beside him again but this time he didn't take the time to look for her. Instead he packed his bag and crept silently out of the house. He wasn't sure where he was going but he'd figure that out later. Driving eastbound into that apocalyptic orb that he had seen out the window just a little while earlier, a John Fogarty song began building in crescendo in his head.

"... I see a bad moon risin', I see trouble on the way, looks like we're in for stormy weather .... don't go out tonight, it could mean your life, there's a bad moon on the rise ... .Oh right."

The farther he drove, the less idea he had about what exactly it was that he was doing. Was he running away from Debra or was it just the situation? Would he solve anything by leaving the situation to solve itself? Wasn't that what he had just accused Debra of? Then again, would it make any difference one way or another, anyway?

With that last thought weaving in and out of the Bad Moon Risin' that kept echoing through his head, Joey realized that he really didn't want to leave Debra at all. Try as he might, he couldn't run away from **this** problem. So, slowly letting out a deep sigh composed of equal parts of resignation and relief, he turned the car around and headed back home ... away from that awesome moon.

When he got home, he left everything in the car and walked silently into the kitchen. Debra was not there but that piece of junk book was. Joey turned his back on it and crept softly up the stairs. The bedroom was dark but he could hear Debra's steady deep sleep breathing. Dropping his clothing quietly on the floor, he tried to slide under the covers without waking Debra but she rolled over almost immediately.

"Where have you been, Joey? Why did you leave like that?"

He sighed deeply and tried to compose his thoughts but he was caught off guard. "Well, I took off thinking that I was going to just ride off into the night away from all of this confusion but when I got a few miles down the road, I realized that I didn't have anyplace to go."

He waited silently for what seemed like an eternity for her reply.

"Oh, Jesus Joey," she mumbled as she rolled away from him, "go to sleep."

It was a long time before sleep came.

Chapter Sixteen

A MONTH DOESN'T SEEM like a long time when your whole world is going to shit . . . but, in the four weeks since his disconcerting experiences with Debra and the moon, it seemed that way to Joey. It felt like just yesterday that all of the parts of his life had been optimistic and upbeat, enthusiastic and hopeful . . . but lately things had gotten disjointed, almost out of control . . . on the outside as well as the inside. The old one step forward and two steps back routine looked as if it were taking over his life and, with no relief in sight at the moment, Joey felt powerless to stop it's progression.

Here his best friend, J. C., had split the sheets with his wife Betty Jo who was off trying to find some kind of inner being that she just **knew** was there. While Debra in the meantime was getting goofier by the minute and it scared Joey when he realized that she acted more and more like her sadistic Momma everyday. Sometimes when she was in one of her moods he would look at her and see Momma's face where hers should have been. It gave him the creeps.

More to his great consternation, Joey's old buddy, Jimmy Jeff Stewart (for whom Joey had sacrificed greatly over the years) and Debra had become tighter than a cheap pair of underwear recently. It didn't help Joey's uneasiness when he faced the fact that, even though he didn't have any hard evidence to prove anything, it was becoming increasingly obvious that even if no hanky-panky was occurring at the moment, Jimmy Jeff was thinking about it. He didn't **even** want to consider whether Debra was thinking about it too.

Joey Hews might have been one of the more pure refugees of the decades of change labelled Fifties and Sixties. Although brought up smack dab in the middle of the cultural revolution of beatniks, hippies, pacifists and other social outcasts of the era, he had maintained some semblence of common sense and order in his life. It wasn't necessary for him to carry a banner for any cause as most of the followers of his generation felt it necessary to do. He was, however, quite outspoken on his feelings about war, peace, love, hate, socialism, capitalism and other major issues of the time.

A strong believer in the free enterprise system, he took a hard stance against the socialistic bent of the women and minorities in the United States and, along with that, the majority of the recent alumni of the college system. He took an even stronger stance on the moral issues of the time. He felt pretty comfortable with monogamy after his first few experiments with the opposite sex. Like most young guys full of testosterone and immortality in the Sixties (sexties?), given the relative acceptance of sexual freedom at the time, he availed himself of the pleasures at hand. But soon the novelty wore off and, tiring rapidly of the modus operandi of the New Woman Era, he decided early on that one woman at a time suited him just fine.

In his constant quest to avoid becoming one of the mindless sheep of the era, he developed an unusual style in that, instead of working out a basic "pick up line" to use at the meat markets indigenous of the times, he would enter the arena more as an observer than a participant. Preferring to sit on the sidelines and look over the action rather than burst into the thick of things. He liked the "Old Bull, Young Bull Theorem." You know the one in which the old bull and the young bull are standing on a hillside overlooking the heifer crop. The young bull in a fit of passion cries, "Let's run down there and service one of those sweet young things!" To which the old bull replies, "No, let's **walk** down and service them all!"

Like all free thinkers, he had the requisite bevy of groupies (hoping that some of his "brilliance" would rub off on them) as well as a myriad of detractors who were so jealous of his ability to see the "whole picture" (one that they would never comprehend) that they innately tried to destroy him. It would take years for him to be able to differentiate between his true friends and the traitors since they both harbored the same disguise. Ironically, later on, when both became obvious to him, it would still come as a surprise . . . like that jab in the ribs when you least expect it . . . only much more devastating.

The results of this particular behavioral pattern were and are sadly predictable. Joey, being the "money makin' machine" that he was, attracted all kinds of interesting people . . . most of them interested soley in their own welfare. This period was the augury of his business downturn and our good ol' boy Joey never even saw it coming. While he was out kickin' ass and takin' names in the world of big business, his peers were smiling crookedly at him and trying to figure out what it was that he was doing. While his friends looked at him rather obliquely and wondered what the hell it was that he was trying to say (just like all those teachers and professors had), his competitors weren't hiding the fact that they were trying to put him away for good. After all, they justified, this guy was just trying to make things tough on everybody else! Why didn't he do things the way that they had always done them? Why all of this innovation and new thinking? Didn't this dickweed realize that things had always been a certain way and always would be that way? Why was this idiot so intent on rocking the boat?

As an outlaw of the status quo in the business world, Joey suffered greatly. His innate pragmatism, although propelling him rapidly upward, was also pissing off a great majority of the old school business owners in his line of work and, collectively, they were trying to sink his ship before he whipped their asses. It seems that, as it is with most businesses, the old guard had gotten rather complacent and were content to sit back and collect what they considered to be the dues that they were owed for all of their previous hard work. While doing so they neglected to realize that in sales it doesn't matter what you did yesterday but rather what you are going to do tomorrow that counts. Having no past history to fall back on, everything that he did was new to Joey and this caused him to be running amuck in their eyes.

It was around this time that the old established firms began openly raiding his little company. They would watch carefully as he developed a specific product line and, when it reached a money making level, they would begin a campaign to convince the factory to drop Joey's little company and come with theirs. They invariably would point out the fact that he didn't have the size nor scope of organization and manpower that they had and, therefore, they would do a better job.

After his initial surprise at being fired by a couple of what he thought were his most trusted suppliers, Joey decided that, in order to keep the rest of his business together, he would have to staff up just as he had implored his old partner to do a long time ago. Unfortunately, this didn't quite work out as planned. Repeatedly, after hiring a new salesman and investing a lot of time and money in the guy, the salesman would leave and go to work for one of his competitors. It was hard for him to believe that they would do all of this just over a few dollars but, invariably, that was the key to their decisions. His competitors, when made aware of any new talent that he had acquired, would just raise the ante until his salesman acquiesced. What to do now, Joey?

Well, he tried everything that he could think of to try to stem this onslaught by his fellow businessmen but he always came to that same dead end, people with deeper pockets than his. It should not have come as a surprise to him that, in a capitalistic system, money was the ultimate king. And it also should not have come as a surprise to him that there were alot of folks out there who considered business as war and therefore all of their competition as enemies. What overwhelmed him most, though, was the part that greed played in the equation.

For years he had heard greed defined in a number of ways, such as: ambition, the will to succeed, the desire to excel, etc. These things had been drilled into him in school, on the football field and in the church on Sunday for as long as he could remember. The confusing part was how could those same people exposing those things as virtues jump up and call greed a sin? Well, damn! Weren't they all the same?

Yeah, they are all one and the same, Joey, they are just cloaked in spiritualism or, cynically, in selfishness. Really now, if all of the original thinkers would just band together and protect each other, a lot of people would be that much better off. Think about it. If all of those people that are trying to better themselves at everybody else's expense could organize and recognize what they could accomplish united as opposed to the fact that alone they merely open themselves up to someone else's greed . . . well hell, they might rule the world! Or at least live pretty good until some other guy caught on . . . and after all, that would be another day, wouldn't it?

216

That the system didn't work this way at all was very hard for Joey to comprehend. Instead of his business continuing to increase through his high ideals, things started to fall apart. As fast as his business had grown through his hard work and industriousness, it now was starting to falter at much the same rate. A bunch of the people who had been so instrumental in it's rise began to also fall by the wayside.

Joey, in his naivete, began looking for the cause of it all, thinking that he could turn things around. He turned to some of his friends who had encouraged him to get started originally. He knew that they probably had the answers . . . and they did . . . but they were reluctant to tell him what they were. They had seen young ambitious souls like him come and go over time but they were unwilling to point this out to him. For the most part it was because they genuinely liked Joey and didn't want to see him hurt but in reality it was because that they felt that this was the natural progression of things and that they, or anyone else for that matter, were powerless to stop it. That what was going to happen was going to happen. That the best didn't always get the best. That goodness didn't always beget goodness. That even if all the things someone did were right it didn't really amount to a box of rocks . . . and a box of rocks was what poor old Joey was getting.

Joey's business started to falter in other ways too. Some of the relationships that he had so carefully cultivated over the years began to deteriorate. People that he knew and trusted started making unexplainable decisions and, when he confronted them, would present him with mealy-mouthed excuses for their actions. When he would call his manufacturer friends to try to get explanations for these phenomena he was met with poignant silence rather than an explanation. Old friends and accomplices were of no use at this time. No one knew what the solutions to his problems were . . . or maybe they did, but they couldn't or wouldn't tell him. Much to his chagrin the downturn of Joey's business brought with it other problems . . . or maybe they were there all along and just became more evident because of the deterioration of his state of mind.

Not only did he begin losing his business friends but his social friends, with the exception of J. C., began to cop out on him also. A lot of those good folks at the country club began looking the other way when he would go there. So much so that he stopped going there as often. It bothered him that even as he went there less and less Debra spent more and more time there . . . and more money.

So began to unfold a trite but true tale about men and women. As Joey's business unraveled so his marriage began to come apart also. He still wasn't cynical enough to link the two together but everyone has heard the old story time and time again. As the purse strings tighten and the pressure mounts nerves get frayed and fiscal fears begin to overwhelm the married pair. The results are always black or white. Either the pair in question gets tighter than two bugs in a rug or one or the other takes a turn in the opposite direction.

At the outset Joey was so involved in trying to save his business that that is all that he concentrated on. But as it became increasingly obvious to him that, no matter what he did, the business, although far from going bankrupt, would never be the same again, he began to look around at the rest of his life. He thought about what it would be like to be without Debra and he didn't like what he thought. He thought about growing old alone or like his dear friend J. C. and that wasn't too appealing either. But he also thought about continuing in the business world and found that to be the least attractive of all. So he started to assess his alternatives.

He and Debra were at the kitchen table one morning and he started the conversation.

"Say, Debra, I've been thinking . . . "

"Uh-oh," Debra rolled her eyes, "that could be dangerous."

He grinned but she wasn't smiling back at him so he continued rapidly on, "It's not like that at all, darlin'. What I was thinking is that summer is coming on and the business can pretty much take care of itself for a while. Why don't we load up, just you and me, and go somewhere warm and tropical for a couple of weeks? I was thinking maybe Hawaii or the Carribean or something along those lines."

Debra brightened a little as she thought about getting away but then her face darkened a little. "How are we going to afford this little jaunt if business is so bad? I mean, that's all I've heard about for the past few months is how bad business is and how everyone is screwing you. I've had to cut back on my spending and everything because of it."

"Yeah, well the two most important people in my life are right here at this table, darlin' and, even though alot of my business friends have let me down they can't eat me. The business will survive. It might not be as big or as profitable as it once was but it will

218

still provide comfortably for us. The most meaningful thing in our lives should be each other and I think we need to get away for a little while, just the two of us."

With this he reached out for her hand but she did that little move that you see on television all the time and, instead of grabbing his, she picked up the plates and headed to the sink. Busying herself with tidying up and putting things away she began to talk in a rational yet resigned tone.

"Is this supposed to be one of those second honeymoon type of things, Joey, because if it is you sure took your damned time getting around to it. This is probably the first time in the last six months that you have even taken the time to talk to me. Hell, I was beginning to think that I was the maid or part of the furniture or something."

With this Joey got up and went over to her and put his arms around her waist. He gave her a little nip on the neck (not too sexy or suggestive yet Joey. You know the trouble that can cause. This is a delicate time.) "I know that I haven't paid nearly enough attention to you recently but you know what I've been going through. I think the worst is over and I can leave for a while. I apologize for not being what I should be to you but I just couldn't stand by and see everything that I have worked so hard for go down the drain. Yeah, it will cost a little money but we always have American Express to fall back on! Let's just pack up and get the hell out of here!"

Debra turned around and put one hand on each of his shoulders. She then pushed him gently back at arm's length and gave him a crooked smile. "You know, to be such an asshole sometimes, you're still kind of cute. I'll go to Hawaii with you but you've got to know that I have felt mighty left out of your life recently. Things aren't exactly like they used to be . . . "

"Of course they aren't darlin'," Joey rushed in anxiously, not wanting to hear the rest of this discourse, "things aren't ever the same. They change every single day. But we've gotten through the rough part of this crap and now we can get back to normal. Let's erase all of this uptight bullshit that's gone on for the last six months and pick up where we left off. A couple of weeks away from here would do us both a world of good."

Debra looked skeptical but amenable as she acquiesced to the trip. I mean, after all, it was a trip to Hawaii that he was talking about. That meant some new clothes and being able to tell all of her friends that she and Joey were going off alone just the two of them

. . . and getting away from Momma for a while. Since Joey began having his business problems, Momma's smug looks and snide comments about his plight had been starting to wear very thin on her.

"So Joey's business ain't so hot anymore, baby? Why, you'd think to talk to him that he knows ever'thang about ever'thang. Well, if it gets too tough, we might be able to loan y'all a few bucks just to help you get by. That's what family is for!"

This last was said with such obvious rancor that it made Debra turn her head away and light a cigarette. When she turned back, the wicked smile on Momma's face made her turn away again so that she could compose her thoughts and, even though in the past she had always taken anything that Momma offered, she knew that her pride would not allow her to accept Momma's unmistakably cruel offer.

Mustering up all of the composure that she could at the time she smiled genuinely over at her and said, "It hasn't come to that point yet and I don't think it will. Joey is a smart man and a hard worker. I'm sure everything will work out for the best."

This last came out a little lamely and Momma headed right in on it. "You don't have to be proud with me, Debra. I've heard lots of stuff over at the club about what's goin' on. I told you in the beginning if he was so damn smart what was he doin' sellin' auto parts, anyway? Why ain't he a insurance salesman or a lawyer or somethin' respectable like that?"

"Let's talk about something else, Momma. Joey has been a good husband and given me everything I've wanted all along. Don't you be cuttin' him down. By the way, when's Daddy comin' home. Seems like he's been gone forever."

This, of course, was Debra's touche and she knew that it would cause Momma to give her the old "well, you know Daddy, he's always worked real hard to give us the best of everything" speech. It would also cause her to find someone else to pick on besides Joey, more than likely J. C. or Betty Jo. It's probably best that Joey couldn't see the look on Debra's face at the moment because the smug yet snide smile that she was laying on Momma was actually the mirror image of her mother just a few minutes before.

The next day Joey called several of his friends and all of them suggested that he stay on Maui so he called the airline and burnt up some of his frequent flier miles to get them free tickets. After settling on The Banyan Tree Hotel, a favorite of one of his business friends, he called the hotel direct to make sure that he could get a room overlooking the ocean and that they had a breakfast buffet, horseback riding on the beach, sunset cruises and all of the good stuff. He wanted this trip to be the most memorable one that he and Debra had ever taken together and he wasn't going to be disappointed.

As the time drew near for them to leave, Joey noticed that Debra was getting more and more uptight. She was especially having trouble deciding what outfits to take. Apparently making vacation decisions is tough for the female of the species especially in the clothing arena as appearance seems to take precedence over most every other facet of character. Isn't it interesting that women often complain about being considered sex objects and yet they tend to dress like hookers? Is it women or those light in the loafers designers of haute couture that dress them that way? At any rate as the time for departure neared Joey was beginning to second guess his conviction that a trip to **anywhere** together would be a good idea.

It was about two days before they were going to leave and Joey was sitting in the kitchen after dinner, drinking a beer and looking out at another one of those gorgeous Texas sunsets. He tended to go off into mind neutral while staring into all of the beautiful colors of nature . . . the same kind of hypnotic trance that you can fall into staring at a fire or at a candle for a long period of time. So it startled him when Debra burst into the room on the verge of tears.

"Joey, I can't believe it! Aren't you ever going to pack? We're leaving for Hawaii the day after tomorrow! Look, don't expect me to pack for you! You're a big boy and . . . oh, dammit, nothing looks right on me, anymore!"

By this time Joey, completely taken aback by this outburst, was standing up with both hands held up in front of him trying to quiet her down and get to the bottom of whatever it was that was bugging her.

"Hold on now, Debra," he had to raise his voice a little to slow her down before she became hysterical, "I'll be packed before we go to bed tomorrow night. Don't worry about me! And there is no reason to get so bent out of shape about a vacation. This whole experience is supposed to be fun and relaxing, you know . . . not tense and upsetting."

Joey walked over and tried to invoke the General Law of Womanhood but before he could enfold Debra in his arms and tell her that he loved her she spun away from him and stomped over to the sink. It was obvious that she wasn't having any of that particular

221

charade today. So, in order to ease the tension in the room, he tried to reason again.

"Hey, look darlin', you're gonna look great no matter what you wear. Tell you what, just take over an outfit for the trip and we'll buy you some new clothes when we get there. How about that for a deal?"

At this Debra turned, frowning, and said, "C'mon Joey, we can hardly afford this trip and now you want to spend a whole bunch of money on clothes? Don't patronize me! I'm not a dumbass! Just get yourself packed so I don't have to worry about that, too!" and with that she stomped out of the room.

Whew! Joey thought, another great beginning to a blissful, romantic holiday.

Chapter Seventeen

TWO DAYS LATER THEY were on their way to the airport with Joey humming a little Hawaiian tune that he couldn't name but that had been ringing in his head all morning. He had packed his bag in about thirty minutes the day before but it had taken Debra until about thirty seconds before they walked out the door to get all of her things in order. All of Joey's gear fit in a fold-up hanging bag but somehow Debra had required two large suitcases, a hanging bag, a makeup bag and was carrying a purse and a tote bag onto the plane. The atmosphere in the car on the way to the airport was chilly to say the least. Joey decided not to come too near to Debra lest he get frostbitten and that was probably a prudent course of action.

He checked the baggage outside the terminal and, handing Debra the tickets, went to park the car. The remote parking at DFW is so far away that you have to take a tram to get back to the terminal and the round trip takes about fifteen minutes. By the time he got back the plane was already boarding. He wasn't very concerned because he had used his frequent flyer points to get them first class tickets but as he approached the gate area he saw Debra frantically going through her purse and tote bag.

Getting into his vacation mode, Joey walked up grinnin' like a possum in the moonlight. "Whatcha lookin' for, darlin?"

"Dammit, Joey, where have you been? I can't find the tickets and they are already boarding! What are we going to do?"

"Well, let's see. Where did you go when you came into the terminal?"

"I went to the bathroom and then to the newstand . . . but why did it take you so long to get here? I've been going crazy trying to find the tickets! Why aren't you ever here when I need you?"

"Look, just calm down, Debra. It takes a while to park the car and then you have to take a train to get back here. I got back as quickly as I could. You go look in the ladies room and I'll tell the gate agent our problem and run to the newstand. You didn't take them out of the airlines envelope, did you?"

She shook her head no as she headed to the lady's room and Joey went up to the podium to talk to the gate agent. She smiled sweetly at him as he showed her his i.d. and frequent flier card.

Punching a few keys on her computer, she started nodding her head, "Yes, I have you here. Mr. and Mrs. J. Hews, two first class seats to Maui. Tell you what, it looks as if Mrs. Hews is pretty upset over this whole ordeal so why don't we just file a lost ticket report and you can go right on board."

Joey thanked the gate agent profusely and turned to confront an out of breath Debra hurrying for the gate. He could tell from the way she looked that she hadn't found the tickets.

"Everything is all right, sweetheart, we filed a lost ticket form and we can go right on board. Thanks, again, ma'am!"

He smiled at the gate agent and for the first time realized how cute she was. My, my, Joey thought, that is one little darlin' there and look at that cute little poop chute . . . As he looked up, she met his eyes and there was no mistaking the electricity in her glance. Even though these events didn't take more than a few seconds in total, Debra didn't miss a drop of what was going on between he and the agent.

"Thanks alot!" she spat icily at the agent all the while grabbing Joey and pushing him down the jetway. Joey couldn't help chuckling as she walked quickly staring straight ahead the whole time. He thought about how most of the time, he had to slow down and wait for Debra no matter how slow he walked and now he could hardly keep up with her. Nervously, he started to hum a little of the "Silver Shells" that had started drifting through his head earlier that morning.

Debra was about ten paces in front of him and accelerating so fast that since he couldn't catch her anyway without breaking into a run, he slowed down to his regular pace. As she blew around the corner into the first class section, her tote bag caught on the door of the coat closet and he watched in dismay as everything in it spewed out onto the floor. By the time he got to her, she and the flight attendant were bouncing off of each other as they tried frantically to rescue all of the items she had stuffed in the tote. Joey bent down and tried to help but Debra angrily pushed him away and hissed at him to sit down. With that he took his seat and ordered a beer from the flight attendant to soothe his jangled nerves.

Debra finally got her tote squared away and plopped down next to him as the flight attendant served him his beer. As the beer passed in front of Debra on its way to Joey's outstretched hand, she looked at it as if it were a piece of roadkill that had been laying in the Texas sun ripening for a few days.

Pivotting her head slowly around until she was looking out the window she said out of the side of her mouth, "Isn't it a little early for that, Joey. It's not even eight o'clock in the morning for chrissakes!"

Trying to lighten things up a bit, Joey smiled back as if he didn't see the look, and said, "It's all right, darlin. It's almost noon where we're going and, besides, we're on vacation. Why don't you have a little orange juice and champagne? What do they call that thing again?"

It took what seemed like forever for her to answer but when she did she had softened up just enough so that she was now at least civil. "They call it a mimosa but I don't want anything right now, thanks."

Feeling the lessening of tension in her, Joey decided to lay low for awhile and pretended to be real interested in the baggage loading going on out the window. Actually, he wasn't going to take a chance on anymore small talk until she initiated it. Just sit back and relax and enjoy your beer Joey, she'll either loosen up or not and it will be a lot easier to deal with either way if you sip on a couple of brewskis. He smiled at himself . . . inwardly not outwardly.

"Good morning from the flight deck, ladies and gentlemen, this is your captain speaking. We'll be leaving in just a few minutes for beautiful Maui in the Hawaiian islands. The flight will take us about eight hours at thirty-five thousand feet. So sit back, relax and sip on your favorite beverage as we take you to an island paradise in the middle of the Pacific ocean."

The takeoff was uneventful and soon they were cruise climbing to altitude. Joey excused himself and went to the lavatory to unload the first beer of the day. As he passed the flight attendant, she smiled at him and asked if he'd like another beer. After a thoughtful pause, he said, "Yeah, what the hell. I **am** on vacation, right?"

"You bet!" she smiled back as he closed the door behind him.

When he came back to his seat he was surprised to see Debra smiling up at him and holding a mimosa in her hand. He smiled back at her and said, "Do you want the window, darlin'? You might like it for the first three hours or so. After that there won't be anything to see except water 'til we get to the islands."

"That's okay," she said, still smiling, "I've got a book to read."

He gave her a little hug and a peck on the forehead as he squeezed by her into his seat but that was all he was going to risk at the moment. Even though she was smiling, you could almost cut the tension in the cabin with a knife. He hoped that after a few mimosas she'd either loosen up or go to sleep. Either one would be a blessing now, he thought, as he stared out the window at the barren west Texas landscape flowing by beneath him.

About thirty minutes later, breakfast was served along with some more mimosas. This time Joey also tried a little orange juice and champagne. Debra looked up from her book long enough to give him a curt little smile but she didn't offer any conversation and he knew better than to initiate any at the time. After breakfast, he ordered another beer and she buried her face back in her book. Joey took out a deck of cards and started playing solitaire and so it went for the next few hours, Joey playing solitaire and Debra reading, each in their own separate little atmosphere.

After a while, tiring of reading, Debra slept and Joey continued to play solitaire. When she awoke, she got up and went to the bathroom. Joey, in the meantime, took the opportunity to order another beer. When she came back, she looked refreshed and happy and to his surprise ordered a mimosa.

Sipping her drink she grinned over at him and said, "Would you like to play some gin rummy or something or do you want to play solitaire all day?"

"Love to darlin'," he said pulling down her tray table and getting out a pad and pencil. "Here, shuffle and deal. What would you like to play for?"

"How about a blue jay ?" she grinned a little tipsily back at him.

Blue jay was their code word for that particular sexual pleasure that men seem to love the most. This indicated to him that the mimosas were doing their job and he quickly ordered another one for her and a beer for himself. Now we're getting somewhere, he thought as she dealt out the first hand of rummy.

"That's more than fine for me, darlin'," he said in his syrupiest voice, "but what do you want if **you** win?"

"Well, if **I** win, I want to have things the way they used to be when we first met. I want to go out on dates and go dancing and have fun. Just like when we were learning about each other and everything was new and . . . different."

She said it with a smile but her eyes were telling another story. Dammit, Joey thought, everything was trending correctly and now she's into this horse manure again. Well, maybe the best thing to do is to go along with it. If I try to make sense out of anything she'll probably go ballistic again and that wouldn't be worth a flip.

So Joey, in all of his brilliance, smiled radiantly and said," Hey, no problem, darlin'! Why don't we start pretending right now. Look, I just met you in the bar in the airport and we decided, on the spot, to take off to Hawaii. You know, I think we can have a great time with each other. We can go out and dance, lay on the beach and drink . . . and maybe even have some horizontal fun. Your draw, baby."

Unhappily for Joey, his comments came off a little facetiously and probably not as sincerely as they should have. Needless to say, Debra didn't take them in exactly the spirit in which they were offered. As a matter of fact, she looked at him with that withering glance that he had been seeing way too often lately. Joey couldn't believe how swiftly things were going to hell in a hand basket and all he could do was smile like a dumbass. After waiting for what seemed like an eternity for her to draw, he finally handed her a card and she gave him a terse "thanks." Since he didn't know what else to do, he continued to try to lighten up the atmosphere a little.

"Hey look, maybe you're right. Maybe what we need is to lighten up a little bit. You want to go out on dates and I want to eat a date. Maybe we can meet somewhere in the middle!"

He said this with tongue in cheek but she met it with tongue out-stretched. It was hard for him to look at her with that sneer on her face. Not only was her tongue out but she had that **look** again !

What the hell was he supposed to do about that **look**! How was the best way to wipe it off her face. No, No! Not that way, Joey!

Barely controlling the urge to get physical, he regrouped and tried to make the most of what he had. He figured that, if he pretended nothing was wrong, nothing would be. This is the habitual male farce, that hopefully manufactured inanity that is supposed to take the place of reality. That longshot that will ease the awkwardness and make things bearable again. The odds on favorite to melt her heart. Tough dooky, Joey! It ain't never and ain't ever gonna happen! A sad state of affairs for our old friend, eh?

So now, with the lines drawn, both of them played the game in earnest, determined to win. It was no longer simply a card game that they were using to pass the time and enjoy each other's company. Now it was a battlefield and each one was determined to beat the other. Although they both pretended to be having fun there was a strong hint of malice when either of them would win a hand and the smug smile of that winner would only piss the other one off more. It made each of them more determined than ever to kick the dog out of what used to be their friend and now was just another opponent in the war between the sexes.

About half way through the game it suddenly occurred to Joey, who had a hefty lead at the time, that winning the game might not be in his best interests. He could almost predict what would happen if it were the case. Debra would start out the trip indignant and it would take him the best part of the first couple of days to get her nose back in joint. The irony of the situation almost overwhelmed him as he remembered that, in the early stages of their relationship, she liked for him to win at games because it proved how smart he was and she wanted him to be smart . . . even if it was at her expense.

He'd win and she'd grin . . . with that sleepy sexy look and say, "I guess you're just better at this than me sweetheart."

His reply would be something like, "Just luckier, darlin', luckier because I have you." This would usually lead to a little apres game nookie which meant that they were both winners anyway. That happy thought wouldn't be the case in the present situation and hadn't been the case for far too long a time for Debra and Joey. It seemed that now Debra was in constant competition with him. Instead of being his cheering section, so that she could show the world how smart he was, she actually wanted to best him so that she could show the world how dumb he was . . . or how smart **she** was . . . or . . . hell, he didn't know . . . something. This situation didn't necessarily apply to a game, it applied to anything. Even the simplest conversations were turning into contentious debates. When she won she was almost unbearable in her smugness and, if she lost, her derisiveness was equally insufferable. Not to mention the fact that intimacy of any type or degree was totally out of the question for some period of time in either case.

That's probably what struck Joey on this particular occasion and brought him out of his combative mindset. Look idiot, he thought, if you win you lose but if you lose you just might win. So lighten up and let her squeak out a victory. To his delight the plan worked like a charm and after she won they spent the rest of the flight sneaking kisses and copping feels and promising each other all kinds of sexual favors when they got to Maui. They even played another game and this time she let **him** win.

They walked off the plane a little bit drunk not only with alcohol but with each other. Joey was ebullient, almost glowing in the warmth of her body which was glued to him as they sashayed off the plane into the humid Hawaiian moonlight. Debra on the other hand seemed lost in the fantasy that she had wanted so badly. To her, they had just met and were off on an innocuous and yet wicked little sojourn. The kind that you read about in all of those romance novels . . . kind of dirty, a little bit nasty and yet at the same time . . . **romantic!**

When they got to the hotel everything went so smoothly that he thought they might be in a dream. The bell clerk met them as they got out of the hotel limo and their bags were whisked away as if the staff had been waiting for them for weeks. All he had to do to check in was sign his name and then the concierge suggested that they have a nightcap on the lanai as the staff arranged their room. The lanai was a kind of balcony with a bar and a native guitar picker who sang with a particularly haunting soprano for a man of his size . . . with that big blue-gray moon shining over his shoulder as if it had been painted there. The setting was so beautiful and the music so unearthly that neither of them spoke a word as they finished their drinks. When the musician began packing his bag they both sighed audibly and headed for their room.

Joey and Debra's suite was airy and light and the smell of frangipani seemed to be everywhere . . . as if they were in the middle of a plumeria lei, their bodies together in reverent subservience to this fragrant nirvana. Yo! Pretty heady stuff, this, eh? Well this night went on and on and on and on . . . until, finally totally worn out with each other and with the ambience of the moment and that of their subconscious longings, they fell into a deep refreshing sleep.

When they woke up in the morning, they were still on the same movie set. One of those old Doris Day things where they shoot the whole picture through vaseline so that no one can see a flaw in anything or anybody. Suddenly as if someone commanded it, there was a knock on the door and in came a bellboy with a sumptuous breakfast of native fruits and breads along with some wonderful smelling coffee. Joey had the young guy, who was looking at him as if he were a little strange standing there in his skivvies, put everything out on the table on their veranda and, as he signed the check, ordered a couple of Diet Pepsis to go along with their feast.

"Why did you do that, Joey?" she asked, and he blanched (yes "blanched"; to all of you oblivious to what goes on in these goings on, he kind of scrunched up his eyes and flinched) because he knew what was coming. "He didn't mean any harm. You didn't like him because he was yellow, wasn't that the deal? Or is it just the way you are? You are a bigot, you know. That's the only way to describe the way that you treat people."

"Well, you're probably right. I probably am a bigot. I think everybody is . . . in a way. We're all a little bigotted or chauvinistic or selfish by nature but it's not something to be ashamed of. Besides, I didn't notice that I was being especially rude or anything to that guy and he didn't seem to be upset with me or with the tip for that matter. What did I do wrong?"

"Oh, it's just the way you look at people and the way that you seem so much better than them. They're just as good as you, you know, even if you don't think so. Maybe they don't have the same education as you do and maybe they aren't as smart as you but they're still just as good as you are. Don't you see?"

The fact of the matter is that Joey didn't see. Not only did he not see what he had done that was in any way discourteous to the hired help but also he was aware that, although his station in life was obviously higher than the guy that was waiting on him, he still had thanked him and tipped him well. Was Debra reading something into the simple events that had just occurred or was she transposing her thoughts on his treatment of her or someone else into the scene?

In any event, he could see that this could be the beginning of one more of the "debates" that she liked to get into lately that were dead-end streets for their relationship and he wasn't going to abet the situation. So he judiciously changed the subject.

"Holy cow," he exclaimed, throwing open the curtains on the lanai," look what a georgeous view! And listen to the surf! Isn't this the next thing to paradise? It sure beats the hell out of sitting in Dallas watching the grey winter clouds, doesn't it?"

Grudgingly, Debra agreed, but she wasn't giving up her self-inflicted sparring match that easily. "I still think that you could have been nicer to that poor guy. He can't help it if he was born Japanese and he certainly can't help it if he has to work in a hotel waiting on wealthy white people."

"Hell, don't worry about it, darlin'. He got a nice tip and he could be in Japan jammed up with all of those people starvin' to death and besides it's just too damned nice a day to worry about it. What do you want to do today, anyway? Want to go down to La Haina and do some shopping? Maybe take a swim down at Makena Beach? Have a couple of drinks and eat some fresh fish or pork for lunch? What do you think?"

Well, what she thought wasn't nearly what Joey thought. As a matter of fact, what she was thinking and what Joey was thinking were miles apart. He wanted her to be a part of his dreams and she wanted him to be a part of hers. As you can probably guess, the two were not even in the same millennium. Of course, what Joey wanted was the third definition of that word, millenium, "a hoped for period of joy, prosperity, peace" and, sure enough, what he got was just the opposite.

Debra shook her head gently and opened her eyes as if coming out of a dream. She sure looked pretty in the early morning light. A little bit tousled and soft yet smooth, almost ethereal in the soft trade winds breeze. He wondered how she could be so hard and so soft at the same time.

"Come on, darlin'," he beamed, almost like the sun over their heads, "Let's get up and go on into town and have a nice, laid back day. We'll eat and drink and lay around just like rich white folk. By the way, I wonder what the poor folk are doin'?"

Seeing almost immediately that he was being offensive to her

231

liberal self again, he tried to save the moment. It's intriguing that, even though he was so good at it with his business associates, he couldn't begin to cut the ice with the ice maiden.

He didn't think about the fact that her basic feminine liberalism would always clash with his candid conservative nature and isn't that the way that it is with most men and women, anyway! Perhaps it would be better for men to save this side of themselves for other men rather than for the women that they want to spend time with.

"What do you mean "poor folk"? The only reason that we are here is because we have good credit. We certainly don't have much money these days!"

"You're right, darlin'. Just kiddin' around a little. Don't be so serious. C'mon, let's get up and go see what's goin' on in "La Hiney"!

He said this last with such little-boy innocence and enthusiasm that she couldn't help but smile. So, melting at least a little bit inwardly as well as outwardly, she pulled him down next to her and paid back her gin rummy debt. He in turn, blown up, so to speak, by this turn of events, returned the favor in kind and decided that maybe all of that piddlin' crap from a few moments ago hadn't occurred at all. After a sweet little nap curled around each other, they got up and showered together, shared in a little bathroom afterplay and walked out of the hotel arm in arm like a couple of newlyweds.

As they strolled by the banyan tree in the square, Joey started singing his song for the day about the little fish that has a name longer than it's body. Here's the answer to the poser of the day, yes it's the humahumanukanukaapuaa, pronounced hum-a-hum-a-nooku-nooku-a-poo-a-a. It's a real fish about an inch and a half long that **is** just a little bit shorter than his name but so much for this digression, on to the two newly met, married too long, goin' on forty, just about crazy, honeymoonin' harbingers of misfortune.

Well, Joey and Debra had a really great day. First they browsed all of the shops that he could handle in downtown La Haina, then they went to brunch where she had several mai-tais and he had several beers, all the time looking into each other's eyes. Then they went back and seriously went shopping and they bought her several sarongs and two or three swim suits and for him a straw hat that some derelict alongside the road was selling for whatever he could get. On a whim (actually on his whim), they packaged up all of their new purchases, bought a twelve pack of beer and a cooler at the 7 Eleven, rented a car and headed down to Makena Beach where they spent the afternoon.

Most of it was totally delightful for both of them . . . except for the last part. They hugged and swam and drank and carried on for the best part of the day . . . until Debra got drunk, that is. It started out easily enough but then things kind of deteriorated. She went from giggly, to horny, to wanton, to mad in such a short period of time that Joey, in his laid back, semi-inebriated state (you know that one dontcha guys?) couldn't keep up with the series of events. It happened so fast that he still thought that she was huggin' him when she hit him. As a matter of fact, when she hit him, she hit him so hard that when he came to he was laying on his belly with a mouth full of sand and a mind full of wonder.

Looking around (the whole scene had taken place in a nanosecond), he finally focused in on her striding licentuously down the beach in her new bikini, returning every dirty look that she enticed, with a come-on-to-me smile that couldn't be mistaken by anybody on the beach. Joey jumped up, kind of groggy but still semi-coherent and began running after her. It was like he was in a dream. You know that one in which you are running in sand and, even though you can see the one you're chasing, no matter how hard you dig in you can't catch up. It didn't take a long time for him to realize that no matter how fast he ran after Debra at this point, he might catch up to her physically but it was an almost certain presumption that he wouldn't catch up to her emotionally. To take this one step further, even though Joey didn't want to accept it at this time, he and Debra would more than likely **never** be in synch again spiritually.

Joey finally caught up to Debra but she was striding along at that pissed off pace again. You know the one. The one in which they stare straight ahead and pretend you're not there and only respond to some macho guy about ten years your junior and thirty pounds heavier that can see the weakness of your position at the time. It was easy for Joey to see why men would respond to Debra at this moment because, when she was in a state as agitated as the one she was in now, she was one hell of a striking woman. He finally had to grab her arm to slow her down and she did that typical woman thing. She slung his hand off her arm a couple of times before she stopped dead in her tracks and whirled on him in order to make "the scene" more dramatic, just like in all of those inane soap opera productions.

"What in the hell do you want, Joey? What **do** you want?"

What he really wanted was to give her a shot up along side the head just like she had done for him just a few long minutes ago. Looking around, though, he could see that the two of them were the center of attraction on the beach at the time and all he wanted to do was get her back to a semi-rational emotional state. Joey, for whatever reason, wasn't cognizant that he had somewhere along the line lost the ability to pacify her. Even though he had pulled off this particular hat trick many, many times in the past, something changed that day on the beach and, try though he might, it never did get changed back to the way it was.

"First I want to know why, when we were having such a great time, you chose to hit me and . . . well, what in the world is wrong with you? Here we are in paradise, having a great time and you have to spoil it all and I don't have a clue as to what went wrong! Hey, look, we don't have to air this crap out here in the middle of all of these people. Let's go somewhere where we can talk."

With this he attempted to take her hand and walk back to their stuff but she did the woman thing again and, to his astonishment, took off down the beach in that same exaggerated hooker strut, throwing a, "We don't have anything to talk about!," over her shoulder. This time she wasn't just returning looks, she was staring right into the eyes of everyone of the opposite sex on the beach as if choosing her next dance partner.

After he overcame the initial shock, Joey began to get mad. The hell with her, he thought, she wants someone else let her have him. That thought immediately turned his bowels to the consistency of cold cream gravy but, having been duly humiliated in front of all of the people on the beach, he had to regain some face. So he spun around and went back the other way, gathered up their towels and other paraphenalia and headed for the car. As he drove off he noticed that she was already drawing a crowd of young guys exuding testosterone and temptation. She was the only one that didn't look up as he drove away.

His first stop was to get some cash out of the ATM and then to the store for some more beer. His plan was to go back to the hotel and sit out by the comforting surf with his beer and try to figure out what to do next. Imagine his surprise when, after stashing their stuff in the room, he was walking down toward the beach with the cooler under his arm and he looked back over his shoulder to see Debra getting out of a car in the parking lot driven by an older couple who looked at him like he was a known criminal. To hell with her, he thought, I'm going to stick with my plan.

He was sitting in the sand trying his damndest to deep-breath the cream gravyball in his stomach away when he felt her shadow pass over his back. Fearing the worst he tightened up ready for one of her patented shots to the head followed by another big scene. Much to his surprise she walked right on by and then, just like in the soap operas again, she turned slowly around, smiling, and walked back up to him.

"Hi. My name's Debra and I couldn't help noticing how lonesome you look out here all alone. Do you mind if I join you?"

"Come off it, Debra! Its not that easy . . . . Dammit!"

By this time she had moved around so that the sun was in his face, just like the kamakazis did in WW II, so that he was kind of blinded and had to squint and put his hand over the sun to even see her silohuette against the glare.

She put her finger over his mouth to shush him as she continued. "You haven't even told me your name much less offered me a beer. If you want to be alone or you're with someone else, I'll go on . . . Well?"

Joey slumped in the sand, the tension of the day all of a sudden tiring him completely out. He could see now that for some unknown reason she was play-acting their first meeting here on the beach but he was just too mind-weary to buck the tide. So he decided the hell with it! They had a couple more days left on their "vacation" and **his** plan wasn't working worth a damn, was it? Why not help her live out this fantasy that she was so intent on. After all, the way things looked, if she didn't live it out with him she might do it with someone else and, at the moment, he didn't **even** want to consider that alternative.

"No, please sit down and have a beer with me. I just got in town and must be suffering a bit of jet lag or something . . . "

And so it went for the rest of what he later would call "Hawaii Hell." Everytime that Joey even got close to attempting to come back to reality she would put her finger over his mouth and change the subject. If he tried to talk about anybody back home or anyone else that they hadn't specifically met on this trip together she would do the same thing and finally he just gave up and played the game her way. They looked wonderful together. Both of them tanned and fit and holding hands but, laying in the dark in their room at night, Joey couldn't remember ever being more alone . . . with that little dark cloud lurking in his subconscious and no music playing in his head.

On the way home on the airplane, Joey again tried to broach the subject, but using her finger over his lips and smiling sweetly, she continued the pretense. Since they were getting along so well and, actually, since he was totally dumbfounded by this strange turn of events, Joey continued to go along with this make-believe situation. At least that was the way that he rationalized it to himself but, in reality, Debra's vacation fantasy, this eerie pretense, scared him to death.

Chapter Eighteen

THE FIRST THING THAT Joey did when they got back to Dallas was to call J. C., hoping against hope that his old friend could help him make heads or tails of this far-fetched turn of events. Debra was still pretending that they had just met in Hawaii and continued avoiding any possibility of confrontation. Over the phone J. C. allowed that it would be best to let things go along as they were for a while as long as everything stayed on an even keel . . . at least until he and Joey could get together and talk. This made sense to Joey since, he had to admit, he and Debra were getting along better than they had in a long, long time. Her abrupt mood swings had evened out and her temper was the most upbeat that he had seen in months.

Joey and J. C. met at Hebert's the next day at lunch. He hadn't let any of his business associates know that he was back and J. C. said he could get loose so they met just before lunch in the bar. Despite all of the weirdness that had taken over his life, he was so happy to see his old friend that Joey found himself smiling genuinely for the first time in what seemed like weeks. They had a couple of beers and a couple of laughs to get the edge off and, after they ate some lunch at the bar, the three musketeers minus one got down to business. Joey opened the subject by telling J. C. how relieved he was to be back among friends (friend?).

"Damn it's good to see you again, pardner! Seems like I've been gone to beautiful Hawaii forever. Everything okay with you?"

"Yeah, I'm finer 'n' frog hair but, look, I can't stand the suspense any longer! Let's get on with it! Has Debra gone completely batshit or what?"

"Hell, what do I know? It's funny, here in the last little bit of what was once a great life, I have gone from witty, brilliant and charming to dull, stupid and rude. I've gone from rich and successful to struggling and losing but all of that bushwa doesn't make a damn bit of difference right now. By the way, are you comfortable? This may take a while, amigo."

"Yeah man," J. C. had that lopsided grin he got when the beer was beginning to hook up and the glow was starting to come on him, "I'm as cozy as a pig in mud. Bring it on!"

Joey then went through the whole diatribe beginning with the awful days leading up to their trip to paradise and through the events leading up to their fiasco at the gate in the airport.

"The only mistake that I can find so far, Joey," J. C. interjected with that smile on his face again, "is that you didn't get that ticket agent's name. Hell, if you weren't going to do anything about it, you could have at least taken care of your old pardnuh!"

Joey smiled and thought, ol' J. C.'s on point as usual! Then he continued on about the upturn in Debra's state of mind as they got farther and farther away from home and she got a little tipsy. He went on about what a great time they had that first night in Hawaii and the mystery of what set her off the next morning with the Japanese waiter (as it turned out he was Korean). He was frowning by this time but he continued as best he could about how she quickly changed back to his lover and what a delightful day they had . . . until that afternoon.

"She's really got me buffaloed this time, J. C. I figured that crap in the beginning was just because that's the way women get before a trip. You know what I mean. Kinda uptight and edgy because they think that they're forgetting something or somethin'. Then that deal with her losing the tickets at the airport and . . . but the things she was doing didn't have any form or fashion . . . or any rationale for that matter. I couldn't tell what was going to happen next and you know that's a great state to be in when things are going in a positive direction but when you can smell the ozone in the air and almost hear the ticking of the time bomb, it's not a good feeling at all. You don't know what's going to happen next but you feel sure it's gonna be bad, you know what I'm sayin'? Does any of this make any sense, buddy?"

By now J. C. had lost his beer glow and was listening intently to everything that Joey said. "Hey man, anybody who has ever been involved with a woman has been in that same situation. They all get uptight before they travel and usually start off their vacation by making you miserable as sin. But if you just let things run their course, everything usually works out for the best. There ain't no way to explain it. It's like the best booger you'll ever get is right after they're just about to walk out on you. I can't for the life of me explain why they got to fight before they can have a good time. Maybe that's the only way they can get their passion up, hell, I don't know!"

J. C. was trying to get that loose-lipped, laid back look back on his face in order to ease up the tone of the moment but it wasn't working too good for either one of them. He did manage a smile but it made Joey turn away and that didn't help things a bit.

So he ordered them another beer as Joey got up and went to the men's room.

When Joey got back, J. C. got up and did the same thing. He thought that letting Joey be by himself for a few minutes would probably do both of them some good. J. C. knew for sure that a few minutes alone would help **him** compose his thoughts a little bit anyway. He didn't like the irrational tone of the story that he was hearing. Especially considering what he had recently seen happen to Betty Jo. After all they **are** sisters, he thought, and their mother is a certifiable loon. Maybe it runs in the family.

"You had enough of this babble, my friend?" Joey smiled as J. C. slid back into his chair. Joey looked more relaxed and refreshed than he had since they had gotten together and J. C. wondered if maybe he'd scored some kind of pharmacutical in the bathroom or something.

"Sheeit, we've just gotten started pardner. You ain't gonna make me go back to work and screw up my whole day are you? You got something else you have to do or do you just want to be with your old buddy this afternoon?"

Joey grinned at the look of thoughtfulness and concern written all over J. C. at the moment. He not only looked like he was worried over Joey's plight but Joey could almost feel the empathy in the air. This buoyed him up more than anything had in what seemed like forever and Joey's smile broadened in direct proportion to this warm feeling that was washing over him in wave after wave of delectation (another fantastic word).

239

"Okay, just remember that you asked for it." and so Joey began anew and related the rest of his strange tale. The weirder it got the more J. C. wondered about what Joey had done in the bathroom. He knew Joey as well as he knew himself, though, and was confident that if he had scored any wacky-tobacky, or anything else for that matter, he would at least have shared it with his pal.

Betty Jo had gone erratic enough with all her "I, me" double talk and her blathering about why she couldn't accept her role as a wife and mother anymore but at least she hadn't acted as bizarre as this thing about her sister that Joey was relating to him. It disturbed J. C. greatly that as Joey got deeper and deeper into the story the one thought that kept occurring to him over and over was "the end is near, the end is near." He hoped it wasn't mirrored in his eyes every time it crossed his mind.

By the time Joey finished, J. C. had to hit the head again. As he got up to leave, he said, "Order us up a couple more beers, Joey. We've got to talk some about this crazy crap you're laying on me. I need a minute to think this over."

When he came back , he didn't even wait to sit down to start.

"Look, I got to ask you one question and you've got to look me in the eye and answer it honestly." Joey started to raise his hand in protest but J. C. grabbed it and put it back on the table as he locked onto his eyes. "Tell me the truth, buddy, no bullshit! You haven't made any of this up, have you? You weren't real stoned or drunk or something and dreamt all of this up? You didn't go get loaded in the john a little while ago did you? Tell me!"

"Look, I know this all sounds crazy as hell," Joey couldn't help giggling nervously at J. C.'s concern. "As a matter of fact, merely thinking about it has been driving me nuts but I swear on my mother that that is exactly the way things happened. Hey, if you don't believe me, go get Debra on the phone and say you'd like her to come down and join us. I'll give you odds she'll tell you, and anyone else that calls for that matter, that we're going to be real busy for a while. She's caught up in this fantasy thing and I'm not sure that she wants to get out of it. For all I know she **can't** get out of it!"

That ain't the only problem you've got, pal, J. C. thought, the biggest problem you've got is that, when and if she does get out of her little dream world, she'll probably get out of your **life!** J. C. knew that he should warn Joey about what he suspicioned but at the

240

moment Joey was so vulnerably intent that he just couldn't bring himself to say it.

"Here's my advice, Joey. As long as things are going along smoothly stay in there and have a good time. There is no explaining why people do what they do . . . least of all women. There will probably come a time in the near future, though, when she'll want to talk about whatever it is that's buggin' her. So be prepared to be patient with her no matter how far out it sounds. If she doesn't start coming out of this state in the next few weeks I'd consider getting her some professional help. It sounds like her elevator ain't gettin' to the top floor these days."

Unbeknownst to J. C., Joey, too, was beginning to feel that this could be leading up to an unacceptable conclusion and subconsciously he was pushing that feeling out of his mind with all of his might. Given all that had transpired in the recent past he knew that there was no way that he could entertain the thought of her leaving or the end of their relationship for that matter. Of course, the Great Procrastinator was sure that he could face it sometime . . . some **other** time, that is.

Feeling simultaneously that their conversation was over, they stood up in unison and hugged each other, J. C. muttering those hackneyed phrases that are meant to make friends feel better but never do.

"Let's face it, my man, one thing is for certain. Things can only get better from here on out and, besides, you've always got me. You know I'll be your friend forever. She'll probably get up tomorrow morning and be totally different . . . I mean, you know, back to her old self . . . Well, maybe not her recent old self but the one from a couple of years ago . . . aw, you know what I mean!," he finished lamely. "You want another beer or what?"

Both of them knew it was time to leave since they were at an impasse that neither wanted to vocalize. Neither one of them wanted to say out loud that Joey and Debra's relationship, like so many others in the chaotic eighties, probably wouldn't survive her middle-age crazies. He hoped that the relief he felt didn't show too much when Joey refused and shambled wearily out the door. Joey turned to wave as he walked by the front window and his melancholy hound dog face was almost too much to bear. It was obvious that Joey sensed the fragility of the once solid relationship that he had with Debra and that he was at a loss as to what to do about it. Having been through much the same thing recently with Betty Jo, J. C. knew the fruitlessness of that particular orientation. Joey had absolutely no control over the direction that he and Debra would take at this point. It was kind of like when she made up her mind that they would get married. Isn't that amazing?, he thought, you chase 'em and then they catch you and, finally, when they get tired of you, they just shuck you like a bad habit. It was sad but he knew that the outcome of this dilemma was totally up to Debra and her severely convoluted psyche. She was becoming totally immersed in herself and her fantasies and she alone would control the outcome of their relationship . . . whether that was right or wrong.

As is usually the case, somebody's law states that when one's marriage starts to go bad so does his business and vice versa. This instance was no exception to the rule. Joey's business, which he knowingly had allowed to downsize in the last year or two so that he could try to salvage his marriage, all of a sudden took a turn for the worse. It didn't help that, with all of the upheaval in his personal life, he was losing his taste for the politics and posturing necessary for him to make a living.

It wasn't that he had to grovel or beg in order to be successful but he did have to pander to some genuine lunatics and it was getting tougher and tougher for him to do so. Some people suggested that he was suffering from "burn-out" since that was a common occurrence in his business. In all honesty he had begun thinking about that very thing more and more lately and the more he thought about it the worse it got.

As the tension from all of his problems began to mount, instead of meeting them head on and resolving them as he would have done in the past, he found himself going to great lengths to avoid them. This caused him to sink into an incredible depression which was in direct contradiction to his usually jovial, upbeat self. Joey, who for all of his life up until now had been the life of the party, was suddenly changing into a wall flower. His friends and business associates, who often called Joey in the past to hear the latest jokes or just for a little mental pick-me-up, were getting tired of his constant carping and depressing conversations. As a result his phone was not ringing nearly as often lately and when it did the result of the call wasn't **more** business but usually **less**.

As his business spiralled downward and he became more introverted, he noticed some other danger signs. Not only was the music not playing in his head, not even in the morning or at any other time for that matter, but these days he found it almost impossible to listen to country and western music. He loved country music because he felt that the writers were the last true poets but most of their songs were so melancholy that he'd get a lump in his throat after only a few bars. What he didn't know was that a sure sign that you are **over** a bad relationship is when you can listen to country and western music **without** crying.

Finally one August morning two days before his birthday, as he was sitting in his office trying to figure out how to play hooky for the rest of the day, the phone rang. Much to his surprise it was one of his largest competitors.

"Good morning, Joey, this is Sid Glick. How are you today?"

"Well, hi Sid. I guess we haven't seen each other or spoken since the show last fall. How goes everything in the world of **big** business?"

"Business is fantastic!," he said with way to much enthusiasm, "so how goes it with you? Everything okay? Business good?"

His name should be Sid Glib, Joey thought, I haven't heard anyone this slick on the phone since they tried to sell me aluminum siding last year. I know this guy really detests me but he sure sounds congenial this morning. Wonder what he wants from me?

He knows damn well that things aren't good with me, Joey reflected pointedly, what's this sly bastard up to? As was his wont, Joey decided to get right down to the meat of the matter. The only way he knew to handle guys like this was to call their bluff.

"Yeah, business is okay but it's not as good as it has been by a long shot. As you know, I've taken some pretty big shots here lately. I've had much better years but I'm sure that I'll survive. As a matter of fact, I was just doing some planning and projections for next year when you called."

"Naturally, I've heard some of the stuff that has happened to you lately," Sid went on, "This is a tough business we're in but you've managed to do amazingly well over the years. That's kind of what I wanted to talk to you about. What say we have lunch and talk face to face day after tomorrow?"

That's what he wants to talk to me about? About my hard luck in business? What the hell is going on here? Does he just want to rub it in or what? Joey could feel the sharks circling in earnest!

"I'd love to, Sid, but that would be on my birthday and I try never to work on that day. How about today? I could use a break from all of this forecasting."

"Tomorrow would really be better for me, Joey. I've got a luncheon with Walmart today. What say we meet at Farfallow at eleven-thirty. I'll get the reservations handled."

"I can't make it that early, Sid. I've got a late morning appointment at AAFES that I can't break. You know how the military is."

Joey really didn't have anything going tomorrow but he wanted to look as busy as Sid was. Besides, if Sid were going to be at Walmart by noon, he'd have to be calling from the airport and Joey didn't hear any air terminal noise in the background. This whole conversation had turned into a poker game and Joey wondered who was bluffing whom?

"You know it probably **would** be better to go over there a little later. The lunch crowd is pretty noisy. Why don't we have a late lunch, say one-thirty. That way it'll be a little quieter and we can just plan on making an afternoon of it. Does that sound better?"

"It's a date Sid. Looking forward to it! Give 'em hell up their in Bentonville this afternoon!" Joey couldn't resist that last jab at his biggest rival.

Farfallow was a trendy north Dallas restaurant. One of those places that are way overpriced so that only the upper crust frequent them. Joey had been there for drinks and dinner a couple of times with some of the highrollers from the country club and, even though it was not his kind of place, he had found the food and the service excellent. It seemed odd to Joey that Sid had chosen this particular place for luncheon. Sid Glick was known for his success in business but more so for his legendary tightfisted ways with money. Well, Joey thought, since **he** asked **me**, we'll stick him with a tab that might just give him a touch of indigestion!

That evening he wanted ever so badly to talk to Debra about this latest turn of events but she was still in her make-believe world and dodged every effort he made to entice her into a serious conversation. In the past he had often talked with her about his business problems. It seemed that in talking the problems through the solution would present itself more often than not. "You teach best what you most need to know" or however that goes.

So it was that as the appointed hour for their luncheon grew closer Joey grew more and more not really nervous but kind of agitated or awkward . . . at any rate, he felt out of synch. Not his usually self-assured persona. You know how sometimes when you're speaking on a subject everything just kind of flows into place naturally while other times you stumble and fumble around and still can't find the right words? Well, that's how Joey felt as he drove up into the parking lot of the restaurant.

He had taken the time to get his car washed and his shoes shined and was wearing a dark pin-striped Cardin suit that he knew was flattering to his lean physique. He had found it somehow comforting, given his peculiar situation at home, to work out more and more often. As a result he had gotten into the best physical shape he had been in in his life.

Joey pulled up in front of the restaurant as the first wave of lunchers came out to get into their cars. There was a lot of confusion as the valets scurried around taking care of the regulars, but when he stopped the car one of them appeared out of nowhere at his door and had it open before he could reach for the handle. Joey smiled as he handed the young guy a couple of bucks and, by the time he reached the front door which was opened for him by another valet, started to regain some of his customary confidence.

Quickly scanning the dining area he couldn't find old Sid anywhere so he headed for the bathroom where he checked himself out in the mirror gaining more confidence as he went along. When he came out he caught a glimpse of Sid in the bar mirror nursing what looked like a martini. All right!, Joey thought, maybe he's a little nervous too! Well, let's let him wait a few more minutes while I make an unnecessary phone call, he reflected as he instinctively dialed J. C.'s number.

"Hey, buddy, what's up?" J. C. sounded extremely relaxed and upbeat and the effect on Joey was immediate and soothing.

"Oh, I'm over here at Farfallow about to sit down with one of the biggest guys in my business, Mr. Sid Glick! He called a couple of days ago out of the blue to invite me to lunch. Wonder what the hell he wants with me?"

"Listen, pardner, I can guarantee you that he isn't interested in your views on the state of the economy or whether or not you're screwing your secretary. If I were you, I'd listen up real close and keep my hand on my wallet the whole time. You can bet your last dollar that whatever that guy wants it will be in **his** best interest, not yours. I've heard of a lot of people getting into deals with him and he's always come out on top!"

245

"Hey, how do you know so much about this guy? He's in **my** business, not yours."

"One of his ex-salesmen came to work for us a couple of weeks ago and every damn day he's got another Sid Glick story for us. The guy is slicker'n owl shit. He's one of those guys who have made so many millions in business that money isn't the object anymore. Now it's just a game to him and nothing seems to give him more pleasure than to kick every gentile's ass that he comes up against. One thing this guy says, though, is that even though Sid kicks a lot of ass, everyone he makes a deal with somehow makes big money. Whether they know enough to keep it or not is another story but he swears that all the guys that hang out with Sid seem to get well in a hurry."

"That's comforting to know, my friend. Well, I think I've made him wait long enough. I better get in there and see what's on his mind. Meet me at Hebert's later?"

"Yeah, I ought to be able to get over there about five-thirty or six. I'm serious though, watch the guy carefully but keep in mind this could be the chance of a lifetime."

"Thanks alot for the info, J. C. I wish I'd talked to you sooner. I had no idea you'd even heard of this guy much less knew so much about him. I've been on pins and needles for two days trying to figure out why he called me. See you this evening."

As he turned from the phone and headed into the bar, Joey was suddenly more settled and confident than he had been all day. Instead of making him more wary, his conversation with J. C. had whetted his appetite to play in the big guy's arena. Let the games begin, he beamed inwardly and outwardly at the same time as he found himself standing right in front of a smiling Sid Glick.

"How are you Sid? Pretty day, isn't it?"

"Yeah, it sure is. Hey, I'm sixty years old today. Look pretty good for an old fart if I do say so myself!"

By this time both of them were laughing and slapping each other on the back. I'll be damned, Joey thought, I wouldn't meet him tomorrow because it's my birthday but he can meet me today and it's his sixtieth! The son of a bitch does look good, though. Wonder if I'll ever get to be that old? By the time that thought had begun to sink in, the bartender was in front of him and Joey asked for a beer as Sid ordered another martini, extra dry and straight up.

"C'mon, Joey, it's my birthday! Why not have a martini?"

"Thanks anyway, Sid, but all I drink is beer or the occasional bottle of wine. I don't even drink champagne on New Year's very often. One of those things you're drinking would set me right on my ass . . . but I can drink beer till the cows come home. By the way," he said raising his bottle, "Happy Birthday!"

Sid raised his glass in return and said, "And Happy Birthday to you a day early. How old will you be tomorrow?"

"I'll be thirty-eight. I guess I should apologize, though, I didn't know it was your birthday today or I wouldn't have agreed to lunch. Birthdays to me are private times. Times to be spent with family and friends, not in some business meeting."

It was obvious that Joey was sincere in his apology and Sid was impressed by his barefaced honesty. As impressed as Sid could be, that is. Sid was a very realistic man. So realistic that he had very little time or tolerance for the values that most people live by. To him everything was very cut and dried and most everything that he did was involved with money and practical means to accumulate dollars and put them to work. But for some reason Joey's genuine almost naively open form of expression, instead of being a sign of weakness, as Sid would have interpreted it in most people, was somehow appealing to him. It might have something to do with the fact that Sid had two daughters and one son and the son professed to be not at all interested in his father's business or in material possessions, a pretense long ago perfected by the offspring of lots of wealthy people (the Kennedys come immediately to mind).

"Don't worry about that, Joey. When you get past forty, birthdays are more a sigh of relief than a celebration. It's real good to be alive and you realize that you are probably on the downhill side of your life but you don't want to dwell on it. It might just be superstition, but sometimes I feel that if I pay too much attention to it, life that is, that it might suddenly be over."

Embarrassed by this, for him, emotional outburst, Sid changed the conversation back to business. Or maybe that whole diatribe was just to put me off balance, Joey mused. No telling what he has on his mind right now. Take your time, take your time he kept repeating to himself inwardly, let this guy proceed at his own pace. He obviously has something pretty profound on his mind.

"But enough of that nonsense, let's go have some lunch and talk a little bit about our business." With this he drained the last of his martini, got up and headed for the dining area which at this time was practically empty. Not waiting to be seated, he walked back to a secluded corner table and motioned Joey to join him there. It was obvious that he was familiar to the staff here and could do just about anything he pleased in the restaurant.

By the time Joey made it to the table there was a waiter at hand and the guy did that little maitre d' thing where they pull out your chair for you and place your napkin in your lap in one fluid move. This move as well as the attitude of the whole staff toward Sid impressed Joey a bunch. This guy clearly has made some kind of impression on these people. Money talks and bullshit walks, he reflected wryly.

Sid ordered steak, lobster and salad, so Joey seconded the motion. "What the hell, kid, it's our birthday, after all. Let's have another toddy while we're waiting. What do you say?"

"I say, since it's our birthday, we ought to just take the rest of the day off and celebrate. Bring it on, my friend!"

They went through lunch like two old friends, both of them a little put off by their immediate intimacy with each other but neither one of them wanting to relinquish the moment. They talked about the commonality of their business interests and their attitudes about business and life. Sid had a lot more experience and insight into people and the workings of big business but he was impressed by Joey's grasp of the general picture of modern commerce. Finally, after they finished lunch and ordered another drink, he got down to the meat of the matter.

"I guess you're wondering why I called this little get together, Joey, and I have to say the reason isn't the same now as when I originally called you. You are a much deeper person than I assumed from our little bit of exposure in the past and I have to say that I am impressed. I've been watching you for the last couple of years and, quite frankly, along with most of our competitors, waiting for you to fail. To your credit you haven't, but it's no secret that you have fallen on tough times. I guess what I'd like to know is what you want from your business life from here on out?"

Joey took a minute to ponder the question at hand while he motioned for another beer. "I won't beat around the bush, Sid. You seem to be a pretty straightforward individual even though your reputation is that of someone who is pretty crafty and ruthless in business. I am probably not nearly a match for you in that respect but I have to admit that you come off a lot differently than what I

248

have been lead to expect and, for some reason, I think I can trust you. At any rate, I have nothing to hide, so here goes."

Taking a long swallow of his fresh beer, he continued. "I got into this business by accident ten years ago. I was casting about and didn't know what to do with my life. I'm sure you know that I got hooked up with that kook in the beginning through a mutual acquaintance . . ."

"Yeah, I never did understand that one," Sid interjected, "I wouldn't have picked that match-up in a month of Sundays!"

"I wouldn't either as it turns out but, what the hell, live and learn. However, when I figured out what the deal was, I split. The first thing I knew some of the manufacturers began courting me and the rest is history. None of this was planned, it just kind of fell into place. That's all yesterday's news, though, and what you wanted to know was what I wanted to do in the future."

"Quite frankly, I haven't given that a whole lot of thought. I pretty much have just gone with the flow up until now. I guess I don't have much choice since this is the only business that I know. I don't believe at this point that I could take a real job. I like to do things at my own pace and that nine-to-five routine would probably be my undoing. Besides, this business is a lot of fun and I think I have a heap of good years left. On top of that, I don't know what else to do."

"Well, here's a thought for you." Sid piped up like a reporter at a news conference with his hand in the air, "As you probably know my only son has no taste for my business. As a matter of fact, he thinks that it is far beneath him. He looks at us as peddlers rather than marketers and to him this whole arena is rather sleazy. You, on the other hand, are very good at what you do but you're not nearly mean enough to survive. Well, maybe you'll survive but it will continue to be a struggle and your growth will be limited from here on out. You've already upset a bunch of your competitors with your sales ability and, even though they all predicted your early demise, your longevity has pissed them off even more."

He held up his hand for silence as Joey began to protest and continued.

"Listen to me for a minute. I've been in this business a lot longer than you and, besides, it's **my** birthday not yours. So hear me out!"

"Here's what I want you to think about. I own the largest company of our type in the southwest and one of the biggest in the nation. You're at that point in your business career in which you will certainly either go up or down in size but you will definitely not remain in the position you're in today. I'm here to tell you that if you want to grow you're going to need a lot of money and a lot more manpower than you now have which will increase your headaches by some major multiplier. If, on the other hand, you don't grow there is a strong chance that you won't survive."

At this point Sid paused and was pleased to see that Joey was listening intently as he looked directly into Sid's eyes. Now that Joey had no objection in the offing, he continued.

"Here's my proposition. I'll buy you out and you come to work for me. You'll handle some of our major accounts in an executive capacity and, if everything works out well, you'll get a shot at ownership in the future. Look, neither one of us is getting any younger and, although you're good at what you do, you might be able to learn a few things from me."

At this point the beers were running through Joey like crap through a goose so he excused himself and headed for the restroom. Besides, the enormity of what he had just been offered was beginning to sink in and he needed a few minutes to think things over. It didn't take him long to realize that what old Sid was saying was a pretty accurate assessment of his situation and that, as J. C. had intimated, this just might be the chance of a lifetime. Even though he loved the entrepreneurial experience, it was a dog-eat-dog world out there and it wouldn't hurt for him to see what it was like to deal from strength for a change. The guy had said that there would be an ownership opportunity in the future, hadn't he?

When he got back, Sid was nursing another martini and there was a fresh beer on the table for Joey. He smiled as he slid back into his seat and Sid smiled back in a surprisingly clear-eyed fashion. Earlier it had looked like the martinis were taking their toll but there was no sign of that now. Joey noticed that he, too, was a lot more clearheaded than he would normally be after several beers at lunchtime.

"You don't have to make a decision at this time, Joey. Go on home and think about it for a day or two. Talk it over with your wife. Let me tell you from experience, this lot that we've chosen in life is very hard on marriages. I may be one of the few successful guys in our field that still has the same wife. It didn't hurt, of course, that her daddy was in the same business that we're in. She knew what to expect."

"On the contrary, Sid, I'm no fool and it doesn't take me long to make a decision. I love the business but I'm getting tired of fighting my way through it. I realize the power you have in the industry and I can't help but think that I could be a whole hell of a lot more effective if we worked together. I know I'm good at what I do but I'm sure you could teach me a lot if you wanted to. Both of us bring a bunch to the party. Let's try the deal and see where it leads us. It looks like a win-win situation to me!"

With this they shook hands and spent the rest of the afternoon in one of those euphoric states brought on by the optimism of the moment and fueled by new friendship and alcohol. They made their plans rapidly and were surprised by the reality that, other than on a few minor issues, they agreed on most every aspect of Sid's buy-out of Joey's company and their future plans together.

At some point, Sid looked down at his Rolex and saw that it was getting close to supper time.

"I'll tell you what, Joey," Sid said, standing and extending his hand, "we've got a deal but we also have a lot of work to do between now and the show in November. I've got to get on home so my family can celebrate my getting closer to the grave. I want you to know that I have thoroughly enjoyed this birthday . . . more so than any that I can remember recently.

"Let's get out of here. I think we've beaten this old horse as much as we can in one day. Call me day after tomorrow and we'll get together and iron out the rest of the details. Have a Happy Birthday!"

"The same goes for me, Sid, this has been a great afternoon and a wonderful beginning. You've made my birthday for me! Have a great evening and I'll talk to you in a day or so."

With that they headed out of the restaurant, Sid for his car and Joey for the men's room. He could hardly wait to get to Hebert's to break the news to J. C. but the beer was knocking urgently at his bladder door. He checked the time as he was leaving the bathroom and saw that it was five-forty-five. Perfect!, he thought as he got into his car, this time tipping the guy five bucks. A couple of beers with J. C. and then home to Debra . . . this last thought sobered him up a ton.

When he got to Hebert's he didn't see his friend anywhere so he ordered a beer and went back to the phone to check in with Debra. He was so excited that he started to tell her about his meeting but she quickly changed the subject to his birthday and, his balloon somewhat deflated, he didn't bring up the subject again. She would fix a nice steak dinner, ready about seven-thirty and wondered if he could stop and pick up some red wine on the way home. As he hung up and went back to the bar, he wasn't quite as fired up as he had been when he walked in but he was close to it. He wasn't going to let Debra or anyone else bring him down on this blue ribbon day.

J. C. showed up just as he sat back down at the bar and Joey ordered him a beer also. He quickly related his good fortune to his pal and accepted his congratulations with a hearty laugh. They only had time for a couple of beers so he made it short but it was almost impossible for him to contain himself. As they walked out of the bar laughing and hugging each other, they promised to get caught up the next day as J. C. offered to take the day off with him on his birthday.

Joey stopped by the liquor store and picked up two bottles of some vintage Cakebread Cellars cabernet along with some fresh bread from a local bakery. On a whim he picked up a small bouquet of roses for Debra also. Cruising down the highway on the way home, smelling the roses and reflecting on the exhilaration of the day he couldn't help feeling extremely optimistic about the future. Boy, this is going to be strange, he mused, working for someone else after all of this time. The very thought of it was peculiarly comforting to him at the moment.

Chapter Nineteen

DEBRA HAD POTATOES COOKING in the oven and the grill going on the patio as Joey entered the house. There were no lights on but she had some votive candles lit and placed around the kitchen and even more candles in the dining and living rooms. When she came down the stairs, she was dressed in one of those see-through summer dresses that she used to wear when they were going out in college. It seemed like forever since then but at the same time just yesterday. She was stunning in a shimmering kind of offbeat way, almost dreamlike in quality.

He took her in his arms and kissed her sweetly. She returned his kiss and the heat in it made him forget completely about what had transpired earlier. Joey broke away just long enough to present her with the roses which she quickly put in a vase and the next thing he knew they were locked in an erotic embrace again. It seemed like only an instant and then they were naked in the living room, she on the couch and he on the floor in front of her. They made love with a heat that he remembered from a long, long time before and when it was over a saccharine wave of days gone by flowed smoothly over his spirit. It was just an instant ago when he didn't think that he could ever be this happy again.

They finally got up and, as Debra went into the kitchen to finish their dinner, he went upstairs and changed into some shorts and one of her favorite shirts. The dinner continued in the dreamlike state of the events preceding it. One of those deals where everything appears softly diaphanous. The look in her eyes that sparkled from the flickering light of the candles between them only accentuated the lust that was all pervasive in the room. They ate in silence devouring the food with relish and each other with their eyes. It was like one of those passages from an Old English love story with lots of wine sipping and lip smacking and finger sucking overtures. Toward the end of the meal, Joey opened his mouth to say something but she put her hand over it and shook her head no. Getting up from the table she lead him out to the patio for dessert.

They woke up some time later naked on the chaise lounge, their clothes strewn between the dining room and the patio. The candles were still giving off their ethereal glow and the air had that soft warm quality that is peculiar to Texas on summer evenings. It seems to caress the skin with a lightness that is piquant and yet satisfiying, soft and warm but tittilating at the same time. Again Debra took his hand but this time she led him past their clothes and the dinner table to their bedroom where she made love to him solo until finally, exhausted, they drifted off into a profound sleep.

When he got up the next morning he felt as if he had slept for days. He took a shower and came downstairs to a glorious Texas summer morning. There was not a trace anywhere of what had taken place the night before. The dishes were off the table and the dishwasher was still warm but empty. Their clothes had already been picked up and Debra was nowhere to be found. Opening a Diet Pepsi he walked down to the barn but on the way he noticed that her car was gone. When he got back to the house he found a note by the telephone telling him that she had gone shopping and that she would be back about dark. Perfect, he thought, and he left her a note saying that he would be back around the same time. Me and J. C. can have a hell of a birthday this afternoon, he beamed to his innerself.

He called J. C. and they decided that since it was such a pretty day they needed to be outdoors. Joey met him at a park out by Grapevine Lake that they liked because during the week it wasn't very crowded and they could lay out, drink beer and talk to their heart's content. Sure enough, they were two of a very few people in the park and they got their choice of picnic areas. Texas lake parks all have the same motif. If you've ever been there you know those plain concrete pavillions with a roof over them and concrete picnic tables with concrete benches under them. Joey and his buddy picked the one nearest the water, got out the cooler that J. C. had filled with beer, cheese and bread and sat down to enjoy the day.

"Happy Birthday, Joey, my dear friend. May every day of the rest of your life be as good as this one is going to be. We are going to indulge ourselves today and I have just the right thing to get things going. Here try one of these."

J. C. pulled out an ice-cold beer and passed it to Joey. As is usually the case, cold beer and a glorious day produced some esoteric results. It only took a moment and there they were rehashing old times . . . times that were so poignant that at times they laughed and at times they cried. The first thing they knew the sun was moving toward the horizon and the beer was gone. As if coming out of a dream, they looked around and vaguely remembered the sounds of children playing and boats racing by pulling water skiers, and the sound of airplanes turning final over the lake for their landings at DFW International Airport. Now all was silent. The children, the boats and the airplanes were all gone . . . and it was time for them to go, too.

They got up in unison, slowly, savoring the moment. The moment between light and dark. That time when time stands still . . . the instant that the islanders look for the green flash. That place in history that is now . . . and now . . . and now. As if waking from a simultaneous trance Joey and J. C. came to. Still in some kind of somnulistic state they wished each other goodbye and headed home. Each one had their respective stereos turned up as loud as they would go and were smiling as they cruised carefully down the road to home . . . J. C. to his imagined dream world and Joey to Debra's dream world.

It struck Joey as he motored steadily down the road that even though life was wonderful at this moment it could turn on him swiftly as it had in the recent past and that thought almost sobered him up . . . almost. But his will was strong and his heart just wouldn't have it. His downfall or downturn if you will was when in search of the perfect song to fit his mood he happened on a country station and suddenly he felt the saltwarm tears running down his cheeks. Riding along by himself on his birthday, boohooing like a baby, he felt so achingly alone and at the same time so inexorably satisfied that he had to pull the car over to the side of the road and take stock of the situation. Sitting there rocking back and forth in his seat to the music he looked up and who should drive by but his used-to-be friend Jimmy Jeff Stewart in his beat up old pickup truck. JJ was so intent on where he was going that he looked neither right nor left never noticing that it was Joey along side the road in his car.

Without thinking about why he was doing it Joey pulled out slowly and began following the old pickup, being careful to stay back far enough so that he wouldn't be seen. When JJ pulled into the motel by the airport, Joey was and wasn't surprised to see Debra's car parked in the lot. He cruised down the street a block or two and found himself suddenly wide awake and alert. Turning the car back around he pulled into the motel parking lot and started walking down the row of rooms until he heard Debra's laugh coming from, of all things, room number one-thirteen.

By now Joey was acting purely on instinct and adrenaline, not planning anything or thinking of the consequences of what he was doing. He put his ear to the door and could clearly hear Debra and Jimmy Jeff talking and laughing together. The adrenalin suddenly hooked up and, taking a step backward, Joey kicked the door with all of his might. The door cracked a little but it took two more swift kicks for him to knock it off its hinges.

The scene in the bedroom wasn't nearly as bad as he had imagined it would be. Both Debra and Jimmy Jeff were fully clothed sitting on the edge of the bed with a glass of wine in their respective hands. Debra's shoes were in the middle of the floor but JJ still had his boots on. Joey came powering through what was left of the door as JJ came to his feet sloshing wine all over him and Debra. Debra started to raise her hands in protest but Joey had already gotten off his first punch which opened JJ's left eye up like a ripe peach. He was in such a frenzy that even when it was obvious that JJ was out on his feet he continued hitting him with combinations that actually kept JJ erect. Sort of like those guys in the rodeos who keep a can in the air by shooting it with a pistol repeatedly.

Joey finally began to flag as the adrenaline burned all of his energy. As JJ began to wobble down though, he hit him with a magnificent left to the temple that propelled ol' JJ right out the door onto the sidewalk where he laid out cold as a mackerel. He turned to Debra who was still sitting on the bed and it occurred to Joey that if she had made a sound during all of the ruckus he hadn't heard it. She still had her glass in her hand and was kind of absent-mindedly wiping at the wine that was all over her blouse. Slowly raising her head to meet his outraged gaze, big tears began rolling down her cheeks.

256

"That ain't gonna work, Debra! You've gone way too far this time. I don't know what the hell is wrong with you and I really don't care. I'll just leave you here with that piece of shit lying out there on the sidewalk. The two of you deserve each other."

With that he turned and walked out the door where the motel manager and the room clerk were bent over JJ trying to find out what happened and where he was hurt. Joey pushed his way through them and looking JJ right in the eyes kicked him as hard as he could in the crotch. JJ doubled up in pain and began vomiting at the same time losing control of his sphincter.

"Just a little something to remember me by you asshole." Joey hissed in his ear, "I want you to know that wherever you go the rest of your life you better be looking back over your shoulder. Because if I am anywhere in the vicinity I'm gonna whip your ass just like I did today and that's a promise! I hope you two pigs are happy with yourselves."

Joey could hear the sirens in the distance as he got in his car and headed home. When he got there it was just a little before seven o'clock. Just in time for the last few minutes of happy hour he thought sardonically as he reached in the refrigerator for a beer. The house was quiet and lonely and the sounds of the refrigerator door closing and his footsteps were magnified by it's emptiness. The sound quality in his ears was like one of those Italian westerns with Clint Eastwood, tinny and loud and irritating. He turned on the stereo to keep him company but the only music that his frazzled nerves could stand was some chamber music on the public broadcasting station.

He was sitting out on the porch working on a fresh beer when the phone rang. He let it ring a couple more times trying to compose himself but when he reached for the receiver he noticed that his hand was shaking. It was Debra and she was sobbing hysterically, babbling almost incoherently that she was sorry that she had made an almost tragic mistake.

"But nothing happened, I promise you Joey! I ran into Jimmy Jeff while I was shopping and we had a couple of drinks at the mall and then he said why don't we get some wine and . . . "

"Shut up, Debra, I don't want to hear all of the gory details. If this is what you consider a happy birthday you are a lot sicker than I would have ever believed. I hope you two are proud of yourselves."

257

"Oh, Joey, I know I've been stupid but it's all over with now. I don't know what I was thinking. I guess I just got lonely with you working all of the time and traveling all over the country. The last month or so has really been confusing to me. It's like I've been in a dream . . . it's been all I could do to get out of bed in the morning. I swear I don't know how we ended up in that motel room. Everything is blank from the bar to there."

"Well, I hope you two are very happy together because I'm going to the lawyer in the morning . . . "

"No, no, Joey, don't do that! I'm sorry and I swear nothing like that will ever happen again. It's like I just woke up from a bad dream and all I want to do is come home and go back to the way things used to be. You're the only one I love, Joey. You just forgot to pay any attention to me and I got scared. Please, Joey, let me come home and let's talk about it. I'm sure we can work it out. Please?"

Joey was torn between what he wanted and what was. Deep down he knew that their relationship was over, that Debra had committed what to him was unforgivable. He knew that they could never be the same again and yet, as men are wont to do, he hoped beyond hope that what she was saying was true even though he knew that it was all a lie.

"Okay, Debra," he sighed resignedly, "come on home but I can't promise you what you'll find when you get here. I've had about all of you and your screwed up friends and family that I can stand. I can't believe your goddam timing! Here it is my birthday and I finally got my business squared away and . . . I'll see you later. Goodbye, Debra."

Joey hung the phone up and stared out the window into the deepening dusk. He pulled another beer out of the fridge and walked back out on the porch where the moon, which was as big and bright as he had ever seen it, started peeking over the horizon. Damn, it's gonna be a beautiful night, he thought, as he watched the moon rise up over the trees.

Yeah, a beautiful night . . . but for what? For sitting up and listening to your crazed, soon to be ex-wife try to convince you that what she has done was your fault or her mother's fault or her daddy's fault? That the lie that she has been living was a product of things out of her control and that all of that didn't matter anyway because now she has recovered her "self-esteem" or found her "true

258

purpose" or some such crap as that and things will go right back to normal just like nothing ever happened?

Sure that's a nice easy out isn't it, Joey deliberated, trying to prepare himself for her return. But things don't just get fixed like that he mused unhappily. What was it the man said about a leopard not changing it's spots. How in the hell can I ever trust her again and do I really want to anyway? Damn, why did I tell her to come on home? Am I some kind of masochist or what?

Yeah or what Joey! You aren't a masochist you are a man and men fold up like you're about to do all of the time. Men don't like to rock the boat. They like things to flow smoothly and comfortably without disruptions of this kind. They like their women to be clean and faithful not dirty and untrustworthy but they are unrealistic enough to believe that the apple doesn't always fall close to the tree. That just because her family is totally messed up doesn't mean that their little darlin' is. If you're going to play in this game, Joey, you've got to pay and you better be sure your soul can afford the price.

As he heard Debra's car coming up the drive a feeling of dread passed over Joey. He had no idea what he was going to do or say to her when she walked through the door and had even less of a clue what she had up her sleeve. The moon by this time was in its shining glory, lighting up the countryside almost as if it were daylight. Maybe that's what the problem is! Maybe the moon has caused her to go stark ravin' mad! Lord knows, she got there somehow!

About this time Debra came busting through the door, ran up to him and hugged him in what was almost a deathgrip, the whole time babbling about how much she loved him ad nauseum. This whole situation seemed extremely awkward to poor Joey and depressing too. Carefully, he extricated himself from her embrace and, pausing to dig a couple more beers out of the fridge, headed out to the porch with Debra in tow. He had no idea what he was going to say or what was going to happen from here on out but he did know that he had to get back outside . . . back out to that blazing orb continuing to rise brighter and brighter from the east.

They sat in silence for a long time mesmerized by the candle in the sky. Neither one able to start the conversation that both of them dreaded but knew that they had to have. It wasn't just the fear but the reality that, since both of them assumed that these things would never happen to them, neither one of them knew how to proceed much less where they were going to go from here. So they sat in the

259

moonlight like a pair of gawky teenagers sipping their beers, each waiting for the other to break the ice.

At last, they turned in unison and began to speak at the same time. They each stopped and then started to speak at the same time again. The third time this happened, Joey raised his hand for silence and said, "Why don't we just wait until tomorrow to talk, Debra? I don't know about you but all of this stuff has really worn me out. Let's have one more beer without saying a word and just go to bed. Anything we have to say from here on out can keep til morning."

When they finally wobbled up the stairs Joey fell immediately into bed while Debra went into the bathroom. When she came out he was on his side staring hypnotically at the moon filling the east facing window. She got into bed and tried to curl up next to him but he wasn't having any of it tonight.

"Go to sleep, Debra," he mumbled moving farther away from her and pulling the pillow over his head, "just go on to sleep."

Chapter Twenty

THAT NEXT DAY WAS the beginning of about a month of what seemed like an eternity to both of them. Joey started out by calling his office and telling them that he wouldn't be in until Monday. He vaguely alluded to some family problems that would take a couple of days to solve. He then put the telephone answering machine on the first ring so that they could talk without interruption. As it turned out they had so distanced themselves from all of their friends and acquaintances in the last few months, it didn't ring anyway.

Debra started out by suggesting that they try counseling again but Joey, remembering the Phyllis farce, was totally against that idea.

"Look, Debra, we don't need to go through that Chinese fire drill again. If we can't talk this thing out just the two of us then I think we ought to call it a day. I mean, hell, look at it from my side. In my mind by doing what you did you gave me a pretty good indicator that you don't want me anymore and I'm not going to try to force myself back into your life. Either you get your act in order and convince me that this whole deal can be salvaged or you can have your damned Jimmy Jeff Stewart!"

"Don't keep giving me ultimatums Joey! If we are going to work this out we've got to do it together. This has been a very tough time for me. I've gone through a lot and I don't need you threatening me with leaving."

"**You've** been through a lot! What the hell do you think **I've** been through and **who** do you think put me through it! Damn, Sam! Don't try to turn this thing around as if it was anybody's fault but yours! You didn't walk in on **me** in a motel room with somebody else! That was you in there and I didn't see anyone holding a gun to your head!"

This, of course, puffed Debra up immediately and she broke into that typical cop-out that married people use when they get caught with their finger in the wrong pie. "Maybe if you had stayed home a little bit more, I wouldn't have had to turn to anyone else to keep me company and talk to me. I just got tired of waiting for you to come home that's all! You drove me to find someone to talk to!"

"Get off that tack, Debra, this isn't Geraldo or Sally Jessy Raphael or any of those assinine pieces of dirt that try to pass for reality. This is the real thing. Nobody but you caused what happened yesterday and what you did was wrong. I may have had the same feelings as you but I didn't go out and find someone else "to talk to" because of them. After the weird way you've been acting the past year or so, **I** should be the one looking for companionship not you . . . but I didn't give up on our wedding vows . . . you did. If we are going to get anywhere with this you're gonna have to take responsibility for your actions."

"That's right Joey make it all my fault. You haven't exactly been a prince either. Why can't you see how I felt with you never around?"

"I can see how you felt and that's one of the main reasons I decided to sell my business and uncomplicate my life. So that I could be home more. But I can't see that as justification for you to go slipping around like a goddam alley cat. You broke a promise that you made to me a long time ago. One that we both agreed on and one that I have not broken to you. You not only broke it but you did it with someone who was supposed to be my friend. How would you like it if you found out I was screwing one of your girl friends? Don't tell me you'd understand that crap!"

262

Seeing that this tack wasn't going to work in the face of reason and the facts at hand, Debra leaned back on all of that pyschobabble doubletalk that is in those women's magazines. That trash about "wants" and "needs" and "innerselves" and all that tomfoolery that is supposed to explain people's dishonesties. As is always the case, the stuff is based on such irrational premises that it goes down hill until the psychobabble turns into just plain babble. Even the person spouting all of that drivel gets confused by its outright banality and this was the case with Debra. She was trying so hard to justify the unjustifiable that she finally confused even herself and had to pause for a while to try to think up a plausible argument to change over to.

And so it went for the rest of that day and through the weekend, Joey citing facts and Debra citing *Redbook* or *Self* or some other irrational source. During this period Joey tried to work but naturally the quality of his labor was impaired by his personal problems. He found it hard to concentrate and he noticed that even though he hadn't lost the ability to do well in his job he certainly was losing the desire to do so. He knew he could conceal this loss of drive and spirit only so long in the competitive world of sales but the constant frustration of Debra's circuitous arguing continued to drag him down no matter how hard he resisted it.

Finally, late on a Sunday afternoon almost a month to the day after he had found Debra and JJ together, Debra had had about enough of his commonsensical approach. It was directly after her latest attempt to substantiate her substandard behavior which he had picked apart way too easily for the umpteenth time.

"That's the only way you can think, isn't it Joey? Logically! Why can't you think with your heart?"

"Because if we all thought with our hearts we'd have no rules to live by and without rules we'd have chaos! Look, darlin', at some point you've got to take responsibility for your actions or we'll never get over this hump. If you keep thinking with your heart and not your head we'll just end up in this same mess again. Tell you what. I have to go out of town to a meeting tomorrow. While I'm gone you need to come to terms with the fact that you have violated the most basic trust that a man and a woman can have. If you want to keep us together you need to determine what it is that you have to do to resurrect that trust in our relationship. We've ridden this old mule about down to the ground with all of your late-model nonsense. It doesn't take an Einstein to tear all of your arguments apart so why don't you just drop it and come up with a plan for our future? I don't want to talk about it anymore until I get back."

With this he went outside to run for a while. Running was becoming more and more of a crutch for Joey these days. It worked almost like a drug as it cleared his mind and eased the tension of the situation. After a few miles he would become a lot more calm and in control. He did notice that the music was still not playing in his head and try though he might he couldn't get it turned back on.

The next day he left for his out-of-town meeting with mixed emotions. On the one hand he was relieved to leave the emotionally charged atmosphere that he had been living in for what seemed like forever. On the other hand he was hesitant to leave Debra alone because he knew that she was pretty unbalanced and, he feared, totally untrustworthy. One more incident like the one in the motel and he would be forced to do what until recently was the unthinkable . . . well, maybe more unfathomable than unthinkable.

The meeting was with a prospective manufacturer who was one of the biggest in the automotive industry. In the past they had used their own in-house sales personnel so for them to hire a company of the type that Joey now worked for would be an extreme departure from the norm for them . . . and a huge windfall for Sid's company in volume as well as philosophy. Nevertheless Joey was having an extremely hard time concentrating on the business at hand. He kept finding himself drifting off into daydreams about all kinds of things. Very few of them, surprisingly enough, had anything to do with Debra or his personal strife. It was like a defense mechanism for his ego that would kick in every time that he began to feel insecure or nervous and take him into a relaxing dream. He would come out of these mini mind-vacations (they would only last for an instant, although to Joey it felt like hours) and be slightly confused for a few seconds. He didn't think his prospective employers noticed but he knew that Sid wasn't missing a thing.

It was after the meeting at the bar before dinner that Sid confronted him.

"Come on over here and sit down, Joey," he smiled, gesturing to a table back in the corner of the bar, "Let's talk a minute before everyone gets down here."

"That's okay, Sid, we can talk right here at the bar. No one's here and they won't be down for thirty or forty minutes believe me. They've got a lot to talk about between now and dinner. Here have a seat!"

Joey sat down and Sid joined him reluctantly, not wanting to start off this conversation with a confrontation.

"So, how goes it on the homefront, Joey? You've been looking a little preoccupied lately . . . not your usual self. Everything okay? Nobody in the family sick, are they?"

Joey knew that he would eventually have to confide in Sid about his difficulty with Debra (especially if it reached that conclusion that he couldn't bring himself to dwell on) but he had hoped that it would all go away before that was necessary. By his very nature he couldn't cover up what was going on so he tried to tell Sid in twenty-five words or less what was happening in his life. After a ten minute synopsis of the problems at hand Joey sat back took a long pull on his beer and smiled . . . shakily but sincerely.

"C'mon now, Sid. Don't look so damned concerned. Like the bartender said to the horse as he ordered a drink, "Why such a long face?"

Sid chuckled at the old saw and it seemed to relax him a little but he still had his game face on.

"I don't have to tell you how important this meeting is to me and to our company. If this big guy comes over to us this could be

265

the start of a trend back toward leased sales agencies like ours and away from direct sales forces. The result could be a bonanza unlike anything we've seen in this business in several lifetimes. I need you to be as sharp as you know you can be for the rest of the time that we are here and for the immediate future. Personal problems weigh heavy on us all Joey, but believe me it's a hell of a lot easier to deal with woman problems when you've got a pocket full of gelt. Let's bear down and bring this baby home!"

Between the beer, the pep talk and just being away from home and those endless harebrained discussions with Debra, Joey could feel his old persona beginning to reemerge. He walked into the can to take a leak and comb his hair and on the way out he found himself smiling confidently. Striding positively back into the bar he clapped Sid on the back and ordered them each a drink.

"My pity party is over, Sid. I guess every now and then we all have to feel a little sorry for ourselves, at least I do. Look," he said, sidling confidentially up to Sid, "Here's what I think we need to do to clinch this deal . . ."

With that the two sat close together until the rest of the group arrived cheerfully planning how to "get the order." As it turned out they had already done a better job than either one of them had thought. Joey, because he was too preoccupied with his own problems and Sid, because he was too preoccupied with Joey's preoccupation but both of them had unconsciously said exactly what the committee had wanted to hear. They had a few more drinks with the group all the while Joey and Sid entertaining the bigwigs with jokes and tales of times on the road. The laughter continued through dinner and the president of the company proposed a toast.

"Gentlemen," he said looking directly at Joey, "I propose a toast to our combined futures together. We have no doubt that you and your organization will give us the added impetus that we need to dominate our industry. We are proud to have you on board!"

They all drank and then he turned to Sid. "We have already prepared a contract for you and I want you to take it home, read it and send me back a signed copy. I think you will find it to your satisfaction. I've got to tell you if all of your people are like Joey here we're going to hit a bunch of home runs from here on out!"

After a final drink they all headed for their rooms elated at their future prospects together. Joey, riding an adrenalin high so strong that he knew sleep was a long way off, decided to walk around the block first since it was a beautiful September evening in Houston. As he walked out the revolving door he was immediately struck by the almost full moon rising in the east. Whoa, he thought, all this and a full moon, too. Maybe the moon was the cause of all of the rigamarole that had been going on lately. Whatever the cause nothing could attack that salesman's high that he was on at the moment. After completing the second circle of the block, the adrenalin wore off abruptly and, like a little puppy, he went directly to his room and was asleep almost before his head hit the pillow.

That next morning Joey suggested that since they were only a few blocks from their new client's offices they should call and see if they could go over and finish the contract signing in person. Sid called and their new employers were elated that the two could spend the day with them. Finally, after the standard plant tour and lunch with the key players, they signed the contract and looked up to see that they only had a few minutes to catch the last flight home. So with a hurried goodbye they raced to the airport and made their flight.

On the way home Joey and Sid celebrated by upgrading to first class and the wine and conversation flowed for the entire flight. Upon their arrival they wished each other a good night and hurried laughing to their cars. Driving west from the airport to home Joey looked in the rearview mirror at the ascending luminous globe in the east. It was so large that it overflowed the mirror and lit the landscape in front of him so brightly that it seemed like twilight rather than the almost midnite that it was. Gradually the adrenalin that had

267

kept him so high on his successful trip drained away and with it the ebullience that he had felt earlier on. The closer he got to home the lower his spirits flagged until as he pulled into his driveway he was confronted with a dark, cheerless appearing house. Not a light was on anywhere and, as he opened the garage, Debra's car was nowhere to be seen.

The house was neat but empty and the one dish in the sink had obviously not been used recently. Joey pulled a beer out of the refrigerator and went out on the porch to look at the moon. A few beers and a few hours later, Joey awakened with a start to the phone ringing. It was Debra and she was crying.

"Joey, I think we need to get a divorce," she sobbed into the phone.

"Where are you, Debra? Don't you think we ought to get together and talk this over?"

"We've been talking for weeks and it doesn't do any good. I can't believe that you would want me back anyway after what I've put you through."

"Yeah, maybe you're right," he sighed resignedly, "I guess there just isn't any going back, is there?"

When his mouth said the words it was as if someone else were in the room with him making the pronouncement. He heard his own words as if someone else was standing in the doorway saying them and the finality of what he heard was almost overwhelming. Suddenly he could no longer listen to her voice as she was rambling along about being sorry and always "being there" for him and other doubletalk of that ilk. So he hung up the phone and went to get another beer.

For the next few hours Joey sat in the kitchen drinking beer and staring alternately out the window at the moon and at a picture of Debra on the window sill. Sometimes he slept and when he woke he would get another beer and stare at the moon some more. Finally he achieved a sort of phantasmagoric state . . . somewhere between

268

consciousness and unconsciousness. He was vaguely aware that he was running out of beer and moon at almost the same rate. The kitchen was dreamlike and comforting and it surprised him a little when he looked down and found the gun in his hand. He didn't even remember going and getting it in the first place and wondered hazily if this could be a dream.

He watched abstractly as the gun slowly came up and entered his mouth. It was just like before when his mouth said the words but it sounded like someone else had said them and he could only hear. Now he could only watch the scene as it played itself out unable to do anything about it. I wonder what in the world's going to happen now he mused. Now he was kind of above and behind his body which was sitting in the chair at the kitchen table facing that amazing orb filling the kitchen window, its light spilling all around him and casting a crooked shadow behind him on the tile floor.

To his alarm he could see his finger begin to tighten on the trigger and he felt powerless to stop it, like in that dream that you have where you're trying to get away from something or someone that's threatening you but its like moving in slow motion. The harder you run the more bogged down you get and no matter what you do whatever it is is gaining on you . . . always gaining. You're running in glue. So it felt to Joey as he sensed that something bad was about to happen and he felt powerless to stop it.

Although it seemed as if hours had passed, this all had taken place in only a few moments but Joey was suspended in time and out of his body . . . maybe even out of his mind. He watched as his finger (someone's finger!) continued to tighten on the trigger. He tried to cry out to himself to stop, to put the gun down, to S

T

    O

       P

        !

Bang!
Bang!

Two shots rang out and the sound in the kitchen was deafening. Waking with a jump that almost toppled him out of his chair, Joey was amazed to find himself in the midst of all the smoke and the smell of cordite, the still warm gun in hand. He looked up to see the remnants of Debra's picture floating through the air like confetti at a parade. Shards of glass littered the floor and the window sill. The soft September breeze wafted through the hole where the window used to be. As the smoke cleared Joey could again see the moon and he could swear that it smiled and winked at him. Now sober as a judge Joey smiled and winked back at the moon and giving ol' man moon a salute, went up to his room. He changed into jeans, an old comfortable shirt and some tennies and brushed his teeth. Then he packed a bag with only comfortable clothes and his shaving kit. Carrying the bag over his shoulder he walked methodically through the house bidding each room and stick of furniture adieu. His goodbyes complete he grabbed the last two beers, walked out to his car and drove off to the east into that glorious warm friendly orb that now smiled down on him. Almost immediately the music was back with him . . . a friendly old Jimmy Buffet number and he sang along with it as he drove down the highway sipping his beer.

Wasted away again in Margaritaville
Searchin' for my lost shaker of salt
Some people claim that there's a woman to blame
But I know . . . It's my own damn fault.

Epilogue

WHEN JOEY DROVE OFF that night he knew without knowing where he would go. Dropping his car in the airport parking lot he bought a one way ticket to Key West on the first flight out that morning. He still had the two beers left in his bag so he sipped on them as he sat in the empty waiting lounge and wrote letters to Sid and Debra. He told both of them that he would be gone for awhile and not to wait for him. Kind of ironic, he thought, that I would even think that waiting for me would cross Debra's mind.

Then he called J. C. and woke him up.

"Sorry to wake you, old buddy, but I'm on my way out of town and we gotta talk. You got any beer in the house?"

"Sure pardner. Come on over. What time is it anyway?"

"It's five o'clock in the morning but I'm already at the airport and my plane doesn't leave for about three hours. Would you mind loading up a twelve pack and comin' out to the airport for a while. I'm in terminal 2E at gate 13 and there's some details we need to talk over real quick before I get out of here."

"Sounds like you're about to make a getaway my friend. What in the hell's goin' on?"

"You might say that. Come on out and I'll tell you all about it."

They sat on the floor against the wall in the empty waiting lounge which was suddenly full of their love for each other. Joey talking and J. C. smiling like an idiot as Joey related the whole crazy tale. They laughed and toasted and had a great time and finally heard

271

the last call for his flight. They looked up to see a bunch of strangers looking curiously at them and the pile of beer cans at their feet but no one could dampen their enthusiasm at this point.

Standing up unsteadily to hug his buddy goodbye, Joey promised to let J. C. know where he would be and how to get a hold of him. J. C., in turn, promised to take care of his car and contact his divorce lawyer and get all of that together for Joey who didn't want to let those kind of details drag him down right now. With just the hint of a tear in his eye Joey broke away and bolted for the door of the plane laughing almost hysterically and waving like a man possessed. The stewardess couldn't help but smile at his happiness as he flew by so freely.

And so it was that Joey Hews, boy wonder, auto parts maven, victim of the perilous changes of the seventies' decade of decadence, ended up that evening down in Key West. Sitting close to the sidewalk at Captain Tony's watching the tourists stream by on their way to watch the sunset at Mallory Square; talking to Captain Tony and listening to his tales of days gone by of Papa Hemingway and fishing and smuggling and partying.

It was late and the Captain had gone on home when Joey picked up a bar napkin and began to write.

"This is a story that explores some major changes that have taken place in our culture in the past couple of decades and, even though it's fiction, you may recognize someone you know or maybe even yourself in these pages. The years in question were pivotal for the masses . . . ."